Praise

Dream Helper

"*Dream Helper* is vivid, carefully researched historical fiction that brings to life an exciting and important period in early California. The characters are well-drawn, the story of Cayatu is dramatic and engaging, Willard Thompson is a writer to watch."
~Leonard Tourney, author of *Time's Fool*

"In telling the tale of the early days of Mission Santa Barbara, Willard Thompson spins a yarn worthy of James Fenimore Cooper. His Dream Helper is a vivid portrait of the triumphs and tragedies of the Franciscan friars who carry the blinding light of Christ into the hinterlands of New Spain, the naïve Chumash people who become their slaves, and the Spanish soldiers who keep a predatory eye on them both. Those who've grown up in Southern California will particularly appreciate Thompson's longingly rendered landscape of stark hills, sere grasslands, and coastal fogs."
~Broos Campbell, author of *No Quarter* and *The War of Knives*

"The missionaries, conquistadors, settlers, and Native Americans of Dream Helper spring to life in this historical novel of early Santa Barbara. The lively cast of characters with their hopes, dreams, and cultural clashes, are sure to provide the stuff of great book group discussion. With historical accuracy and great attention to detail, Thompson illuminates the California history you were never taught in grade school!"
~Carol Clement and Jane Eller, discussion leaders of the Santa Barbara Inklings reading group

"A delightful fresh look at the American Indian experience as told through the eyes of a woman. The writing is lyrical and sweeps one along with all the passion and drama of an iconic movie."
~Christina Allison, Actress/Playwright

Dream Helper

A Novel of Early California

Willard Thompson

Rincon Publishing
Santa Barbara, California

ISBN 10 0-9797552-0-4
ISBN 13 978-0-9797552-0-0

Cover design: Cathi Stevenson
Interior design: Gwen Gades

Thompson, Willard, 1940
    Dream helper : a novel of early California / Willard Thompson. --1st
    ed. --Santa Barbara, Calif. : Rincon Publishing, 2008.
        p. ; cm.
        (Chronicles of California)
        ISBN: 978-0-9797552-0-0

    1. California--History--Fiction. 2. Santa Barbara Mission
    -Fiction. 3. Chumash Indians--Fiction. 4. Missions--California--Santa
    Barbara--Fiction. 5. Historical fiction. I. Title. II. Series.

PS3620.H698 D74 2008
813.6--dc22 0803

Rincon Publishing books may be purchased for book clubs, educational, business or sales promotion use. For information please write Rincon Publishing, P.O. Box 50235, Santa Barbara, CA 93150

Disclaimer:
This is a work of fiction. All persons, places and events depicted herein, except those clearly in the public domain, are figments of the author's imagination or are used fictionally. Any resemblance to actual persons, living or dead, is unintentional.

Printed in the United States of America

Dream Helper

A Novel of Early California

Willard Thompson

For Jo,

the love of my life who never stopped believing.

With special thanks to Anne, Shelly, Leonard, Matt, Abe, Sid and especially Carol Clement who was literally there for me from start to finish.

Chapter One

Sounds in the dry grass alerted Cayatu. Her fingers curled around the handle of her flint knife. Rising cautiously from her cooking fire, she hardened her resolve to do whatever she had to in the next few minutes to protect herself. Her skirt of tule fronds rustled against her legs as she moved to the bank of the small stream that flowed by her lean-to. The clamshells in her necklace danced between her breasts, making soft, tinkling sounds. The valley around her lay parched. Days of dryness had given it a stale smell that signaled the end of another acorn-growing season.

Knife poised, she waited, ready to defend her life, only to see two gray-robed Franciscan monks, wooden crosses swinging from their rope belts, emerge on the far bank. Open-mouthed, the two men stared at her.

Cayatu watched as the older of the two missionaries drew a cross across his chest with his fingers.

"Alavado sea Dios!" His words meant nothing to her and she continued to stare. Then he spoke haltingly in her language. "Put knife away, *niña*. You have nothing to fear from us."

She giggled at his awkward speech and relaxed. "I was afraid," she said.

Franciscans were familiar to Cayatu. As a little girl she

remembered them walking into her village as they journeyed along the coast, always curious to learn her language and curious to see how her people lived, and always accompanied by leather-jacketed soldiers. After each visit, Qoloq, the shaman, would warn the village about them.

A smile came to her now when the old monk, and the other one in his middle years, hiked their robes above their knees, showing white legs, and waded the stream.

"I am Esteben Salamanca," the old one said smiling, showing teeth dulled by his years. He might have been a tall man when he was younger—as tall as her father, she guessed—but now age stooped him over. Sparse white hair circled his head like a wreath, leaving his crown bald and sun scarred.

"This is Brother Fermin Ortiz," Salamanca introduced the younger man. "We're going to the *Presidio de Santa Barbara*."

Salamanca paused. Cayatu watched him look around at her lean-to and cooking fire. He seemed to struggle for words.

"Why aren't you in your village? Why are you living here?"

She drew in a breath, let it escape her lips. "I am outcast," she said.

"Outcast?"

"Qoloq banished me here during the last acorn-growing season."

Fermin Ortiz had kept silent so far. The intense way he stared at her gave Cayatu a shiver. It was a stare her people would have called rude. She backed away a step. He took a step toward her.

"Your village—how far?" he asked.

Though he spoke her words, Cayatu had to puzzle their meaning for a moment. Then her face brightened with understanding. She pointed toward the ocean. "A short walk."

Ortiz turned to examine the rabbit sizzling on a wooded spit at her cooking fire a few yards off. Turning back to her, his Chumash words came slowly. "We're tired. Hungry.

Still a long walk."

"We'll go to your village," Salamanca told her. "It's not much out of our way." Cayatu saw the frown Ortiz gave Salamanca but didn't understand its meaning.

"Will you lead us?" Salamanca asked.

"If you'll keep me safe," she replied.

She led the Franciscans back along the main trail to a side path that branched toward the ocean. The village's round huts, built of bent willow poles covered with tule mats, clung to the edge of an oak grove. The oaks gave way to a sand beach, and the beach disappeared under calm waters that rippled over sand and pebbles.

Cayatu watched tiny waves lapping against the planks of two *tomols* pulled up on the beach. The sight brought a smile to her face. She looked around for other canoes before moving down the path but didn't see any.

Walking through the village, she studied the huts. Some needed repairs. One or two had fallen down since her banishment. The smell of simmering acorn gruel, rising into the pale morning sky with the smoke from cooking fires, awakened her hunger and brought back memories of happier times.

In front of the shaman's hut Cayatu called out for her sister. She smiled her joy when Tanayan stepped from the dim interior into the strong morning light. Older by almost twelve seasons, shorter and rounder, Tanayan stiffened on seeing her. She rubbed her eyes as if to rub away Coyote's trick, and then ran to embrace Cayatu, tears sliding down her fleshy cheeks.

"Little Sister, I've missed you," she whispered. "I've missed you every day...I was wrong—"

"—You *were* wrong, but I forgave you long ago." Cayatu gave her arm a reassuring touch. "I've come to the edge of the village often hoping to catch some sight of you."

"—So, you've come back." Qoloq swaggered from the hut, a bear tooth necklace bouncing off his chest with the abruptness of his movements. He leered at Cayatu and waved a baton made from a deer's leg bone as he spoke. The bone was inset with obsidian flakes that caught the sunlight as he waved it. It seemed to Cayatu, Qoloq was sprinkling his words about like sparks in the morning air.

"I knew you would," he gloated. "I told Tanayan you would come back. I knew Coyote—"

He stopped short. Open mouthed, Qoloq pointed the baton at the priests. "Why are the grayrobes here?"

"To visit your village," Esteben Salamanca said, understanding Qoloq's gesture with the deer bone.

Fermin Ortiz added haltingly, "Your people join our missions."

"—You steal them!" Qoloq hissed. He pulled himself erect, pointing the baton directly at Ortiz.

Ortiz straightened. "We don't steal. They come freely."

"We'll have a new mission in Santa Barbara," Salamanca interrupted. "Your people will do God's work there."

"Your god is nothing!" Qoloq sneered, puffing out his chest and shaking the baton at the missionaries. "First People are real—Sun and Eagle and Coyote of the Sky, Lizard, Moon, all of them. You lure our people away with false promises. If my people don't return, Coyote will punish them."

Cayatu watched the priests stand their ground. Their eyes were fixed on Qoloq's lips, struggling to understand the words he flung at them. Each man fingered his wooden cross. She turned to look at Qoloq, staring belligerently back at them, holding his baton like a shield.

Cayatu felt Tanayan take her hand. Standing beside her sister, Cayatu smiled again when she saw her nephew racing up from the beach. His long hair flowing behind him in the breeze brought a quickening to her heart.

"I saw you...On the path...I was at the *tomols*...You've come back," he said, catching his breath and hugging her. "I hoped you would."

Cayatu held him in her arms. Grown almost to an adult, Massilili was a strong, agile young man.

"I will give the girl my permission to return to the village," Qoloq boasted to the missionaries. He turned to her, looking smug, then back to the priests. "She's an orphan. Her sister and I raised her when her parents traveled across the Rainbow Bridge to the Peaceful Place. Now, I've picked a man for her to marry. He's paid me well because he desires a young beauty like her. He wants to lie with her and run his hands over her breasts. She'll live in his hut. Bear his children—"

"—I won't! I won't lie with a man just to ease *your* life!" Cayatu's voice rang with anger. "I'd rather live alone and move about as I please." She confronted Qoloq, moving forward so her face pressed close to his, not letting him see her tremble. "You banished Ysaga—I'll have no other husband. You have no power over me anymore, Qoloq." She stopped to look around, then pointed to the other huts. "Our village grows smaller. People leave. They go to the missions of the Spanish. I'll go too."

Tanayan rushed in front of Qoloq and fell at his feet, "Let her stay and find her own husband. Don't drive her away again."

The pleading in Tanayan's voice seemed to anger Qoloq.

Cayatu watched his face contort.

"I took her in as an orphan; she must do as I tell her," he shouted at his wife.

The priests withdrew several steps, looking uncertainly at Qoloq.

Cayatu tensed at Qoloq's words. She hesitated only a moment before turning to Massilili. "My father—your grandfather—led the Brotherhood of the Canoe and I have a rightful high place here. I won't obey Qoloq. I won't live in the village unless I can live free as I was born to live."

"You can't—"

Cayatu turned on Qoloq. "I'd rather die from Rattlesnake's venom than live out my seasons controlled by you." She turned to the missionaries. "Will you take me with you?"

Salamanca and Ortiz spoke rapidly back and forth in Spanish.

"Hmm," Salamanca mused after their brief discussion, "Praise God." Turning to face Cayatu, speaking haltingly again, he said, "We'll take you to Santa Barbara, *Niña*. We'll baptize you. But the mission's not built. Hard work lies ahead. Hardship—you should wait."

"I will go with you now," she said, edging away from Qoloq when she saw anger burn in his eyes like the coals in a cooking fire. "I won't live here!"

Qoloq sneered, "You live in the valley like an animal. You have no Dream Helper to guide you. Your chance of having a man fades with your beauty, like each season fades into the next. Your safe life is here with a man I choose for you."

Cayatu turned her back on him. She hugged Massilili to her breast and reached out for Tanayan's hand. "I'll come back to visit," she said.

Tanayan nodded understanding.

"Coyote was right, you're a cursed woman," Qoloq grumbled.

Cayatu wiped her tears with the back of her hand and forced a smile at Tanayan. She looked up into Massilili's angular face and put her hand on his muscled shoulder. "I helped your mother raise you—"

"—The way I raised Cayatu after our mother went to the Peaceful Place giving her life and your grandfather was lost in the ocean," Tanayan told her son.

"You're almost grown now," Cayatu said.

"Qoloq teaches me the healing secrets," Massilili told her. "I'll be shaman after him."

Tanayan went into the hut. Cayatu felt a lump rise in her throat when her sister reappeared holding a sea-otter-skin skirt. It was the same skirt Qoloq had stripped from her in anger the previous gathering season when he sent her from the village for lying with Ysaga. "Wear this," Tanayan said. "I'll paint village colors and weave shells in your hair so you can go proudly. Show all the light-skin men the dignity we have."

"No!" Qoloq ordered. "It's not allowed."

"Stop!" Tanayan scolded him. "She's my sister."

The Franciscans frowned. Talking in hushed voices, they averted their eyes while Tanayan painted Cayatu's face and breasts. After she finished the symbols, Tanayan went back inside the hut a second time. She emerged holding a slender-necked shell basket, woven of tules with designs of dark rushes and sumac shoots. Wiping a tear, Tanayan held it out to Cayatu.

"Our mother wove this while she waited for you to come into our world, Little Sister. It contains all the love she had for her unborn daughter. She died giving you life, but this basket still holds her love. Take it with you to your new life."

Chapter Two

Cayatu and the Franciscans walked the length of the parched valley. They skirted the marsh fed by ocean water, alive with the shrieks of ocean birds and the smell of souring vegetation.

Stopping on a slight rise to admire the scene, Salamanca placed his hand gently on her shoulder.

"He was the one you readied the knife for," he said, more than asked.

She stayed quiet but nodded slightly.

"You are safe with us," he assured her.

Cayatu followed the Franciscans. Soon the priests fell into their own words, paying her no attention.

"So, our task begins again Brother Fermin," Salamanca said to the younger man. "And a new role for you."

"*Aí*, and no easy task. These people seem slow to learn, lazy. They have human form, but it's hard to believe they belong to mankind. Look at the heathen symbols painted on the girl."

"They'll come to our mission, you'll see. Soon, we'll have our hands full." Salamanca looked deep into the younger priest's face, but without criticism. "Try a gentler approach, Brother Fermin. You may learn a lot from these people. Learn to speak their language."

"That's no easy task, either," Ortiz responded. "God help me, my tongue stumbles over my teeth when I speak their words—Look there!" Ortiz interrupted himself to point at a hawk floating down from the mountains crowding the valley in the north. Its tail feathers shone reddish-pink in the afternoon light. "The hawk's a hunter." Ortiz gave Salamanca a hard look. "God ordains it to rule over this valley."

Cayatu saw the hawk had spotted something in the dry grass. She stayed still but her eyes went back and forth from the bird to the two Franciscans.

The hawk hovered overhead. Cayatu drew in a quick breath when it folded its wings and plummeted out of the sky, diving so fast its feathers quivered. The bird leveled off inches above the ground not ten paces away when its talon pierced its prey. The trio standing by the marsh heard a squeal. The hawk called a triumphant kee-ah, kee-ah.

The hawk flew to a rock a few yards off. Cayatu watched the bird preen, holding a mouse securely on its claw. She watched the priests caught up in the drama.

As the three watched, the bird began to retract its claw, holding the rodent with its beak. When the mouse came free of the talon it gave a sudden twitch that seemed to surprise the bird and cause it to open its beak to get a better grip. In that instant, Cayatu saw the mouse drop to the ground and wedge itself against the rock.

She suppressed her grin so the grayrobes wouldn't notice. She guessed a creature from the World Below, some mischievous spirit, had intervened. The thought amused Cayatu at first. But then, as she considered the unpredictability of life in the Middle World, it gave her pause. Spirits were capricious, she knew. They could change the path of any life for their own amusement.

For several minutes she watched the hawk's efforts to

reclaim its meal. The bird stormed around the rock, an explosion of wings and slashing talons, but the curve of its beak and the overhang of the rock gave the bird no way to snag the mouse. It uttered one final, defiant *kee-ah* and flew off.

Esteben Salamanca resumed the walk, urging the others along with him. He stayed quiet for a short way but then turned to Ortiz. "We strive to know God's ways," he said to his companion, "but his ways are always a mystery to man."

Late in the afternoon the trio entered *El Presidio de Santa Barbara*, a stockade dominating a slight rise overlooking the ocean. Ortiz put his hand over his nose to block the stench of animal and human waste, mingling with the smells from cooking pots outside soldiers' quarters. The odors clawed at his stomach, reminding him of his growing hunger.

He watched a band of soldiers moving about the dusty parade ground. He saw their eyes follow Cayatu.

"She's a comely girl to tempt these men," Salamanca said, as if reading Ortiz's thoughts. "Look how those shells sparkle in her hair."

"Like stars on a winter night in Santander," Ortiz said with a wry laugh. "But I think these men are more interested in her bare breasts."

Ortiz and Salamanca led Cayatu across the open plaza to the center of the fort where the red and yellow banner of Spain fluttered from a pine flagpole. She still clutched the basket her sister had given her. A soldier in blue tunic and buff pants, Toledo blade at his side, strode across the open space toward them. At a distance, Ortiz saw only the bushy blond beard hiding the man's face. But as the soldier came closer, Ortiz felt the intensity of his cobalt eyes blazing out from deep sockets. He judged the soldier to be in his middle years, handsome, taller than average, solidly built, with skin as fair as his hair.

Salamanca whispered to Cayatu that the man approaching was Lieutenant Don Jose Maria Demetrio de Alba, *Comandante* of the *Royal Presidio de Santa Barbara*. She showed no emotion at Salamanca's words that Ortiz could detect, but he watched her fingers slowly turning the shell basket in her hand, much the way he might finger his rosary.

De Alba greeted the missionaries, asking politely about their health and about their journey in a tone Ortiz judged condescending.

"A hard journey," Esteben Salamanca told him. "This land is dry and barren. It gives us nothing but sore feet as we plod the paths between missions. I pray God to release me from this task soon so I can return to Majorca and end my days there."

"Fine enough for you," Lieutenant de Alba said. "I fear I'm destined to serve my king here for all eternity. My superiors have forgotten me. They've left me to rot in this hell hole— forgive me, father—but I'm afraid I'll never see *Nueva España* again. Pray to your God to send me home."

Fermin Ortiz stepped closer to de Alba.

"We'll pray for your safe return home, sir," he said, looking up into the soldier's eyes, "but surly there are opportunities here for men of courage. Not the silver of *Nueva España* perhaps, but land. Land that gives its own kind of wealth to those who grab hold of it."

Salamanca abruptly turned to stare at Ortiz, "Brother Fermin—" he started, but de Alba cut him off.

"—Fine-enough land for you *padres* to build your missions on, I suppose. Fine enough for sheep and cattle. But worthless land; no more than a buffer. Few settlers will ever come. And for me—an officer of the army of King Carlos—a bleak end to my valiant career."

They're blind to the wealth of this land—The thought startled Ortiz. Salamanca has no eye for it, seeing only souls to save. Lieutenant de Alba wants to go back to Mexico City. If I possessed this land I'd produce wealth beyond the ability of either one to imagine.

De Alba's eyes shifted to Cayatu. "Why is the girl here?" he asked.

"We've come to build the mission Junipero Serra planned—God rest his soul," Ortiz said. "This girl will be our first baptism."

Salamanca said, "Pray God we do the right thing for her in Christ's name and protect her from evil." That said he stared at de Alba.

"Send her away! She doesn't belong here." De Alba used a sweep of his hand to show his irritation.

"Tomorrow we'll take her to the mission site. Tonight she'll stay with us," Ortiz told him.

The soldier shrugged. "That will be on you. I won't be responsible. No place here is safe for her. Look how my men stare. With so few women... Just soldiers' wives..." He hesitated. "Sooner or later this God-forsaken land gets the better of us all, *Padres*. I know my men. I hear them boast at night. It will be hard to keep her safe."

"Surely for one night you're able to protect her from your own men," the old priest said.

Ortiz smiled but De Alba ignored Salamanca's remark.

De Alba dropped his hand to rest on the hilt of his sword.

"Keep her with you until dark, then lock her in the chapel," he said. "Let the Virgin protect her. Get her out of my fort early tomorrow." Returning again to his polite but distant voice, still gripping the sword hilt, he added, "After you've put her away I'd be pleased to have you take your supper with me, humble as it is. We've made two rooms available to you until your mission is built, but stay clear of my men. Don't interfere with me."

After praying in the *Presidio* chapel, Ortiz and Salamanca took Cayatu to a kitchen yard in the far corner of the fort, where a large pot hung over a wood fire. Ortiz ladled out a bowl of pasty white gruel. *"Atole,"* he said, offering it to her.

She tasted it and spit it on the ground.

"Come, woman, eat it," Ortiz prodded. "You'll be eating it often enough from now on."

Salamanca soothed her. He urged her to try again. Ortiz watched Cayatu look at Salamanca with wide-open, questioning eyes that showed her reluctance to eat more, but he saw her hunger win out. After only a slight hesitation she scooped a handful from the bowl and stuffed her mouth, gagging it down her throat.

After she ate, Ortiz led her back to the chapel. "You'll be safe here tonight," he told her, opening the heavy door. "To be sure, I'll lock you in and come get you in the morning."

Cayatu's look told him she was unsure of what he intended to do.

He pointed to the iron lock and key. "I'll lock the door to keep you safe," he said, searching for the right words. Then he gave up and used his own language. "Understand, child, I'm doing this for your safety. Jesus Christ and Holy Mother will watch over you during the night. Tomorrow you can live in the open again until our mission's built."

Cayatu still balked at entering the dimly lit chapel.

"Come now, go inside," Ortiz urged, using his hands and pointing to supplement his words. "My supper's getting cold. I haven't eaten enough today to satisfy a small child. My stomach begs for the roast meat and good Spanish wine the *Comandante* has waiting for me. You'll be safe in God's hands tonight. Move along."

He put his hand on her shoulder and pushed her through the door, turning the key in the lock when the door closed behind her.

Ortiz sat with Salamanca and Demetrio de Alba at a wooden table in the third room of the *Comandancia*—de

Alba's quarters in a corner of the *Presidio* not far from the chapel. It was dimly lit and smoky from crude candles giving off a pungent smell that filled the room. One of the *Soldados de Cuera*, a soldier of Spain's frontier army, served them. Ortiz heard the sounds of men and animals outside, quieting as darkness spread over the fort.

Inwardly, he rehearsed his disappointment at the meal. The beef was so tough he wondered if the hide had been served by accident. He'd worried he might lose a tooth as he gnawed away at it. No vegetables were in sight. A bowl of *pozole*—the same barley gruel the Indian woman had spit on the ground—with bits of meat afloat in it, was their side dish. Oranges and grapes were plentiful, but Ortiz judged them tasteless compared to the fruits he'd enjoyed at the Queretaro missions high in the *Sierra Gorda* Mountains of *Nueva España*. Even the wine was disappointing. Instead of the *Rioja* made from Spanish grapes he'd expected, the large tumblers were filled with *aguardiente*—crude brandy— that his host poured without reserve. Not at all what he had hoped for, Fermin Ortiz thought.

But perhaps it was all that could be expected here, so far from Spain, far even from *Nueva España*. De Alba was right. It was a forgotten frontier, only a buffer really, he realized, protecting Spain from her enemies to the North. His brother Franciscans saw it as fertile new ground on which to plant Christ's cross. So be it; he'd made up his mind to make the most of that zeal to gain visibility among his superiors, visibility and stature, maybe more comfort.

"My apologies for the meal," de Alba said, catching the disdainful look Ortiz made no effort to hide. He shoved back, reaching behind him for a cheroot in a box on a wooden side table, and signaled for the soldier. "Miserable compared to the delicious food we ate in the City of Mexico, is it not? But what can we do? We're just an outpost."

De Alba turned to the soldier who came by his side. "Look deep in my trunk. I think we've one or two bottles of fine port left. We'll share one with the *Padres*."

Turning back to the Franciscans, de Alba said, "Nothing like the feasts we enjoyed before, eh? We knew how to live in New Spain, didn't we? The food and wine, the beautiful women, dancing long into the nights on verandas where the moon seemed to bow down to caress the *señoritas'* shining hair... *Aí* that was the life for a soldier. Now we're fortunate if the ship arrives from San Blas. When it does, it brings only a few pleasures."

De Alba paused to light his cigar from a nearby candle. He took in a long draw and blew out the smoke toward the ceiling, while he looked at Ortiz. The soldier filled their glasses from the new bottle.

"What news from Monterey?" De Alba asked, after a long drink. "Any word of our enemies?"

"Nothing," Ortiz answered. "The Russians stay north of Mission Dolores content to trade for pelts. The British are farther north collecting their own furs. All's quiet—"

"—And forgotten," de Alba threw in quickly. "We would all be better off in *Nueva España*. Here's to a speedy return for us all." He raised his tumbler and tossed down the port.

Ortiz took a mouthful of the sweet wine and let it tease his senses, moving it from cheek to cheek then trickle slowly down his throat, as he listened to de Alba.

When he had swallowed he turned to the *Comandante*. "Mission and fort will be closer here than at the other Presidios," he started.

"Indeed. An excellent opportunity to show the governor how well we can work together."

From the corner of his eye, Ortiz saw Salamanca's face screw up in a skeptical look.

"It's a concern to me and Brother Salamanca that your soldiers and our Indian neophytes will be so close," Ortiz continued. "As you said earlier, it may be difficult to keep them separated."

"True," De Alba nodded slowly. "Father Serra planned it this way and it's not to my liking at all. Your mission should be in the valley to the east, away from the *Presidio* and *pueblo*, but Serra said there wasn't enough water there. In truth, I think he was scared of the bears." At this, De Alba gave a humorless, grunting laugh.

"But done is done," he continued. "If the governor gets word to the viceroy we live without strife so close together, he may reward me with a recall to Mexico City—let's work together for that, no? It's your task to protect the Indians, not mine." With that, he gave both missionaries a silent stare.

Ortiz took the measure of the Lieutenant in the ensuing pause. He judged Demetrio de Alba to be of only middling intellect. He might be able to command this small garrison but he wasn't bright enough for bigger assignments. He didn't seem to have the toughness or diplomacy Ortiz had seen in other leaders, certainly not the toughness and diplomacy Ortiz knew he had. In fact, he wondered if the *Comandante* didn't show just a trace of fear. And yet de Alba might be useful.

Esteben Salamanca mentally withdrew from the conversation in order to study the two men seated with him. He reached his hand up to smooth his bald pate, a reflex that often accompanied moments when he was deep in thought. He let his aging fingers comb through the sparse fringe of white hair. Who were these two men he might spend the rest of his life with?

De Alba was like other military men he'd known for almost forty years of doing the Lord's work. He lacked all trace of humility. Salamanca had seen plenty of soldiers like this one. He knew how to handle them—stay humble, praise and pamper them like the hunting hounds they were. Throw them a bone now and then, but stand firm and strong in the name of the Christ when there were important matters at hand. De Alba could be handled, Salamanca decided. He drank too much and talked too freely... Too boastfully. So did Ortiz. In many ways they were two of a kind. De Alba had something on his mind, some scheme to get sent back to *Nueva España*. He'd need to be watchful.

And what about Fermin Ortiz? Salamanca pondered this young priest he'd been thrown together with. Look at him empty the tumbler again. Where is his moderation? How does he fit the mold Saint Francis cast for us? Poverty sits on Brother Fermin like a Jesuit sits on a mule.

"I'm sure you *Padres* will have your Indians growing crops here in Santa Barbara soon enough," de Alba broke the silence. "Then you'll supply my poor soldiers with all the food we need, no? And better *aguardiente*, I hope. These Indians are smart enough—they'll learn quickly."

"Soon enough indeed," Salamanca nodded. "Gardens and orchards and vineyards will bloom as they've bloomed at other missions along the coast." His face turned more serious. "But only after the mission is built and the neophytes are cared for."

"You'll have to do better than that," de Alba snapped. "I urge you to move with due haste to produce food for us. My men are scrawny from our meager diet. Near starvation. The crops from *El Pueblo de Los Angeles* are insufficient. With your new mission so close, we look forward to eating better."

"In God's time." Salamanca smiled.

De Alba laughed harshly, draining his tumbler of the port and refilling it. He handed the bottle to Ortiz who refilled his own glass.

Salamanca thought de Alba was starting to slur his words. "Brother Fermin," he cautioned.

"If these heathens don't work fast enough lemme know," de Alba interrupted. "I'll work 'em. Keep 'em under control, work 'em hard, or they'll overwhelm us."

"The king commands us to care for these Indians," Salamanca said.

"And feed my soldiers," de Alba shot back at him.

Chapter Three

When Fermin Ortiz turned the key in the lock, Cayatu was alone in semi-darkness. She sat on the dirt floor with her back propped against a wall. In the dim light she could barely make out a statue of a woman and infant. The Franciscans' mother spirit, she guessed, remembering Ortiz's words. She held her own mother's shell basket in both hands for several minutes, turning it slowly to inspect the intricate designs. She tried to picture her mother weaving it.

When darkness blanketed the *Presidio*, Cayatu could see Evening Star had followed her into this new world and was watching through the window. She heard the sounds of men, laughing and singing in the plaza outside. Then a shadow came between Evening Star and the window, almost invisible against the night sky. It peered in at her and stood silently watching. Then it disappeared. Moments later she heard sounds at the door. The door shook and slammed against the door frame for several minutes before it stopped. The shadow reappeared at the window, staring at her again. Then it was gone. Was it real? Had Coyote followed her?

Fermin Ortiz unlocked Cayatu from the chapel the next morning.

"Last night something watched me," she said, pointing to the window. "It tried to get in."

"Mother of God! *Los soldados* are a scourge." Ortiz spoke rapidly in Spanish, but reached out a consoling hand to touch her shoulder.

She flinched, backing away, and looking at him with questioning eyes. "It might have been Coyote. Do our spirits come to your fort?"

He stared at her. Cayatu's large, dark eyes, sparkling with flecks of reflected sunlight, made him forget for that instant she was an Indian—made him forget he was sworn to celibacy. Her face was a soft oval, with full lips. He admired the way her black hair cascaded around her shoulders and down to the swell of her breasts. He felt sensations in his groin and thought about the other woman in the church in Mexico City.

"There are no spirits," he told her, using gestures to fill in for the words he didn't know. "But stay away from the soldiers."

Her look told Ortiz she didn't understand. "We need soldiers. To protect us from foreigners, protect us from Indian attacks," he said. Then he shrugged. "No harm done."

He willed his feelings away but asked no forgiveness for having them. "Be still now. Come along. We've a hill to climb," he said, trying to make her understand.

When they reached the hilltop that looked down on the few mud-brown adobes that made up the tiny *pueblo* of Santa Barbara huddled around the fort, Ortiz let his horse browse the dry bunch grass while he studied the land stretching east and west along the coast. His gaze swept the broad bench lands behind the beach, flat to the western horizon but sloping gently from high mountain wall to teal blue ocean. A man could become a lord with cattle on land like that. Praise God! Ortiz thought.

His horse gave a sudden whinny, side stepping and pawing at the ground.

"Coyote plays a trick on your horse," Cayatu said, laughing.

"There are no spirits," he told her sharply. "It was only a lizard." He pulled himself back from his musings and allowed himself to admire her naked breasts again, enjoying the stirrings in his body.

"Find shelter here," he told her. "We'll build the mission on this hill." Then he kicked his horse and rode off.

Over the next weeks, the missionaries prepared Cayatu for baptism. They came regularly to instruct her at the sheltered spot she'd chosen along a stream in the canyon behind the mission site. It was in a stand of sycamore trees where the ground was carpeted with dried leaves and patches of low-growing wild grape. Redbud bushes spotted about lent privacy. Esteben Salamanca led the lessons as they sat beside the stream flowing down from the high mountains to its union with the ocean. With dappled, mid-afternoon light filtering through the leaf canopy, Salamanca used phrases he'd mastered at the mission in San Diego to teach the catechism, his words punctuated by the tapping sounds of woodpeckers in the live oak trees.

One afternoon, Cayatu saw Salamanca coming alone along the path.

"As I approached I heard you singing," he greeted her. "What was it you sang?"

She smiled at the old Franciscan who was smiling back at her. "When I'm alone I sing songs from my village. It was a song to Morning Star I sang to my nephew when he was a baby and I was a young girl."

"Teach me your songs and about the spirits you sing to?" the priest asked her. "Your voice is as pure as a night bird's call, Cayatu. It has the gentle sweetness I remember in my mother's voice long ago. I hope you'll sing in our mission choir."

"Singing makes me happy," she said. "I used to sing on the beach by our village when I collected shells."

It seemed to her a lifetime, since she'd walked along the beach in her village, singing, picking up perfect limpet and purple olivella shells Tanayan fashioned into beautiful jewelry. Sometimes, as she collected, she stopped to watch her father building canoes with his men, and sometimes she took her nephew Massilili down to the water's edge where his eyes delighted to the cold water tickling his toes.

"Ah," Salamanca's face beamed, "I used to sing on a beach, too, but my beach was far from here, on an island called Majorca in *España*. There I sang to a beautiful young woman, as lovely as you are now, Cayatu." He stopped and she watched as his eyes took on a faraway look. After a pause he continued, "Tomorrow we'll baptize you in the *Presidio* chapel. I've brought new clothes for you to wear. You'll put aside your animal skin and dress like a Christian woman."

He set the garments down on a nearby rock.

"When I put on these clothes I'll be Christian?" she asked.

Salamanca grimaced. "Well, no, *niña*. Being a Christian is more than clothes."

After he left, Cayatu delayed trying on the new clothes. When she finally did, the blouse restricted her arms. She tripped on the hem of the skirt walking to the stream, and recoiled at the sight of the reflected image she saw in the water. With just the tip of her finger she prodded her breast, and her stomach and her hip. In the slow-flowing waters, it looked to her as if she were touching some other woman. She despaired that her breasts were covered; despaired that the new skirt hung limply around her ankles. A feeling of sadness came over her. You're not Chumash anymore, a voice in her head taunted her.

Feeling uncomfortable in the white *camisa* and skirt, Cayatu stood with three Chumash men in the *Presidio* chapel. One, a younger man, smiled at her. She returned the smile and quickly looked away.

Lieutenant Don Jose Maria Demetrio de Alba stood beside her in his full dress uniform of dark blue pants and tunic, with ruffled white shirt and red velvet waistcoat. His blond hair was slicked back and the smell of his pomade tickled her nose. He stood erect, his hand on the golden hilt of his sword that jangled in its scabbard when he moved. Solemn-faced, he agreed to be her Godfather and promised to protect her Catholic faith. Cayatu sensed de Alba's eyes straying to her from time to time. It made her tremble.

Behind him, the people of Santa Barbara, mostly soldiers and the wives who had come with them from New Spain, watched with smiles and approving looks.

Wrapped in a gray robe, with beggar sandals on his feet, Esteban Salamanca went to each of the converts, taking water on his fingertips from a bowl and pronouncing a new Christian name for each. "Tomas, Nuncio, Miguel," he said to them in turn. Feeling his wet fingers on her forehead made Cayatu cringe. "Henceforth we will call you Clare," he said to her, "in honor of Clare of Assisi, founder of the second order of Saint Francis."

When the service ended, *Comandante* de Alba lifted his hand from his sword, tugged at his beard with thumb and forefinger, then reached out to clasp her shoulder. She flinched again, as she had when Fermin Ortiz touched her. She grew rigid, watching him as his expressionless blue eyes scanned her face and body; feeling shivers race up her back to the base of her neck, where the hairs seemed to bristle. He said nothing, but stood looking at her in silence. Cayatu felt his fingers tighten on her shoulder then slide across her blouse to touch her hair at the base of her neck. She felt faint. The moment passed. He gave her a quick smile and turned away to join the others outside the chapel.

On the *Presidio* parade ground, Cayatu joined the small group milling around in the sharp, early winter sunlight that etched precise shadows on the hard-packed earth. De Alba walked over to Fermin Ortiz, who began gesturing to him and counting on his fingers as he spoke. She saw de Alba glance her way and say something to the priest.

In ones and twos, some of the olive-skinned Mexican women came shyly to her side, dragging their reluctant soldier-husbands and children behind them. They spoke words without meaning for her, but their smiles and the sing-song lilt of their voices told her they meant to be friendly. She watched white-haired Esteben Salamanca, across the parade yard, walk among the people, speaking a few words to each, smiling at the children, reaching out a hand occasionally to touch one of them. One woman, with dark ringlet curls cascading down to her shoulders, stopped him and pointed at her. Together they approached.

"Do I know you?" the woman said to Cayatu, using the priest to interpret her words. Before he could finish she went on, "*Aí*, I do. I do know you. From the feast in your village when I came with Guillermo and the other *soldados* to build the *Presidio*. That terrible journey."

"You're Josefa," Cayatu said.

"You remember!" A smile lit the woman's round face. "At the baptism I guessed it was you. You've left your village."

Cayatu nodded.

"I'm pleased to see you again," Josefa said. "Perhaps we'll see each other often; we can be friends. I told you that night we feasted at your village your life would change, eh? Now it comes to pass. Already you wear civilized clothes. Soon you'll be living a Christian life and all your old ways will be gone."

Chapter Four

The young Chumash man, who had smiled at Cayatu at the baptism, fell in beside her as they walked along the horse path up the hill to the mission site.

"So, we all have new names from the priests today," he said, offering her a smile. "They call me Tomas now. And you are Clare."

"My name is Cayatu," she said, with an edge to her voice.

"The Franciscans won't allow that, you know. Everything is to be new. The old traditions, our spirits, names, all are gone now. Father Ortiz said we are born again in their God."

Cayatu regarded the man, and judged him to be a summer or two older than she was, plain-looking, not handsome like Ysaga, but with gentle eyes.

"I am Cayatu," she told Tomas again. "Muniyaut, my father, and the village seer named me at birth. Let the missionaries call me what they will, I'll always be Cayatu. You should cling to your name, too. If you let them, they'll take away all that is you."

"I hope we can be friends at the mission," Tomas said. "But you seem angry."

Cayatu stopped walking and squatted down on her haunches on the path so that her skirt billowed around her.

She looked up at him with an unblinking stare. A nascent smile slowly turned up the corners of her mouth but she still held him locked in her gaze.

"Angry? Yes, I'm angry, but not with you, Tomas," she answered him. "I'm angry the missionaries place no value on the lives we lived before they came here. It's as if we didn't exist before they marched along our beach—the way they try to replace everything that is ours, like our names, the way we dressed."

"Why did you come to the mission, then? Why did you choose to be a Christian?"

"I had no choice… But I don't think I'm a Christian just because I have a new name and a cloth skirt."

Looking at the baggy pants Tomas wore, with a shirt made of the same coarse cotton, Cayatu broke into laughter.

A hangdog look dropped over his face. "Why are you laughing?"

"Your clothes."

"They're fine clothes. The missionaries gave them to me."

"I've never seen a Chumash man wear so many clothes. You don't look like a man. You're made of cloth. You're hiding your man-thing." She laughed again. "You're a hiding man."

"What about you, Clare?" Tomas reached down to take hold of the sleeve of her blouse, rubbing the material between his thumb and forefinger. "You're just as strange-looking as I am. Where are your breasts? You're a doll woman for little girls to play with."

She looked Tomas up and down while her laughter grew. "Look at us," she said, almost choking on her words. She stood and took his hand. "Look at us!" Her eyes accepted him. "You're right, we're dolls. Dolls for children. Not real anymore."

They stood on the path, looking at each other, shaking with laughter. Together they stood close, holding on to each other, laughing until tears rolled down their cheeks.

"Like dolls," he repeated, holding her hand just a little tighter as the laughter choked him.

"We'll be friends," she told him, offering another smile. She decided Tomas was a man she could grow to like. "Tell me why you came to the mission, Tomas," she asked.

Tomas turned serious, dropping his hands to his sides as they started to walk again. "It seemed better than staying in my village," he said. "My father wasn't respected. He had no *tomol* and those who did wouldn't let him fish with them. He couldn't teach me to fish because he didn't know how. My mother worked all day to gather enough food. She only wore a straw skirt—not even a deerskin. She was not respected. I left the village as soon as I heard about the mission, to have a better life."

Cayatu took an involuntary step away from Tomas. She was annoyed with herself for taking it but it was done before she could stop. She felt her pride pushing her. "My father led the Brotherhood of the Canoe," she said. "He built strong *tomols* for other men." She paused, searching out his face for a reaction before going on. "He built a canoe for a man whose son was my friend. One day my father went out on the ocean with that man. They fished and my father caught a great one, perhaps the greatest fish our village had ever seen. It was *'Elye'wun*, the swordfish, his dream helper. *'Elye'wun* was so strong he pulled my father from the canoe."

Tomas stopped walking to listen. His face soured. Cayatu saw dullness creep over it; his eyes went a little dim and the edges of his mouth turned down.

"The others tried to reach him," she went on, wishing she could stop but knowing it was already too late, "but the swordfish dragged him a long way off. When the others got to him my father was no longer struggling, only floating in the water. Sun took him home that day. After that I lived with my sister and her husband."

When she finished she studied him again, waiting for him to speak, hopeful she hadn't killed their friendship before it had found roots. Tomas looked down the path toward the *pueblo* and rubbed his toes in the loose earth, before he looked back at her. Then in a hushed voice he told her, "It's not right for me to walk with you."

"Why not? I thought we could be friends." She was hurt by the quick shift in his manner but not surprised. She looked away so she wouldn't have to see the shame she had brought on him, silently cursing herself.

"My mother only wore a straw skirt. Your mother must have worn a sea otter skirt if your father was such an important man."

"She did." Cayatu paused and let her thoughts drift into the stillness of the trail for a moment. "I never knew her," she said when she spoke again. "She died giving me life. My sister and I both had sea otter skirts…"

Cayatu reached out to take his hand. "At the mission we all wear the same clothes, Tomas. The missionaries say we're all equal. Your family's place in your village isn't important here. It isn't important to me."

Tomas snatched his hand away. "It's best if we don't walk together," he said, shaking his head as he moved up the path ahead of her. But after a few steps, Tomas turned back to face her. "Your father's important place in your village came from his mother, just as my father's low place came from *his* mother. No matter how hard I worked, my life would have been the same as my father's. When the Franciscans told how everyone at their missions worked together, I decided to come. I'd like to have respect for a time in my life. Or at least know my children would not be laughed at." He thrust his hands into the pockets of his cotton trousers and quickened his pace up the hill ahead of her. "Watch me," he called back after a few more steps, "you'll see that I can earn your respect at the mission."

Chapter Five

Esteben Salamanca rose slowly from the crude bench on his side of the makeshift confessional. His aging joints ached from the damp chill of the Santa Barbara winter, but he was beginning to feel better now that spring was returning. Still, it took him a moment to straighten all the way up and adjust his robe.

Josefa emerged from the other side of the hastily built confessional that had only a screen of tules between the two benches. She dabbed a cloth handkerchief on her cheeks and waited until the old monk could walk outside with her.

"Pray for the soul of your lost child, *Señora*—you and Guillermo," Salamanca told her as they walked from the church to the crest of the hill.

"We will pray, *Padre*." She looked away but he knew her tears. They walked together in silence near the heavy cross on the brow of the hill that overlooked the infant *pueblo* of Santa Barbara and stood out like a warning beacon to intruders on the ocean. "The mission grows so fast," she said when she could speak again. "Soon you'll have a large *ranchería* of neophytes here."

Salamanca nodded, but inwardly he grimaced at the thought. "These Chumash are clever. But they don't take well to our discipline. They seem always going off on their own or finding a different way to do a thing. They're the cleverest people I've worked with in my years as a missionary, but they need instruction. Brother Ortiz and I are like parents giving guidance to our wayward children."

Josefa nodded. "The Indian woman I spoke with at her baptism?"

"Ah, you mean Clare. She has the voice of an angel. And a sweet face to match. We're teaching her to weave."

For a moment, Salamanca was seeing another pretty young woman back in Petra, the small farming village on Majorca where he was born sixty years before. Josefa's dark curls cascading around her smiling face reminded him of that other woman. She had a full round face, too; a face burning with life, unafraid of her sexuality. At night, when the low hills drew the stars about them like a secret cloak, Esteben and the girl lay wrapped in each other's arms. He played his guitar, singing her songs filled with his passion. She had returned the passion without guile, giving herself over to him.

That was before his boyhood friend, Miguel Jose Serra, coaxed and chided him to attend the University in Parma, and from there into the Franciscan Order. Miguel Serra had taken the name Junipero and Esteben had taken holy orders, sorrowfully saying farewell to the girl. For more than forty years he'd answered Serra's call and toiled among simple people. At the start, he burned with zeal to bring them the word of God. Now, the fire burned with less heat, and he prayed often for an answer to the question of whether he had done the right thing.

"I'm teaching Clare to sing hymns for the Mass," he told Josefa, returning from his reverie. "We'll have a choir soon. The discipline of our music challenges her. She resists. She seems trapped in her old life." Salamanca gave Josefa an optimistic smile. "Soon, though, they'll all accept our ways, and our choir will sing for you here in our new church."

"That will be good," Josefa said, turning back to look at the wooden church the neophytes had built. "The women look forward to bringing their husbands to Mass here, and getting to know your Indians so we can be friends with them. I'll bring my Guillermo. We'll pray together to the Virgin for our lost child and ask her for a new one."

Salamanca's attention drifted from Josefa, whose face had turned somber again at the mention of the lost child. He watched a rider approach on a gray Arabian stallion, whose hoofs seemed barely to touch the ground as it galloped its way up the hill. The rider reined the horse to an abrupt halt that had it rearing on hind legs and snorting excitement as it pawed the air. Lieutenant Don Demetrio de Alba, *Comandante* of the *Presidio* jumped from the saddle and lifted his plumed, tri-cornered hat to Josefa.

"*Buenos diás, Señora*, Good day *Padre*." De Alba bowed to each of them, then turned to inspect the work going on around him. "Your mission grows," he said. "New buildings. Soon you and Father Ortiz will move up here from my fort, no? I'm anxious to have you gone so I can use your rooms for other purposes."

"In time," Salamanca answered, giving de Alba a look that said he would not be rushed out of the fort. It was also intended to tell de Alba Salamanca wasn't intimidated by his disdain. "The neophytes are building rooms for Brother Ortiz and me, as well as storerooms and a kitchen. Already we must plan for a larger mission because the Chumash come to us freely. Brother Ortiz visits the villages and new converts come almost daily."

"So, you've plenty of workers for your tasks," de Alba said. "That's good; the work will go quickly." He turned to Josefa. "You're Guillermo's wife. I see you at the *Presidio*, but you don't live there with the other families."

"No, *Comandante*. Guillermo paid some Indians to build a small adobe outside the walls for us. So we could be alone." She giggled.

Watching de Alba as he spoke with Josefa, Salamanca couldn't help but feel the lieutenant's look wasn't proper for a man speaking to another man's wife. He couldn't put a name to his concern, it was more a sense of discomfort than anything tangible, but he thought he saw a look in de Alba's eyes that seemed too intimate. Salamanca saw de Alba glance at the swell of Josefa's breasts against her blouse—for an instant it took him back again to Petra and the swell of another breast—and it took more effort than he liked to bring himself back.

"Guillermo's a good soldier," was all de Alba said before his horse nudged him in his back to show impatience to be on the move again.

Josefa took Salamanca's hand and kissed it, then gave the two men a quick curtsy and an animated farewell smile that took over and lighted her whole face. "I'll go back to the *pueblo* now. Tell Clare hello. I hope to hear her sing when we come to Mass. I'm pleased to see you, too, *Comandante.*" She walked off down the hill and Salamanca watched de Alba's eyes follow her.

When she'd gone, Salamanca turned to the lieutenant who was stroking the Arabian's muzzle. "What brings you and that fine stallion up the hill today?"

"I need workers, *Padre,* if our plan to show the Governor how we prosper together is to go forward quickly."

"Our plan, *Comandante?* We both have our work, is that what you mean?"

"My plan, then," de Alba barked. "But I need the mission's help. I can't hire enough heathen Indians in the *pueblo* for the work so I need to borrow some of your neophytes to work for me."

"I don't think that will be possible," the old priest said. He gave the soldier his sternest look. He heard the familiar warning in the back of his head telling him to go carefully.

Here was just the beginning of the demands de Alba would make. If he gave in now his life, and the lives of all his neophytes, would be burdened. Why had Miguel— Junipero—been so foolish as to allow this mission so close to the *Presidio?* "The Indians are here to learn to grow crops and raise animals so they can have their own lands when they're ready." he told de Alba. "They're not free labor for you."

"We'll pay them," de Alba shot back.

"With beads? Red beads? I think not. What can they do with beads? Or pay with *aguardiente* perhaps? No Lieutenant, they're not available. We need them here, doing the Lord's work. They belong to us."

De Alba grabbed the reins of his horse and mounted without further word. He jerked the horse around to start down the hill, then jerked him back to confront Salamanca, a dark scowl, like a gathering storm, clouding his face. "I remind you once again about being our neighbor, *Padre.* To survive we need each other. You need our protection and we need workers to build our defenses. Think well on it. If you lose our friendship, it could be hard to regain." He galloped off, his horse kicking up dust in Salamanca's face.

Later in the day, Esteben Salamanca worked side by side with his neophyte Christians in the new garden in front of the mission. He knelt in the soft soil planting seeds, with his gray robe pulled up between his legs and tucked into his rope belt.

"It's a glorious afternoon, isn't it, Clare?" the old priest greeted Cayatu as she came into the garden with several other women from their morning work at the looms and dropped down on her knees beside him. "Smell the warm earth," he urged. "It's God's gift. Smell the earth, smell the air, fragrant with lemon blossoms. Soon we'll have abundant food."

"Our land always blooms after the rains," Cayatu said. "It

turns green, food becomes abundant again. It always has."

"Hmm. I suppose so. But now we'll teach you how to grow foods so you'll never go hungry."

"We were never hungry before you came," she said simply.

Why couldn't these clever people grasp the glorious gifts of the Lord God, maker of Heaven and earth? Salamanca thought. Deep inside him a voice answered: because they've lived here without knowing God or Jesus Christ and they've gotten along pretty well. Why should they accept our teachings unless we find ways to blend them with their own? But the first voice responded: They must become civilized Christians or die in the fire. He reached over to put his hand on hers for a moment and then they continued poking holes in the warm earth with sticks and dropping seeds into each hole.

Salamanca looked up from his digging to see Fermin Ortiz striding purposefully toward the garden from the horse corral on the other side of the mission. Jimeno, the soldier assigned to teach neophytes how to tend cattle, accompanied Ortiz and pushed Tomas roughly along in front of him. When Ortiz stopped in front of him, Salamanca saw he stood rigid, meanness on his face.

"We have a runaway, here," Ortiz demanded of Salamanca. "This man tried to leave the mission to return to his village. We must make an example of him to show the others we won't tolerate runaways."

Still kneeling, Salamanca looked up at Ortiz. "Surely not a runaway, is it?"

"Jimeno here can tell you."

"*Sí, Padre*, a runaway for sure. I watched him ride off from the herd."

"Hmm, let the man tell what happened," Salamanca said. "Speak to me, Tomas," he said so Tomas understood his words. "Why did you leave the cattle?"

"I wasn't running away, Father Esteben," Tomas said and

smiled a quick, shy greeting to Cayatu.

Ortiz scoffed. "Jimeno says he watched this man ride off from the other *vaqueros*. He watched him ride toward the large village near the *estero*. Jimeno went after him and brought him directly to me."

"I did, *Padre*. I brought him straight back."

"I was only going to show my mother and father the horse I ride," Tomas insisted when Salamanca asked him again, "I wanted them to see how I work cattle for the mission."

Salamanca rose slowly to his feet, the strain of authority feeling like the ache in his joints. He reached up to run his fingers through his fringe of hair as he considered his course of action. Cayatu rose too, silently inserting herself in the discussion.

"Is this so?" Salamanca asked Ortiz.

"It's possible, Brother Esteben. He didn't try to hide. Just rode off in front of Jimeno."

"That doesn't sound like running away, now does it?"

Ortiz paused. "Nevertheless, we cannot have it," he said after a long moment. "*Vaqueros* can't leave whenever they get a mind to visit their village. We must stop this now, before others try. Make an example of this one."

"Yes, I see that you're right," Salamanca replied. "We can't allow it. And what do you suggest?"

"A whipping."

"That's not called for here."

"A day in the stocks then, where everyone will see how we treat runaways."

Salamanca grimaced. Finally, he agreed. "Just an afternoon though, Brother Fermin, and no harsh treatment. A little time in the stocks and make sure he gets water."

Padre Ortiz blustered some, but nodded and said nothing. He moved away, with Jimeno pushing Tomas in front of him again. Salamanca stood holding his planting stick, watching the trio retreat toward the corral, wrestling in his mind with the question of Fermin Ortiz.

Cayatu tugged at his robe. "No one can go back to their village?" she asked.

"It's not allowed," Salamanca answered, kneeling again and resuming his planting. "Not without permission. Once baptized, we expect you to stay with us."

"Are we your prisoners?" she asked, still standing and looking down at him.

"You're neophytes who must learn our ways. We'll teach you to speak our language and live as we do," he told her. "That takes time. In time you may be allowed to move away from the mission. In time... Not now. That's our plan."

"I would like to visit my sister and my nephew Massilili."

The look on her face worried him. He dropped his planting stick to reach up to reassure her with his hand on her arm. "I'm sorry, it's not allowed."

"Why not allowed?"

"When I was at Mission San Diego, neophytes went to their villages and brought warriors back with them," Salamanca told Cayatu. "They tried to burn the mission. There was fighting, many were hurt, *pobre hijos*. Now we only allow visits to villages when we approve them—a few at a time. You'll see. You'll be able to visit your family in a year or two, when the mission is the bountiful place we're working to make it. After each harvest you might be allowed long visits to your village."

She pulled her arm away and planted it on her hip. "What about Tomas?"

"He'll be fine. Only a few hours in the stocks."

"What if he leaves again?" she persisted.

Salamanca looked at the anguish on her face. He wished he could give her a more reassuring answer. "The soldiers bring back fugitives," he said.

"Would he be put in the stocks again?"

"Perhaps. We would try to correct his ways, teach him

ours. We can't have runaways when there's work to be done, now can we? How could the mission prosper without the hard work of our Indians? If the stocks aren't a strong enough lesson there are other ways." Salamanca was uncertain about the right words to use so he included some hand movements to make her understand. "Sometimes a whipping. Or a leg will be broken. Don't speak of this now. We must get back to planting our gardens and talk about new hymns for the Mass. Kneel down beside me again, Clare. Don't think about running away. Warn Tomas not to leave."

Cayatu backed away and turned her head to look around the familiar hilltop. When she turned back, the old priest saw a new look in her eyes. Was it anger? Defiance? He couldn't be sure which, but it troubled him.

Chapter Six

The day was sharp. Golden light flooded the weaving room on the back side of the mission. A breeze, drifting down from the mountains, filled the room with the smell of new-cut hay, and hinted another rainy season wasn't far off.

Cayatu threw a questioning look at Nuncio, the *alcalde,* who had come with Esteben Salamanca's message she should go immediately to his cubicle. She stood up from her loom as he approached. He shrugged, as if to say he didn't know what the priest wanted with her.

"I can't keep up with all that's happening anymore," he said, turning his hands up in a display of indifference. "So many baptisms and new people here now, I can't know everything. The priest said you should go to see him; that's all I know." He turned away before Cayatu could ask anymore questions.

She looked to Dolores, the girl at the loom next to hers. Younger than Cayatu by several years, Dolores was a slender reed whose hair hung short and straight. She'd come to the mission just after the last winter rains when food was scarce in her village. Afire with the zeal of her new faith, Dolores's eyes grew large and shone with conviction when she spoke of the Virgin. Cayatu frowned to herself but never questioned Dolores when her voice took on an almost mystical tone as she recited what the missionaries had taught her about the Holy Mother.

"What could the *padre* want?" Cayatu fretted. "It's never good when the priest calls you to his room."

"The priests say fornication is going on in the *ranchería* with so many unmarried men and women now," Dolores said, averting her eyes from Cayatu's, but speaking with a righteous ring to her voice. "Father Ortiz told me when we prayed together in his room. He asked who I fornicated with." Dolores struggled to say the word and blushed with embarrassment. "How could he ask?" she went on when she regained her composure. "I strive to live my life like the Blessed Virgin."

Cayatu didn't respond. She moved to the door and stood there for a moment adjusting her eyes to the bright day. As she walked to the front of the mission, the breeze played at the hem of her skirt and swirled dust devils on the path in front of her. The smell of *atole*, now familiar, but still not much to her liking, filled the air along with voices coming from the kitchen.

Absorbed in her thoughts, Cayatu rounded a corner, colliding head on with Tomas, who was walking with two of his fellow *vaqueros*. Tomas dropped the horse blankets he carried, reaching out to catch her before she fell. He held Cayatu in his arms for a moment. She gave him a shy smile but he responded by setting her on her feet and pulling away. His friends laughed at his awkwardness and stooped to pick up the blankets.

"Tomas, I'm happy to see you," Cayatu said, still holding his arm so he couldn't pull back too far. "Our paths don't cross. With so many new families here, and you with the cattle, I miss seeing your face. I want to visit you in the evenings. I'd like that; would you?"

His two friends clicked their tongues against the roofs of their mouths in a teasing way; she felt a flush of embarrassment and hoped it didn't show.

Tomas held back, but his face grew a smile that spread,

turning up the corners of his mouth, as she spoke. "Oh, yes, it would be nice to visit with you, Clare. At night I visit with other friends and sometimes girls come by to sit outside the hut with me. You could come too."

"My name is Cayatu," she reminded him, but kept the warmth in her voice. "Please call me that. I'd like to hear about the cattle. Do the other girls ask about your cattle?"

Tomas's face lit up. "Oh, yes, the girls are very interested." He darted a look at his friends and Cayatu saw them smirk. They responded in a kind of sing-song together, "Oh, yes, the girls love *vaqueros*," and broke into laughter.

"I have a fine horse to ride," Tomas cut them short. "Our herd is growing now. We had lots of calves born during the spring and some heifers are heavy now. It would be nice if you came to visit." He stopped awkwardly and looked at her. "Are you sure you want to visit with me?" he asked.

"Oh, yes, Tomas. Quite sure. I'll visit soon."

Cayatu found Salamanca in his sparse, cell-like room where several candles competed weakly with the daylight from a single window looking out on the front of the mission. He looked up and pulled himself erect at his wooden desk when she knocked on the open door.

"Sit there, Clare, and talk with me," he said, wrapping his woolen robe tightly around his shoulders and pointing to a stool across from his desk. He chose his words carefully. "I have a new song for us to learn. It's a song for evening called *Alabado*; not a song for the Mass like our other songs." There was excitement in Salamanca's voice as he spoke of the music that brought almost a glow to his worn face. "This song will end the day with words to help the neophytes remember what we've taught them about Mary and Joseph and the son of God. It's a beautiful song."

"I like your music," she said. "It's my happiest time here.

You told me once you wanted to learn about my music, too."

"We'll have to do that one day when we have some time together. But now let me play this one for you." He took his guitar from a shelf behind him and began to play simple chords, singing in a strong, deep voice.

"It's a fine song, Father," she said when he finished. "Is that all? Should I go back to my loom now?" she asked, surprised that the priest had called her for so little reason but pleased by the new song. She rose and started for the door.

"No, Clare. Sit back down," the priest said. "There is one more thing I must tell you. The carpenters have finished building the women's quarters, the *monjerio*. You'll sleep there from now on."

"What are women's quarters?" she asked.

"Where all our unmarried women will sleep."

"I'm happy sleeping in my hut in the village," she told him.

"We want you to move to the women's quarters for your safety. We wouldn't want anything happening to a voice as sweet as yours, now would we?"

He said it with a kindly tone, but underneath Cayatu heard sternness.

"There are so many at the mission now—and that's good," he continued, setting the guitar aside. "The baptism record grows every day, praise God. But we can't look out for each and every one of you, now can we? All unmarried women will sleep in the *monjerio*. Each evening, Nuncio will lock you in with the other women. If you marry, of course you can move to your husband's hut."

Cayatu looked at Salamanca in shock. "Locked in? I don't want that. When you found me in the valley I moved around freely, day or night as I wanted. I could sit by my shelter and watch Moon rise and Evening Star take its place in the sky." Cayatu felt her world closing in, pinching her smaller.

"We do this to protect you from promiscuity," Salamanca interrupted her, continuing to speak gently but with firm resolve. "It's the rule at all our missions. There's no choice, Clare. Move your possessions from your hut to make it ready for a new family."

Dryness caught in her throat, making her gasp to take in enough breath. "I want to see the stars and hear the night sounds," she protested—"

"—Don't argue with me, Clare. This is all decided."

"What of Tomas? My other friends? I want to visit with him at night."

"You and Tomas aren't married. Do you fornicate together, Clare? That's sinful."

"A man and a woman lying together is not sinful. It's what First People want us to do."

"No Clare," Salamanca almost shouted. "We will not tolerate that."

"We live differently than you do, Father." Panic was taking control of her as she fought for words that would change Salamanca's mind. "Each morning you send me to the weaving room. It's dark and damp, even while Sun warms the earth. You live in this small room where air can't reach you and the smells don't leave. No, *Padre*! I can't live locked in with other women. I would run away."

"You must," he demanded, his voice rising into a strident tone. "And I'll hear no more about you running away. If you do, we'll hunt you down and punish you. We'll punish you if you don't move to the women's quarters. You have no choice, Clare. You must move your things immediately."

Anger born of her frustration and fear took control of Cayatu. She felt as if her stomach might erupt in front of the priest. "I will not," she shouted at Salamanca. "I don't need protection from Chumash men; I can protect myself. I won't live penned up like the horses and pigs. I won't let you build your high walls around me. I'll live freely as I always have."

Cayatu didn't wait for him to speak. She jumped from the stool and ran out of his cubicle.

Chapter Seven

Cayatu burst out of Salamanca's cubicle fighting for breath. She ran along the mission veranda onto the hard-packed path, raising a dust cloud the breeze swirled behind her. She fled from the old priest's room as if he were a demon from the World Below telling her she would never be free to watch Moon dancing with the waves again. The memory of her night imprisoned in the *Presidio* chapel added to the fear pummeling her like a stormy ocean. She ran past the new church, rising higher day by day with each new adobe brick the workers added. Then she ran onto the narrow path that led into the protective dimness of the wooded canyon that smelled of decaying leaves. Racing along the bank of the slow-flowing stream, her hair spilled in her face. She stumbled, tearing her long cotton skirt on a low alder sapling, but she kept on. At her old shelter, she sank onto a rock at the water's edge.

She sobbed until her sobbing numbed her. Finally she rose and walked along the stream, eating a few berries picked from toyon bushes as she considered her plight. Simple enough, she decided, she'd leave the mission and find a new place to live out her life.

But where? Her whole life had been lived in the valley

hugging the ocean. Valley and mission—the valley along the coast where she lived freely but in fear, or the mission that protected her the way a penned animal was protected—the only places she'd ever lived. Neither was safe.

Cayatu walked deeper into the canyon, where willows and cottonwoods clung to the banks and sycamores stood on higher ground. She left the cool-smelling woods and followed a path climbing the canyon wall toward the dry brown peaks, already shimmering with mid-morning heat. She climbed out of the green canyon into scruffy, gray low-growing sage and buckwheat and coyote brush.

As she climbed above the trees, she looked down on the landscape spread out below her. She gasped at the sight of a world far bigger than any she'd ever imagined. Far to the west, she saw dark dots upon the land and thought they might be grazing cattle. Was Tomas with them now? To the east she saw all the way to her old valley where tendrils of smoke hung in the air. In front of her, the ocean rippled, flashing points of light at her. The islands floated on the horizon like sleeping whales, and the ocean beyond stretched forever.

The knot in her stomach grew tighter when she thought of leaving this land of her mother and father and their mothers and fathers who had lived here since First People showed them how to be free. A moaning sound escaped her as she understood how much of her old life was lost.

Lost were bright days when she went with Massilili and Tanayan to the beach, collecting shells at the margin of sand and ocean, where rotting kelp's familiar stench assaulted their noses. So too were the evenings when she knelt at the cooking fire with her sister grinding acorns into coarse meal, as smoke rose outside a hundred huts. Lost was a young girl, standing proudly beside her father as he launched a new *tomol,* smelling of the pine pitch and tar that would keep it dry on its voyage to Limuw. All she clung to now was a memory of the young man, Ysaga. But he was lost, too.

When Cayatu turned back to the trail she was startled to see a stag standing motionless no more than ten paces away. His sleek head boasted heavy antlers. His large eyes watched her. He stood for just a moment, then turned and walked a few steps up the thin trail, stopping to look back at her.

She took a step toward the stag. He stood unmoving, watching her approach over his shoulder. Cayatu came within inches, timidly reaching out her hand to touch his hindquarter with the tips of her fingers. His bristly hair felt soft. She could smell his wildness.

The stag moved a few more paces up the trail and stopped again. She followed. Her trembling fingers gently touched his shoulder and neck. Unafraid, the stag watched her with unblinking eyes. A third time he moved upward and stopped. Again Cayatu followed until she could stroke his head, rub it softly, lay her arm across his neck. She felt him quiver at her touch, smelled again his animal scent. For another moment he stood there. Then the stag disappeared.

Cayatu blinked. Had she imagined him? She raised her eyes and saw him far up the faint trail. Feeling uncertain, she sat again. Her eyes traced the trail as it wound up the steep slope, disappearing here and there around outcroppings, dipping into gullies carved by streams, but always reappearing again higher up. The trail followed a narrow ridge along the summit and disappeared on the other side.

Cayatu started up the trail. It was a steep climb and she was soon sweating. She wondered how long it would take her to crest the summit. Where would the trail lead then? What mysteries? What spirits lurked for her on the other side? Like pesky gnats, her questions swarmed in her head so that each time she made a decision a dozen new questions undid it.

She retreated into the coolness of the canyon to gather

food for the journey. She paused by an oak tree to pick up some acorns. Would she ever again have acorn meal? It was a fleeting thought, but it vexed her. She sat by the stream, trying to get control.

She thought about her shell basket back at the mission and wanted to go back for it. Cayatu thought about other things at the mission she should take with her, too. Several times she started back along the trail, taking a few steps toward the mission, then retracing them in a quick little dance, the way a sandpiper chases the tide.

She wrapped toyon berries as best she could in large leaves she moistened in the stream and she crushed the acorns on a flat rock. As she worked, her thoughts went to Tomas. Maybe she should go back to tell him how fond of him she was.

Cayatu was startled alert by the sound of someone coming along the stream, hidden from sight by the thick willows that grew along its banks. Fear fixed her where she stood, and only after a moment's indecision did she look for a place to hide. Across the path redbud bushes offered concealment and she took a step. Too late, a soldier rushed at her.

The words he shouted meant nothing, but the rough sound of his voice told her what she needed to know.

Cayatu grabbed the hem of her skirt and started to run, but the soldier was quicker. He covered the space between them before she took a single step. He grabbed her by the arm. She twisted away from him and started to run, but again he was too fast for her, and this time his hand tightened on her wrist.

She cried out, trying to pull away. She twisted her arm back and forth, trying to break his grip. With her free hand she hit him in the chest but her blows were ineffective against the padding of his leather jacket. She kicked him, but he held on to her while she lashed out.

Cayatu continued kicking at him and flailing her arms, desperate to loosen his grip, but her efforts were no more a bother to him than yapping dogs from the *pueblo* might be. Growing tired of her struggle, the soldier threw her on the ground and stood over her. On her hands and knees, wild like a trapped fox, she looked up into his dark, impassive face and her desperation turned to panic. On the ground in front of her a rock no larger than a grinding stone lay within reach. She grabbed for it and jumped to her feet all in the same motion, striking the man in the face.

He staggered, a surprised look contorting his face. Blood trickled from a cut above his eye. He jumped back. She followed, smashing the rock into his face around his eyes and nose several more times before he could recover. He crumpled to the ground. Now she stood over him. "Let me go," she sobbed, repeating it over and over. Cayatu dropped on her knees beside the soldier and smashed the rock into his face again, then several more times, unable to control her anger. Spent finally, the rock slipped from her hand and she fell beside him. The suddenness of her act shook her body.

Cayatu lay there a long time, prisoner to the horror of what she'd done. When she was able, she sat up and looked at the soldier. She trembled. She stared at the blood and bone and flesh of his face, and knew he was dead. Fear replaced her remorse. She knew *Comandante* Demetrio de Alba's other soldiers would track her, hunt her like an animal, and bring her back to the fort for killing this man. They'd done it to others.

Almost at a run, Cayatu started for the steep trail again, but soon stopped, her plan of escape dissolving like morning mist in the sunlight. She had to go back. She couldn't leave the soldier's body exposed by the stream. They'd know. She'd have to hide it before she could flee.

At the sight of him again, lying on his back across the

path, Cayatu felt weak in all her muscles. Her mind filled with fog, but she gripped his black boots and dragged his corpse toward the shallow stream. Moving him, even a little, was a big effort, but bit by bit she was able to pull him into the water. Not far upstream the water slowed and pooled into a deep hole and she pulled his body there, bumping it over the rocks. She listened for footsteps or voices, but only the jays accusing her from the treetops, and the stream taunting her as it crackled over rocks and pebbles, broke the quiet.

Cayatu worked to keep her mind blank. Giving his boots a final push, she watched the body, weighted by the leather jacket and leather boots, sink into the deep pool, not disappearing from sight as she'd hoped but only blurring under the shivering water.

A chill gripped her as the afternoon sun abandoned the canyon to twilight. How many men would come looking for this one? If she ran now they'd all know. They'd track her down. Perhaps it would be better to bide her time, pretend she was never here, wait for the right moment before disappearing over the mountain.

She went back to her shelter, undoing all she'd done, leaving no trace she'd been there. Wetting a willow branch from the stream, she washed away the blood. With another branch she erased the footprints. When darkness descended, Cayatu crept back to Mission Santa Barbara, going straight to the women's quarters where she found the straw mat on which her shell basket and other belongings had been placed—moved there by Nuncio, she guessed. She pressed the basket gently to her lips, mumbling a plea for help to her dead mother. When the other women came in she feigned sleep. After awhile she heard Nuncio's footsteps come near her sleeping mat and stop briefly. Then the footsteps moved away. The heavy wooden door closed and a key turned in the iron lock, trapping her with the other unmarried women.

Chapter Eight

Lieutenant Demetrio de Alba studied Fermin Ortiz, opposite him behind a rough, pine plank table, still smelling of sap, that passed for his desk. De Alba slouched in the airless room's only other chair. A cheroot pointed like an accusing finger at Ortiz from the corner of de Alba's mouth. From time to time, he exhaled a column of smoke that hung in the air beneath the low thatched ceiling like a threatening cloud, and gave the cubicle a fetid smell.

What manner of man was Ortiz, de Alba asked himself. Not like the Franciscans he'd known in Spain or Mexico City—not like any of them. This one had an air about him de Alba couldn't put his finger on, almost an arrogance. Ortiz wrapped the façade of humility about him, and yet, unspoken, let everyone know how important he thought himself to be. De Alba had sensed it the first time they met and his opinion of Ortiz hadn't changed in the year and a half since.

"So, we're settled on this other matter, no?" the Lieutenant asked. "The Indian girl is here. You understand my needs? You'll take care of the rest?"

"It will be taken care of," Ortiz responded. "I've called for the girl. My apologies. Brother Esteban alerted the

57

mayordomo needlessly. When the girl ran from his cubicle I think he assumed the worst. Now we know she was at the mission last night." Ortiz rose from his desk and walked past de Alba to the door and opened it. The smoke cloud sailed out into the still morning.

"*Bueno.* We'll speak no more of it then. I see your cattle herd grows, *Padre,*" he offered, moving on to other matters. "When I rode up the coast some days back there were steers everywhere I looked."

Ortiz agreed. "These Chumash *vaqueros* haven't learned much about herding them. They let cattle roam about so they can charge after them on their horses. They're like children at play."

De Alba threw off a deep guttural laugh and nodded his head. "Like children." Punctuating his words, he spit tobacco juice out the door onto the wooden veranda that ran along the front of the mission buildings. "This land supports a large herd. How many graze?"

"In truth, soon there will be more than we can count. The *vaqueros* aren't good at keeping tallies, and Jimeno has more to do guarding them than he can handle. We know steers stray. But you're right about the land, *Comandante,* it's rich. It grows abundant feed. Cows fatten quickly."

"There's land in Spain like that. Land in the south, where I was born. What I wouldn't give to be back in Andalusia now instead of this forgotten outpost."

Just for an instant, de Alba's mind went back to his childhood in Torcina, outside Sevilla. The land was soft and giving, and his youthful days were indolent. His older brother tended the family's cattle—soon to be his own—and paid Demetrio not the least attention. When their mother and father journeyed to Madrid to bow before the King and beg for the court's largesse, Demetrio was left to fend for himself. His memories of days spent riding the land were bittersweet.

He learned to trust his horse, the companion that never failed him. But the vast rolling hillsides where he perfected his horsemanship dramatized his loneliness, too, and taught him to fear unseen dangers. It was only the memory of evenings, pampered and protected by his governess, that brought a secret smile now, hidden beneath his straw-colored beard.

"You should think about land here, not in Spain, Don Demetrio," Ortiz chided, bringing him back. "You could raise your own cattle. Surely the King would grant you land if you petitioned for it."

De Alba exhaled another cloud of smoke, hiding Ortiz's face. He waited until it drifted out the door before looking squarely at the priest. "To what purpose would *I* raise cattle, *Padre?*" he asked in a steely voice, shaking off the old memories. "I am commander of the King's army here. I'm no *vaquero* chasing cows about this treeless wasteland; I'm an officer. Besides, the mission herd supplies our needs."

"For now," Ortiz replied. "But there could be other opportunities. If, as you say, you'll never return to your homeland, there could be opportunities here. You could grow rich. We should speak more about this."

There it was again, de Alba thought. Insinuations that leave his meaning vague. This Franciscan thinks about land, about riches, when he's taken a vow of poverty. What hand does he play? De Alba felt unsettled when he couldn't read a man. "We should indeed—"

He was interrupted by a soft knocking on the open door.

"Where have you been, Clare?" Ortiz's stern voice asked without preface as she entered the room.

Cayatu looked down at the hard-packed floor, not speaking.

"You know not to leave the mission. You disobeyed our rules," Ortiz pressed her.

"I didn't leave the mission," she said in a soft voice.

"You ran from Brother Esteban and didn't return to your loom."

"I wanted to run away when Father Salamanca said I'd be locked in the *monjerio* at night, but I didn't run away. I hid down in the fruit orchard all day. I knew it was wrong; that soldiers would look for me, so I came back. I slept in the *monjerio* last night."

"You vex me, Clare, right from the start you've vexed me. You push against us."

The *Comandante's* silver and gold scabbard clanged against the chair as he unwound from it and stood. His black boots gleamed, rowels on his spurs jingled, as he stepped toward the door. "We sent men out to hunt for her," he told Ortiz in Spanish. "Perhaps this one is too smart. She tries to outwit us." He paused and then said as an afterthought, "One man hasn't returned yet." De Alba stepped onto the veranda, his frame blocking the doorway. The sun cast a glow on his blond hair. He looked back at Cayatu, memorizing her features. "She's a fine-looking one," he said.

"Isn't she?" Ortiz replied.

"I wonder if she's as innocent as she acts." De Alba's cold blue eyes searched her for signs of guilt. "We'll talk more on this other matter," he said. He tossed the cigar stub on the dirt, and strode out into the bright light.

I didn't run away," Cayatu lied after de Alba left. "I slept in the women's quarters. I'm ready to live there." She felt her words sticking at her throat.

"If only it were that simple. If only we could say you didn't disobey. Then we could go back to the way things were as if nothing had happened. You'd like that, Clare, wouldn't you?"

Cayatu heard the irony in his voice. "Oh, yes—"

"—But we can't," he snapped. "We can't allow it! We

can't have every neophyte walking away from us whenever they want; thinking they can sit in the fruit orchard all day. Oh, no, I won't tolerate that. Perhaps Brother Esteben would, but I will not. He's old. He wants no trouble. He's loath to write reports to the *Padre Presidente*, but I have many years ahead and ..." Ortiz stopped in mid-sentence.

"There must be a punishment," he continued after his pause. The flesh of his cheeks turned an angry hue. She felt his eyes burn into her. "It speaks in your favor you went to the *monjerio*, but still, there must be a punishment so others will be warned."

Ortiz paused again, his words echoing off the bare adobe walls. The crucifix hanging behind him frightened Cayatu and cast a pall over the room. He gave her another stern look. Cayatu shifted from foot to foot, feeling weakness in her legs and wanting to sit. She twisted the fabric of her skirt in her hand while she waited. She tried to look steadily at him, but in her mind the image of the dead soldier dominated her thoughts.

"The *Comandante* tells me his men need blankets before the rains come," Ortiz continued after the pause. "I'm sending you to weave them on the *Presidio* loom. You'll stay at the fort until the work is done, weaving on their loom by day and sleeping there at night. You won't be free to move about as you please."

"A prisoner?"

"Not a prisoner, but doing penance there. I think it's the only way we can convince you that it's useless to disobey our rules."

"Not the fort," she burst out. "I didn't run away."

"Say no more, I've decided. The *mayordomo* is waiting now to take you. I hope you find humility during your time at the *Presidio* so we'll have no more trouble with you."

Fear poured over Cayatu like a winter storm tide. She wanted to plead with Ortiz. The stocks—any punishment, as long as it kept her at the mission so she could plan her escape. But she saw the set of Ortiz's jaw and she heard Tanayan's parting words in her head—"Show the Spaniards the dignity we have." She let not the slightest hint of her fear show. She narrowed her eyes to stare defiantly at the priest. Then she turned and walked out of the cubicle without another word.

Chapter Nine

Cayatu was taken to a musty weaving room as soon as she was delivered to the *Presidio*. Slightly larger than the loom it held, the room's only light and air came from the door and a small window high on the opposite adobe wall. She sat on a rough wooden bench in front of the loom and picked up the shuttle. From habit formed over a hundred other days at mission looms, she passed the shuttle through the coarse warp threads. Left to right then—*womp*—she brought the beater sharply toward her, ramming the threads tight.

Her feet found the treadles. The small metal holders jangled as the warp threads shifted into alternate positions. Right to left, *womp, jangle*, and then left to right, *womp, jangle*—a mindless cadence in the silent room underscoring her palpable fear. With each pass the coarse-textured cloth grew a fraction. She turned the handle on the cloth beam to roll up the new work. *Womp, jangle, crank, womp, jangle crank.* The cloth grew, the hours passed.

Images of the dead solider haunted her as the shuttle moved back and forth. Did they know? Had Father Fermin Ortiz sent her here to await punishment? *Womp, jangle, crank.* All day long the treadles of her mind alternated between her panic and her plan to flee the Spaniards.

Outside, she heard soldiers' wives talking to each other and calling words she didn't understand to their children. She heard whinnying horses— large and powerful animals unknown before the invaders trampled her special seed-gathering places—stomping their hooves as they came and went on the parade ground. She heard dogs barking and the rush of men shouting harshly to one another while the cadence of the loom recorded the passing of time. *Womp, Jangle, Crank.*

The smells of the fort grew with the heat of the day: food simmering in outdoor pots, animal wastes unmucked in stalls, human sweat from unwashed bodies, all told their own tales about the Spaniards and their Mexican foot soldiers.

Early in the evening, a bowl of *pozole,* with bits of meat bobbing to the surface like suffocating fish, was left at the door. After setting the bowl down, the soldier stood for a long moment in the doorway staring at her. She backed away from the loom and stood pressed against the far wall, watching his every movement with unblinking eyes. Then he smiled, spoke quickly, and hurried away. Too scared to eat, she laid down on the hard dirt floor at the foot of the loom.

At dusk, the thick body of a sergeant blocked the waning light coming through the doorway. With a grunted command, he motioned for her to get up. She held back so he grabbed her by the arm and dragged her outside. Moving rapidly, he led her across the quadrangle, quiet of activity now, stopping to knock outside a door near the chapel. The door opened. The sergeant pushed her inside and left.

Standing with her back tight against the door, she saw the room was large and connected to other rooms. A plank desk, wax-encrusted from dripping candles in wrought iron holders, sat against one wall with a simple chair pulled tight to it. More candles burned in holders on the walls. A musket and sword, whose gilded scabbard glowed golden, stood in one corner.

Comandante Don Jose Maria Demetrio de Alba's turquoise eyes were fixed on her. She returned his stare. After a moment, with their eyes still locked, he approached her, the smell of food crumbs buried in the curls of his blond beard gagging her when he stood before her. He pointed to her blouse, but she didn't understand his meaning, continuing to match his stare. He came closer and slapped her face. Then de Alba reached out a large hand to capture one of her breasts. Stunned, she jumped back. He pushed forward, still looking into her face with his stone eyes, still holding her breast and squeezing it until it hurt. As he began pulling the blouse up over her head Cayatu cried out for help.

There was no help. Cayatu stood alone and desolate as de Alba began to humiliate her. He dropped his hand and roughly began pulling up the fabric of her skirt. She worked to deaden her senses, making herself numb to his touch, but the foulness of his breath, standing so close now, clawed at her. De Alba would do whatever he wished with her. Her only choice was numbness. She struggled to push his breath, his stone blue eyes, his thieving hands, from her mind and retreat into a world where the beach was bright and the water calm.

When the *Comandante* started moving his hands over the rest of her body Cayatu couldn't stop herself. She launched her fist into his face and tried to squirm out of his grasp. He recoiled back several steps, giving her a startled look. Then de Alba laughed and gave her another open-handed slap across her face. Not a hard slap, just stinging enough so she knew he had control over her. For the first time since she'd entered the room, a smile lightened his intensity.

De Alba slapped her a second time and the act seemed to brighten his face further. He gave a low, guttural laugh that bared his teeth. He pointed to the cot in the next room. When

Cayatu failed to understand his intention quickly enough, de Alba's hand shot out again and slapped her hard this time. Laughing, he grabbed her by the wrist and dragged her to the mattress, forcing her down with a painful twist.

When he'd finished with her, breathing hard, de Alba motioned her to the floor. From the table next to his cot he opened a leather pouch and took out a handful of red beads. He handed them to her and stroked his hand over her hair. Several more times during the night De Alba repeated his thrustings, meanly, as if he were driving a stake into the ground. And each time he finished he pushed Cayatu to the floor.

The next day Cayatu was at her loom, the pain of the previous night accentuated by long hours sitting on the hard bench. The memory of her degradation hurt her heart.

The pattern was repeated again that evening: the sergeant took her to the *comandancia* where she spent the night on the thin straw mattress and on the floor, rewarded with red beads. No mention was made of the missing soldier; no words were spoken at all. Deep in her heart she felt shamed by her treatment; wounded by the knowledge she'd become powerless in her own land.

When the sergeant came on the third evening to take her again to de Alba, Cayatu resolved not to allow herself to be humiliated another time. When de Alba pointed to the cot she didn't move. He approached her with an angry glare and she backed up against his desk. Reaching behind her she felt the solid weight of a candle holder and gripped it behind her back. When de Alba came at her, intent on ripping off her blouse, Cayatu's hand shot out, aiming at his head with all the force she could summon.

His hand was quicker. He grabbed her arm at the height of its arc and squeezed it until the iron holder clattered to the floor and the candles died in the dirt. He stood there, with her arm pinned high over her head, just looking down into her face. Cayatu shook with rage and fear mixing together, watching his eyes narrow to slits and seeming to penetrate her; seeing inside at everything she tried to conceal. She waited for the final blow, the smashing fist into her face, the thrust of his sword. But de Alba stood unmoving for a long moment, looking into her, seeing what she had done.

He dropped his hands but kept his eyes fixed on her for several more moments, as if trying to gather his thoughts or perhaps compose his fury. Then, De Alba relaxed and let another of his guttural laughs slip from the side of his mouth, baring his teeth again. Once more he pointed to the cot and barked a command. Still shaking, she went to it, understanding his meaning without knowing his words. When he was done Cayatu watched him rise from the bed and go to his desk where he sat well into the night, smoking a cheroot. She was afraid to close her eyes.

After seven days of confinement, the *mayordomo* came to take Cayatu back to the mission. She was eager to leave the fort but had to stand by the flagpole in the plaza under skies turned leaden while he and the sergeant of the guard spoke back and forth in a hurried exchange. Gray clouds came scudding in from the ocean. The wind from the northwest told of a storm, still at sea, but coming. Already waves were forcing their way down the channel and slapping the beach with an endless assault of whitecaps.

Whirling dust devils hurried across the sand of the quadrangle. Cayatu hunched her shoulders and flattened her hands at her sides to keep her skirt from billowing up. As she stood waiting, Josefa hurried through the gate, wind whipping her curls into a dark froth about her face. She came breathlessly to them, trailed by an old Chumash man carrying water in a wooden bucket. With just a quick nod and weak smile at Cayatu, she spoke rapidly to the soldiers. The man set the bucket down and stood by respectfully.

"She's asking about a missing soldier," the old man told Cayatu after listening to the conversation. "Her husband. These men say they've searched for him without success. They've given up. They think some animal may have attacked him, but I think Coyote has hidden him." He laughed at his own cleverness.

Cayatu shivered. Dryness gripped her throat so tightly she choked for breath and turned her face away.

Finally, Josefa turned to her. "My husband is dead. I know it. This bitter land of yours has robbed me again. A son and now a husband. What will I do?"

The old man translated as fast as he could.

Cayatu was reeling but tried to offer some solace. "I don't know what you will do," she said. "I'm sorry for you."

Looking up at the gathering clouds, the *mayordomo* started to move. He put a hand behind Cayatu's back, pushing her away from Josefa toward the gate. Cayatu resisted, thinking she should say more, but too stunned to know what. The sergeant kept pushing her away.

Across the plaza, Cayatu saw the *Comandante* watching them, one hand on the hilt of his sword, the other on his hip. She stared back for several moments. Then, resisting the *mayordomo's* shoves, she reached into the pocket of her skirt and took out a handful of red beads. Still staring at de Alba, Cayatu raised her hand high over her head so he could see it. Then she dropped the beads through her fingers onto the ground, like drops of blood staining the sand.

Chapter Ten

After the *mayordomo* left Cayatu in front of the *monjerio*, she stood for a moment staring out at the Channel waters. The ocean and sky seemed one without start and end as rain-laden clouds rolled in, hanging low over the hilltop and mountains behind it. The islands were gone, swallowed by a mean sea. She looked up and down the coast, searching for familiar landmarks but the world was gray and becoming dim. There was no clarity, nothing familiar, just the opaqueness of the landscape smeared before her.

Her mood was darker than the clouds, hanging so low over the mission she thought she could reach up and pull the grayness down around her to become invisible. The wind tugged at her skirt and scoured her with grains of grit, stinging her arms and legs like summer flies. She winced at the pricks on her skin and turned away from the hilltop. She crossed the path and went inside the empty women's quarters.

Tears clouded her eyes when she saw the shell basket next to her sleeping mat. Sinking to her knees, consumed by loneliness, she took it in trembling hands. How had she come to such a miserable end to her life? she asked.

"Not ended," the voice beside her said.

"I'm cursed by spirits," she responded without thinking. "Coyote plays with me. With threads attached to my arms and legs, he jerks me into a dance for his amusement."

She stopped short. Where had the voice come from? She looked around. The room was empty, save for an old woman who sat cross-legged on the mat next to her. Cayatu studied the woman's weather-creased face, heavy with darkness. It was a face of smallness, from the narrow circles of her eyes to the tight-set lips. She had small hands and feet and a frail body. Cayatu found nothing remarkable in the woman except her shining black hair.

"Who are you?" she asked, staring at the old woman, uncomfortable with a vague feeling of familiarity.

"Don't you know me?" the woman asked.

"I don't know you. I've never seen you. And yet… It feels like I know you," Cayatu answered her. "Who are you?"

"You came from me," the woman said. "I gave you your life. You took mine in return."

"Mother? Sioctu?" She stared at the woman dumbstruck.

The old woman nodded.

"You're dead. Gone over to the Peaceful Place."

"Your sadness calls me back."

"I *am* sad. Sadder than I knew possible. Take me with you across the Rainbow Bridge."

"No. You have a life to live." Sioctu moved close in front of her, holding Cayatu's eyes captive with her own.

"How can I?" In a sobbing voice Cayatu told her mother all that had happened.

"I know without you telling me. I've watched."

"The pain's too strong, mother."

"You will survive. Think of your family; live for us. You have proud blood to carry forward into the future."

"What future? Tell me."

"Live your life."

"Look how our world's changed." Cayatu said, crying.

"We're no longer proud people—"

"—We'll *always* be proud! First People gave you life as their gift. Be proud!"

"Mother," Cayatu protested, "night after night the Spaniard stabbed me with his man-thing and gave me beads when he was done, as if I were a child. It might as well have been his sword he used because he killed me with it. His filth is in me."

"I know." Sioctu moved closer to embrace the daughter she hadn't lived long enough to know in her slender arms. Cayatu felt only the faintest of breezes ruffle across her shoulders and caress her cheeks. "We are gentle people," her mother told her. "The light-skinned men bring violence to our villages. They give our women babies. Daughter, you must listen to our spirits. Let them guide you."

"I have no dream helper."

"You're *not* alone. Just listen."

As Sioctu spoke, the storm broke outside, punctuating her words with the sudden drumming of rain on the wooden roof. The rain splashed through the paneless window, hitting the sill and sending a cascade of spray down on Cayatu. The coldness of the tiny drops startled her. She sat still for a moment feeling the rain bringing her alive. As she did, her mother's image dissolved. Sioctu's face and body faded to transparent until Cayatu sat alone.

She rose, and walked outside to the crest of the hill. By the time she got there her wet clothes were weights dragging on her. The wind was a gale but she let it have free play, whipping her skirt and streaming her wet hair in thin ropes. She lifted her face to the sky and felt water drip from her forehead, off the tip of her nose, rolling into the corners of her mouth. It tasted good. She lifted her arms, holding them out to the horizon in a welcoming embrace.

It felt cleansing to her. The rain soaked her garments and reached her skin to take away the filth of the *Presidio,* all the animal smells, the stench of *atole,* stale cigar smoke and rancid candle wax. At least she could be clean on the outside, she told herself.

"What are you doing out here in this storm, Clare?" a voice called out. It was Dolores hurrying along the path from the weaving room.

"Cleansing myself," she replied.

"Come inside where it's dry. I have to get out of my wet clothes."

Cayatu laughed at the younger woman. "When we lived in our villages we bathed in the rain, Dolores. Don't you remember? We didn't have so many clothes to get wet."

"I remember," the girl said uneasily. "But those were our heathen days. Now the missionaries teach us new ways, they tell us to cover our nakedness."

"Is that so good?"

"They've brought us the Christ and Blessed Virgin. For me it's better. You, too, if you follow our Lord's teachings. Come inside."

Dolores took Cayatu by the hand in a timid gesture of friendship and led her back to the women's quarters. "Tell me where you've been. For seven nights your mat was empty. I counted. I moved my mat next to yours. I worried you had run away so I prayed for you."

"Your prayers never reached me. Father Ortiz sent me to weave at the fort. I didn't run away, Dolores." Cayatu saw a flicker of fear in Dolores's eyes.

"I would not like to weave there," she said. "Those men are a rough lot—even the ones who have their women with them. How was it for you?"

"Not good."

"The weaving?"

Cayatu studied the young woman she hardly knew, wondering what to say. Dolores had a sweetness about her Cayatu liked, and a desire to please others. Her instinct told her not to tell Dolores too much, but she needed to share the ache inside. "A man used me."

Dolores had a questioning look. "Used you? Who was he? How?"

"He used my body. What the priests call fornication."

Dolores gasped. "God have mercy on you," she said.

"On me?! Your God should take vengeance on the man."

Dolores looked at her without speaking. Cayatu watched a blank look capture her face, as if the words were having trouble being understood. Finally, Dolores reached out her arms to embrace her. "You must pray, Clare. Pray as I do when Father Ortiz invites me to his room. Pray to the Virgin for guidance." Dolores still held her by the shoulders but pushed Cayatu back and looked into her eyes. "Ask Her to calm your anger," Dolores said and Cayatu heard the innocence in her voice. "She'll answer your prayers if you pray with openness. She will show you how to live your life. I'll pray with you if you like."

"Does the Virgin guide your life?" Cayatu asked. "Does She tell you how to live in balance with our world? Like a dream helper?"

"That's our old world, Clare" Dolores scoffed. "The Virgin listens to women who pray. She gives us strength."

Chapter Eleven

Demetrio de Alba strode across the parade grounds to Josefa after Cayatu and the *mayordomo* disappeared out the gate.

"No sign of your husband," he said. *"Lo Siento."*

Josefa looked up at him with sad, dark eyes. She swept back the nest of dark curls the wind had blown about her face with her hand and gathered her *rebozo* tightly about her. "He's dead, Lieutenant." she said.

"I believe so. *Lo siento, por Dios.* I can't continue the search. Accept my sympathy."

"We've searched everywhere without a sign, Josefa," the sergeant of the guard added. "If Guillermo were alive, we'd've found him."

"So... I'm alone..." she said, pausing for a moment to look around at the familiar *Presidio* grounds. "This is a harsh land... May the Virgin protect me."

"Hard on us all," de Alba said, offering her a sympathetic smile. He used it as an excuse to look her over. Sturdily built, not fat, but soft and round. A welcoming body that fit well with her full face, always smiling, even in the depth of her sadness. Her face reminded him of the sultry governess he'd had growing into adolescence in Spain, another dark woman he could never forget even though there had been dozens of other women since her.

He reached out a consoling hand to touch Josefa's shoulder. He let it rest there. "Look at me—alone like you," he said. "No one to comfort me. The wind blows right through my walls. And the winter coming on… I envy my men who have women to care for them. I envied your husband because he had such a beautiful woman to hold him at night."

Josefa's face warmed to his compliment. "Perhaps you should take a woman," she said.

"A wife?"

"A woman to comfort and care for you. This is a hard land in which to be alone. The *padres* smile on holy marriages."

"Yes, the *padres*… Tell me Josefa, what will you do now, if—"

"—Stay here. There's nothing for me in Guanajuato, where I was born. The Virgin will watch over me and the Franciscans will help. I'll be all right."

"I'm at your service." De Alba kept his hand on her shoulder, giving it just the faintest pressure. "Call on me whenever you have a need."

"We can help too," the sergeant spoke up, trying to be helpful. "You could petition the king for the land Guillermo was promised."

De Alba shot the sergeant a look that quickly shut him up.

"What would I do? Become a farmer?" Josefa came close to laughter then hesitated. "…I'll think about this land you talk of."

De Alba's eyes shifted to two horsemen coming through the gate. One was Father Fermin Ortiz, riding a chestnut mare, accompanied by Jimeno, the guard of the *vaqueros*.

"*Buenos Días, Padre*," he called out as they rode up. Josefa and the sergeant nodded to the priest.

"A blustery day, *Comandante*. We'll have a storm before nightfall." He bent down from the saddle to put his hand on Josefa. "May the Holy Mother be with you," Ortiz told her. "We pray your husband's soul is safe with the Lord.

Brother Esteben will say a Mass for Guillermo. We'll help any way we can."

"*Gracias, Padre.*" Josefa bowed to Ortiz and de Alba, then, tears filling her eyes, she turned and walked away toward the cluster of mud houses outside the fort. The old Chumash man still followed behind her.

"What brings you here?" de Alba questioned the priest when Josefa had disappeared out the gate.

"Jimeno and I ride out to the cattle. It's the day for *Matanza* so we ride out to see the steers slaughtered and make sure the correct tallies are kept. I invite you to ride along with me so we can talk and you can—"

"—On such a day?"

"Especially today! You'll see, Lieutenant."

De Alba heard the intensity in Ortiz's voice and it took him by surprise.

"It will be worth your time, Lieutenant," the priest promised, "well worth your time. The weather should hold off until we're done. We'll only have to ride a few leagues west of the *pueblo*. You should ride with us."

"Very well. Jimeno, go to the corral and see my horse is saddled," de Alba ordered. "Bring my sword and pistol, too."

"No need," Ortiz said.

"Get them, Jimeno," de Alba repeated.

T he trio rode along a well-worn path west of the *Presidio* and small settlement that clung to it for protection, winding through stands of live oaks and around grass-covered hillocks. Emerging on the headlands west of the *pueblo*, they rode along bluffs overlooking the beach. Offshore, the gray was thickening.

"*Padre*, you sit a horse like a man who rides well," de Alba commented as they reached open ground and picked up their pace. "A rare gift for a man of the cloth."

"I rode as a boy in Spain. My family raised cattle in *Cantabria*. The *Padre Presidente* prefers us to walk, more humble, you know, but this land is so vast. Without horses it would be a chore."

"Without a horse a man is nothing," de Alba said with a grin softening his face as he sized up the priest. "Perhaps a race?"

Ortiz chuckled. "*Comandante*, I hardly think I could keep pace with the magnificent stallion you ride."

"No wager," de Alba said. "Just a friendly race to the *matanza* where your *vaqueros* work." He threw down the challenge with a condescending smile but didn't wait for a response. "*Vamanos!*" he shouted, and dug his spurs deep into Esperanza's flanks.

The gray Arabian responded instantly, bolting ahead, dark mane and tail streaming behind him. Esperanza stood fourteen hands, short, like most of his breed, but with a full barrel chest built to run long distances at full gallop. His finely formed head held eyes that burned, challenging eyes that kept other horses at a distance.

Jimeno and Father Ortiz were left far behind, although they also kicked their horses into a gallop. De Alba guided his mount effortlessly, jumping small bushes for the pure joy of it. He ran the gray stallion full speed far ahead of the others. When he arrived at the milling herd of cattle, he reined the horse up so short it reared on hind legs, pawing the air with his front hooves, snorting triumphantly. While still in the air, de Alba pivoted him around so that he came back to earth facing the other riders who were just approaching.

"It's well we didn't wager," he laughed. "No one can match me on Esperanza. We are superb."

"Indeed you are, Lieutenant," the priest answered him. "But our *vaqueros* have become fine horsemen, too. They might give you a good race."

De Alba wheeled Esperanza around to study the men working the cattle. "This is a joke you make, *Padre*, no?" he said turning back to the priest. "You must be making sport with me if you say these Indians could match me."

"Perhaps, Lieutenant, but watch awhile." Then Ortiz turned to Jimeno, "How many to slaughter today?"

"Thirty, perhaps forty, *Padre*. The slaughter grows each week now to feed your neophytes." Jimeno called out to two of the *vaqueros*—Tomas and Vicente—asking them for the tally. Tomas rode over and handed Jimeno a short oak branch with notches cut in it. Turning back to the priest, Jimeno said, "They've already killed thirteen."

Astride Esperanza, de Alba watched the slaughter. Tomas, Vicente, or one of the other *vaqueros* in turn rode toward the cluster of cattle, milling about, snorting, bellowing, kicking up clouds of dust with their hooves. The rider shouted and spurred his horse into a full gallop, charging into the bunched up steers. Coming as close alongside as many of them as he could during the charge, the horseman reached far out over his saddle to plunge a long knife—almost a short spear—into the hump of each animal just behind its head. The steer staggered to the ground, dead. The rider pulled the killing knife out and went on to stab the next, and again the next steer, plunging the long blade into each panicking animal he passed. The horsemen made quick work of the killing. De Alba was startled at the way Indian and horse seemed to flow together, merging so that each was the mind of the other as they cut sharply left or right pursuing a steer.

Other Indian men and women followed the *vaqueros,* skinning the downed animals and butchering them. But while he took in all the activity, de Alba's eyes never strayed from the horsemen charging through the herd. Abruptly, he shouted to Jimeno over the din of the slaughter, "Stop the *vaqueros*! Gather them by that oak tree and wait for me."

Both Jimeno and Ortiz shot him questioning stares.

De Alba rode to Jimeno's side. "The Chumash ride well," he said.

"Sí, *Comandante,* as if they were born to be horsemen. They learn quickly. They live for their time in the saddle. Sometimes they ride just for the joy of riding."

"So I'm told," de Alba said. "Let's see how good they really are." De Alba pointed into the distance. "Tell them to race their horses as fast as they can to that far tree to the east and back."

De Alba watched Jimeno instruct the other riders, feeling the thrill of competition rising in his chest. When all the riders burst into motion, almost as one man and kicking up dust behind them, de Alba dug his spurs into Esperanza.

The far tree they raced to was half a league away. It sat silhouetted against the sky on the bluff overlooking the beach. The plain sloped toward the ocean over rough ground of small hillocks and hidden depressions, but it was familiar ground for the Chumash men working the cattle. Excited by the thrill of the race they urged their horses on. First one, then another of them took the lead, but they all stayed tightly bunched as they sped over the ground, shouting friendly taunts to each other as they raced.

De Alba held Esperanza in check, riding confidently with the pack until they approached the tree.

Mayhem broke out as all eight riders tried to round it as tightly as they could for the return gallop. Horses snorted and whinnied, hooves a blur, coming in contact with each other as their riders maneuvered them for advantage. One *vaquero* got too close to another. Their horses bumped, throwing each off stride. Their riders clung to their saddles.

De Alba approached the turn alongside Vincente. He swung Esperanza wide and then reined the stallion hard to the right, aiming the horse as close to the tree as he could. Esperanza protested with a shrill whine. The Lieutenant's gambit trapped Vicente between Esperanza and the tree trunk, forcing him to pull up sharply. Vicente's mount bellowed fear as Vicente tried to avoid the tree. The horse reared. Vicente fought for balance. The horse veered off to the left, tripping on his own legs, and stumbled to the ground on top of its rider.

De Alba didn't look back. He spurred Esperanza to greater speed. He caught up with the pack and raced past three of the riders, including Tomas. There were still three riders ahead. He urged Esperanza to greater effort. The stallion forced his way into the pack of leaders. Now they all ran together, hooves flashing and slashing the ground, coming dangerously close to each other. The staccato of sixteen hooves pounding the earth together sent a flush of excitement coursing through the Spaniard.

In response to de Alba's leg pressure, Esperanza veered right then left, forcing the horses next to him to give ground. The aggressive gray bullied his way through the pack. Only one *vaquero* was still running with him.

The two horses were closing fast on the finish line, running side by side as one horse. Esperanza was blowing blood-flecked foam from his mouth. The look in his eyes was fire. De Alba drove his spurs deeper into his flanks where drops of blood already oozed from his withers. With only a slight head movement Esperanza bared his teeth. The other horse lurched out of reach. It was enough for Esperanza. He flew by Jimeno a full length in the lead.

As horse and rider recovered their wind, de Alba pulled up alongside Jimeno. "These riders could be a threat to us if they chose to rebel," he shouted, short of breath. "We'd best be careful. If I weren't such a fine horseman—"

"—Why would they rebel?" Ortiz interrupted, turning in his saddle to give de Alba a questioning look. "They are peace loving. We give them all their wants. ...And we keep a strict hand on them. We're alert to danger but we're always in control."

"Still," de Alba said, "they could be a threat if many of them rode against our small garrison. Take their horses back to the *Presidio,* Jimeno. Get the Indians lesser mounts."

Chapter Twelve

Ortiz ignored de Alba and waved his hands impatiently at Jimeno. "Get these Indians back to work. Finish the *matanza* before the storm hits," he called out. "No more play." Then he urged his mare into a slow trot toward the beach, motioning de Alba to follow. Half a league to the west he descended a gentle slope that ended on the sand in a small cove protected by headlands reaching into the sea on either side. Ortiz reined in and sat for a moment looking out at the gray-green sea. A smile came ever so faintly over his face, as he peered into the thickening gloom. Offshore, he heard the constant cadence of breakers no longer visible in the grayness. His smile faded when he turned to face de Alba.

"So, *Padre*, you bring me here for what? For *this*? Just to see a storm coming?" de Alba chided before Ortiz had a chance to speak.

"Precisely, Lieutenant."

"This is a waste. There's nothing here."

"Look about you, *Comandante*. Look carefully."

De Alba let Esperanza's reins go slack and gave the stallion a reassuring pat on his neck. He turned in his saddle to stare into the grayness. His eyes swept back and forth, scanning the beach and the headlands jutting into the ocean, fading behind a gray curtain drawn over sea and sky, anxious with wind and waves. He stood in his stirrups, looking out for a long time over the dim water, scanning the horizon.

"*Madre del Dios!*" he muttered, so softly Ortiz could barely hear him. Turning to the priest, with an angry tone coming into his voice, de Alba said, "I cannot believe what my eyes are showing me."

"I saw it this morning from the mission, well off shore, probably looking for a safe harbor to ride out the storm away from the eyes of the *Presidio*."

"No flag. It's not our ship. You should've told me immediately."

"When the storm abates it will sail on," Ortiz said, keeping a calm tone. "But think, Don Demetrio; how many ships sail by unnoticed? How long before another puts in for water—or sees the cattle—out of sight of your men? How long before foreign sailors want to trade here?"

"Not allowed," de Alba said. "My men would stop them. Trade with foreigners is forbidden."

Ortiz studied his companion then looked away in a moment of reflection. His hand reached down to run slowly along the smooth leather of his saddle as he tried to gauge de Alba's mood. Don Demetrio's face was screwed up tight. The priest watched as de Alba fixed his stone blue eyes on the two-masted brig riding beyond the surf, only the vaguest outline of hull and masts visible; so vague as to challenge detection and mock the certainty of the two men on the bluff.

The sour smell of kelp thrown up by the waves caused Ortiz to draw in a deep breath before starting. "I told you there was opportunity here for men of action, with the vision to see the future," he began. "We won't be alone for long, Don Demetrio; too many nations envy us. Our land's too rich to stay empty."

"How can you say rich?" De Alba's response was full of disdain. "This land is barren, few trees. Not like the Valley of Mexico I long to return to. That lush land gave us all our wants. Not the barrenness of this forgotten coast."

"Most of the king's officers will return home to Spain or *Nueva España*," Ortiz acknowledged. "But they'll return as poor as they came, second and third sons with nothing to support them and no way to enrich themselves."

To Ortiz the opportunity seemed obvious and he wondered at de Alba's failure to comprehend it. Only a dimwitted man or one of insufferable arrogance could fail to see the riches *he* saw for the taking. The future was clear to Father Ortiz, full of promise, if he had the *Comandante's* blessing. "Land is the great wealth here," he continued. "Cattle will be the currency in which wealth is counted, of that I'm certain. If you have the will we could prosper."

"Prosper? We? How?"

De Alba's puzzled look told Ortiz he would have to go very carefully. "I was told in Monterey before coming here that Bostonmen would buy sea otter furs on their way to the Orient if they could, and stop for cattle hides and tallow to take back to New England. Think about them bringing us all manner of goods for the people living in the *pueblo*. We could trade for those goods." Ortiz waited, studying the soldier again, letting the thought work its way into his mind and watching to see how he would digest it. "It could be us," he said after the pause.

"The king forbids trading with foreigners."

"But it will happen. Soon enough some Yankee ship captain will try. Someone will trade with him."

Esperanza shifted impatiently, pawing at the sand. De Alba straightened up in his saddle, pulling himself erect and glaring at Ortiz. "I take my oath seriously, *Padre*."

"And well you should, Lieutenant. But did the king intend for his subjects here to suffer unnecessary hardships? I think not."

De Alba thought for a moment, then he acknowledged Ortiz. "My men lack food, uniforms. They receive no pay when the San Blas ship doesn't arrive."

"Precisely. The law is obsolete now because the Motherland can't keep us supplied. She fights too many wars in Europe. And what harm is done really? Who would know? But, *Comandante,*" Ortiz hurried to add, "I would never suggest that you break the king's law. Never."

"I worry for my men," de Alba said, turning in his saddle again to look out at the brig lying off shore. "I have no cattle, *Padre*. No land. Nor do you, a monk sworn to poverty. How could it be us?"

"There's opportunity here if we take hold of it," Ortiz said again, looking hard into de Alba's face. "We're alike, you and I. We must do for ourselves what our fathers couldn't do for us. Those problems are easily solved. The mission has more cattle than Jimeno can count. Steers wander off into the canyons."

"You would steal them from the mission?"

"An unpleasant word," Ortiz said. "The mission will have more cattle than it needs soon. A few cows wouldn't be missed. Some could be slaughtered, their hides ready when foreigners come looking to trade. All that's needed is a place to hide them away from the mission herd and a few *vaqueros* to keep watch. Do you understand what I am saying?"

"You want me to assist you in stealing mission cattle and trading with foreigners, do I understand *you, padre?* I cannot do that. I am an officer—"

"—Oh, no, Lieutenant. No! I would never suggest that you do those things. Perhaps all I suggest is that you look in a different direction when a foreign ship comes near our shores. You could help Josefa in getting a land grant from the king. Compensation for Guillermo's death. That's not breaking any law. Soldiers are entitled to land when they retire. Leave the rest to me."

De Alba sat silently in his saddle, looking questioningly into his companion's face. "I see," was all he said after a moment's reflection. "Tell me, *Padre,* you are sworn to poverty…"

Ortiz shrugged. The mare he rode whinnied her discomfort. "In the end we're alike, Don Demetrio. We're impatient men. We both want to live out our days in comfort wherever we're destined to live them. And we must make our own way in life. Together we could do that. All you would do is petition the king for land here away from the *pueblo* and turn your head from time to time. We could share the profits."

The wind came in strong gusts from the sea, blowing foam off the wavetops and stinging their faces with sand driven off the beach. De Alba shuddered a little in his tunic. He started Esperanza back up the trail to the bluff, looking back only once at the ship hove-to just offshore, sitting high on the water, pointed into the wind, bare masts and yards ready to ride out the tempest bearing down the channel. "Let's ride to the fort," he called to Ortiz. "The weather is closing fast. I could use a glass of fine port. I'm sure you could too. No race, but let's get back quickly. Port and more talk, no? As you say, in some ways we're alike."

"Yes, port," Ortiz agreed. "And perhaps some roast meat."

Chapter Thirteen

On the eve of the acorn festival, as Sun finished his journey across storm-threatened skies, Massilili nervously watched the torches being lighted around the dancing place. A few old men and women had come to sit behind a low wall of stones, but most of the villagers stayed away; some playing the dice games at their huts, while others traded with men from the *Pueblo*. As smoke from dying cooking fires disappeared in the darkness, musicians went into the dancing place with clapsticks, flutes, panpipes, and rattles made from turtle shells.

Three men of the *'Antap* cult came from the shadows. Massilili joined them and they all started dancing. They wore skins and feathers of the animal and bird spirits who lived before the great flood. Their dance told the story of creation. Swirling and twisting in the fire-glow, casting shadows that danced out among the watchers, Massilili moved to the rhythmic staccato of the music. It was his first dance.

"Look how you've grown—almost a man now," Tanayan had told him. "Your father gives you a great honor for so young a man."

Qoloq danced with the others. "Dance with all your strength. All your courage," he had urged his son. "You've grown tall, strong. The strength of your dance tonight will show your commitment to First People. Your first ceremony—show you will be a strong leader after me."

Now, as Qoloq moved to the music, slowly at first, but gaining intensity as he danced, Massilili saw his father's thick body lose its ungainliness. Qolog's leaps and jumps and spins were precise but frenzied. He *became* Coyote, the Wily One, teaching others to use power. Coyote showed the Chumash how to travel great distances in an instant and how to drink Old Woman Momoy's water so they could have spirit dreams and find dream helpers.

Massilili tried to keep up with Qoloq's intricate steps but couldn't. He wanted his father to be proud of him. He wanted the villagers to think he was worthy of leading them. But as the dance continued he grew tired. Qoloq seemed to draw energy from the music, from the flickering torches, from within himself. Massilili danced self-consciously while Qoloq danced with abandon, his eyes closed, enraptured, giving himself up to the spirit world. Massilili felt the ache in his gut and knew it was more from shame than from his effort. He watched Qoloq's body twisting and jumping in the torchlight, and he knew his father's spirit had risen to the World Above.

That was a world Massilili didn't know and thought little about. His was the Middle World of beach and ocean, fishing and paddling long distances to the islands to trade. Mountain cat was Massilili's dream helper. It had come to protect him during the dreaming ceremony when he passed into manhood. He was proud to have such a powerful guide in his life, but he felt no connection to the spirit world of his father.

Qoloq uttered sounds from deep in his throat, primitive sounds without sense, in counterpoint to the flutes and pipes growing louder as he danced. His spinning and leaping continued long after Massilili and the other dancers had tired and moved to the edge of the dancing place. His shrieks grew louder. And still he danced, eyes closed, legs and arms jerky, uncontrolled, flailing. Late in the night he fell on the ground, trembling and moaning, still enraptured in the mysteries of the three worlds.

Opening his eyes, Qoloq aimed a feral stare at the handful of old people in front of him. Massilili watched Qoloq draw himself to his hands and knees in an animal pose. "Where are your sons and daughters?" Qoloq growled at them. "Where have your young ones gone? Your babies are dead in your huts," he shouted. "Dead from diseases the foreigners have brought us. Lost forever!" He got to his feet and staggered off through the village.

Massilili followed behind. He knew few of the villagers still followed the old ways and he worried about what his father might do. He saw Qoloq weaving among the huts, shouting at villagers who sat around their fires throwing the gambling stones, and his only thought was to protect his father. Qoloq kicked at the dirt, swearing curses at the usurpers of his land. He came upon two traders from the *pueblo* sitting cross-legged on the ground, using hand signs to trade for small stone carvings of whales and pelicans. The Mexicans offered crystal beads and a pigskin of *aguardiente* in return. Helpless to stop his father, Massilili watched from the shadows as Qoloq leapt into the middle of their circle, picking up a handful of the beads lying on the ground. "Worthless," he shouted. He tossed the beads into the night and stood glowering down at the men.

Both traders jumped to their feet. The two villagers scrunched crab-like into the darkness. Qoloq continued raving at the confused Mexican men, while Massilili stood fixed to his spot in the darkness, watching, asking himself if he would ever find the spirit strength his father had. He wanted to be a canoeman, speeding across the shining ocean in a great *tomol* searching for strong fish or valuable items the islanders would trade for. His father had a different future planned for him, a future of spirit dreaming and healing, but Massilili didn't want it.

Qoloq reached out to grab the pigskin of *aguardiente* away from one of the men. The man backed up but Qoloq pushed forward, trying to get at it. The other man came from behind, wrapping his arms around Qoloq's chest, trying to pull him back.

The first man was angry his beads had been scattered on the ground. He swore at Qoloq and then raised his hand into a fist, smashing it in Qoloq's face. Qoloq crumbled to the ground as the other man let go of him.

Massilili charged into the firelight, picking up a piece of oak firewood from a nearby hut and swinging it wildly. The traders looked at each other in panic. "Get away!" Massilili shouted. "Leave the village! Don't come back." He swung the wood with more purpose, connecting with one man's arm just below the shoulder. The man winced and backed away. The other one, the man who had hit Qoloq, stared at Massilili, standing tall and defiant in the firelight. Massilili took another swing. The wood connected with the man's head, knocking him to his knees. Massilili stood over him. "Go! Now! Before I kill you." The trader crawled a few feet off, then got to his feet and ran into the darkness following his partner. Massilili scooped Qoloq up in his powerful arms and carried him, still shouting oaths, to their hut.

Chapter Fourteen

The day after the storm drenched the small settlement of Santa Barbara, leaving a sun-bright, well-scrubbed morning in its wake, Cayatu hurried to leave the mission weaving room when she finished her allotted length of new cloth.

"Wait for me, Clare," Dolores called to her when Cayatu paused in the doorway inspecting the day. The mountains framing the mission church stood out in finely honed relief against a cloudless cobalt sky. Ocean waters in the channel below her had given up their wind-tossed confusion and returned to a gentle swell.

Together, the two went to the *monjerio* where Cayatu put on a clean blouse and skirt and took a brush to her hair, smoothing the long dark strands that hung down to her shoulders. She continued brushing until her hair glistened like the obsidian flakes on Qoloq's baton. As she did, her thoughts slipped back to the days when she brushed her hair to a luster before going to Ysaga.

"Do you have a man in the village?" Dolores asked.

"The Franciscans call him Tomas. He's a *vaquero.*"

"I've heard other girls talk of him."

Dolores's voice had a restrained note to it that got Cayatu's attention. Her head bobbed up, hair still hanging about her face. "Other girls?"

"They gather at the men's huts when the *vaqueros* come in from the cattle."

Cayatu tossed her hair back off her face and stood. "I don't want other girls there. I'll chase them away," she said, half laughing self-consciously to make it sound like a joke but there was a look of resolve on her face.

The women walked together to the kitchen and waited for their food. Tomas stood waiting too. When he saw her, Cayatu watched his face change from somber to excited. "Clare, where have you been?'

"At the fort." She gave Tomas her brightest smile, but looked at him steadily with serious eyes. "Please say my real name."

"You know the priests don't allow our real names," Tomas chided. "Father Ortiz said what existed before the Franciscans came doesn't matter."

When the meal was over, Cayatu led Tomas away from the others, but before she could speak to him, he spoke first, concern showing in the creases of his forehead. "The fort was not such a good place, eh?"

"Not good," she answered. "We won't talk about it." She smiled at him, touching his hand, sending a silent message. "Tell me about your work."

Tomas swelled with pride. "I'm one of the best *vaqueros*," he said drawing himself up and puffing out his chest. "We round up calves and drive them to Jimeno, the soldier guard, so he can add them to the tallies," he told her. "We slaughter steers for food and hides. Today only half rode to the herd because of the heavy storm. I stayed here with some others to care for our horses. Oh, what fine animals our horses are! I love tending my mare—brushing and feeding her. I've never had anything to care for before. She takes me wherever I want to go."

"So," Cayatu teased, "You love your horse; other men love women."

Tomas stared down at the ground without comment. "Come with me," he broke the silence, "You'll see."

Tomas led Cayatu down the path to the corral where the smell of manure and warm hay and horses hung in the air. A dozen horses grazed in groups of twos and threes along the low stone fences that were topped with dry bones to keep them from escaping. When he whistled, a chestnut with black mane and tail raised her head and looked over her shoulder at them.

The mare, her coat glistening in the afternoon light, trotted to the fence gate in front of them. Tomas stroked her nose, speaking quietly. "You can touch her," he said.

Cayatu caressed the softness of the mare's nose, stroked the sides of her face, touched her fleshy lips with hesitant fingers. She cupped her hand over an ear, drinking in the mare's unmistakable scent. The horse stood quietly, with large, unblinking eyes watching Cayatu. Then she nickered softly.

"Could I ride her?" Cayatu asked.

"Here? Now?"

Cayatu tugged at his arm. "Could I learn to ride?"

"Jimeno wouldn't allow it."

Cayatu was drawn to the mare by a force she didn't understand. "Let's go into the corral, Tomas." She didn't wait for an answer, taking his hand and leading him to the gate. Looking around, to make sure they were alone, Tomas threw up his hands and lifted the latch.

The mare came over to them. Standing close to her, Cayatu felt the horse's size and power. It sent a shiver of excitement through her. "How far can she take you?" she asked Tomas.

"I could ride her all day."

"Show me how to get on her back. I want to feel what it's like to ride." Cayatu stepped closer to Tomas, so she could put both her hands on his shoulders and coax him with her smile. "No one's here. Show me."

"I shouldn't..." He turned around again to make sure they were safely alone. "But for you..." He walked to the far side of the corral, taking a blanket from a wooden stand. He tossed it on the mare's back, then a saddle.

Cayatu studied Tomas's skillful work. A tinge of fear, mixed with the anticipation of a new adventure, sent a shiver up her spine. What a capable husband he would be, she decided.

"I shouldn't do this," he said again, adjusting the cinch, his eyes scanning the path once more for trouble.

Cautiously, Tomas took Cayatu to the mare. He showed her how to mount and helped her put a sandaled foot into the thin iron stirrup. When she stalled half way up—one foot in the stirrup and her hand gripping the pommel—he clasped hands for her to step on and lifted her the rest of the way.

Giddy with joy, Cayatu giggled as she settled herself. From this new, high vantage point, she felt tall. She felt the strength and power under her. Looking off in all directions, she could see farther than she'd ever seen standing on the ground. From the mare's back she could see trees in the lemon orchard the priests had planted down the hill from the corral and beyond them to the rooftops of the adobes in the village and the walls of the fort down the hill. She could see the sails of a ship, brightly lit by the arcing sun.

Even Tomas seemed smaller when Cayatu looked down from the saddle. Her world had a new dimension. She felt the thrill of a new kind of freedom. The mare's flanks breathed in and out, a gentle sensation under her. Cayatu trembled. No wonder a horseman has so much power, she thought. She reached down with her hand to stroke the mare's neck. The mare moved forward.

A new swell of excitement surged over Cayatu as the horse took a step, shifting her weight from one side to the other. She was moving. Without any effort she was moving forward. If she knew how to direct this horse it would take her wherever she wanted to go. It would take her away from the mission, she thought.

"Oh, Tomas," she called out. "I'm free."

As Cayatu turned in the saddle her heels accidentally nudged the mare's flanks. The mare walked forward, catching Cayatu unaware and off balance. In an instant, she was tossed out of the saddle and lying on the ground. The mare stopped and stood beside her. Tomas ran to her side, dropping to his knees, panic on his face as he reached for her hand.

"This wasn't a good idea," he fretted. "I told you that." He started to scold. "Are you hurt?"

On her back, Cayatu looked up at him, watching concern darken his face, tightening the skin around his eyes and mouth. She stared at him several moments' longer, thinking how much he cared for her. She started laughing, forgetting for the moment her imprisonment at the fort. Tomas's startled look evaporated when he saw she wasn't hurt and he began to laugh with her.

Together in the afternoon stillness, Cayatu on her back on the soft dirt and Tomas on his knees beside her, they laughed till tears dripped from their eyes and her sides hurt. Tomas edged closer to her. Cayatu grabbed his arm, pulling him down beside her. They laughed together, lying on their backs looking into the sky. Their feelings for each other flowed back and forth through their fingertips.

"Run away with me, Tomas," she said, still looking up into the clear sky. "Let's take a horse and ride away from the mission—live free again."

Tomas rolled onto his side so he could stare incredulously at her.

"What's going on here?" The strident Spanish voice shattered their moment.

Tomas jumped to his feet, brushing leaves from his pants, face to face with Jimeno. "I'm... I'm showing my horse to my friend," he stammered.

Cayatu got to her feet and stood behind Tomas, flush in the face and composing herself as she adjusted her skirt. The mare trotted off to the other side of the corral.

Jimeno looked down on them from atop his own horse, and Cayatu saw the meaness flashing in his dark eyes. "*Your horse*," he spit at Tomas. "You fool. These mounts aren't your play things. They're not yours at all. I've told all you worthless men these horses belong to the King of Spain. We only let you ride them to do our work."

The words flew out of Jimeno's mouth, each one a prickly barb that bit into Tomas. Tomas could only nod and look down sheepishly at the ground.

"You'll get a whipping for this," Jimeno continued his tirade.

"No whipping," Cayatu said, pushing in front of Tomas and pointing to herself. "My fault," she tried to make the Spaniard understand. "I asked him to show me his horse."

Jimeno dismounted and put his hands on his hips. "Who is this woman?" he demanded of Tomas. As his eyes swept over her, Cayatu felt a chill run up her back. She saw a smirk come over Jimeno's face. He walked up close to her, staring at her, standing so close his breath scorched her. "I know who you are," he said, his barbed words now biting into her. "The lieutenant's whore, aren't you? Everyone at the fort knows of you."

Cayatu stood still, not knowing what to do, but she was angry this man had invaded her day, ruining her time with Tomas. Most of Jimeno's words sailed off into the afternoon sky without leaving any meaning behind, but she saw the hurt look on Tomas's face and knew she had to end this confrontation.

Before she could, Tomas pushed between her and the soldier. "Do not talk to her with those words," he said. "Talk to me as a man and leave her alone."

Jimeno took a step back from the force of Tomas's outburst. "You stupid Indian," he snarled. "How could you dare to speak that way to a soldier of the king? I'll whip you till you beg for death."

Cayatu understood the words for whip and death. The fear they brought pushed her into action. "No whipping," she shouted at Jimeno. "Tomas and I will leave now. If you don't let us go I'll tell the *Comandante* how you treated me. He likes me. He'll be angry, maybe whip you."

She took Tomas's hand and led him from the corral, not looking back to see Jimeno's reaction.

Chapter Fifteen

Esteben Salamanca clung to the altar rail with arthritic hands. His skin was paper-thin, translucent blue veins bulged against his knuckles like boulder-clogged streams. He looked out over the bowed heads of his congregation from listless eyes. Almost all color was gone from his face.

Before him knelt the people of the *pueblo*—*gente de razón*, Salamanca and the other pure-blooded Spaniards called them. They were the Mexican soldiers and their wives and a small band of other men and women who had come north from New Spain to build a future or escape a past. Spaniards were their leaders, highborn men, both priests and officers, but it was the *mestizos* recruited in the mining villages of Sonora and Sinaloa sitting in front of him that Salamanca knew would be the true foundation of the *pueblo*. Kneeling behind them, the mission neophytes stirred as he intoned a final prayer for Presidio soldier Guillermo Tapia.

His gaze fell on Josefa Tapia kneeling alone in the front row, a black lace *mantilla* covering her head and shoulders. Ringlets of soft, dark curls peeked out around her forehead and cheeks. Her white *camisa* set off pale olive skin and her handsome face held shining dark eyes. Those eyes were dry now as she prayed, but Salamanca knew the unbearable heartache of her loss had drained them.

He made the sign of the cross and bid the mourners go. Then he moved to Josefa's side. "Are you at peace, *Señora?*" he asked.

"*Sí, Padre*, I am. A body to bury in the ground would ease my mind but that may never be. Do you think an animal killed Guillermo? Or an Indian?"

"In truth, Josefa, what does it matter?" Salamanca said. "We may never find him. There are bears in the mountains. Large cats come down to drink at the streams, I'm told." He paused for a moment before going on. "Probably an animal. We've asked many Indians and not one knows anything about your husband. So, what can we do for you? How can we bring some comfort to your life?"

"Don't trouble over me, I can care for myself. I lived by my wits in Guanajuato and I'll do it here." Josefa forced a smile that turned up the corners of her mouth and parted her lips. "I was poor there—orphaned before my twelfth birthday. I worked even then for food and shelter. Guillermo told me we'd live better in this new land so I came with him."

Salamanca put a fatherly hand on the young woman's shoulder, admiring her beauty, just on the verge of fading into her middle years. He was troubled by the rough path that lay ahead for her. "It could be more difficult for you here than it was in your home village," he told her.

"Already *Comandante* de Alba helps me," she said. "He's given me work at the fort, washing his clothes and cleaning his quarters. Other soldiers' wives look out for me, too."

"And land?" Salamanca asked. "Brother Ortiz tells me you might get land from the king."

Josefa laughed wryly. "Do all men want land? Don Demetrio wants to petition the King for land as compensation for my loss. He says it was Guillermo's right as a soldier to have land here when he retired. Land can wait.

When the time is right I'll take the land. For now I'll stay in the *pueblo*."

"*Padre* Ortiz and the *Comandante* seem more interested in land for you than you are," Salamanca mused. "Is there nothing else we can do for you, then?"

"There is something, *Padre*. I'm chilled at night and I have only these thin clothes and worn blankets. I need new ones. For that I need cloth if you have cloth to spare."

"We do," Salamanca reassured her. "Come with me." He moved toward the doors and stepped out into the bright morning light. Neophytes and townspeople still milled around, warming themselves from the chilling dampness of the church, coming alive like lizards crawling out from rocks into a noon sun. "Clare," he called from the steps.

Cayatu left the others to join Josefa and the priest. Standing so close to Josefa, she trembled, but worked to still her emotions, not letting her face reveal her guilt over Guillermo's death. Looking at Josefa she remembered their first meeting at the feast in her village five acorn seasons before the building of the mission, when Josefa and the party of settlers first made their way along the coast. She remembered Josefa as the attractive light-skinned young woman who had taken such a fondness to Massilili, patting his head like a small animal and pampering him with tidbits of food at the feast the immigrants shared with the village.

Those first feasts with the newcomers had been innocent ones. When Qoloq warned of the dangers, few paid attention. Cayatu remembered taking Josefa to the beach with Massilili to show her where they hunted food along the shore and where they collected shells. Neither could speak the other's language, but they found ways to understand each other and tell the boastful stories strangers often tell.

Now Josefa smiled, showing even teeth. She held out a friendly hand to Cayatu.

"Clare," Salamanca started, "It's our Christian duty to help Josefa. Her husband went looking for you. He never came back—"

"—Did you see him?" Josefa interrupted. "Do you know where he is?"

Cayatu looked from woman to priest, understanding their words and feeling nervous. Do they know, she wondered? "No, Josefa. I'm sorry that your man is gone, but I never saw him. I never left the mission," she said and stood stone-faced while Salamanca translated.

"Josefa needs blankets and clothes for the rainy season and she asks us to help her," Salamanca continued. "I've given my permission for you to weave cloth for her. Each day, when you finish your allotted amount for the mission, you can weave Josefa's cloth and take it to her in the *pueblo*. ...And let us have no more trouble from you," he warned her as an afterthought. "Your rudeness gave me quite a worry. We wouldn't be so lenient next time."

Salamanca spoke again to Josefa and was ready to say his farewell, but Cayatu broke in while he was speaking.

"Why don't you teach me your words?" she interrupted him. "You promised you would. Then I could speak to Josefa myself."

The old missionary seemed annoyed by her outburst, or possibly annoyed by her question. His wrinkled face turned accusatory. "We haven't had time," he stammered. "Building the mission takes all our energies—mine and Brother Ortiz's too. Look how it exhausts both of us. It's no easy thing to provide food and shelter for all of you who are arriving each day. Or to instruct you in our faith as we're called to do. We do our best. It takes time."

"You don't teach us your words," Cayatu persisted. "All you teach are the words of your songs so I can sing at the

Mass. Strange words, nothing more. Maybe you want to keep me silent so I will do as you tell me. As you command all of us at your mission." Even before she'd finished, she knew she shouldn't have spoken that way.

"Clare, I'll have none of that," Salamanca snapped. "I thought your disruptive attitude was gone when you came back from the *Presidio*. The missions must serve everyone's needs—*pueblo*, fort and you neophytes. When the time is right, when we weary priests have the strength, you'll be taught."

Cayatu watched Josefa brightened. A glimmer of understanding made her smile as she listened to Josefa speak. "I can teach her," she said to Salamanca. She pointed to Cayatu. "When she brings the cloth. It would be my way of helping her become a better Christian and I won't be as lonely. *Aí*, I'll teach her."

Chapter Sixteen

As Cayatu's shuttle flew back and forth in the Mission's weaving room, she was haunted by the image of Josefa's husband, Guillermo, lying dead beneath the water of the stream in the canyon. The weaving she did for the *Padres*—ten varas a day—was easily done, even when her hands were numb from the damp cold leaking from the room's adobe walls as winter set in. How sad for Josefa, Cayatu thought, but how could she have known who Guillermo was? The fear that her crime might be discovered nagged at Cayatu from the back of her mind, hidden away in the same place she kept her shame, but poised to spring on her if she ever let down.

Eager to learn the new language, Cayatu suppressed her fear of being discovered each time she made a trip to Josefa's adobe house. She believed knowing how to speak the new words was her best way of outsmarting the priests and soldiers. One day, after Josefa had finished making her practice saying the new words the Spanish used, Josefa's face became excited.

"Come, we've worked hard enough for one day," she announced. "It's time for a treat."

Cayatu watched in amazement as Josefa sliced off a piece

of something—she didn't know what—from a long brown loaf and put it in a cooking pot and poured hot water over it. Then Josefa attacked it with a three-pointed wooden stick—a *molinillo* she called it—and beat the hot brown liquid by rubbing the stick between her palms. Cayatu watched in wonder as froth formed on the liquid under Josefa's flying hands.

"This is the way we like it," Josefa told Cayatu, smiling as she poured the liquid from the pot into a cup and handed her a cup, "Hot and frothy. The cacao comes from *Nueva España,* pressed together with sugar, cinnamon and vanilla. Drink it. It's a treat we enjoy only when the ship brings it from San Blas."

Cayatu was uncertain about the drink and decided to watch Josefa to see how the Mexican woman would act.

"Taste it," Josefa commanded."

At first sip, the steaming liquid felt strange on Cayatu's lips. Then the sweet aroma reached her nose, and she felt the sensation of warm froth on the edges of her mouth. A smile spread across her face when she tasted the richness of the first drops, tickling, almost burning with sweetness, at the back of her throat. Her eyes widened with delight.

Josefa beamed at Cayatu's pleasure. "This is chocolate!" she said in a singing voice.

After more sips, Cayatu's smile became a laugh that started slowly and grew. She giggled like a child as she tasted the wonderful new drink, feeling the warmth deep inside her and the sweetness of the dark drink clinging to her lips.

"It's like the foam a wave leaves on the beach," Cayatu told Josefa letting the tip of her tongue flicker in and out at the corners of her mouth dabbing at the froth.

They sat together, each sipping her sweet drink. Cayatu beamed with joy. For the moment, all unpleasant thoughts of Josefa's husband were safely tucked away in the secret place at the back of her mind. Nevertheless, she knew her crime might be revealed at any moment.

Over the next weeks, Cayatu wove more cloth than needed so she could return to Josefa's adobe often. She was drawn by the sweetness of the chocolate drink, but something stronger she didn't understand was pulling her down the hill to the *pueblo*. As their ability to speak together continued to grow, a bond formed between the two women. Cayatu wondered if Coyote the Trickster had played a mean trick on her. Had he entwined her life with Josefa's, binding her to Josefa with a sinew of guilt? Cayatu felt pain, like an animal in a snare as she tried to understand her feelings about Josefa. As much as she tried to resist going to Josefa's adobe and vowed to stay away, she knew it was more than the chocolate drawing her back each time.

One afternoon, as the sun glowed golden through the glassless window of the adobe, casting pink light on the mountain cliffs outside, Josefa began to tell Cayatu the horror of her journey to Alta California. The two women sat on benches across a wooden table from each other sipping their drinks.

"We traveled such a long distance through the deserts of *Nueva España* to reach Alta California," Josefa began. "We were a band of settlers. Mostly loafers and shiftless men and women who wanted a new start, traveling with soldiers coming to build the fort. It was a chance at a new life for Guillermo and me. Oh, sweet Jesus, what a long trip—hot, dusty it was, most of the way. And no water at all many days. None! But we reached the coast, and oh, Lord, when we saw your village and knew we were almost done, what a blessing."

Josefa stopped to sip her chocolate. Cayatu sat still, looking about the darkening room that had become familiar to her, listening to the words Josefa spoke. She saw mist forming in Josefa's eyes. Josefa looked down into her cup, as if studying the residue on the bottom, before speaking again.

"But how sad for me," she continued. "To lose a *niño*, my baby boy. The desert was so dry. So hot! I carried him on my back or next to my breast in my *rebozo* the whole journey, and I didn't mind at all. Joaquin was my firstborn, he was my whole life. But the sun beating down... and no water—it was more than the little child could endure."

Cayatu listened more intently now. She could see Josefa's grief spread across her face and feel the sorrow in her own heart. Josefa paused to find the next words, sadness dulling all her features. "The cattle bellowed night and day for water," she went on. "It was like walking through sand on fire. It wore the animals out. Wore us out, too. Joaquin whimpered all the time." She set the cup down on the table to run her hand across her face and through her curls as if she were feeling the heat and the dryness. Cayatu could see the sweat beading up on her forehead.

"We traveled at night, but still, it was a taste of hell crossing that desert. All we could hear in the darkness were the sounds of the suffering animals. Many animals died. They dropped where they were when they could go no further.

"Finally, we came to a wide river. Guillermo raced ahead to get water. By then little Joaquin's belly was bloated like a pig bladder. It was so terrible for Joaquin. Terrible for us all. He suffered. We gave him sips—that seemed to quiet him. After a while he went to sleep. We all slept when our thirsts were gone."

Josefa stopped again, her face twisted with grief, all the prettiness vanished into sunken cheeks and eyes that sought refuge deep in their sockets. She rose from the bench and moved slowly to the window, looking at the mountains dying with the day. She looked out for several minutes. Cayatu sat silently waiting. When Josefa came back to the table, Cayatu saw no tears, but the pain in Josefa's eyes was terrible to see. She wanted to hear no more of Josefa's story. She wanted to get up from the table and run outside. In her mind she saw Josefa and Guillermo fretting over the baby. Josefa and Guillermo. Cayatu tried to force the image away.

"In the morning Joaquin was gone," Josefa said quietly. "He went to sleep beside me on the ground, but he was gone when I awoke. We searched the camp but there was no trace of him. Just tracks where an animal had dragged him into the rocks. A coyote, our leader said. I wanted to follow, I wanted to find my Joaquin. I screamed my pain and struggled to run in search of him, but our leader and Guillermo held me back. They said it would be too terrible to find the body. Joaquin may have died during the night. He made no sound when the animal took him. We'll never know. I cried and cursed God and struck out at Guillermo. He held me tight in his arms until I was too exhausted to fight. We built an altar of rocks on the river bank. I put a cross of sticks on top. Then our leader said we had to move across the river into Alta California."

After sitting quietly for several minutes when she finished her story, Josefa reached across the wooden table to take Cayatu's hand. "Joaquin is gone to heaven but he lives on in my heart," she said, dabbing her eyes with a trembling hand. "And now God adds to my grief. Guillermo is gone too. Lying somewhere dead and unburied. Like Joaquin. Carried off by some animal that picked over his bones—like Joaquin."

A storm wave crashed over Cayatu in that instant. Shaking, she moved slowly, as if she were moving in a dream, to Josefa's side. Hoping her own anguish didn't show, she took Josefa in her arms, cradling her there and rocked her gently back and forth.

Chapter Seventeen

Days later Cayatu returned to Josefa's adobe. At the door Josefa took the cloth from her and put it inside, laughing, "Enough, Clare. There's more cloth than I can use in a year. *Padre* Salamanca will wonder, no?" Then she led Cayatu by the arm. "We'll walk through the *pueblo* today and learn new words," she said. As if reading Cayatu's thoughts, she added, "Don't worry, we'll have our chocolate when we return."

The small pueblo sprawled in no particular order in the shadow of the fort a mile above the beach, halfway between the harbor and the mission. The two women threaded their way between crude homes, one- and two-room adobes, scattered about randomly. Thin wisps of smoke from outside cooking fires rose into the clear sky, carrying assorted smells that perfumed the air.

As they walked, Josefa pointed to things and gave them names. She called out greetings to women working at the cooking fires outside their homes. But mostly the two women just talked together, using words and hands to make each other understand. Well into the rainy season now, it was a rare afternoon of clarity, the kind of day that often follows a storm, when all the land seems scrubbed. The hills were vibrant but spring was still a long way off. Both women knew more rain was just over the horizon, but the brightness of the day put both of them in high spirits.

In her mind's eye Josefa could still see the city of her birth tucked in among wooded peaks, pock-marked with mine shaft openings. She stood on the steps outside the entrance to *La Valenciana Inglesia,* clutching her icon of the Virgin, praying for Guillermo's safety. It was a colorful sight of yellow and ochre and sienna buildings spotted here and there with blue and white ones, all made dim and ugly by the sight of barely alive men crawling out of the shafts. They were covered in grime after twelve hours in hell, scratching away inside the earth to make other men—Spaniards—rich with gold and silver. Guillermo was among them.

"It's a good land here," she said to Cayatu, indicating the shifting and shimmering blues and greens of the ocean and verdant hills in a single sweeping gesture. "My Guillermo was excited about coming here. He thought it the best land he'd ever seen."

"It *is* a good land," Cayatu agreed. "My people have lived here forever. There has always been plenty."

"*Aí*, land! Land is the way to get rich—Guillermo told me, and I believed him. I'll have my own land here one day soon. And when I do it will be mine alone. No one will take it from me."

"Did you have land where you came from?" Cayatu asked.

"Oh, no. We were poor in Mexico. So poor! Guillermo worked long days. So did I, but still there was never enough. He wanted more for us. He joined the army to give us a better life than we had there."

Cayatu looked puzzled. "What is poor?"

"Poor is a terrible thing," Josefa said. "Poor is when the ribs of your child press on his skin; when there's no money to buy the maize growing just outside your town or the milk that will keep your child alive. Poor is when the ache in your belly lets you steal from your neighbors without regret."

"Were you always poor?"

Josefa stood in thought for a moment, reflecting back to her days in Guanajuato before she'd met Guillermo. Those were days when she'd lived by her wits, knowing at a young age that men found her attractive, and knowing as a last resort she could count on her looks and pleasing attitude to provide food to eat and a place to sleep, but not much more. "I've been poor all my life, yes," she told Cayatu. "I was an orphan," she said. "But it was different for our people before our land was conquered. Then men like my uncle and his father worked the fields and raised enough food to feed their families. They traded for other things they needed. No one knew they were poor then, only when the Spaniards sent men into the ground to dig their silver did we learn how poor we were."

Pausing, Josefa's face took on a frown as she studied her new friend. "My ancestors were Indian. Like you. That was a long time back. I have Spanish blood—we all do now because the conquerors took our women to bed with them. But we aren't Spaniards—they don't treat us as equals. We're Mexicans, working to make them rich. We've learned to live with them—we survive well enough. You will too, in time. Soldiers will make babies with your women. Your children won't be Indian anymore either. They'll be *Mestizos,* like us. That's our life, soon it'll be yours. There's nothing to do about it. You'll learn how to survive." Josefa shrugged. "It's God's will. Come along now. Let's go back for chocolate."

As they turned to go back to Josefa's adobe, a leather-jacketed soldier raced his horse along the dirt path towards them.

"*Buenas tardes,* Josefa," The rider called out as he pulled his mount to a sudden stop in front of them. "Good news," he called down from the saddle. "*Comandante* de Alba has heard from the governor in Monterey. Your petition for land has found favor with him so he's sending it forward to the viceroy. Don Demetrio sent me to find you and send his regards. Soon the land will be yours."

"If God wills it," Josefa replied, smiling indifferently up at the rider. "Tell Don Demetrio I thank him for the news."

Cayatu watched the solider gallop off. Then she turned to her friend. "Do all your men charge about on their horses like that?" she asked.

Josefa broke into a laugh. "Men charge about. They are too lazy to walk so they ride everywhere. Without horses they would go nowhere."

"Horses are powerful animals," Cayatu said, thinking for an instant about her brief moment astride Tomas's horse. And women?" she asked. "Do women ride strong horses?"

"A few. Rich ones in Mexico City, I'm told."

"Is it hard to ride?" Cayatu pressed. "Can women ride?"

"I think it isn't so hard. But the men don't want women riding around the country. They want them to stay in one place."

Cayatu shrugged indifferently. "And this land the soldier talked of? It is good for you to have it?"

"Very good. It's what Guillermo wanted for us. Having our own land was why we came here, all the *soldados* were promised. With land I can raise food. Land is the way to become rich." Josefa stopped talking abruptly and looked sternly at Cayatu. "But I don't let others know how I feel about the land. Men will try to take land away from a woman. Especially the lazy men here. A woman must be cautious. When I get it I'll fight to keep it."

"Your men are mean."

"Some are, and some are lazy. But most are good men. They come from lives without much joy; they've learned to turn inward."

At the adobe, Cayatu watched as Josefa boiled water and prepared the chocolate. "Is it hard for you to live here without a man?" she asked.

"Yes. Hard," Josefa said, rubbing the stick vigorously between her palms, whipping the drink, then pouring it into clay cups and handing one to Cayatu. "Life alone is hard. I should have a man to protect me from all the harm of this place. I do all the work, I need children—a young boy to help with the chores would be a blessing. Even a daughter. But no hope of children now unless a man marries me.

"You are lucky, Clare," Josefa went on, talkative now as they sat at the table next to the room's lone window. "You're in the hands of the missionaries. They'll care for you. Provide food, a place to sleep safe each night. I have none of that. I must do for myself without a man. God plans different paths for each of us, eh? I don't complain but his path for me seems very hard; alone, far from the place of my birth, only my wits to keep me safe. Would I choose this life for myself? I would not. But I pray to the Virgin of Guadalupe to keep me safe. She watches over me. I'll live out my days and die here—if it's God's will—and I'll do my best to be comfortable until that day comes. You're young. If I had your beauty, your soft hair instead of these coarse curls, perhaps I could attract another man. Your hair shines in the light, like the ravens that circle above Valenciana near my birthplace, Clare. It attracts men, no? Who knows what God's will is for you? Perhaps you'll find a man and bear his children."

Chapter Eighteen

Hard rain hammered against the roof tiles. Inside the adobe Don Jose Maria Demetrio de Alba was reaching the climax of his passion. His feet pushed hard against the wall at the bottom of the bed. His body was rigid. He was raised up on both hands, every muscle taut.

The woman beneath him was his newest partner in a long string of willing women dating all the way back to the olive-tree-studded hillsides of Andalusia, the place of his birth and his coming of age. In Alta California the commander of the royal *Presidio* of Santa Barbara no longer took his sexual pleasures for granted so he was determined to take advantage of every opportunity that presented itself.

Infidels were gone from Spain when Demetrio was growing up but in their retreat they left dark-haired Arab women and clandestine Jewesses in the back alleys of Seville. They were the women who had initiated Demetrio in the art of lovemaking for a few pesetas. Left alone by a mother and father at court, young Demetrio had been an eager student. So eager was he to practice his new-found manhood that he began an adventure with his young governess when just the two of them were alone in the family's estate house. The adolescent Demetrio thought he had found lasting love—solace from his solitary life—in her bed, but she tired of him quickly and broke his heart when she fled to Seville. He went on to deflower the daughter of a local lord and at that point his life changed forever.

In the nobleman's extensive gardens, hidden from view by box hedges, with Moorish fountains murmuring a water song, the young girl had eagerly given herself to the handsome and experienced young Demetrio. When they were caught behind the hedgerows on a far lawn by the girl's suspicious mother, shame descended like a thundercloud on Demetrio's family. The young girl was dispatched to a convent near Madrid where she gave birth to a baby girl. Demetrio's father banished him to military life at a garrison in Castile, securing a commission for his second son in exchange for a number of favors called in at court.

In the army of the king, Demetrio de Alba found a safe place. He was comfortable taking orders and was always able to find a safe vantage point when serious conflict threatened. His love for horses grew apace with his sexual appetite, both fed by a military life. It had been a fine time to be a Spanish officer. Women in New World ports freely offered their favors and he never turned them down. When he arrived in *Nueva España*, the mother lode of gold and silver, he found it was also a mother lode of opportunity. Beautiful *criolla* and *mestiza* women sought out the blond-bearded officer with chiseled features and penetrating blue eyes. Eagerly they seduced him, hoping for marriage or pregnancy to improve their place in the social order, and happily he succumbed, although the thought of marriage was always a distant stranger.

When he bedded the fiery-eyed wife of a superior officer in her hacienda in Mexico City, paradise was lost. Upon discovery, the lady swore she had been taken advantage of. The cuckolded officer brandished a glove in Demetrio's face, demanding satisfaction. Offered flight over fight by his commander,

Demetrio was soon marching to a life of exile in Alta California at the head of a fifty-man garrison for the new *Presidio*.

Demetrio's breath exploded in short, wheezing gasps as his buttocks pumped up and down. His fingers clung to the sides of the bed as if he would plunge into a viper pit if he let go. His heart pounded just below his throat. Then he was done in a series of jerks and twitches. His muscles sagged. He collapsed on the body beneath him. His breathing continued to rasp for several more minutes.

Under Demetrio de Alba another body stirred. Her eyes opened reluctantly, still clinging to an unfinished dream. Her private thoughts gave her a distant, slightly petulant expression. The intense color of copulation drained slowly from her face. Her curly dark hair lay damply in disarray on the coarse sheet and little sweat beads danced on her upper lip.

Almost immediately she expelled him and shifted her body to a more comfortable position. She nudged Don Demetrio aside, closed her legs and raised her buttocks to prevent any leakage. But she leaked anyway, adding a new stain to the cloth-covered straw mattress.

"*Qué hombre,*" she said without much enthusiasm. "Such a stallion."

Demetrio seemed not to notice her tone. He beamed with pride. "*Qué Magnifica,* Josefa! You and I make a wonderful pair, no?"

"For an afternoon of rain?" she shrugged. "An afternoon of pleasure? Why not? We are so few here."

"Our lives would be easier if you were my woman and we had more time together," he urged her.

"Don't worry, Demetrio, I won't leave." Josefa came alert at de Alba's words. They triggered warning bells in the back of her head.

"We could build an adobe on the land the king is granting you."

"The king's land, you say? Where is it?"

De Alba didn't seem to hear the hint of sarcasm in Josefa's voice. "West of here," he said. "It sits above the ocean, between canyon and beach—vast stretches of land."

"What will I do on my land, Demetrio? It's leagues away from the *Pueblo*, with no one else around. What would I do?"

"You won't need to do anything, Josefa. You'll have cattle. Let them roam the hills and our herd will grow. Indian *vaqueros* will tend them. *Padre* Ortiz says there might soon be a market for those cattle. We could grow rich there and we would have our times alone."

The warning bells in Josefa's head sounded alarm. De Alba let his fingers caress her curls and the side of her face. His touch felt good to Josefa but she was determined not to be distracted. "*We* could? *Our* herd? What is this about, Demetrio?" Josefa rose up on one elbow to look directly into de Alba's face. "I want a child to take the place of Joaquin," she told him. "A child to love, the way I loved Joaquin. And a child to help me as I grow old. Are you offering to be my husband and the father of that child?"

After a long silence, de Alba said finally, "So, it's agreed. We'll raise a family on your land grant."

Josefa noted the lack of enthusiasm in his voice and continued to stare at him skeptically. "So, you will marry me, Demetrio?" she demanded.

De Alba hesitated. "We could, I suppose. But here on the frontier we don't need to be so formal."

"As I thought." Josefa sat up, pulling her knees up to her chest and holding the sheet up to her chin, giving him a sharp look. "Why would an officer of the king marry a peasant? True love? Ha!" It was a bitter laugh that escaped her lips. "How foolish you must think me, Demetrio. No, not agreed." She laughed heartily, tossing her head to straighten her matted hair. She reached out for de Alba's hand and patted her belly with it. "We can have our afternoon romps, but nothing else until there's a baby here," she told him.

A knock at the door interrupted their conversation. Josefa rose quickly, pulled on a thin *camisa* that clung to her sweat-damp breasts and stepped into a long skirt. She motioned to de Alba to dress. "I'm coming," she called out. "Just one minute." She shot a look at the *Comandante,* "Marriage is the price of the land," she said.

De Alba shrugged and reached for his trousers. Josefa went into the front room of her small house and opened the heavy wooden door.

*H*ola, *amiga,*" Josefa greeted Cayatu, still arranging the fall of her skirt with one hand and fussing at her hair with the other. "Such rain. Such a day to be out. But a day for visitors it seems. What brings you?"

Cayatu hesitated. "There was no work at the mission. The smell of chocolate drew me down the hill," she giggled self-consciously, but returned a serious look to her face. "I have something I must ask of you."

Josefa returned the laugh, looking back over her shoulder at de Alba. "Come in but be patient. I'm finishing with the *Comandante.* We'll talk when he leaves." Josefa grabbed Cayatu by the wrist and pulled her inside when she hesitated. "*Ven, muchacha.* Don't stand out in this rain. I'll lend you dry clothes."

Josefa left Cayatu in the main room, dripping wet, standing in front of de Alba, while she continued through a narrow doorway into the sleeping room. The *Comandante* sat on a rough-hewn chair tucking his trouser legs into high leather boots. His tunic, only partly buttoned, revealed his strong, smooth chest. His hat hung on a peg near the door, with his sword and scabbard underneath it. He stopped tugging at his boot to stare up into her face and a harsh grin of recognition shown through his beard, turning up the corners of his mouth.

Josefa hustled back into the room carrying a worn camisa and skirt, "Put these on for now," she told Cayatu. "Take off those wet things." Josefa paid no attention to Don Demetrio's presence, but began tugging Cayatu's wet blouse over her head.

At first Cayatu thought about running into the other room so de Alba would not see her body again. But why should she hide? Look how he stares, she thought. No one knows what he's done. How he wants to touch me again. But here he cannot. She smiled at the sight of his discomfort. He averted his eyes and busied himself with a boot. It was her small triumph.

Cayatu's eyes darted around the room, searching for a weapon. If she could find a knife within reach she would stab at his heart. Her hatred boiled beneath the surface. Her mother's words emboldened her and Josefa's presence made her feel safe. But his sword was too far away on the peg and no other weapon was in sight. But perhaps there was another way, she thought.

Instead of running, Cayatu brushed Josefa's busy hands aside and slowly continued lifting her blouse up over her head. She set the wet blouse down on the wooden table next to de Alba, letting her breasts almost brush against his hand. When he shifted uneasily on the chair, it brought a smile to Cayatu's face. She dropped her skirt and took down her undergarment. She turned toward the soldier again and watched his eyes grow large. Then she stepped into Josefa's offered skirt.

De Alba sprang from the chair. One hand shot out to grab his hat and sword from the peg on the wall while the other pulled at a boot that was still only halfway on. "I must go to the fort," he called over his shoulder to Josefa. Then he was out the door, still tugging at the boot. Cayatu felt a small thrill of triumph as he hopped out into the rain.

Chapter Nineteen

Josefa stood with her hands on her hips, showing a mixture of amusement and surprise on her face after the *Comandante* fled into the rain. "Aí," she said, beginning to laugh, "What was that?"

Cayatu was quick to put on Josefa's dry clothes. She looked at Josefa, feeling satisfaction and feigning innocence.

"You can't fool an old whore like me," Josefa continued to laugh. "Where did you learn to tease like that? In your village? Shame on you, he's your Godfather."

"In the village that wouldn't be allowed," Cayatu's voice had the embarrassed tone of a child. "I'd be punished. When women tempt men it disrupts order."

"So, you *were* teasing." Josefa laughed but quickly grew serious. "You're wasting your talents. He lies with me, not you. I may not have your firm breasts or shining black hair but I make up for it in other ways. Don Demetrio has his needs, I take care of them. God knows there are few enough men in the *pueblo* worth opening your legs for. We must take our pleasures where we can, eh? Anyway, enough of this," she said, tossing the conversation off as if it had no more importance to her than garbage she threw out for the dogs that roamed the streets, "So, you came to talk?" Josefa turned from the table, where she had gone to pick up the wet clothes, to study her friend. "Come over here," she ordered Cayatu. "Stand by the window. Take down your skirt again," she said not waiting for Cayatu but tugging at it herself. "Let me see."

Cayatu held back.

"As I thought," the older woman said. "You're carrying a child."

Cayatu sat down abruptly on the chair de Alba had abandoned.

When Moon's first cycle had passed without her woman-flow Cayatu had paid little attention, but when Moon showed her fullness a second time, she began to worry. She lay awake at night, prodding at the soft flesh of her abdomen with angry fingers. It wasn't that she didn't know the symptoms of childbearing—Tanayan had taught her years before when her sister bulged with Massilili. It was the horror of thinking about having an unwanted baby that made her fingers probe angrily. A horror that made her breath come in short gasps, catching in her throat. She had *his* baby inside her. It would be a half-breed child who belonged to neither world, suspended between two worlds like an insect trapped in a spider web. She hated the thought, hated the seed growing inside her.

Ever since the first time she lay with Ysaga near the beach she'd imagined carrying his child. Even when Qoloq banished them and she lived her lonely life in the valley while Ysaga was sent away, she dreamed how she would care for their child. In her mind's eye she could see them caring for an infant in a hut near the beach. Now, there was a devil child inside her, a monster worse than any of the creatures from the World Below. Anger and fear consumed her together.

She searched for a way to rid her body of the seed, but didn't know how. Qoloq would know, she told herself. Secrets like that were the shaman's alone.

She kept her growing panic to herself, going about her daily work at the mission, numbly, as if in a spell. Who could she tell? Who could help her? She pondered the question over and over. The answer came back the same each time—perhaps Josefa will know what to do.

We never hear you laugh or join our conversations anymore," Dolores had said as they entered the *monjerio* one evening. I pray for you, Clare. I ask the Virgin to comfort you. Is there something I can do?"

"You're a fine friend," Cayatu answered the younger woman, "but there is nothing you can do for me. I must do for myself."

"Perhaps confession with the priests would clear your conscience. Have you gone to them?"

"No. No confession. Do you, Dolores?"

"I do…" Dolores hesitated. "I confess to Father Ortiz. I try so hard to do as the *padres* tell us but I fail. I tell him my sins and I feel better. Sometimes I don't know what I should confess though," Dolores added. "Before, I knew what was right or wrong, but the priests have different wrongs and more of them. For me now it seems best to confess everything. Madelena confessed to Father Ortiz she had impure thoughts about a man in the *Ranchería*. He made her pray on her knees all afternoon in his room while he stood over her, Madelena told me."

"Do you have thoughts about men?"

Dolores blushed. She turned her head to the side. After a while she whispered, "I have never been with a man but sometimes I think about it. Should I confess, Clare? I don't want to spend an afternoon on my knees in the priest's room, but if my thoughts are unclean… What do you think?"

Cayatu laughed. "Thoughts of men aren't unclean no matter what the priests say. Women think of men, just as men think of us, in ways that would make the priests blush. Maybe Ortiz has impure thoughts about you."

"Oh, Clare!" Dolores turned her head away again.

"He's a man. I don't think you should confess. I have thoughts about a man I wouldn't want to tell to the priests."

"Tomas?" Dolores asked.

A surprised look came over Cayatu's face. "My thoughts are for a man who's not at the mission."

"How sad! Sad for you, sad for Tomas. We all know Tomas would like you to be his woman and have the wedding ceremony the Franciscans insist on."

Cayatu couldn't control her feelings of despair. She began to sob at the thought of a lost life with Tomas.

Dolores came to her side, embracing her in comforting arms. "What is it, Clare?" she cooed.

"I might love Tomas," Cayatu said, "but I can't think of marrying him or any other man. I have a child in my belly." She blurted it out, tears flowing down her cheeks. Immediately, she wished she hadn't been so careless. "You must keep my secret, Dolores. I only tell you so you will know what troubles me."

"I will," Dolores gasped, reaching out to wipe away Cayatu's tears with the hem of her skirt. "Who gives you this baby?"

"At the *Presidio*."

"You must tell the *Padres.*"

"My shame is more that I can live with, Dolores. Don't ask me again. Keep my secret."

Cayatu rearranged the borrowed skirt as Josefa handed her the chocolate drink she'd made, but today the drink left a bitter aftertaste in her mouth. Josefa was like one of the *pueblo* dogs shaking a bone in its teeth. "So who is the father?" she pried. "Some handsome buck in the mission *ranchería*, I'm guessing.

An accident? Or do you want a child? Maybe you would tease Don Demetrio so you could name him as the father? But he would never lie with an Indian."

Cayatu gave Josefa a prying look. "The father is my secret. But I'll tell you this, Josefa. I don't want this baby. I want to rid my body of it. A devil child is growing inside of me, the seed of a bad man, and I don't want it."

"You were forced? Have you told the priests? They'll know soon enough. Don't think of getting rid of the baby, Clare. That's a sin. Let it live—"

"—It's evil! I have to be rid of it," Cayatu interrupted, spitting out the words and then dissolving into tears. "Can you help me? I came today hoping you knew how."

Josefa came by her side, embracing Cayatu in her arms, hugging her to her large bosom. "It's the baby inside getting you confused. You must have the child. You *will* have it, the *padres* will see to it. It would be a sin to kill a baby. Pick a man at the mission so the priests can marry you before the birth. *Padre* Salamanca will understand."

"I don't want this baby!" Cayatu shouted, rising to her feet and looking down at Josefa. "Nothing will change my mind. I don't care about being married in the church."

"Pray for forgiveness for your sinful thoughts, Clare," Josefa snapped back at her. "Women like me long to have babies they can love and care for. Pray for guidance. Perhaps God will send down an answer. Get on your knees with me now and pray."

Chapter Twenty

Fermin Ortiz let the chestnut mare's reins go slack as it carried him up the hill from the fort. The rainy season was coming to an end and the hills behind the mission still shone a brilliant green in the afternoon sun. Letting the horse plod slowly along the dusty path to the mission, he was silently taking stock of this new world to which his God had sent him. A trace of smile played at the corners of his mouth. His God had done well by him. He'd brought him to this unique land, this perfect place to get rich while others sleep. Fermin Ortiz felt sure he was ready to take advantage of his God's gift and that brought a self-satisfied feeling, a feeling of smugness.

Turning in the saddle to let his eyes sweep far out over the gently undulating land along the coast, he thanked his God for blessing Santa Barbara like few other places. Look how the grasses grow knee high and thick. Grass for a million cows. No wonder these Indians are lazy, the land spills out its blessings everywhere you look.

The mare jerked to a stop, startled by a lizard that scurried across the trail and climbed a nearby rock, where it paused to inspect horse and rider before scurrying into the underbrush. Ortiz reassured his mount with a soft hand on its neck. The horse slipped back into its slow walk.

Not just the superstitious Indians, Ortiz mused. This land lulls everyone. Truly, a land of milk and honey as God promised Moses, a soft, lazy land. No one needed to work very hard to survive. But a smart man like me could bend others to his benefit. That thought pleased Ortiz. He was not prone to hard work. Up till now the priesthood had been the right calling for him, but it had its limitations. It was time to move on, time to prosper while foolish men lolled about.

The third son of a minor official, Fermin Ortiz knew early in life there'd be no patrimony. A soft, bright child, growing up in Santander on the storm-bound Bay of Biscay, he daydreamed of reckless adventure, winning great fortunes through bold actions. His mind was fertile with schemes for gaining riches, but his body resisted all strenuous activity that might have furthered his ambitions. He sought the easy path to his goal. When the path became difficult, he changed the goal. He drifted through the small abbey school where he learned about the contemplative life of monks. It sounded agreeable, and the Franciscan order fit him.

Yet he knew from the start his devotion to a life of ease was stronger than his devotion to God and Saint Francis. His appetites often overpowered his self-discipline. He turned his head at the sight of a beautiful woman. He had his fantasies. He enjoyed meat and drink far more than was modest. Being sent to Mission Santa Barbara was a true blessing, it gave him a large measure of freedom. Brother Salamanca was old and tired, not strong enough to oppose him.

Dismounting at the corral, he greeted Jimeno, handing him the reins. The soldier started across the corral with the mare. "Wait," Ortiz called him back. "What's the tally?"

"Several hundred calves, *Padre*. More each day," Jimeno said.

"It's time to start a second herd," Ortiz told him.

Jimeno's face was impassive as he looked at the Franciscan. "We're well ordered now," he replied after a pause.

"Indeed. The Lord's work goes very well. Now is the time to plan the future. Start driving half the newborns and their mothers to the small canyon up the coast. Assign your most trusted *vaqueros* to move them and keep them separate, Jimeno."

"Why go to that effort?" Jimeno questioned.

"Get them started tomorrow. It will be to your benefit."

"And how might that be?"

Ortiz saw a greedy smile spread across Jimeno's pock-scarred face as he looped the reins around a set of horns atop the corral fence, and thrust a booted foot against the stones of the lower fence. Ortiz thought his voice took on a more defiant tone, too. He made note of it.

"Just what would a poor priest do for a leather jacket *Soldado* like me?" Jimeno's voice almost seemed to taunt.

"You'll be rewarded. I'll see to it," Ortiz said, deciding Jimeno needed watching. "But it would be best for you to keep your questions to yourself. Trust my word. Tell your *vaqueros* only what's necessary and keep them quiet. I've discussed all this with *Comandante* de Alba and he agrees. Get started in the morning."

Striding up the path to the mission church, where a knot of neophytes waited for him to hear their confessions, Fermin Ortiz reminded himself he needed Jimeno and de Alba's cooperation. Jimeno would go along, untroubled by the theft of cattle, he'd take his orders from de Alba. Ortiz wasn't worried about the commander's greed. De Alba had finally come to see the profit in their venture and now his enthusiasm was more than a match for his oath of allegiance to the king. De Alba wasn't troubled by the thought of stealing mission cattle. He had no love for Franciscans and he would simply turn his head. After all, who suffered if a few hundred head were missing? And who benefited?

Ortiz hurried past the waiting neophytes into his tiny room to change his robe. Looking around, he assessed the sparseness of his current life—straw mattress, simple chair, plank desk, barely enough light from a small window and a few candles— not much to show for twenty years of devotion.

He brightened as his thoughts turned to the meeting he'd had with the captain of the Boston ship *Reliant*. He and Jimeno had lit a bonfire on the beach. When the captain sent a boat to find out who was signaling, Ortiz was rowed out to the brig where he struck a bargain to trade hides for goods the captain would bring from New England. Ortiz had suggested the captain might spread the word to other ships trading the Canton, Sandwich Islands and Sitka route. Looking to the future, the priest could see a day when he would live handsomely far from the mission's limitations.

Reflecting on Don Demetrio's slowwittedness as he adjusted the cross hanging from his rope belt and headed toward the church, Ortiz saw that maybe it was another blessing. He could easily manipulate the lieutenant into doing what he wanted. If only de Alba would move faster on getting the land grant it would make the venture safer.

"I tell you," Don Demetrio had said as they shared a leg of mutton at the fort an hour earlier, "The crown is reluctant to make land grants."

"Surely, his majesty doesn't refuse a poor widow, like Josefa. Now is the time to put our plan into action, Don Demetrio," Ortiz had urged. "The land beckons. The riches are there if we just seize the opportunity."

De Alba raised his glass in a toast. "Here's to our riches. And the petition is going forward from the viceroy to the

King. But we can't rush this. Josefa hasn't agreed."

"Are there problems?"

"Not problems, conditions," de Alba responded, his voice bristling. "Josefa wants a baby."

"It's a subject I can't help with, Demetrio," Ortiz said with his best piousness. "You must marry the woman."

"It's not that I *can't* give her a baby, *Padre*." De Alba had paused until Ortiz nodded his understanding. "And I suppose I must marry her. A *mestiza*. I've never wanted a wife or a child. In truth, I don't want one now, especially a Mexican woman. I don't want to be tied to this place. If the viceroy called me back to *Nueva España* I would be on the first ship to sail. I would beg God's forgiveness for abandoning her, but I would leave Josefa and a child behind."

Fermin Ortiz chuckled to himself as he entered the confessional and arranged his robe around him. Maybe it was an advantage after all to have a slowwitted partner, he thought.

Chapter Twenty-One

Dolores shivered at the back of the church, waiting her turn in the confessional. She pulled the *rebozo* closer around her shoulders against the chill and dampness, but that didn't help. It was her coming confession that sent spasms of fear through her body so strong she had to lean against the church wall for support. How could she speak her sinful thoughts?

She yearned for the soul-cleansing to come but she still dreaded the next few minutes. Confessing her sins was part of her new faith—the act made her feel pure—but as she waited the stern voice in her head told her she was unworthy.

Still, Dolores felt more at ease with the ritual about to take place than she had ever felt as a young girl in her village. From childhood, she'd been indoctrinated in the old ways of the elders. She'd been taught her people were at the mercy of powerful spirits whose moods and whims were unpredictable. Those spirits were capable of rewarding a person for no reason or just as easily punishing them. Dolores was confused by the uncertainty of life in her village. More than confused, it frightened her so much that her shyness was magnified tenfold. Longing for security, she withdrew from village life, but found it when the missionaries came.

She saw Father Ortiz enter the church, survey the waiting line and take his place in the confessional. Slowly, the line moved forward amid a low, mumbled mixture of Spanish and Chumash. A neophyte entered the booth when another slunk away, head bowed. As she moved closer, Dolores's apprehension grew, giving her a lightheaded feeling. Her breath came in short gulps. You are a sinful girl, the voice inside scolded, you're dirty in the eyes of the Virgin.

When they came to her village, the Franciscans had painted pictures of a purposeful Catholic life for her. Shortly after they left, the Virgin appeared to Dolores one day when she ventured out to collect mussels along the rocky shore for her mother. The Virgin came to her from across the ocean, floating above the water and shimmering, so real Dolores knew she could reach out to touch her robe. The Virgin said no words, floating above her in the air, arms outstretched, calling Dolores to her bosom. Dolores heard her voice inside her head, speaking in her own language, as if in a spirit dream. Dumbstruck, she fell on the sand and let the wavelets wash over her, sobbing, "Mother of the new God, show me a life." And the Virgin answered her, "Your life is in Christ. Get to a mission so you can know him."

Soon afterward, Dolores left her parents.

Forgive me Father for I have sinned," Dolores began, using words the priests had taught her. She sat precariously on the hard edge of the narrow confessional bench so she wouldn't feel too comfortable. Her pulse raced, throbbing against her temple, as she searched for her own words to begin. How could she start? She couldn't tell Father Ortiz how shameful she'd been. She tried to think of minor indiscretions but her mind was blank.

"Well, child," Ortiz said, speaking slowly in her language from the other side of the screen.

She took a breath. "I took extra food yesterday at dinner and didn't share it," she began at last.

"And?"

Again, she paused, not anxious to reveal her wickedness. "When I wash my clothes I look at my face in the water to see if I'm pretty."

"Is that all?" Ortiz asked after a period of silence.

"No, Father. …Not all."

"Well…"

She let her breath out slowly. Her heart raced. She thought she might explode with the tension in her stomach. Finally she said, "At night, before I sleep, sometimes I think about lying with men. I touch myself."

Ortiz was silent on the other side of the confession screen. After a moment that seemed a lifetime to Dolores, Ortiz cleared his throat and told her to continue.

"I think about them planting their seed in me so I can have a baby." The words poured out now, cleansing her, sweeping Dolores along with them, so there was no way for her to stop. "Feelings come over my body that make me touch myself."

Again Ortiz was silent. Dolores could hear him shifting about on the other side of the screen but he didn't speak again for a long time. Finally, his words came hoarsely. "Having babies is God's way. Babies are God's gift to men and women joined in marriage. It's lying with men before marriage that's a sin, child. Is that what you think about when you touch yourself?"

"Sometimes," Dolores almost sobbed. "I try not to. But my friend has been with a man. Now she carries a baby. I can't stop thinking about having my own baby."

"Who is this friend?" Ortiz asked.

Dolores was startled into silence.

"What woman carries a baby?" Ortiz asked again.

Dolores sensed his tone hardening. "Oh, no—" Too late, she felt the danger.

"—You must tell, child. That woman has sinned. It's a sin for you to keep her secret. Tell who the woman is."

"I can't." Dolores felt faint.

"You must," Ortiz demanded, "if you want your sin absolved."

"Please, Father, I swore to keep her secret."

"Your oath was a blaspheme against God," he charged.

Dolores heard the emotion rising in Ortiz's voice, raising it to a higher pitch that took on a whining tone. "In the name of Jesus and Holy Mary you must say the name. Then pray for forgiveness with me. Tell me now."

The fear of telling Ortiz about her feelings was replaced now by angry rumblings deep in her stomach, as if she would spill her last meal on the church floor at any moment. She couldn't betray her friend and she couldn't run out of the confessional. I'm lost, she heard the voice in her head say. There is no way out. Weakly, she called out loud, "Mary, come to me." Her mouth went slack and dry.

"Tell me," Ortiz demanded again.

Her breath wouldn't come and the faint feeling grew. When she finally spoke it was with a weak, shaking voice. "The woman you call Clare, Father. Cayatu. Don't punish her. Punish me. I've sinned against her," Dolores said. She rocked slowly forward and fainted onto the earthen floor.

Chapter Twenty-Two

Hola, Cayatu," Tomas called out. He stopped short. "What is it?'

Cayatu wobbled unsteadily toward Tomas. Food smells outside the kitchen were sending waves of nausea surging through her stomach. She tried to smile, but her face was a poor mask. "Nothing, Tomas," she protested. "For a moment my stomach... Now I'm fine."

"You're sick. Come rest at my hut. I'll make root tea. You'll feel better."

She didn't resist. Loosening her blouse from her skirt so that it draped over the slight bulge in her belly, she followed him along the path. "You're good to worry about me," she said, forcing the best face she could and reaching out to take his hand.

She was self-conscious about the child she carried and hoped Tomas hadn't noticed. Was this Qoloq's curse, she wondered silently as they walked the path to the *rancheria* together? His punishment for leaving his village? Had Coyote taken the *Comandante's* form to put this monster in her belly? Even though she had come to accept her love for Tomas, having him for a husband was a choice she could not make. This gentle man would tie her to the mission, tethering her like a mule plodding in circles grinding corn on a stone wheel. Not freedom at all really.

Leading her down the path toward his hut Tomas brightened. He pointed to the mission gardens stretching down the hill toward the ocean just below the cluster of neophyte huts. "Look how the land awakens," he said. "Smell the air. The familiar smells of our land, not the Spanish smells. It's a new season, Clare, a time of new birth."

Cayatu hesitated, afraid he'd guessed her secret, but she allowed no surprise to show on her face. "Tomas, I am Cayatu, please use my Chumash name. It is a good time," she agreed, hoping to change the subject. "Do you have calves?"

"New calves daily. We have two herds now." Tomas puffed up. "Vicente and I are in charge of one herd of young steers in a canyon up the coast." He laughed so that his eyes sparkled and his lips curled up to show his teeth. "Jimeno says the herd's a secret we must not talk about. He threatens to whip us if we do, but cows are cows, no? They stray. These newcomers to our land are strange—with their secret herds and their new foods that don't smell good. It's because we're good *vaqueros* that Vicente and I were chosen."

"Does Jimeno punish you for our time in the corral?"

"He's still angry. He doesn't speak of it, except once when he took me to the far side of the corral. He said he'd find a way... Now, he watches me, looking for reasons to use *Señor* Lash. I give him none. I do his work. He knows I am good with his herds. He's no trouble to me."

The animation on Tomas's face as he spoke, pleased Cayatu. At the same time, it gave her a hollow feeling in her heart. If only he were scared of Jimeno or the Franciscans, or the soldiers the way she was. "Why another herd?" she asked, working to show interest.

"No one can say. There are more cattle now than we need. The priests give meat freely to people in the *pueblo*. We feed the soldiers at the fort. It's a plentiful time for all. Jimeno won't say, but it's a very serious thing with him. He keeps *Señor* Lash behind his saddle every day now." Tomas shrugged. "They're strange men, Cayatu. Perhaps they want more hides. Or tallow. Already meat rots in the fields."

Sitting outside Tomas's thatch-roofed hut, the same kind of huts the Chumash built in their old villages, Cayatu watched the small children playing nearby in the dirt. The little wooden toys they played with reminded Cayatu of the figures Muniyaut had carved for her to play with while he built *tomols*. The memory brought pain with it, and a loneliness that caught her off guard. It seemed only days ago she stood by Ysaga's side, feeling soft breezes flowing through her hair, as together they watched their fathers put the final touches on the large canoe. Ysaga pointed toward the islands as they stood together, boasting what their lives would be like when he was grown and had his own canoe and could build a hut for her.

Cayatu tried to imagine a life with Tomas as they sat together. A pleasant life, free from want, she decided, with a sturdy, dedicated man who would care for her and give her Chumash babies. They would carry her rank. But that would never happen. She knew she was foolish to dream of the old life. Tomas was a good man to love, she was sure of that, so why did she fight so fiercely against a life in his hut?

A flurry of activity down the path aroused them. Cayatu and Tomas watched Father Salamanca hobbling along on his spindly legs. Stooped with age, he barely acknowledged people he passed. Tomas rose to greet him.

"*Hola, Padre*. A fine, warm day."

"Is it?" the Franciscan huffed, pausing for breath. "I've no time to enjoy it. Always trouble for us poor shepherds, it seems. Trouble for me. I've come for you, Clare. I've searched high and low. Come with me."

Cayatu rose, adjusting her blouse again. "Why?—" she asked.

"—No questions. Come with me. We'll speak with you later, Tomas."

The priest turned and started back down the path. Cayatu walked a step behind him, trying to think what she'd done that was likely to bring a punishment. She'd never known Father Salamanca to be so cold. He hobbled toward the mission as fast as he could, oblivious to all that was going on around him and hardly paying attention to her. And what did, "We'll speak with you later, Tomas" mean?

They mounted the veranda that ran the length of the front of the mission and went to Salamanca's cubicle. Inside the dim room, with the Christ staring down obliquely from his prominent place on one wall, and Saint Francis watching from another wall, the old man dropped into his accustomed chair. Already seated, Fermin Ortiz sat expressionless. Salamanca fixed his stare on her while gathering strength to speak.

"So," he finally started, "you carry a baby. Is that true, Clare? Don't lie to us!"

"Yes," she answered, stunned by their knowledge.

"Pull down your skirt so I can see your belly," Ortiz said.

"No. I won't."

"Who is the father?" Ortiz demanded.

"I won't tell," she said.

"You must. Tell us now. It'll be easier."

"I think Tomas. You spend so much time with him," Salamanca said. "I think he's the one who has brought this disgrace on you."

Cayatu retreated in the room, backing against the door and pressing against it, feeling her nails dig into the rough wood. "Not Tomas," she answered them.

"Then who?"

"I won't say."

"Perhaps a whipping for Tomas would tell us if he's the father," Ortiz said.

"Whip me if you must," Cayatu confronted Ortiz. "It's not Tomas."

"Then who?" Ortiz demanded.

She was overwhelmed by the storm pounding her. Qoloq's curse? She looked from Ortiz, who stared belligerently at her, to Salamanca, slumped down to nothingness behind the plank writing desk. These men are not from my world, Cayatu told herself. They were men who didn't care what happened to her—to any of her people. If she didn't escape they'd destroy her and all the others. In a burst of anger she blurted out, "One of your soldiers did this."

The priests went silent. They looked at each other. Cayatu saw her words were no surprise.

"Which one?—"

"Tell us his name—"

"Point him out—"

"He'll be punished—"

The two men were speaking at once and she barely caught their meaning. When she did, she let out a laugh that startled Salamanca and Ortiz. "You say you'll punish a soldier but I know you won't because you have no power. If I said the name I'd still be the one punished—only worse. Do what you will with me, the father is my secret. I'll carry the child and give life to it."

"That you will," the younger Franciscan affirmed, "But it's of great concern to Brother Salamanca and me. We must make reports—"

"—What you've done is sinful. We can't let you set this example for the rest of the unmarried women," Salamanca interrupted. "Pray for forgiveness, Clare. We'll speak to Tomas."

"No, Father, don't let him know... or about the solider."

"We'll do our sacred duty," Ortiz said. "You must do your

penance. Go back to the women's quarters now and stay there until the child is born. Your meals will be brought to you. You are not to leave—"

"—You would make me a prisoner?" Her voice rose in panic. "How can you be such cruel men?" Cayatu stared at the priests to be sure they understood her words.

"We'll give you and the unborn all the care we can." Salamanca said. "The unmarried women will see you there all day. It will teach them not to whore."

"We'll make you an example they won't forget," Ortiz added. "Come over here now. Sit on this stool." Abruptly Ortiz got up and went to her, grabbing her by the arm and pulling her to the wooden stool.

"No," Salamanca pleaded with Ortiz. "Not that."

Ortiz came behind her, grabbing her by the hair, pulling it tight over her head so that it hurt. "Oh, yes," he replied. "She's sinned. She must be an example others won't forget. Give me the knife."

Salamanca sighed. He picked up the finely honed Toledo blade that lay on his desk and handed it to Ortiz. Then he slouched deeper in his chair and looked away.

"Such fine, beautiful dark hair," Ortiz said, suddenly calm, smoothing it out now to its full extent. "Such a beauty. So soft to the touch." He continued to pat and stroke it, intoning, "You are a sinful whore." He took the knife and began sawing and hacking at her hair. She sat immobilized on the stool, as if she were watching some other woman being shorn, as strand after flint-black strand dropped to the floor. Ortiz continued to mumble, "You're a sinner."

Tears overflowed her eyes. They streamed down her cheeks but she kept silent as the hair she cherished grew in piles on the floor around her. She sat helpless. She was in the hands of the priests. Lost. Anger replaced her tears. These were godless men, not men of God. They will destroy us all in the end for the sake of their beliefs.

Silently, she recited her sister's words over and over. "Show the dignity we have."

Salamanca limped across the room to brush some of the hair from her shoulders. Cayatu reached up to feel the wiry stubble. She choked. Ortiz continued cutting like a man possessed. Cutting closer and closer to her skull, mumbling over and over, "Sinful whore."

Chapter Twenty-Three

When Cayatu heard the key turn in the iron lock she rose from her straw sleeping mat. Combing her fingers through the wild stubble of her hair, she ran the few steps across the women's quarters to crouch down along the wall next to the door. As it swung open, letting in a burst of strong light and the soft scents of blossoms from the orchards, she tried to bolt through it.

Wise to her escape attempts, Nuncio, the old *alcalde*, blocked the opening with his leg as he had done repeatedly since her confinement. He set the food bowl down inside the door and closed it behind him.

"You've gotten wild as a deer," he scolded, pushing her back inside. He was old, with a wrinkled face that seemed to sag into his neck. His eyes smiled knowingly. "You won't get past me, Clare. Not till the baby comes."

"Let me out."

"How could I? The *padres* would punish me if I did, wouldn't they?" he said, putting hands on hips. "And I've no taste for their lash or the stocks." He gave her an almost fatherly smile. "Be patient, Clare. Soon the baby comes— look how you bulge. You'll be free soon enough."

She rushed at him again, using her fists to pound on his shoulders and chest. "Let me out!" she shouted. "Can't you see I grow weaker each day? I'll die if I stay here."

"No you won't." The old man took her wrists firmly and led her away from the door. "Get back on your mat. I've brought you food."

"Ugh! *Pozole*. No more!"

"You need to eat it to be strong for the child." He went back to the doorway and picked up the bowl he'd set down there. "It's got meat to make you strong."

"No more!" she shouted. She rushed him again, knocking the wooden bowl from his shaky hands. It clattered on the hard-packed floor. Gritty white soup splashed out, spreading in a small puddle on the ground. Little pieces of beef and congealed lumps of barley popped up like islands. Cayatu and the *alcalde* stared down at the puddle as it spread over the floor and seeped into the earth.

"You try my patience, girl," Nuncio snapped at her, no longer smiling. "All these months I've cared for you. I shielded you from the Franciscans. And I get no thanks, do I?"

"Don't you see?" Cayatu backed off, her voice subdued now. "Can't you see what they're doing to me? To all of us? If we don't run we'll be destroyed."

"I see it well enough," he answered. "I see it better than you. I go about the mission, I see it. Don't say I don't, Clare. Don't say that because I do see."

"Then leave the mission. All of us." Cayatu edged back closer to the door again, looking for a chance to catch him off guard.

"Get back, girl. You won't get past old Nuncio," he laughed at her.

Tears overwhelmed her. She felt them rushing down her cheeks.

"We'd all like to leave," Nuncio said. "Most of us, anyway. Go back to our old lives, fishing and hunting. Gathering acorns this time of the year. But that life is no more. There's nothing left to go back to."

"We could get far away. To the lake in the big valley," she

said hopefully.

"Many have already slipped away," Nuncio said. "But old ones would die on a journey like that—old ones like me. The priests would send soldiers to bring the fugitives back—they've done it before. There'd be fighting. More might die. No, Clare, it's not possible."

"Then what? Do we fade away here, like foam off a wind-blown wave? Look how the pox kills. The newborns don't survive. Each day, fewer and fewer—the other women tell me death is all about us."

"Yes, some die. And some are whipped till they bleed. But what choice? We have to stay so that your baby will live."

Cayatu flared again. She brushed the tears from her cheeks across the back of her hand and pointed an accusing finger at him, "You say that because you do the *padres'* bidding. You're one of them now. You're too old to leave."

He shrugged and began backing toward the door. "You say foolish things—perhaps it's the child inside making you a crazy woman. The priests made me *alcalde*. What should I do? Say no? Learn not to fight against them, Clare. It's better to get along with them." He opened the door. "They're stronger. Accept the life you have."

"Never," she challenged.

He pulled the door shut again and turned the key in the lock.

Cayatu sat for hours on her sleeping mat during the day when the women's quarters were empty. She sat motionless, almost trance-like, held captive by the stark adobe walls, with one solitary window her only source of light and air. She stared at the small shell basket Tanayan had given her.

Holding it—smoothing the finely woven coils of light and dark tules and cattails that came together in just the right places to form the lightening bolt pattern—turning it endlessly in her hands—she called to her mother who wove it. The mother she knew only as a spirit.

"Oh, Sioctu," she called out in her loneliness, "come to me."

When Cayatu looked up from the basket, her mother sat cross-legged on the mat across from her, weaving new coils of tule into another basket. Expertly, her hands and fingers worked. "I am here, daughter," she said.

Startled, Cayatu looked at the wrinkle-skinned, old woman, whose sleek dark hair cascaded about her shoulders. Tears of joy mingled with Cayatu's sobs of despair at her mother's sight.

"Are you really my mother? Tell me."

Sioctu didn't look up from the coils she was building. "I am Muniyaut's wife. Daughter of the village headman."

Cayatu inspected her seated on the mat, real but not real. "Tell about my birth. Tell why the spirits traded your life for mine."

"You were born after the acorns were stored away." The old voice was strong, unhesitating. Sioctu spoke with authority. "It was a good trade with the spirits. You had so much to bring into our world. It was the new sickness in our village that took me, daughter, not your birth."

"I never knew you. Only the stories Tanayan told. She told of your strong love for our father. Good stories. I cried because I didn't know you. Because I had no mother." Cayatu wanted to reach out across the open space between them to touch her, but hesitated, fearing Sioctu would be gone again in just that instant.

"I wasn't important. It was important you were born to play the part First People have for you."

"What part?" Cayatu laughed scornfully. "Look at me. The spirits are scornful, mother. They abandoned me years ago. They deceived you—"

"—No, not deceived." Sioctu almost cackled her scorn.

"We all have our guides, our dream helpers in many forms, we just need to know where to look for them. You were born to wear the sea otter skirt. But more than that."

"More? What more?"

"To be different."

"You're cruel to say that, Mother."

Cayatu rose from her mat, pacing the length of the room where she studied her mother more distantly. "Your words are too cruel to be my mother's. Look at me. Fat with child. Fattening like some animal penned until time for slaughter. What man would have me now? Have you come from below to torment me?"

"I *am* your mother. What I say is truth." Finally Sioctu's head turned up. Cayatu saw her oval-shaped face, like her own, with eyes deep set under her strong, deeply furrowed brows. Dark eyes, always focused on the work in her lap, but now looking up at her daughter, burning with intensity. Her jaw square and firmly set. "The astrologer said your life would be different. You were born for a purpose. He said a woman born to me with white hair would show the future. It worried the old shaman, Liamu. He returned from the Peaceful Place one night to whisper in Qoloq's ear. To warn him. Qoloq knew and it scared him."

Cayatu ran back to her mat, kneeling by her mother's side, anxious to take her hand and stare into her face to learn the truth. "I'm not a woman with white hair," she said. "What did the seer mean?"

Sioctu looked down at her hands again and resumed her weaving. "Oh, daughter," she said, "your hair is as white as the down feathers of an owl, just as the seer predicted. The blackness is gone. It's a white so pure light shines from it."

"No..." Cayatu spoke slowly, reaching up to touch her hair. "Is it so? Is this another torment for me?" she dropped her hand to her side again.

"It's a mark that you're special," her mother said

solemnly. "You're honored, not tormented."

"Qoloq tormented me. He expelled me from the village for loving Ysaga."

"It's all part of the plan."

"What do you see from your side of the bridge that I can't see?"

"In time, Cayatu. But you can't know now.

"Is it the spirits' plan for me to spend my life a prisoner to these missionaries?"

Sioctu's hands never wavered from her weaving. She didn't look up at her daughter. But now her image grew fainter, dissolving before Cayatu's eyes. She pleaded, "Don't leave me, mother. Tell me the future." Cayatu tried to reach out to embrace her mother, but it was too late. Sioctu's image was gone, drifted back to the Peaceful Place. Cayatu embraced empty space. She sat alone on her mat, still turning the shell basket in her hands.

Cayatu could see the young women of the *monjerio* react in different ways to her confinement. She got sympathy from some and a few condemned her for her sinfulness, speaking in low tones in far corners of the sleeping room and peering over their shoulders at her enough times so that she knew they were talking about her.

Dolores's moods were unpredictable. At times Dolores was caring and solicitous, happy at the thought of the new life Cayatu would bring forth. At other times she scolded her friend for failing to lead a chaste Christian life. And at still other times, Dolores seemed to avoid her altogether, staying away from the *monjerio* as much as she could. But throughout her confinement Cayatu could count on Dolores when she was needed.

"Look how your hair grows so quickly," Dolores had said brightly one day.

"Why haven't you told me?"

Dolores knelt down beside her. "You know?"

"I know."

"We wanted you to stay calm until the birth. We asked Nuncio not to speak of it. It's very beautiful hair, so different from the rest of us."

Cayatu remembered the days when Tanayan had scolded her for always combing her hair until its blackness shown lustrous in the sun. Now her beautiful black hair was gone, replaced by old women's hair.

Just a little more time and the baby will come, she told herself. Then she'd run so far no soldier would ever catch her and if one did, she'd use her dying strength to kill him. Tomas would flee with her. Tomas loved her, he'd go with her. They'd run into the hills.

"My hair wouldn't have been shorn off if the priests hadn't learned of the baby, Dolores. How did they know?" Cayatu asked the girl one evening. "How did they find out?"

Dolores hesitated, backing away a step, before answering. Finally, she said, "I don't know, Clare. No one does."

"I told a Mexican woman in the village," Cayatu mused. "Maybe she told one of the priests. Do you think she did, Dolores?"

Dolores hesitated again, averting her eyes. "Yes," she said finally, "that could be what happened."

Cayatu's eyes drilled into Dolores. She held her stare until the younger girl began to shift from one foot to the other.

Dolores's face took on a far off look. She seemed to drift away. "I told the priests," she whispered. "I vowed to keep your secret but Father Ortiz made me tell. He said it was a sin the Virgin would punish me for." She sank to her knees beside Cayatu. "Forgive me, Clare."

"I forgive you, Dolores." Cayatu reached out to the humbled girl. "You're my friend. What matter does it make now?" She put a hand on Dolores's shoulder.

It was Dolores Cayatu called out to in the predawn darkness. The summer was losing its battle with the invading fall. Her birthing pains had begun. Dolores urged the other women to get water from the *lavendería*, find old cloths and let the missionaries know Clare's time had come. Cayatu propped herself up against the wall in the birthing position she'd seen Tanayan in for the birth of Massilili. She endured the pains which sometimes brought squeaks of anguish from her tight-set lips. She tried to manage her labor with the dignity of a highborn Chumash—the dignity she'd been told Sioctu showed as she was dying—but at times dignity fled when pain took over. Cayatu pushed and grunted and groaned. Finally, she expelled the baby into the hands of one of the women waiting to catch it.

Still attached by the cord, the infant was dried with a soft cloth and deposited on Cayatu's stomach. The new life sent spasms of horror through her. "Get it away from me," Cayatu moaned, squirming out from underneath it, pushing it toward one of the women. "Take it!" she shouted. "Take this monster away!" The other women stopped their chores abruptly, staring at the horror on Cayatu's face.

One held a knife brought by the *alcalde* for the special purpose of parting the baby from its mother. Cayatu lunged for it, trying to snatch the blade away from the woman so she could plunge it into the baby. But it was just beyond her reach. She fell back weakly against the wall.

When the cord was severed the baby was put back on her, sending tremors through her again. She tossed from side to side as if to roll the baby off, hoping to roll on top of it to smother out its weak flame. Weakened from the birth she could not. She could only look down her breast at the tiny, light-skinned baby with a clump of fine black hair in the middle of its head, howling at her.

Just then, Fermin Ortiz burst into the *monjerio* with Nuncio rushing to keep pace behind him. They came to Cayatu propped against the wall and looked down on her and the baby.

"So, it's arrived," the priest said to no one in particular. "God in his mercy has delivered a bastard to the mission. Praise God!"

"Praise God," the women repeated and Ortiz gave them a sardonic look.

Ortiz turned to the *alcalde*, "Take it," he commanded. Nuncio fretted. He clasped and unclasped his hands, standing beside Cayatu. "Take it," Ortiz demanded again.

Looking from Cayatu to Ortiz, he finally bent, lifting the baby off Cayatu's belly. He wrapped a cloth he had brought for this purpose around the newborn. Then he hurried out the door after Ortiz, throwing a quick glance over his shoulder, leaving the other women staring after him as he went out of the *monjerio*.

Chapter Twenty-Four

Torches blazed on the walls of the *Presidio* and around the edges of the plaza, casting shimmering silhouettes of the strolling men and women. Two large fires burned near the center, giving off heat that took the sting out of the evening chill. Overhead, a full moon and star-dense sky added a glow, bathing the couples gathered for the wedding feast in magical light.

Near one fire, two soldiers played guitars, while a Chumash man from the *pueblo* played a concertina. Another man, a neophyte from the mission trained by Esteben Salamanca, played a violin. They played the few songs they all knew, starting over as the evening went on. When they took a break, the soldiers played a dice game the Chumash had taught them with much conversation and laughter between them.

Josefa stood outside the chapel, surrounded by a handful of soldiers' wives.

"So, Josefa," one woman, dressed in a skirt of vibrant red and orange and yellow stripes, said, "a fine new husband for you."

"Aí, the Lieutenant. May the Virgin bless you both with children to care for you in your old age," the woman next to her added.

"A handsome boy, like his father perhaps," another said. "One with blond hair that turns the ladies' heads, just as his father turned yours, and eyes the blue of the ocean."

"Wait," still another interrupted, and now they were all talking and laughing, at once. "It's only her wedding day and already you have her with children."

The first woman gave a knowing laugh. "We know Josefa. She'll have a brood of little ones before you know it."

The women all laughed, but Josefa let only a weak smile drift politely across her face. The sadness of Joaquin lying unburied in the desert haunted her. "In time," she said. "In God's good time, if he smiles on us, we'll have babies for you to fuss over. But Antonia is right, give us time."

"Looking as beautiful as you do on your wedding day, I don't think your new husband will wait too long to start your family," the first woman teased. The others blushed, laughed and bobbed their heads up and down in agreement, like shore birds, as if it were a private joke only they shared.

"*Qué bonita,*" one of them said, indicating Josefa's dress.

Josefa let her smile linger, but she wondered if the dress had been the right choice. It was a tight-fitting, long white gown, with tiers of ruffles cascading down to a tight hem that dusted the ground and made only the smallest steps possible. She'd married Guillermo in this dress ten years before in Guanajuato and brought it across the desert on their long, sad trek to Alta California, too precious to leave behind. It fit her hips much too snugly now, gripping them with threads that strained at the task of containing her and threatened to fail at any sudden movement.

A white lace *mantilla* lay across her head and down over her shoulders, creating a kind of frame for her dark curls, peeking out like sleeping children from under a blanket. Don Demetrio had offered her a red velvet gown with a tight bodice and flowing skirt for the wedding but she had chosen this one to honor Guillermo.

As her eyes swept over the heads of the women to the small knots of men standing around, she remembered how different her first marriage had been from this one. She'd been just a girl then, hardly a virgin, but still naïve and happily romantic. Guillermo was a hard rock miner who spent most of his days deep underground at the Valenciana mine, sweltering in unbearable heat. He emerged grimy at the end of each day, but swaggered around the *colonia* where his family lived each night in search of adventure. Josefa saw him as a self-assured young man, filled with talk of their future together. He had swept her off her feet. His bravado and the pictures he painted of their life together won her heart.

It had taken months of work in the kitchens of the rich mine owners, grinding the maize, molding *masa* and baking tortillas over open fires, to earn enough to buy the dress. Months of hard work, with hands raw from the *metate* and singed over the fire, but the effect, when Guillermo first set eyes on his bride-to-be, was worth every *real*.

What would he think now, Josefa wondered? Secretly, she made the sign of the cross for him and prayed the Virgin of Guadalupe would forgive her. Guillermo would understand, she knew. This land was harsh. It would take a large family to make a new life here; strong sons and sturdy daughters who could chop the wood and draw the water to ease her life.

"The *pueblo* grows," she said to the other women, steering the conversation in a new direction. "I see people whose names I don't know yet."

"*Sí,*" one of the other women said. "That's Irmina." She pointed near the fire. "Her husband's a peddler who travels from mission to mission with another man trading with Indians. They are settling here. They say others will come, too, because our Indians are so peaceful. In other *Presidio* towns life isn't so safe."

"Don Demetrio wants me to move to the land the king gave for Guillermo," Josefa told the women, "but I'll stay in the *pueblo* with you and the new people who come. The Indians help us with our work here—out there I'd have no one."

So, Josefa is pleased with the child?" Fermin Ortiz asked de Alba in a hushed voice as they warmed their hands at the fire and listened to the music filling the night air.

"I suppose she is," de Alba replied. "She kept her promise, but she asks too many questions. What can I tell her, Fermin, when she asks where it came from?"

"Tell her the truth. The child is an abomination, born out of wedlock. We can't have that at the mission, can we?"

"But she asks about the mother, the father. What do I say about that?"

"Demetrio, surely you can find a story that will convince Josefa. Talk with vague words. Show her how wonderful it is to have the child. Tell her it's like a miracle from the Virgin. Tell her whatever you need to, Demetrio. She's your wife now, she'll accept what you tell her."

"My wife." De Alba visibly cringed. "I should have a better wife than Josefa, a *criolla* wife," he told the Franciscan. "I should be in Mexico City choosing a wife there."

"So you've told us often enough, *Comandante.*" Ortiz gave him a stern look. "But in truth, Demetrio, we both know you are probably here for the rest of your life. Here with the rest of us trying to live our lives far from the women of Mexico City of whom you speak so fondly. Josefa is an attractive woman most men would be proud to marry. You have a wife and a child and our plan is complete. Go back to Mexico City if you can, but in God's holy name, Demetrio, stop talking about it."

Ortiz stood by, watching de Alba's reaction to his words. When none was forthcoming he continued, "If you stay you'll be one of the wealthiest men in Alta California. The Yankee captains we've spoken with are all in favor—"

"—How?"

"We keep our eye open for ships. When we see one, Jimeno builds a fire. The ship captains come ashore and we bargain. The red dress was just a sample. Some will bring goods to trade for hides they can carry back to New England, only a few will bring coin to buy them. In a short time the business will be quite successful. Perhaps you'll be able to buy a new uniform, yours is threadbare in spots."

"We haven't gotten our pay or supplies from San Blas in more than two years. I worry these Indians may rise up against us and we'd be unprepared. My men are poorly equipped, their children run about the fort almost naked. I wish there was more I could do for them. What about Salamanca?"

"Leave him to me, Don Demetrio," Ortiz assured him. "Brother Esteben shows his age. His memory isn't sharp anymore. Leave him to me."

"And the Indian mother? Who is she? What've you done with her?"

"She is nothing. We told her about the sins she'd committed. She's a strange one—in some ways she seemed to be pleased to be rid of the child. Go back to your bride and enjoy your wedding celebration now. The townspeople are here to celebrate with you. Look how the *pueblo* grows. It means our business will grow too."

"Here to drink my wine and brandy is more like it," de Alba snapped. He pulled a cheroot from a breast pocket and bit off an end as Ortiz walked away toward Josefa. He pulled a taper from the fire and lit his smoke, relaxing as he blew his first puff into the clear night air.

For the next few minutes he walked about the parade grounds, enjoying the respect his guests lavished on him.

He stopped to talk with a young woman who was new to the *pueblo*. She told him she and her husband had come down from Monterey to settle. As she talked, he eyed her carefully, judging her no more than twenty and noting her pleasant face and ample figure.

"Your bride awaits you, Lieutenant." Esteben Salamanca had come up behind de Alba and now lay a gentle hand on his shoulder, drawing him away from the woman. "Stroll that way with me," the priest said guiding him away.

De Alba cursed the old missionary under his breath but kept a diplomatic smile on his face. "A night to rejoice, *Padre*," he said, taking a long draw on the cigar, letting the smoke out slowly from the side of his mouth.

"A night to give thanks," Salamanca replied. "You have a beautiful bride who will love and care for you."

"We're thankful the king has granted us the land—*Cañada de Corral*, the land grant is called. Josefa will live there as soon as we can build a house for her. We'll pay your neophytes."

"And you'll stay here at the *Presidio?*" The Franciscan studied the lieutenant's face. "So, you'll share the land, Don Demetrio? The deed will be in both your names?"

"The king gives the land to Josefa for the loss of her first husband. Guillermo Tapia would have received it when he retired. But *I'm* her husband now; she'll share it with me."

"How convenient for you," was Salamanca's only response. It made de Alba feel a little uncomfortable, a momentary touch of dizziness that passed as quickly as it came.

"That's land where our mission cattle graze, is it not?" the old priest asked, letting his hand go up to his sparse fringe of hair. "I suppose we'll have to move our herd. Or do you think Josefa will let the cows stay? And such a protected beach. Josefa is well blessed with that land."

It was another little jolt that knocked Demetrio off stride for a moment. He wondered if Salamanca's musings were innocent or if he knew what happened on the deserted beach.

"Perhaps we could ride out there one day so you can show me the land, Don Demetrio," Salamanca said.

"We should. Of course," de Alba stammered. "Whenever you say." Did Fermin Ortiz really have this in hand, he asked himself?

Salamanca now brought de Alba alongside Josefa. "Your new husband wanders off too much so I've brought him back to you," he crooned to her in a way that brought smiles to all the faces gathered around. "It's time for you to dance. The others await your wedding dance so they can join in. Look how our little town grows," he added with a smile. "Our people and the Indians are learning to live together in peace. Isn't that so, *Comandante?*"

De Alba just nodded.

Josefa's face lit up. "So many of them are wonderful, happy people. All the *gente* say so. They get along with everyone and all work together to build our *pueblo*. I only wish my friend Clare could be here to share my happiness tonight. It's been a long time since I've seen her."

"As Brother Salamanca says, it's time for your dance," Fermin Ortiz interrupted, taking bride and groom by the hand and leading them into the center of the quadrangle away from the others. He signaled to the musicians who launched into a lively *jota* from old Spain. The soldiers and their wives, and the new people who had come to the *pueblo* of Santa Barbara, formed a circle around the wedding couple. Demetrio de Alba took Josefa into his arms as the music started. He was cautious of the tiny steps her dress forced her to take, dancing well but sedately, holding her in a strong embrace, but searched the faces around them to see if the attractive young woman was still there. Then his hand slid down Josefa's back to her thigh.

Chapter Twenty-Five

It's time," Qoloq said, a somber, almost sad look knitting his thick brows.

"He's not ready," Tanayan replied. "He'd rather paddle the *tomol* with the other men to *Limuw* to fish and trade with the island people. He listens to all you teach him but only to please you."

"He's not ready," Qoloq agreed. "But still, it *is* time. The headman asks me when he will do the *'antap* ceremony."

"He'll never be a healer, he isn't meant for it."

Tanayan and Qoloq sat outside their hut as darkness crept down from the mountain ridge, leaving the ocean shimmering silver under a quartering moon. Tanayan held her hands together in the smooth lap of her sea otter-fur skirt and looked straight into Qoloq's face. He sat across from her, looking fondly at the woman who had shared his hut for so long. They shared concern for Massilili, too. Qoloq felt it deep in his soul. It gnawed at him like an animal gnawing a leg to free itself from a trap.

"The village will suffer," he answered. "Without a shaman after me to lead them, they'll be drawn to the false life the missionaries promise."

"What's happened to our son?" Tanayan asked, getting to

her feet and pacing near the fire. "He has no power. It seems unimportant to him."

"Who can say why?" Qoloq replied. "Coyote is fickle. But the day for the solstice ceremony approaches and we can't wait. I thought he was ready at the harvest ceremony, but he failed. Tomorrow I'll take him into the sacred place with me. We'll see if the spirits speak to him."

"Don't let him fail, Qoloq." She clasped her hands to her breasts. "Show him how to have your power."

Qoloq looked fondly at his wife but had no comforting words to offer. Then he peered into the darkness, toward the high mountains, thinking of the ordeal ahead.

The next day, Qoloq and Massilili began their journey, naked except for the sinew belts from which a knife and small water basket hung. They took no food, little water. "Our journey will cleanse us," Qoloq explained. "Our minds must be open to messages from the World Above."

"I'll listen for them," Massilili promised.

They walked across the narrow valley lying along the ocean and climbed into brown hills. The damp smells that came from the soil warned Qoloq of the approaching season. Leaves crumbled under their feet. Plants lay dead on the ground, gone for another season, dying back so new life could begin in its time.

Qoloq knew the path well but the climb into the high mountains grew hard and slow for him. He watched his son easily maintaining his pace. So strong, Qoloq thought, as he stopped to rest when he had no breath to continue. What a leader he could be.

They rose into the rock world, where sage and chaparral grew on bald ledges and steep outcroppings. Farther on, they climbed through golden rocks that threw Sun back at the ocean from crumbling sandstone faces. They came to a place where a boulder had blocked the trail, challenging them to climb around it.

"Wait," Massilili said as his father began clawing his way up. And with a strength that startled Qoloq, his son pushed the rock off to one side.

At other places where the path narrowed, they crawled along ledges jutting out over the valley below. "We're climbing into the sky," Qoloq told his son as they made slow progress up the mountain. "Climbing toward the spirit world."

Massilili climbed silently. Qoloq could see his son's look showed respect mixed with apprehension for what lay ahead.

The next day, father and son reached the top of the world and looked out. "The islands are as small as the wooden canoes fathers carve for their sons," Massilili gasped. "So small."

Over the crest they stared down into another valley, toward other mountains on the horizon. Qoloq watched two condors soar in silent circles suspended over the valley, raw red heads against the blackness of their bodies, like blood-soaked blades.

Together, they made their way toward the mountains farther to the north. They began to weaken. Qoloq felt hunger coil like a serpent around his belly. His bark sandals were in tatters. Both men's feet were cut and bloodied. Qoloq talked to Massilili as they struggled onward, telling him of the land and the spirits who inhabited it before the great flood. He forced both their minds away from the hunger and pain. Qoloq could see Massilili, in his own way, trying to help his father keep on, renewing Qoloq's strength by showing him his own and talking of his adventures with the island people.

They kept going until they reached a large valley, flat and dry, dotted occasionally with sparse grasses. It seemed to stretch in all directions without limit. To the east, Qoloq spotted an outcropping of rocks shimmering in the heat that stood like tall sentinels on the horizon. He led Massilili to that secret place where the rocks were covered with pictures painted by generations of shamans.

"Lie down and rest," he told Massilili. "I'll make the drink and you'll dream come nightfall."

Qoloq went to two of the taller rocks and disappeared from sight through a narrow opening between them. It was several minutes before he reappeared, but when he did Massilili jumped up. Qoloq lumbered toward his son, cloaked in the shaggy skin of a bear. The bear's head rested on top of his own, with the dark-furred skin draped over his shoulders. In one hand he held a stone bowl and in the other a small grinding stone.

"This is a sacred place," Qoloq told Massilili when the sun melted into the horizon. He walked around the small enclosure, rolling from side to side, imitating a bear. He struggled to find the words to encourage Massilili, who sat with his mouth agape. "Listen to Coyote of the Sky and the other First People when they speak," Qoloq began. "Let them into your dreams to give you the power of new dream helpers." Qoloq pointed to the red and white and black images painted on the rocks around them. "Paint your dream so the creatures from the World Below will know your power."

"I want that," Massilili said earnestly. There was passiveness in his voice that belied his strength and stature. He sat straighter, thrusting back his shoulders. "I know I failed at the harvest ceremony. I don't want to fail you again."

"Think of the people of the village. Listen to the voices that can guide you through the world of the foreigners and bring the village back to our traditions." Qoloq's voice rose with intensity. "Our people respect power so you must show them yours," he said, putting his hand on Massilili's head. Then he joined his son on the ground. "Be quiet now. We'll start the dreaming ceremony when Sun goes home."

Two coyotes announced the coming of darkness, slinking to within a few yards of where the men sat in silence. They sniffed the air, catching a human scent and sat back on their haunches, as if they would stand guard during the night or perhaps were just curious about the intruders. But after just a few minutes they got bored and crept off into the shadow of the rocks.

Qoloq administered the potion to Massilili. Then he moved off to sit against one of the rocks, still cloaked in the bear skin. Massilili stretched out on the ground and soon fell into a stuporous sleep. The two stayed that way through the night, Massilili sleeping and Qoloq watching over him, occasionally mumbling some words to implore the spirit gods to come to his only son. The youth slept into the next day, shielded from the direct heat of the sun by the rocks towering over him. As the day wore on, heat shimmers rose from the plain and played tricks on Qoloq's mind. Still, he sat in the sun, all but numb now to the hunger and thirst of the past three days. He drifted in and out of consciousness.

In mid-afternoon Qoloq rose from his watching spot and floated into the air. He rose until he reached the level of the tallest rocks and perched on one, looking down. He saw Massilili prone on the ground and himself still sitting against the base of the rock. His vision was acute. Not only did he see the two men below him, he could look into their hearts. When he looked at his son, a sense of pride engulfed him. The lad had a strong body that went with his gentle and loving heart. Qoloq saw the simple joy Massilili experienced living unfettered by heavy thoughts. He could see the life of a shaman wasn't meant for Massilili. That brought a pain to his chest like a fist squeezing his heart.

When he looked down on his own life form, Qoloq saw a different image. He saw a soft body shrouded in an animal skin meant to give fear to others. He saw a heart made hard, hardened to ward off the threats of a new people who wanted to rule the land of his ancestors, men who would destroy the ways of his people without even knowing they'd done so. When he saw the hardness of his own heart a cry parted Qoloq's lips, echoing from the rocks and sounding throughout the wilderness. He hadn't meant for it to be that way.

As he continued looking down he saw people coming to the rocks in ones and twos until they formed a large crowd gathered around Massilili. They crowded close around him when he rose from the ground to greet them. Qoloq heard no voices but he could tell they clustered around his son waiting for his leadership.

When Massilili began to stir, Qoloq roused himself from his trance-like state. His son opened his eyes, looking around at the unfamiliar landscape and saw his father sitting nearby. Qoloq gave him water. Massilili gulped it down quickly.

"I saw you surrounded by our people while you slept," Qoloq broke the silence when Massilili was fully awake. "I know the spirits have come to you. To give you power to lead our village. Tell about your vision."

"I don't know," Massilili stammered.

"Come, son," Qoloq urged. "Tell about the spirits that came to you while you slept."

"No spirits came to me." Massilili stared at the ground averting his eyes from Qoloq.

The feeling of his heart being squeezed returned to Qoloq as the words registered.

"I had no spirit dreams. I'm sorry."

"But I saw our people. They crowded around you, waited for your words."

"Do you mock me?" Massilili stood unsteadily, shouting at his father. "I remember only jumbled pictures. I've failed again. I'm sorry."

"What kind of pictures? Tell me." Qoloq was in a frenzy. "Surely we can find something with meaning."

Massilili wobbled a few steps until he regained his balance. "I'm ashamed to tell you," he said, with a voice close to a sob. "I saw the foreigners—men riding horses through our valley. I saw grayrobes come into the village, wooden crosses swinging from their belts. I saw our young girls going off into the oak groves. Images of the new people you hate so much." Massilili paused, looking down at the ground. When he spoke again his voice was barely audible. "Once or twice I even saw myself with them. I've failed you again, father. I'm unworthy."

Qoloq looked at his son, unable to summon any words. Should he console him? Tell him it was all right? Tell him not everyone had spirit dreams? That's what a father ought to tell a son, Qoloq knew. But how could his son have failed? And how could he tell him it was all right? It wasn't all right. What was wrong with the boy? It was the worst thing that had ever happened in Qoloq's life and he had no idea what to do about it.

The two stared at each other, fear weighing on their faces. The whiteness of their eyes bulged large. Qoloq was unable to speak. He saw Massilili was shaking. They stood like that for a long while. The longer they stood silently apart, the harder it became to break the silence. Finally, it was Massilili who did. He stood tall, facing his father.

"You've done everything you could," he started. "I have deep love and respect for you. But I won't embarrass you any longer because my life follows a different path. Tell my mother I love her. Tell her I'll miss her and always think of her."

With that, Massilili turned his back on Qoloq and walked away toward the west where the sun was falling out of the sky.

Chapter Twenty-Six

Tomas spurred his horse into a gallop. Something was wrong. Cattle were missing. What was going on at the beach? If it had anything to do with *his* cattle Tomas intended to find out what it was.

His thoughts raced as he crossed the stretch of dry grass that was the coastal plain, trying to think of anything he might have done to let strays wander off. He scolded himself for lingering too long this morning at the *vaquero* camp up the canyon. "Don't rush to the herd tomorrow," Jimeno had told Tomas and the other *vaqueros* last night. "Rest in the morning and hunt strays later in the day,"—an unusually kind order from Jimeno. Nevertheless, he knew he should have been up early with his cattle.

What would Jimeno say now? With cattle missing? Would he say it was Tomas's fault? Jimeno was the nemesis for all the men tending mission cattle, but Tomas was the man he seemed to get the greatest pleasure from tormenting. Tomas and the others on this western bench land faced an ongoing struggle trying to please the soldier-guard, or at least not anger him, and avoid his whip. *Señor* Lash, Jimeno called the coiled rawhide with a wooden handle and small bits of metal on the multiple tips. All the men had felt Jimeno's anger from time to time, instant, painful punishment for any mistake or any act that displeased him. Jimeno ruled the grazing land with *Señor* Lash and absolute power.

Tomas believed he was one of the best *vaqueros* at the mission, a horseman who knew his cattle—almost every steer, heifer and calf—by sight. It was important to him to be the best. That usually kept him as safe as possible from *Señor* Lash. If cattle had strayed he could tell. And today, some, a few, were definitely missing. How was it possible?

In the distance he could finally make out several steers kicking up a dust cloud as they disappeared single file down a narrow trail to the beach. Tomas urged his mare to greater speed. He had to rein her back hard as they arrived at the edge of the bluff. Horse and rider were both panting as they looked down the 40-foot slope to the beach.

The scene spreading out before him shocked Tomas, taking what little breath he had left and sucking it from his lungs. What caught his eye first quickened his pulse, and sent a wave of desperate guilt deep in his stomach. Men— not Chumash men, not Mexicans—but men with pale skin, surrounded a small knot of cattle, stabbing them with long knives. The cattle milled around with no place to run, bellowing their pain, taking the steel from every angle, staggering to their knees where other men rushed to their side to slit their throats. The sand ran crimson with blood. Men and cattle slipped and sometimes fell in the gore as the slaughter continued. Dead cows were scattered about the beach where still other men cut them into chunks of meat.

"Careful," he heard a voice shout out to the others in Spanish. "Don't ruin the hides with too many cuts. Take the meat but leave us good hides."

The smell of blood, the smell of intestines and excrement from the dead animals, drifted up. Tomas knew the smells—he'd slaughtered cattle many times before—but this time those smells made his gut retch. His normally placid face tightened into a mask of anger. Regardless of the risk he was going to stop this slaughter. Those were his cattle. Who were these men?

Tomas's next thought was how could he stop them? If he rode back to camp for the others, more cows would be killed before they could return. He was alone, perched on the bluff looking at the *matanza* below. He couldn't wait. He had to take some action. But he held back.

Tomas let his gaze widen to scan the whole scene before racing down the hill. To his left was a large iron kettle bubbling and steaming on top of a log fire that licked at it with flames bright even in the strong morning sun. Men stood around the kettle, pitching slabs of fat into it. "My cattle," he spit angrily, his face flushed. He squinted against the reflected light off the ocean to see clearly. To his right other men were loading dried cow hides into a longboat and making ready to cast off from the beach.

Now, finally, letting his eye scan out to the ocean, he saw the two-masted ship rocking gently two hundred yards off shore, all sails furled. Three longboats were pulled up on the beach, four sets of oars stacked along the gunwales and a tiller swinging free in the stern of each one as waves lapped around them. Those oars would be manned by the men killing his cattle and feeding fat to the cauldron, he guessed.

Poised to race his horse down the steep bank, Tomas hesitated just a moment longer. In that time, his eyes came finally to rest on Jimeno, standing off a short distance from the slashing knives, watching the work as if he were supervising it. And beyond Jimeno, Fermin Ortiz and *Comandante* Demetrio de Alba stood in deep conversation with a light-skinned man dressed in uniform. On the sand between the three lay two large sea chests. The sight of them caused Tomas to hesitate further, and in that instant, Jimeno looked up. He saw Tomas and his horse silhouetted against the sky. Jimeno began gesturing. Tomas only vaguely saw the rage mount in Jimeno's face, matching his own.

Committed now, Tomas rode down the slope, but he didn't race down as he wanted to. He didn't charge into the circle of men killing his cattle, or the men tossing chunks of beef fat into the kettle. Somewhat meekly, he reined up in front of Jimeno.

"Mother of God, what are you doing here, Tomas? I told you to stay at the camp," Jimeno charged at him before he could dismount. "Get away from here now. Now, before it goes bad for you!"

"I saw the dust. I came to see—"

"—Why is this Indian here?"

It was de Alba, striding over, hand on his sword hilt, with Fermin Ortiz hurrying along behind him, hiking up his robe and shuffling through the sand, leaving the third man standing in front of the two open sea chests. Tomas's view was only partial but what he saw surprised him. One chest contained brightly colored cloth, cloth in a rainbow of colors like he had never seen before. The brilliant red and blue and orange and purple hues thrilled him. Wouldn't Cayatu look beautiful with one of those cloths around her shoulders, he thought. The other chest held fancy women's dresses that lay all a jumble. His imagination soared to an image of Cayatu, dressed in a fine, velvet gown with her shining black hair surrounding the collar, looking as elegant as any woman of the *pueblo*.

"Get him away," de Alba shouted. That made Tomas wince. "If he speaks to others it will be trouble. And trouble for you, Jimeno. No more easy time here. I'll send you to Monterey or San Diego where soldiers know hard duty. Get this Indian away from the beach now."

"I will, Lieutenant. This one's too stupid to cause us any trouble," Jimeno told his commander.

Tomas understood—he'd learned the foreigners'

language well—but he showed no change in his face. He kept his rage at this insult locked inside.

"We can't have this," Ortiz fretted. "What if word gets back to Salamanca? To Monterey? It could ruin everything. Jimeno, you have to take care of this man. Make sure he doesn't speak about what he's seen. Do whatever you need to do to ensure that."

"Go back to camp and wait for me. Go! Now! Before it goes badly for us both," Jimeno ordered Tomas.

At the camp, Tomas sat on a rough cloth spread on the ground that was his cover on cold nights. As he waited, his thoughts raced back and forth from apprehension about what Jimeno might do to him to what Cayatu might be doing. In his mind, he saw her with one of those magnificent cloths. He pictured her slender face and hair black as a moonless night framed by a striking red or brilliant orange silk, or maybe softened by shades of blue or green.

Tomas longed for Cayatu. He hadn't seen her since Father Salamanca dragged her off from in front of his hut. Bad enough—he could only hold her image tightly in his mind, recalling her beauty whenever he chose—but worse, he hadn't had any message from her since that day. Not one word. Each day, when he saw Dolores he would rush to her and ask if Cayatu had sent him a message. And each day the answer was the same. "I'm sorry, Tomas. No message. Perhaps tomorrow she'll send word." But no word came. So Tomas cursed himself for *his* failure. If only he were worthy of her. If he could make her see his love. If they could marry and live in his hut...

The thought was interrupted by Jimeno's sudden appearance in front of him. Jimeno hadn't snuck up, but Tomas was so absorbed in his fantasy that he failed to hear Jimeno's boots crunching on the hard ground.

"Follow me," Jimeno ordered.

Tomas jumped to his feet and followed, suddenly filled with fear for what the next minutes would bring.

Jimeno led him into the darkness, well off from the campfire where the other *vaqueros* sat throwing the gambling stones, just as they had in their old villages. They came to a gnarled oak tree, standing sentinel near the canyon mouth. Its limbs spread out in all directions, hanging low to the ground like a giant spider web. Abruptly, Jimeno spun around, grabbing Tomas by his shirt and thrusting him up against the trunk.

"Listen to me, you foul Indian. I'm going to kill you right now. Right here. And no one will know. If they did know, they wouldn't care. That's how little your life means to any of us." Jimeno reached down to his boot and pulled out a small dagger he kept there. He held it up to Tomas's face. "I could stick this into your throat and leave you here to bleed out like a slaughtered steer. And I will do it!" Jimeno's voice rose as he brought the knife down close to Tomas's throat.

Tomas trembled. His legs shook. He thought death was inches away. So be it. Perhaps I'll be in heaven or the Peaceful Place soon. If only Cayatu were here with me so that I could see her once more. Feel her softness. Hear the music in her voice. If only—

"Listen, you dog," Jimeno shouted in his face. "I am not going to kill you tonight. I might decide to do it tomorrow. Or the next night. Or the next. You won't ever know when until I do it. If you have any hope of staying alive, you will seal your mouth from now on. Tell no one what you saw today. If you try to run, I'll hunt you down wherever you go. If there's any word of it—ever—you will die. Understand me?"

By then Tomas had soiled his trousers. They were beginning to smell. He continued to tremble and could only shake his head in response, but deep inside the fires of his rage and embarrassment burned together. The humiliation hung heavy on him and made his rage burn brighter.

Jimeno pushed him away and dropped the dagger to his side. "You are weak," he laughed. "A coward. You smell like a sick dog. I'll show the priest and *Comandante* that I'm in control. That's why you live—for now—to be my puppet. But not for long. Always be where I can see you. Keep your mouth shut and let the priest see that I'm strong. Not you. Not him. The soldiers run the mission. We tell you when to live. When to die."

With that, Jimeno pulled a short leather thong from his pocket and tied Tomas's hands to a tree branch in preparation for the whipping.

Chapter Twenty-Seven

Smiling weakly but barely masking his shock, Tomas watched Cayatu come along the path through the *rancheria* toward him. His jaw went slack seeing white strands of hair peeking out from under her shawl. My beautiful Cayatu, he gasped. The words choked in his throat. Her beautiful hair, black as night on the bluffs, gone.

As she came nearer, sending him an eager smile, the pain he'd felt in his heart as the days crept from spring into summer with no message, no word at all, from her, returned. Wonderful Clare, beautiful, clever, wise—the only woman he'd ever had feelings for—had forsaken him. Clare and his mare were the twin joys that made his life livable. He felt the pain of her rejection deeply. Even so, at the sight of her now, old feelings for her stirred.

"No word from you," he greeted her in a sullen voice, almost a whine. "All this time and no word. I don't even recognize you coming along the path." He knew the words were cruel, but he needed to strike out at her.

Cayatu held her smile. "I thought about you each day."

"But no message," he reproached her again. "Each day I asked Dolores, 'Did Cayatu send me a message?' Each day she just shook her head—'Not today, Tomas.' What was I to think? Didn't you know how I was missing you? How worried I was? How you were hurting me?" Tomas couldn't stop himself from letting his feelings pour out.

"I never stopped thinking of you, Tomas. I would never hurt you. I was angry. It was a bad time for me but I'll make it up to you."

"You were alone all those days in the women's quarters needlessly." He laid a hand on her shoulder and gave up his hurt look. He reached his hand up to touch her white hair tentatively. For just an instant, he felt her pull back. "If you had gotten word to me, I would've gone to the Franciscans and asked permission to marry. You know my feelings. You know I've had them since the day we walked up the hill together." Tomas let his fingers comb through the fine white strands.

"How could you love an old woman?"

"Old woman," he scoffed. "Never! Father Ortiz called me to his room. He told me of your... He accused me of being the father of your child. The *mayordomo* gave me five lashes—"

"—How terrible for you." She interrupted, reaching out to him, laying her hand on the side of his cheek.

"It was nothing. I told Ortiz I was not the father, but secretly I wished that I were." Tomas stood as tall as he could, taking both of her hands in his. "Tell me who and I'll get revenge for you."

"I know you would do that for me, but I don't want revenge, Tomas. I want to live as if it had never happened. I feel safe with you."

"It makes no difference to me about the baby. Say you will marry me and I'll go ask the priests' blessing this afternoon. We'll raise the child together."

"There is no child. Ortiz took it. I never saw it after the birthing."

"How could that be?" Tomas stopped, trying to

understand, trying to picture in his mind a newborn snatched away from its mother. It made no sense so he pushed the thought away. He had long before accepted the possibility of raising another man's child if it meant being with her. In time, there'd be his own son to raise.

"Padre Ortiz came to me after I'd recovered. He called the child a bastard. He said he couldn't have a bastard at the mission. That's all he ever said about it."

"Still, I'll go to the missionaries and ask them, if you say yes. I love you." His eyes shone. His lips parted, spreading his smile to the corners of his face. "...No matter what color your hair is."

Cayatu laughed happily, "And I love you, Tomas."

He heard the words come from her mouth. "You never said that before," was all he could manage.

"Being apart from you I knew my feelings. I knew I have always loved you." She opened her arms to him. "I couldn't tell you that in a message Dolores would bring you. I waited till now to tell you myself."

Tomas stared at her, not sure what to believe or what to do next. Dizziness swept over him. He rocked back and forth on unsteady legs. Without words, she moved closer. They embraced, burying their heads on each other's shoulder. They stood locked like that for what seemed to him a long time.

All thoughts of Jimeno's threats vanished in that moment. If I have only this day, this is enough, Tomas thought.

They kissed, still captive in each other's arms. Then, she took him by the hand, tugging a little to get him to follow her into the hut. Inside, she kissed him again and reached down to touch him. Tomas trembled at her touch. He didn't resist, but he was slow to respond. She took his hand and pressed it to her breast. He felt her firm softness, felt her wince slightly from the pressure of his hand. She pulled her blouse over her head and wiggled out of the cotton skirt. Tomas let his trousers fall. She told him to be gentle, that she was tender from the birthing.

What more could he want in his life? Lying by her side, his hand stroking her belly, still soft and rippled from carrying the child, Tomas felt complete. At times he caressed her breasts, or let his hand wander inside her thighs. This wonderful woman loved him. He had his work with the cattle, his horse. Cayatu made his life complete. They could live their days together.

"So, I'll go to the priests," he said happily, enfolding her in his arms, looking into her smiling face. "We'll let them perform their ceremony and live together here."

Cayatu moved a little, rubbing her body on his, sending a rush of excitement coursing through him again. "There's another way, Tomas," she said, using her hand to smooth his rumpled hair. "We can leave the mission. Go across the mountains to live in the valley on the other side."

"Leave the mission?"

"You could steal a horse we could ride together," she said, sitting up, smiling intently at him. "Or we can walk. The trail in the canyon will take us over the mountains."

Tomas pushed away from her and sat up so he could look into her face. "Is this a joke you play on me?" he asked. Alarm replaced joy.

"You know how much I hate my life here."

"This is the best life we can have." His mind raced, looking for answers to the fear he felt.

Cayatu's hand went to his back, rubbing along the rough edges of his scars. "Look how they've whipped you," she said softly. "I want us to be free, not told each day what to do."

"The lashes are nothing. I can endure them," Tomas said, reaching for his trousers and jumping to his feet to stand over her. "Think what the missionaries and soldiers would do when they had hunted us down as fugitives. Hunted us like animals."

"We'll hide from them," Cayatu implored him. "We can. Many men and women who came to the mission in the beginning have slipped away. Many of them."

"I have my life here. Working. Tending my cattle." Tomas stammered, beginning to move around the hut, not thinking clearly anymore. "Do you want me to give that away? Finally, in my life I have something important to do. I have respect. With you as my wife, my life would be complete."

"I'm sorry," Cayatu said. Bitter defeat came into her voice. "I can't live my life here any more. Come with me, Tomas. Live the life we were meant to live."

He watched tears drip down Cayatu's cheeks. Tomas felt his own tears form and blinked hard, turning his back to keep her from seeing them. "I can't," he said, the agony of his decision catching in his throat.

"You ride off each day," Cayatu snapped, and he could feel bitterness rising in her voice, replacing her anger. He still looked away, out the door of his hut to the mission buildings and church that were his home. "Jimeno sits on his horse and watches you," she continued. "He waits for his chance to whip you. You call that respect? You think you have a better life than the one you lived in your village but you don't, Tomas. None of us has any respect now. You're a slave, like the rest of us."

"No more!" Tomas shouted his pain, turning back to confront her. Despair overwhelmed him. Bitter tears rolled down his cheeks. "Say no more. Don't kill our love with more words. I won't leave."

Chapter Twenty-Eight

Massilili walked away from his father into the twilight. Fear beat against his chest as he saw the emptiness awaiting him, but he told himself that he had to get away from Qoloq, had to leave his father's world altogether. The people of his village didn't care whether he became a shaman, that was only Qoloq's dream.

His throat was parched, he'd had almost nothing to eat or drink on the hard three-day walk to this desolate place and for a moment he wished he hadn't acted so quickly. He knew food stashed away in the rocks would sustain Qoloq on the trek home, but his pride kept him from going back. Weak, hungry, and with his thirst sending waves of bile surging out of his stomach to gnaw at his throat, his prospects of finding anything that night were as dim as the horizon.

Searching the growing darkness, he saw no shelter, only the broad, arid plain he'd crossed with Qoloq, and the mountains, barely shadows in the far distance. The rocks guarded his father's sacred site behind him, throwing back eerie reflections of the dying day. He walked west, toward the purple-streaked horizon. He lay on the ground, still in sight of Qoloq's sacred rocks, now dark against the darkening sky, where his father's food and water urged him to stop being foolish and come back. He felt faint. He wondered if his father would come rescue him. Massilili knew he would not.

Coyotes howled throughout the night, complaining one to the other across long, empty spaces about the human lying on their ground. Night birds swooped past him in the darkness. Once, he heard the sharp squeal of a careless rodent. Chill descended on the plain, and the plain gave off a smell of death as it cooled, a dry, rasping smell that attacked his nose, keeping him awake, reminding him of his vulnerability. He didn't think about his failed vision quest. He knew he would never have Qoloq's visions and knew his life would never follow his father's. He knew the village no longer cared.

Still, honoring Qoloq was important. Honoring him and Tanayan, as the parents who had brought him into this Middle World, was important. It was a new Middle World—not understood by him or the people in the village—lacking the familiar paths to follow—certainly no path he understood—but the Middle World in which he had to survive. Spirit visions, rituals and healings were his father's world. They would never be part of his. Curled up on the hard earth, Massilili shrugged his acceptance of that fact.

But his acceptance brought a profound sadness. He was walking away from the village on the beach where his life had been filled with the joy of adventure and hard activity. In his mind, he saw himself in the *tomol*, paddle in hand, bonded together with other strong men by the water they raced over on their way to *Limuw* or one of the other islands. He traded acorn meal, ground and leached of its bitterness, with the island people for the sharp arrow and spear points they manufactured from the hard, white chert mined near the beach. Acorns for arrow points. It was his livelihood and his joyful life when Qoloq wasn't teaching about the plants that cured sickness or brought on the dizzying sleep that summoned dream helpers.

Now there would be one less man in the *tomol*. Already

there were fewer *tomols* on the sand in front of the village and some of them were no longer able to make the voyage to *Limuw*. The tar that kept the water out was gone from their seams and the milkweed that held the planks together was rotting away. There were fewer men and women in the village beside the ocean now, too. They drifted off in ones and twos like gulls winging across the water to pick and squabble over the leavings in the new *pueblos* and missions of the Spaniards and their Mexican followers.

How would the forces that had always ruled his world, and kept it in balance, survive this new one? What would guide his own life now? Once, he'd found a powerful dream helper in mountain cat. Was mountain cat watching over him now? Still protecting him as he lay here? Or was he alone, abandoned?

At first light, Massilili began walking south toward the ocean that lay over the mountain ranges. "I must find water and food," he repeated aloud as he walked, but he failed to find either on the empty plain. By mid-morning Sun had already brought his fierceness to bear, shining with intensity unfamiliar along the ocean. Heat poured down on this raw land, as if all Sun's anger at the Middle World was concentrated here. He kept on, numb to his surroundings, stopping often, always hoping the respite would bank the fire in the sky or bring water to his lips.

By late afternoon the flat land still stretched ahead. Mountains still loomed far off. His strength kept him going, but he began to feel the pain of his effort. His swollen tongue struggled to escape his mouth. His eyes smarted from the glare, his naked body exploded in pain at the least touch. Still he moved forward.

Willing his body to respond, to do his bidding, as he had disciplined it to keep paddling the tomol when his muscles ached, Massilili's strength kept him going, but he felt that strength slipping away. I need water. The words hammered over and over in his head.

He slept on the ground again that night, and for a second day he staggered toward the low hills and mountains beyond, looming larger now. He willed himself to keep going, knowing the alternative was death. His mind was jumbled, his stride uneven. He stumbled often and lurched from side to side like a man who had drunk too much of the foreigners' brandy. But he kept going forward throughout the day. Night chill engulfed him again. His blistered skin felt as if it were being stabbed by countless knife points. His body gave back the heat accumulated during the day, shaking his limbs and his chest with uncontrollable shivers.

In the dark, delirious now, he stumbled toward a shallow canyon that held the promise of water. Just a little way, he urged his feet, just a few steps more. "There'll be water, berries, seeds, everything I need." But it was all a blur. He wasn't sure if he was talking out loud or in his head.

At the entrance to the canyon, in the dark, he found a familiar berry bush and staggered to it. Grabbing handfuls, he stuffed his mouth, letting the bitter juice run down his face and parched throat. The berries hit his stomach like pebbles and came roaring back in one retching spasm that knocked him to the ground with its suddenness. He tried again, desperate to eat, with the same retching result.

Exhausted, he fell to the ground, rolled on his side with his knees drawn up to his chest. He sank into a numbness that might have been sleep or the coming of death.

A shadow loomed over him blocking the light. Massilili stirred. He blinked several times to clear his eyes, but the shadow remained over him. He struggled to his feet, awake and prepared to fight, but fatigue struck a blow to his legs and he dropped back to his knees.

"You will die," a deep voice came from the shadow.

His first impression of the man standing over him was the wild tangle of black hair growing down to his waist. Then he saw the man's cold eyes, deepset eyes in a gaunt face, skin pulled tight and ears jutting straight out through the wild hair.

"You will die," the voice said again.

This time it connected in Massilili's brain that the man was speaking his language.

"You will die unless you find shelter from Sun, drink cool water. This is hard land. What fool man crosses this land without water? Now, I will take you to water, fool man," the voice told him.

A hand reached down and grabbed Massilili's hair, dragging him back to his feet. The stranger pointed up the canyon and started walking. Massilili followed, still groggy, aching deep in his stomach. They walked—Massilili stumbling along behind—up the slope into the lower reaches of the mountains. The farther they went the slower and farther behind he trailed the wild man who stopped at intervals and waited. "Soon," he said, urging him on. "Water soon." Then the man picked Massilili up and carried him the rest of the way on his shoulder.

The wild man set him down by a small pool hidden in the rocks. For an instant, Massilili's addled brain refused to believe what it saw. Then he broke into a stumbling run, wading into the ankle deep water, falling on his knees, splashing water onto his back and cupping hands to bring it to his mouth. Cracked and blistered, his lips burned with each mouthful. The wild man came up behind him, grabbing him by the hair again and pulled him upright. "Drink too much and fool man will erupt again—like he did last night."

"You saw?"

"I watched to make sure you didn't die," the wild man said.

Massilili showed his surprise. "I thought my life was over."

The man took Massilili farther into the canyon, where overhanging rocks sheltered them from the sun. He gave Massilili a few berries and showed him where to lie down. Later in the day, he roasted a rabbit he'd snared over a fire of sticks. He fed Massilili little strips of meat. Massilili slept the rest of the day and all night.

Massilili stayed under the sheltering rocks three days, sleeping, eating a little more each day, drinking from the pool, hour by hour regaining strength. When he had recovered enough, the wild man began showing him paths that criss-crossed the mountain range, pointing out animal trails, teaching him where to search for water and how to hunt food, skills he'd never needed in the village. He taught Massilili how to build a short bow and arrows from willows growing along narrow stream banks to shoot birds. He showed him how to set snares for small animals and how to scrape a sharp point against a cutting rock. The younger man learned new skills from the older, wild one, and a bond formed between them.

Other days they roamed through the mountains and ranged out into the hidden valleys, tucked out of sight, hunting meat and gathering seeds and berries.

The two became friends. The wild one was happy to have a companion and the wildness of his speech faded with their conversations.

"I'm Massilili. I came from the village called *Mishopshnow* on the beach in the valley that lies along the ocean. Who are you?" he asked one evening early in their acquaintance as they ate by the light of a small fire.

The wild man studied Massilili for several moments in silence. "I know of *Mishopshnow*," he said finally. "I have no village now. I left years ago to wander in these mountains. I've walked from place to place. I've gone far to the north into the big valley where there is a lake so large it takes three days to walk around. Who are your parents, Massilili?"

"Qoloq, the bear shaman, is my father and Tanayan is my mother."

"I know of them," the wild man nodded, with no emotion showing on his face. "Why did you leave? Will you not be shaman after your father?"

"My village is dying. We build few canoes now. Fewer people know the old skills. The people still living there would rather work for the new settlers—drink their brandy—than fish or trade with the islanders."

"Yours isn't the only dying village," the wild man said, getting up from his place by the fire where the two squatted. He walked about in the darkness without speaking, seemingly deep in thought, his heavy brows tightly knit. "As I walk these mountains I see the villages below me," he said after the silence. "Sometimes I come down close to them to watch. Some are deserted; many have only old ones living in them. I've seen our people living around the foreigners' villages, too, doing their work."

"Some go to missions," Massilili said. "The fair-skinned men brought sicknesses from their own land that kill our people in their huts. Babies die, old ones, too. Qoloq can't cure them. People go to the missions because they think they'll survive the sicknesses there. My father doesn't know what medicines to use. His spirit guides give no help. He taught me many cures but we can't stop the dying. Maybe the spirits have left our world."

"You left your people?"

"I've left my village, not my people," Massilili defended himself. "I would never desert them, but I can't lead them. I disappointed my father and mother. Their ways aren't mine. I don't know what I'll do."

"Stay here," the wild man said. "We can live well enough

without the old ways of your village or the foreigners' new ones. With two to hunt, our life will be easier."

Massilili considered staying in the mountains with his new companion—he was well suited to the hard life now that he'd recovered—but the idea sat uncomfortably on him. At times he would go off on his own, walking the rock paths and streamside trails in the mountains, brooding, listening for voices that might show him a way. One day, he announced he would leave the mountains and walk to the coast in a day or two, after he had gathered food for the journey.

The wild one was disappointed. "I knew you wouldn't stay," he said.

"I would stay if I could," Massilili responded. "This time with you has healed my body and cleared my thoughts. I see now I must go back. Staying here is selfish—I wish I could—but there is work for me, perhaps work for us both. Even though First People don't speak to me as they speak to Qoloq, I think they have picked me for a hard task."

"It's best for me to stay here. I've seen the villages, I know the foreigners. When you're ready I'll show you the way." There was sadness in the wild man's voice, matched by Massilili's own sad feeling.

"I owe you my life. I'll come back when I can," Massilili promised, taking the man's arm in a grip of friendship.

It took several days of walking to cross the two mountain ranges and the valley separating them. They followed streams, some dry now, others flowing in shallow trickles. It was a solemn time for the pair—each knew the odds on finding the other again—yet the bond between them grew with each day they spent together. They shared the rigors of the journey, hunting for food and shelter, with the wild man always leading the way, always sure of the path. At last they came to the final ridge. Far below, the hills sloped to the flat land. The ocean winked the sun back at them.

"So many animals," Massilili gasped, looking down at cattle looking more like small ants, grazing far below in the mouth of a canyon opening to the beach at its western edge. "More than men."

"Many more. The mission of the foreigners you seek is a walk to the east. Not far."

"Come with me," Massilili tried one more time, taking the man strongly by the arm and looking into his eyes.

The wild man embraced Massilili in his bear-like arms. "I tried living in the villages of the light-skins," he said with disdain. "I choked on their smells and couldn't keep their food in my stomach. I did their work, hard work making bricks for their houses. They paid in shiny beads. I could endure all that, but I couldn't endure the way they looked at me, like an animal to be used and discarded. To them I was nothing; to me I'm everything. My home is here among the rocks. When the light-skins treat you like an animal, you'll come back too."

Chapter Twenty-Nine

Sitting astride Esperanza, Demetrio de Alba watched hawks circling in the afternoon sky. "A fine day for a dedication, eh, *Padre*?" he said to Fermin Ortiz. "I think God wills this to be a prosperous land for Josefa." De Alba smiled benignly at Josefa and gave the priest a furtive wink.

He kept the bit tight in Esperanza's mouth, restraining the spirited stallion to a slow, prancing walk alongside the high-wheeled black carriage in which Ortiz had driven Josefa from the *pueblo*. She sat beside Ortiz, bundled against the chill.

"Praise God, a fine day," Ortiz responded. "We'll pray our Lord blesses the land so Josefa can enjoy the bounty it provides."

Looking around the narrow canyon bottom on which the cattle grazed, de Alba felt a sense of satisfaction. His eyes took in the whole sweep of land from crescent beach to craggy heights where the hawks hunted. Nice enough for such an abominable land, he decided.

Less than a league back from the trail, one low hill dipped behind another, sealing off the deeper recesses of the canyon from unwanted eyes. It made little difference now because those hills were dotted with cattle. De Alba felt a thrill as he looked at the beasts, but he didn't see cattle—he saw gold. To him each animal was a gold *escudo*, silver *real* or

Yankee coin destined for his purse. And he saw Mexican *señoritas*, tortoise-shell combs tucked in raven hair piled high on their heads. He saw *señoritas* wearing gowns of silk and velvet, the hemispheres of their breasts teasing him with their scant concealment as they swirled around the salons of Mexico City.

If the army wouldn't bring him back to *Nueva España*, he'd go on his own—a rich man—he'd decided. These cows were his passage. The priest had been right, damn him. Ortiz had seen the possibilities before he did. From the day he arrived Ortiz talked of land and cattle. De Alba gave him credit for that; he'd seen only the barrenness.

Esperanza danced sideways on the trail, kicking up a small dust storm in his show of impatience at being held in check.

De Alba shifted in his saddle and laid a reassuring hand on Esperanza's neck. How had he sunk so low here? The question nagged him. The loneliness, that's what did it. Josefa showed how low he'd sunk, the Indian woman even lower. She was nothing—he wasn't sorry—but how could he have been that desperate?

Again he smiled at Ortiz and Josefa in the carriage.

It'll be different in *Nueva España*. Like the old times again. Even without the army—perhaps a small business to invest in. Would the women still come? Another nagging thought.

Not much longer here in exile. Soon he'd have enough. A year, two at most. Then back where he was safe, comfortable. No longer afraid of savages. Under his breath he swore an oath he'd never look back—Josefa, Ortiz, Santa Barbara, just a bad dream.

Fermin Ortiz pulled the carriage to a halt at the base of a gnarled oak tree whose branches spread out in a canopy a dozen yards wide. A flock of crows took flight as he stepped down, complaining of the injustice of his interruption with fluttering wings and a chorus of *caw-cawing*—only to return one by one after they'd expressed their indignation. He offered his hand to Josefa, guiding her down from the carriage. He too held a satisfied grin on his fleshy face.

He let his eyes sweep across the grazing animals boxed in the canyon and congratulated himself. No one is hurt—the mission would never miss these few head of cattle. The Yankee traders and whalers were coming regularly now. He was safe. No one in the *pueblo* knew it was him who had brought them these few luxuries. Oh, they knew the cloth and threads and dresses and utensils and tools and all the other small trinkets they bought were contraband. Did they care? They begged for more. Look how Josefa dresses now, like a courtesan.

Soon though, it would be time to move on. Others would see Spain's weakness, how the Motherland was failing to supply its forts and missions. They'd see the profit and start trading, maybe send armies to conquer the territory. Perhaps the *Padre Presidente* would see it was the only way his precious missions could supply their growing needs. Too many cows and neophytes, too few tools. It would be an easy decision soon.

By then he'd be gone. He'd have made enough to leave the order in a year or so. God hadn't called him to be poor, Ortiz was certain of that. That was Saint Francis's misguided idea.

But what then? Stay here, a defrocked priest? Or move on? There would be other opportunities in Alta California; none in Spain without an inheritance. This land was the future, his future, he was still certain of that. The land was rich, the soil would grow whatever was planted, the hills and oceans teemed with life. What was it the sailors always talked about?—furs, yes, fur, that was it. They said the Chinese at Canton paid a fortune for sea otter furs. Worth more to the traders than our cowhides. He could be a fur trader. Not a fur hunter, certainly, but he could organize the business. He was good at that. He could hire Indians to paddle their boats out to the islands to kill sea otters. In Monterey they said the Russians in the north did that. He wouldn't have to pay them much, either. Then, he'd have the profits without much effort. That was something to think about.

Josefa knelt between Demetrio de Alba and Fermin Ortiz, giving silent thanks. She reflected on the hardships she'd endured that had brought her to this place—Joaquin dead in the desert, Guillermo lost in the canyon behind the mission. Clutching an icon to her breast, she asked the Virgin of Guadalupe to look over her departed loved ones and give her strength to raise her daughter.

So this is my land. A feeling of pride made her shiver. This beach, deep canyon, broad, grassy plain, mine. Beautiful land. But a long carriage ride from the *pueblo*. She'd have to have a horse.

A smile of a different kind lighted her face. Fancy me, a landed lady riding a horse. Never in Guanajuato could that happen; never could it even have been imagined. Perhaps I should have a fine horse like Don Demetrio's so the *gente de razón* will look up to me. …But how could she care for a baby, alone, so far from the pueblo? Perhaps the priests would let her have a woman from the mission to help.

Josefa shifted uncomfortably on her knees, wishing Ortiz would get on with the blessing. *Cañada de Corral* they call this land. She played with the name in her head and liked the sound. What would my Guillermo think of *Cañada de Corral*? Or this baby that Demetrio gives me unexpectedly from the mission? Proud. Guillermo would be proud. His dream is alive here. For them both—Guillermo and

Joaquin—I'll claim this land and never let go of it. I'll keep it for the girl and tell her of the sacrifices that got us here.

If Guillermo were only alive to see this... Josefa stopped. If he were alive she wouldn't have the land, at least not yet, maybe not ever. God had traded her land for Guillermo's life. Not a fair trade, but God had never promised Josefa fairness, only an opportunity. A small sob escaped her throat, causing Fermin Ortiz to stop midway through his blessing to glance over at her. She gave him a weak smile. If God wanted her to have *Cañada de Corral,* so be it. She'd do whatever it took to make the land prosper. To honor Guillermo. She'd fight for it, as she told Clare she'd fight to keep the land her own. No man, not Demetrio, not the mission priests, would ever take it from her. *Cañada de Corral* was her future; her daughter's future, too. She'd guard it with her life. Risk everything for it.

Farther back in the canyon, Tomas was absorbed in the task of grooming his horse, currying it with a rough brush, making her coat gleam. He knew of the trio on the main trail, but he stayed here, with Jimeno and the other *vaqueros,* tending to their own chores and acting dumb to whatever was going on.

Grooming was Tomas's pleasure. He spent hours at it when he wasn't riding. Anger still boiled in the depths of his stomach whenever a ship hove to in the little harbor or when Jimeno ordered another forty or fifty head slaughtered, or when he thought about the dried hides hidden in a lean-to out of sight that the men carried down to the waiting longboats. But he was wary of Jimeno. He gave the soldier no excuse to carry out his threats. In his mind he plotted ways to escape Jimeno's grip, but so far none had ever come to fruition.

Tomas failed to notice the man approaching from the

depth of the canyon, until the man called out to him from a distance.

Startled, Tomas turned at the sound of the unfamiliar voice to stare at a naked man, wearing only a slim belt around his waist and carrying a bow and arrow, walking toward him. The man was tall for a Chumash and strongly built. He had long, wild hair and a flash in his eyes, Tomas saw as he came closer, that contributed to the wildness. He strode aggressively the short distance that separated them, approaching Tomas confidently.

"Stand back," Tomas commanded. "Why do you walk this canyon? You should be in your village. You should not be here."

"I have no village," the man answered. "But I have as much right to this land as any man."

"No you don't," Tomas said.

"I mean no trouble, but I'll fight if you force me," the man said, drawing himself up straight and clenching his fists. Tomas took note of the man's firm body, with tight muscles on his arms and shoulders.

Tomas studied the man's long, thin face. He had an aggressive set to his head and steady eyes that looked unblinking. "There's no need to fight," he said. "This is mission land now. It doesn't belong to Chumash any longer. We work the land for the Franciscans; they promise to give our land back to us when we're ready."

The man laughed. "Ready? Haven't we always been ready? Our ancestors have been on this land longer than anyone can remember."

From the edge of his vision Tomas saw Jimeno approaching. "You should leave now for your safety."

"I'll let no man force me off land I choose to walk. You say it's mission land," the man said. "How do I get to your mission?"

"A long day's walk," Tomas answered, smiling. He reached back to grab the halter of his mount, surreptitiously urging the mare forward beside him. "Much quicker if you had a horse like mine to ride, like the Spaniards," he said, stroking his mare's forehead. "But you don't have a horse, do you? Only mission *vaqueros* like me ride horses. So you must walk."

"What happens here?" Jimeno called out from several paces away.

The man paid no attention to Jimeno, still staring intently at Tomas. "What use is a horse to a man with legs," he said. "I can walk any place I need to go. I have walked all through these mountains and beyond with no need of a horse. I've seen lazy foreigners ride horses but never before have I seen a lazy Chumash man ride."

"Then it's best you start walking now," Tomas said, "before that soldier hears you talk about lazy foreigners."

"Do you know the people at the mission?" the man asked Tomas. "I'll walk there if you point the way for me. I'm looking for a woman named Cayatu."

Chapter Thirty

Cayatu started down the hill as early morning sunlight bounced off the ocean beyond the *pueblo*. She was looking forward to seeing Josefa again after her long confinement, although thoughts of Guillermo's death still gave her a chill at the base of her neck. A chorus of songbirds in the shrubs fringing the trail chirped their greetings. The live oaks midway between mission and *Presidio* were especially welcoming to her, their long, gnarled branches heavy with leaves providing a shaded glen. It pleased her to see the little nuts growing larger on them. She paused to think how long it had been since she ground acorns with Tanayan to make the gruel they ate, far better than the *atole* the priests served them.

When the oaks gave way to low-grass fields stretching down to the fort and the adobe homes surrounding it, she was greeted by the familiar smell of wood fires in the *pueblo*. Smoke rose from cooking fires outside twenty adobes, twice as many small houses surrounding the *Presidio,* as she remembered from her last visit. Muted brays and bellows and whinnying floated up to her. Looking at the new houses scattered about with no plan, she became confused.

She made several false starts toward Josefa's house only

to find her path blocked by a new adobe. Two horsemen dashed by, almost on top of her. They forced her to dive back to the protection of a wall, gasping for breath at the close call. For an instant she felt lost, wondering if she would ever find her way.

Several women, brightly dressed and carrying baskets of food or wooden buckets of water, scurried around her on the dusty paths between the adobes, paying no attention, calling one to the other in their sing-song voices. A plain-looking woman with a friendly smile took pity on her. "Josefa?" the woman said. "Oh, sí, down this path," she pointed. "I'll show you," she giggled. "God smiles on Josefa. She has a new baby. And new clothes. Oh, such fine new clothes." The young woman put a hand on Cayatu's shoulder and pointed her in the right direction.

Cayatu found Josefa tending a small garden in front of her house, wearing a damask dress, as pale blue as a sky at dawn. The dress covered her ankles when she stood and was cinched tightly around her ample waist. Delicate lace trimmed the deep square neckline, framing her chest and exposing the tops of her breasts. Even the sleeves were captured in ruffles. Cayatu had never seen such a fine dress. Its simple beauty made her smile. In her mind she tried to picture how she would look in such a dress.

Josefa looked up at her approach, no sign of recognition showing on her soft face until Cayatu was almost upon her. Then she exploded in laughter that shook the bodice of her dress. "*Hola, amiga*," she called out, still staring hard at Cayatu, but moving to embrace her. "So long since we drank the chocolate together, no? I've wondered about you—how you are. Your hair?—like threads of silver." She reached up to touch its fine whiteness. "What brings you here?"

Cayatu returned the smile. "My last day before the missionaries send me back to my loom. What a fine dress, Josefa. How beautiful you look."

"Oh, *sí*. A gift from the *Comandante*," she shrugged. "Still a fine looking woman, you are," Josefa said, hugging her. "Your child bearing shows no hint. But your hair—white as the priest's surplice, no? How did this happen?" She let the fine, pale strands of hair slip through her fingers. "It becomes you in a strange way."

"It grew this way while I waited for my baby," Cayatu said.

"Ah, a sign from God then. What does it mean, I wonder? And the baby? A strong boy? It's good to have boys. Good news for me, Clare. I have a baby too. A girl."

Cayatu was barely able to stammer, "I didn't know…"

"The mission fathers gave me an unwanted child to raise."

Cayatu steadied herself against the wall of the house. "I feel dizzy," she stammered.

Josefa gave Cayatu a worried look, but seeing her recover quickly, she went on. "But your baby. It's well, no?" she asked, turning toward her house. "Come, let me show you my sweet *niña*." She took Cayatu by the hand, leading her inside. Josefa took her to the back room where a baby swathed in blankets slept in a wooden cradle.

"A fine child for you," Cayatu said cautiously, looking down at the sleeping infant.

"Oh, yes. A wonderful child."

"And I have news, too." Cayatu told Josefa about Massilili joining the mission. "You were kind to him when you came to our village," Cayatu reminded her. She told Josefa about the happy reunion with Massilili in Father Salamanca's cubicle. Telling Josefa helped keep her thoughts away from the question nagging at her.

"Come with me," Josefa commanded her in a breathless, singing voice. She took Cayatu's hand again. "I'll show you the new house they're building for me. You can help me with my *niña*. We'll take the day to go there and back but the *padres* won't miss you, will they? I'll get a carriage from the fort. As we go I'll tell you all that has happened since last we talked. I'm married now. You can tell about your baby. And about your nephew."

Josefa scooped the infant from the cradle, still wrapped in a blanket, and handed her to Cayatu, who took her in trembling hands. Looking down at the infant's face peeking out from the blanket, she was startled by large, round, wide-awake eyes. Chumash eyes, but different, looking up at her.

At the guard house, Josefa spoke a few words to the sergeant. Shortly a high-wheeled carriage, pulled by a dark gray mare, was led up to the gate. A soldier held the reins while he helped Josefa up to the seat with a soft push on her rump, then gave the reins back to her and turned to leave.

Cayatu stared at the carriage. She reached out to touch a spoked wheel but jerked her hand back when the horse took a step and the wheel turned forward, giving off a creaking sound as it did. She clutched the baby tighter to her breast.

"Come, Clare, get in. We've a long drive," Josefa called to her.

Cayatu stood holding the baby in her arms, staring at the carriage and up at Josefa.

"Ah, *mujer*," Josefa laughed, shaking her head. "Don't be afraid. Hand me the *niña*. Step there"—she pointed—"and pull yourself up."

With the baby safely aboard, Cayatu still looked warily at the carriage. Tentatively, she lifted one foot to the step, but the mare shifted again, causing the carriage to rock. She pulled back.

The sergeant, who had watched from his post, came up behind Cayatu and put his hands firmly on her hips, boosting her into the seat, laughing the whole time. "We havta teach these Indians everything, don't we, *Señora* de Alba?" he laughed up at Josefa.

Josefa nodded but made no comment. She handed the

baby back to Cayatu then she flicked the reins, calling to the mare. The horse started off.

When the carriage began to move Cayatu's face turned ashen. She thrust a hand out, grabbing hold of the carriage side to steady herself. She held on with all her strength, but, at the same time, she protected the baby cradled in her other arm. She thought about jumping off to be safe so something terrible—she knew not what—wouldn't happen to her and the child, but when she looked down at the baby, fast asleep in her lap, she knew she couldn't. Thinking they were headed for disaster, she clutched the baby to her breast and still clung to the side of the carriage.

Outside the *pueblo*, Josefa urged the mare into a trot that brought Cayatu new terror. She felt her eyes grow large. The trees and shrubs seemed to be flying past. "Oh, my," she gasped, feeling breathless as the horse speeded up. The carriage was a cacophony of unfamiliar sounds. The axle whined as the wheels turned, the wheels made a crunching sound on the dirt path and the horse's hooves beat a steady *clip-clop* cadence along the bluff overlooking the ocean. Only Coyote can travel this fast, Cayatu told herself. This is not a good speed for a Chumash—too fast.

After Josefa had driven the carriage half a league out of the *pueblo* with nothing bad happening, Cayatu relaxed just a bit, letting her fingers loosen their grip on the side rail and sitting back against the wooden seat, but still holding the sleeping infant firmly.

Growing more accustomed to the sight of the ground flying by so fast, and seeing the mountains weren't really moving when she looked out toward the horizon, she calmed herself. A more pleasant sensation took over. The strange sounds now seemed to blend into a pleasing rhythm in time to her heartbeat. She realized the breeze blowing in her face felt good. The sensation in her stomach brought a smile. Relaxing her grip, she reached up to touch her white hair streaming out behind.

She took a quick glance at Josefa, who held the reins lightly but seemed to control the large animal pulling them along. She avoided looking down at the trail disappearing under the carriage, but watching the mare stepping along, lifting and dropping its feet in a beautiful sequence she couldn't fathom, gave her a great feeling of happiness. She was flying. Flying the way the spirits and the Spaniards on horseback flew. It felt good.

So," Josefa said when they were well along the trail and Cayatu began seeing cattle on the hillsides, "tell about your baby."

"I have no baby," Cayatu answered.

"No baby?" Josefa was startled. She turned to give her a sympathetic look. "Did it die?"

"I don't know, Josefa. The priest took it when I pushed it out and hurried off with it. I never saw it again."

Josefa turned to look squarely at Cayatu. "Boy or girl?" she demanded.

Cayatu sat still for several moments, thinking about Josefa's question and looking down at the sleeping girl in her lap. When she looked up from the baby she turned her face away from Josefa to stare out at the countryside racing by. "I don't know if it was a boy or girl," she said. "The priest took it. It must have died. I think it did."

"I'm sorry for you," Josefa made the sign of the cross while she held the reins. She settled back in the seat. After another silent moment she looked across at Cayatu. "Yes, it must've died," she said and repeated it several times. Then she began talking about the *Cañyon de Corral* land grant the king had given her and how she and the *Comandante* had married, and how Father Ortiz said he would have Indians from the mission build a home in the canyon they were approaching.

"You married the *Comandante?*" Cayatu asked, not allowing her face to show surprise. She felt dizzy again.

"I did. It's better for both of us," Josefa said. "It's a very hard life for a woman alone."

Cayatu sat expressionless, letting the wind tousle her hair and play against her cheeks as the horse sped along. It was better to enjoy the ride than try to understand why a fine woman like Josefa would want Demetrio de Alba in her bed. She laughed lightly when the thought of the *Comandante* giving Josefa red beads each night came to her. Josefa looked over at her and smiled.

Cayatu's silent pleasure was jolted by the baby stirring in her lap. The tiny girl let out a cry and began to whimper. She picked her up and rocked her gently, looking down at her pale, round face.

"Aí, she's hungry," Josefa said, looking over at the child and then to Cayatu. "Can you feed her?"

Cayatu looked uncertainly back at Josefa. "Feed her?" she repeated.

"With your milk. I have none. In the village an Indian woman suckles her. But you still have milk in your breasts, no? Will you nurse my baby for me, Clare?"

Cayatu looked helplessly from the crying infant in her arms to Josefa, whose look seemed to implore her, not knowing what she should do. Gripped by uncertainty, she cautiously lifted her blouse. She cradled the baby's head in her hand, bringing her tiny lips to the nipple. The baby quieted, looking up into Cayatu's face. Then she opened her mouth and began to suck. Cayatu turned her head away from Josefa and the nursing child, staring out over the land rushing by, not seeing it now. She felt the warmth of the girl at her breast, the pulling on her nipple. Voices warred in her head, but the infant was so small and soft and light she silenced them, letting the sensations carry her away. Whose baby? She was afraid of the answer.

Josefa stopped the carriage under a sycamore tree where a scrub jay scolded them. They were well off the trail, back near the entrance to the deep canyon. It was the spot Josefa had selected for her home. To the north, the thin valley wound between a series of hills until it ended at the base of a cliff. In the other direction, Cayatu could see the ocean in the distance.

"What do you think of my new home?" Josefa asked excitedly. "All the land you see is mine. The king has given it to me."

Cayatu's eyes swept the land, taking in the narrow valley rising toward the mountains that cast dark shadows in the deep canyons as the sun moved west. A few clouds in an otherwise clear sky floated near the ridge line, where one cloud seemed to have collided with the highest peak, spilling whiteness that blotted out the crest. Below the peaks, she saw the dark shadow of a hawk drifting in circles.

"How can you own this land, Josefa?" Cayatu asked. "It's the gathering place of another village. Our people share the land."

Josefa laughed. "I do own it. The King of Spain has given it to me and I have his royal deed to prove it."

Cayatu decided to say no more.

Josefa lifted her long blue skirt above her knees and climbed down from the carriage. Cayatu admired the way the dress swirled softly about Josefa's ankles and legs as she stood on the ground. She handed the baby down to Josefa, who nestled her against the pale blue bosom of the dress.

"Clare, I have a wonderful idea," Josefa said, fresh excitement lighting her face. "You could live with me here and help me care for my daughter. I know the mission priests would give permission. Together we would have a good life, share the work. I'll talk with them. Better than the life you have at the mission, no? Jimeno and his *vaqueros* are in the canyon. They'll protect us."

Cayatu didn't respond.

"They're here to watch the cattle," Josefa went on. "To see that no one steals them."

Cayatu saw three riders sweeping down off a nearby rise, their horses kicking up dust clouds behind them that hung low to the ground around their hooves and dissipated only slowly as the horses galloped on. As they neared, she saw a soldier in the lead—Jimeno, she remembered—trailed by two riders in mission clothes. When they were almost on top of her she let out a gasp. Her heart pounded against her chest when she recognized Tomas on his mare.

Jimeno pulled his mount to an abrupt halt just short of Josefa and the child, showering them in dust. Curtly, he paid his respects and asked if there was anything his men could do for her. His quick side glances at her scared Cayatu.

"Build my house," Josefa snapped. "When will it be done?"

"In time, *Señora*," he answered. "In God's own time."

"I want it done quickly so I can live here," she told him.

"It's not an easy task, *Señora*. Workers from the mission must go into the mountains to cut wood. Others must make adobe bricks. I can't spare my *vaqueros*"—the sweep of his hand indicated Tomas and the other man Cayatu didn't recognize—"to build a house for a woman. When Padre Ortiz orders Indians to do the cutting and make the bricks, the house will be built."

"I've waited long enough," Josefa shot back. "This is my land, Jimeno. Make sure you remember that. I expect respect from you, not rudeness. Remember, *Comandante* de Alba is my husband and this child's father now. Be more careful around my baby." She stabbed an impatient forefinger toward Jimeno's face. "Perhaps you should suggest to him that he remind the priest to get this job done. If you don't, I will."

Cayatu shivered at Josefa's words.

"All respect, *Señora*. But I can't—"

"—You can," she interrupted. "Ride to the mission now and tell the good father I'm impatient for my home to be built. Go!"

While Josefa spoke to Jimeno, Cayatu and Tomas stared at each other, unable to speak. Each one's eyes searched the other out, looking for signs; signs of anger, love, rejection, loneliness, any signs. After a couple of minutes, Cayatu took several steps toward his horse. She reached out to take its bridle in her hand and stroked the mare's nose with her other hand. "I remember the day you showed me this horse, Tomas," she whispered in a confidential tone. "That was a fine day. She's a fine horse."

Yes," he agreed. "A fine one."

"I miss you, Tomas. I miss our times together."

Tomas shifted in the saddle. "I spend my time here now, watching my cattle," he said flatly.

Cayatu was startled by a whinnying from Jimeno's horse as Jimeno jammed his spurs deep into his flanks, and tore off toward the *pueblo*. She moved to the side of the mare so she could stand closer to Tomas, putting a hand on his leg and looked up at him, whispering so only he could hear. "I was wrong, Tomas. I hurt you—the man I love most. I'm sorry. If you come back to the *ranchería* I'll live in your hut and never speak of running away from the mission again. I love you."

"I've never stopped loving you," he answered. "But you hurt me. We can talk when I'm back in the *ranchería*."

His words gave no real indication of his feelings but Cayatu thought his face seemed to soften a little. She felt lighthearted. Was it really possible to move out here away from the Franciscans?

Chapter Thirty-One

The sun was bleeding orange into the ocean when the two women arrived back in the *pueblo*. Cayatu said a hasty goodbye to Josefa and started back up the hill.

"*Adiós*, Clare," Josefa called out to her. "Come back soon, so we can talk of setting up the house. I'll speak with the priests."

Cayatu hurried along, going over in her mind the day's events. Would Tomas still want her? If he did, could they live with Josefa in the canyon and near his cattle? Perhaps Massilili, too, if he were allowed. They'd be away from fort and mission. A good plan, even with the baby. She could endure that. It was an almost perfect solution. Almost.

Entering the oak grove, darkness descended around her. The only sound interrupting the stillness was the chirping of tree frogs. She quickened her step, but was barely among the trees when Jimeno lunged at her from hiding.

"My turn with you," he said in a high-pitched voice. "Now I'll taste what de Alba tasted. I've waited a long time for this. You'd better make it worth my wait."

She wrenched herself out of his grasp and darted into the grove. In her flight her foot hit a rock. She tripped, falling on the ground into thick brambles that scratched and bruised her.

Jimeno was on her in an instant, grabbing a handful of her hair and jerking her head back. He turned her over and straddled her, pinning her to the ground with one forearm pressed against her throat. His other hand reached back to grab at her skirt. When she resisted he hit her.

"You will not do this to me," she shouted at him, bringing her knee hard into his groin. At the same time she grabbed a handful of loose dirt and threw it in his face.

He groaned, cursed her through his pain, and started to regain his feet. Cayatu darted deeper into the trees. Running in panic, she fell again, tripping over a fallen branch. Motionless, she lay prone on the ground, choked by the molding smells of oak leaves. Jimeno lunged toward her, framed dark against the darkness of the woods. Helpless, she lay on the ground. Was this Qoloq's curse again? Or was the God of the Franciscans doing this to her? Watching Jimeno come nearer, she trembled.

She heard his footsteps crashing through the underbrush, sure he was about to fall on her again.

But he didn't. His footsteps stopped. He called out: "Where are you, woman? You won't get away from me. Show yourself."

She willed her body to stay motionless and listened to the strange tone in his voice. "Come out here, you whore. I can't see you." A hint of fear sounded. He reached up to rub at his eyes. She saw him stagger off, bumping into the trunk of a large tree. He shouted his pain and turned back toward her again. "Where are you, woman?" His voice was softer now.

Cayatu watched his movements; stumbling, bumping into trees. One time he tripped on a tree root and fell to his knees. Then he stopped to rub his eyes again. As quietly as she could, she got to her feet, but still the leaves and brush rustled at her movement.

"There you are," he roared out and stumbled awkwardly

toward her.

She moved quickly from tree to tree, listening to Jimeno's lunging about the thicket behind her. She made her way back to the trail as his rantings grew more panicked in the distance. On the path again, she ran toward the mission, offering thanks to Coyote, the trickster.

Fermin Ortiz sat hunched over his desk, making entries in a ledger. His face held an unusual smile as he ciphered long columns of numbers. At intervals he mumbled a few words out loud, as if to assure himself of the correctness of his work—estimations of his growing wealth he took pleasure in calculating month by month.

Evening vespers were over, the mission was dark and quiet and Ortiz expected to work in privacy until retiring for the night. So he was both surprised and annoyed at the insistent pounding on his door.

"Who's there? Stop the pounding. I'm busy," he called out.

"Clare. Open your door."

"Who? Oh, Clare. In the name of Mother Mary leave me be. I must work. Come see me in the morning after Mass."

"You must speak with me now," she shouted and beat against the door. "Now!"

Ortiz rose slowly from the hard stool and moved across the cubicle. He removed the wooden bar that held the door securely shut against all possible attacks and pulled it open, bristling at her. "What do you vex me with now, Clare? So late in—"

He stopped in mid-sentence to stare at her silhouetted in the doorway. Even in the dim light coming from the room's candles he saw the cuts and scratches on her face and arms. The dried blood staining her blouse. Her hair was matted with dirt and leaves. "What's happened to you?" His hand went out to her. He led her into the room. "You're hurt. Let me help you."

"A man on the path from town, a soldier," she blurted out.

Ortiz led her to a bench along the wall. He took a cloth and moistened it in a bowl of water that sat on a table near his cot. With great gentleness he dabbed at the cuts and cleaned the blood from her skin. "*Pobre mujer*," he mumbled. "Let me sooth your bruises." His hands moved gently over the skin of her face and arms in a mixture of cleansing and stroking. Brown skin, he thought, so different from a white woman.

But in a way how like that other woman. As he cleaned Cayatu's cuts his thoughts went back to an evening long past at the College of St. Francis in Mexico City. The woman had come into the chapel and begun her rosary without seeing him near the altar. When she'd finished they'd talked together quietly in one of the pews. Ortiz could still remember the sparkle in her green eyes and the highlights of her hair shining in the candle-lit chapel. The soft scent of that hair, freshly washed and brushed to a luster, had aroused him. He remembered his yearnings and reaching out to touch her fair skin.

After that he remembered only the girl running down the aisle and out the door, her blouse ripped, trying to hold it up as she ran so no one would see the breast exposed behind the torn cloth. She'd disappeared into the night but never left his memory. Why had she come to the church to tempt him so? he asked himself afterward.

While he tended Cayatu, dabbing and patting at the cuts and scratches with soft careful hands, she told of being attacked and her escape.

"Once you promised protection, you lied to me." she said.

Ortiz felt attacked by her words. They drove him back a step, still holding the wet cloth in his hand and staring hard at her. Her anger lighted her face. He saw Cayatu's eyes grow large. Her dark eyes sparkling with reflections of candlelight aroused him.

"No king's soldier has done you any harm I know of," he said. "Only the man you won't name with whom you produced the bastard. And I think he was one of your people." He set the cloth and bowl back in place and stood over her, feeling sensations he half fought against. His mouth started feeling dry.

"Do you forget the first night at the *Presidio*?" she almost shouted at him.

What would lying with an Indian woman—this Indian woman—be like? He fought the thought, tried to push it away, as he'd tried hundreds of times before to push similar thoughts away, like he'd tried with that other woman, but they wouldn't leave him.

"Perhaps you call attention upon yourself, Clare. Do you? Do you flirt with men? A handsome Indian like you gets lots of attention, doesn't she? Your white hair turns men's heads more than ever. I've watched them."

Ortiz felt the stirring in his groin, hidden beneath his lose robe. It was not an unusual sensation for him. Unconsciously his hand went to it.

"No," she protested, rising to confront him so that he backed up against his plank desk. "Your soldiers are hunters, always stalking weak prey—that's how they treat women."

"You're not weak, Clare," Ortiz shot back at her. "Look at you—a handsome Indian woman in her prime. You play the temptress. You tempt us with those swaying hips, don't you? The way you move. Your slender arms and legs. Don't you tempt all men—Indian and Spaniard alike? Tempt us with breasts you push out against your blouse."

His words came in short, sharp bursts. He gripped the edge of his desk behind him, trembling a little. "I've often wondered about the man you lay with, what was it like for him? Did you fight him? Claw at his face like a cat? Or give yourself up to him in a meek and wifely way. All men have needs, Clare, don't they? They see a young woman like you and in their minds they dream. Women have needs too, do they not?"

"Not for soldiers who hunt their prey." She almost spit the words.

"Come now, we both know Chumash women are free with their bodies. The soldiers talk of it often enough. Are you free with yours? In my mind I picture our men with young girls. I fight against unclean thoughts—God help me—but sometimes they're too strong. Perhaps, Clare..."

"—Of course I have lain with men. It's a natural thing for a woman—"

"—Perhaps you feel the same stirring in your body that men feel," Ortiz interrupted, his breath coming in shorter and shorter spurts and gulps. "Perhaps you want a man to lie with now. Do you?" Ortiz felt his urge rising out of control as he looked at her sitting on the bench, vulnerable. He stared at her hair, fine and pale as moonlight, her breasts taut against the blood-stained blouse.

"The man from my village has been gone a long time. I loved him—" She rose and took several steps toward the door, away from the priest.

"—But here? Now?" Ortiz came across the room to stand close to her.

She backed away but stopped when her back pressed against the door.

The priest reached out. His hand moved slowly toward her. He couldn't stop it from lightly resting on the soft fabric of her blouse. His throat was dry and constricted. His fingers tightened slowly until he felt the softness of her breast.

Cayatu's hand shot out, pushing him in the shoulder, forcing the priest away. Ortiz staggered back, reaching his hand behind him to catch himself against the writing desk to keep from stumbling. Quickly, he pulled himself upright, straightened his robe and went behind the desk to sit.

"You see," he said, anger rising in his voice. "You tempt men.

You act as if you want them and then you turn on them."

"I don't want you," she spit again. "That thought makes my stomach churn."

"I only did this to show how you act. Look what you did. You struck me. You aren't like the other women here at the mission. You're the devil's child. We can't have that, Clare. We can't lose this mission to the devil who lurks in you."

"It's the soldiers who are devils. Maybe the priests, too."

"So who is the soldier you accuse. Tell me his name." Ortiz's breathing was returning to normal.

"The one with the *vaqueros*."

"Jimeno?" Ortiz paused, thought for a moment. A smile came slowly to him. "Was it Jimeno who tried to assault you?"

"He did," she said, moving from the wall back to the center of the room, leaning toward Ortiz to confront him again. "Will you punish him?"

"He's a mean man, God knows," Ortiz said. He let his eyes wander around the room as he thought about Jimeno, but avoided looking at her. Perhaps an opportunity here, he told himself. Perhaps this troublesome woman had given him the opportunity he'd been seeking. "I'll speak with Lieutenant de Alba about Jimeno," Ortiz said. "I'll say what you accuse him of and we'll see if the *Comandante* will punish him."

"Ha," Cayatu let out a sorrowful laugh. "De Alba will do nothing. He cares little for the likes of me."

"I'd be careful with your words if I were you, Clare. Don't speak rudely of the *Comandante*. Learn to control your words, control your actions, too. We must teach you once and forever to act like a civilized being, not like the animals you accuse the soldiers of being. It's you whose animal instincts let you hit out at people who anger you. You hit out at me just now when I only tried to teach you. You, who ruts, God knows where, with men who give you babies. You have to give up those animal ways and act like a

Christian woman."

Ortiz rose again, but this time went straight to the door, opened it and indicated for her to leave. "Tomorrow I'll order the *mayordomo* to lock you in the stocks for a full day and night—"

"—Put *me* in the stocks? Punish *me*?" she charged. "I've done nothing wrong."

"No food or water. Others will see and know that you disobey us. Pray for forgiveness for your sins tomorrow. I'll pray a day of humiliation will be cleansing for you." Ortiz reached out to put a hand on her shoulder and turned her back to look at him. "We will never speak again of this night, will we? If you do, it will go very hard for you," the priest said.

Chapter Thirty-Two

Oh, Clare," Dolores called out. "To see you like this—what has happened?"

Cayatu watched Dolores approach along the path toward the church, talking, gossiping, laughing with other girls, interrupting each other in rapid, breathless voices. She turned her face away, trying to avoid the disapproving looks Dolores and the others were sending her, but Cayatu knew she was in for a scolding. Dolores was wed to mission life and took every opportunity to chastise anyone who didn't share her strong beliefs.

Cayatu shrugged as best as the restraints holding her arms allowed. "It's nothing, Dolores," she said, but her arms, aching from a day stretched out straight in front of her, compounded the discomfort she felt as her milk dried up. Her anger toward Fermin Ortiz, mingled with the embarrassment of being restrained in the stocks, subject to the jibes of every neophyte who passed her, brought tears to her eyes. She turned her head away to keep Dolores and the other girls from noticing.

"Nothing? In the stocks where everyone sees you?" Dolores chided, coming to stand beside her. "How can you say nothing? What brought you to this?"

"Father Ortiz says I cause trouble—"

"—You *do* cause the priests trouble. You could spend a long time in the stocks for all the trouble you cause." Dolores's weak laugh had a scolding edge.

The other girls shifted uncomfortably, not laughing.

"It's not right. Not right at all." Dolores put her hands on her hips and pointed an accusing finger. "You live in the past, Clare. You live the old life. You'll bring trouble to all of us who want to forget our past until you accept what the missionaries teach. Pray to the Virgin, Clare. Ask for her guidance."

The young women were quick to add their feelings.

"It's true," one of them said. "Life for us is much better when we follow the priests' instructions."

How better?" Cayatu asked.

"The priests don't really care how we live," another one interrupted, "as long as more people come from the villages."

"Our people can't survive in the villages any longer," a third spoke up. "They have to come here."

"The mission cattle and sheep graze the land where our families used to collect seeds and berries," the first girl said. "Then they stop the villagers from burning the fields so seeds will be there the next year."

"The villages won't survive," Cayatu silenced them all, agreeing with the tall, older girl. "We won't survive here either."

"Oh, no," Dolores gasped. "You're wrong, Clare. We will. We'll survive here. That's why Father Salamanca and Father Ortiz prepare us to have our own land. They promise a new life after they teach us to work our land."

"The only life you'll ever have is the life you have now," Cayatu said. "Work each day with nothing at the end of it— that's your new life—your only life. It won't get better. For me it's bitter. Ortiz says I tease men. I told him a solider knocked me down in the woods—look at my face—and he sends me here, saying it was my fault. That's our life, not believed, not trusted, treated like children or punished with whip and stocks. The priests' promises aren't real."

The young women erupted in a cacophony of voices each trying to be heard above the others, some agreeing and some objecting to what Cayatu had said, but all tried to make their point, until one of them toward the back of the group spoke out. "That's always the way for women. It was no different when we lived in our villages, gathering food and preparing it for men. We needed men to protect us then and we need men now. No different."

"And don't forget what they did for us," another of the girls shouted. "Those long shafts they shot into us, their love arrows. How I miss them. Instead I spend each night locked in with the likes of you, no men among us, so we all make do with whatever we can find. Give me a man, any man, to lie with in the dark."

They all tittered and nodded their heads.

"She's right," Dolores interrupted. "If you had a man to care for you, to love you and give you children, your life would be different, Clare. A man like Tomas."

"Another girl interrupted. "I don't see any man protecting you, Dolores. When will you leave the women's quarters for a man's hut, eh? For his strong arms and big man thing?"

The others giggled and teased again, but Dolores silenced them. "Perhaps soon I'll have a man."

"Who will that be?" Cayatu asked, glad the attention had moved away from her.

Dolores looked down at the ground without speaking.

"Tell her," another girl crooned.

Dolores kept silent.

"Your nephew has Dolores's eye," one of the others volunteered. "At night she talks of him all the time but doesn't want you to know. She says how strong and handsome he is."

Cayatu looked at Dolores.

Dolores raised her eyes to meet Cayatu's. "Massilili is a handsome and gentle man, big and powerful," she said. "He might be a good husband, but I don't know if he thinks about me."

"Ask him then," one of the girls teased. "He's coming up the path with Tomas. Ask him now."

Massilili and Tomas gained the summit of the hill. Both men rushed to Cayatu as soon as they saw her locked in the stocks.

"What have they done? You're cut and bruised?"

Cayatu heard an unfamiliar anguish in Massilili's voice. Before she could say any words, he pulled hard at the wooden yoke that held her, trying to wrench it free.

"No use." Tomas put a restraining arm on Massilili's shoulder. "Those are locks the missionaries use. Their locks imprison us and hide things they won't share."

Dolores and the other girls backed off several steps, with some of them making small clucking sounds that Dolores tried to hush with a gesture of her hand.

Cayatu forced a smile. "It's a punishment the priests give."

"For what?"

"My friend, Dolores, from the women's quarters, is here, Massilili," she said, forcing the conversation in a new direction. "Do you know her?"

Massilili seemed to see Dolores for the first time. He gave her a smile.

The other girls cooed and clucked until Dolores gave them another sharp look.

Massilili held his smile. "Are you pleased to see me again?" he asked.

Dolores stood aside with her hands clasped in front of her. "Oh… Yes," she said, averting her eyes.

Again there were giggles and snickers from the other girls.

Dolores looked up at him with a winsome smile. "We're

late for Vespers," was all she could say.

Massilili continued to look at her. "Perhaps you could find a place for me to kneel next to you," he told her.

The others couldn't restrain their mirth, bursting out laughing and hugging their arms around Dolores.

Cayatu watched the sparkle in her nephew's eyes as Dolores and the others walked off toward the church. She noticed that Tomas stood back. She motioned him closer. "Will you be at your hut tomorrow?"

"In the afternoon," he said. "Tell what happened that put you here. Which priest gave you this punishment?"

Cayatu compressed her lips so the words almost hissed out, "Father Ortiz. He said I was lying."

"Lying about what?" Massilili asked.

"I told him Jimeno had chased me in the woods on the path from town. Knocked me down. Ortiz said it was my fault for teasing him."

"Who is Jimeno?" Massilili demanded.

"A soldier. Tomas knows him."

"He's a mean one," Tomas said.

"A dog," Massilili snapped. "What will be done to him?"

Tomas's face took on a sour look. "Soldiers are never punished."

"He should be punished," Massilili said again. "You should have revenge." He squatted down in front of the stocks with a perplexed look. He slammed one hand into the other as he spoke. "This isn't right. You should have revenge, Cayatu," he said again.

"No punishment will be given Jimeno, but I'm not hurt. In a day or two the scratches will go away." Cayatu tried to calm her nephew.

"But he might try—"

"—Tomas," a sharp voice rasped out through the gathering darkness. "Why do you stand about here like some dumb mule too lazy to move? Get along where you belong before I get *Señor* Lash out."

Both men turned toward the voice. Jimeno strode out of the shadows, up the path from the corral, his long steps bringing him quickly to the stocks. His gaze penetrated Tomas who backed away a few steps, knocked back by his stare. Cayatu smiled to herself seeing the skin rubbed raw around Jimeno's eyes.

Jimeno turned to take in Massilill. "Who are you?" he demanded.

"A stone cutter." Massilili returned Jimeno's hard stare and didn't move.

"And you," Jimeno turned to Cayatu. "A fitting place for you. Locked in the stocks. For what? Perhaps you whore too much at the fort with my *compadres*. Is that why you're locked up? Because you drop your skirts for men."

Cayatu strained against the restraining stocks so hard her arms turned white. "Can you see me tonight?" she taunted.

He took a step toward her then stopped, aiming a look that made her tremble. "Be careful, whore."

Massilili's fist clenched and he took a step toward Jimeno. Quick looks from Cayatu and Tomas halted him.

"Stop there, stone cutter, unless you want to feel my lash." Jimeno put his hand on the handle of his whip and thrust his face toward Massilili. After a moment, he relaxed. "So the dumb mule and the stone cutter stand about with the *Comandante's* whore," Jimeno taunted them. "I don't know you, stone cutter, but you should get along before you bring trouble on yourself. These other two aren't worth feeling my lash on your back for. Tomas is a miserable *vaquero*, not worth the horse we put him on. And the woman is nothing. A whore. Get along! Both of you." Jimeno continued up the path toward the kitchen.

"Go," Cayatu urged Massilili and Tomas, "before he comes back."

Both nodded and started toward the church. Then,

Cayatu called out to Massilili to come back.

"Do you see what it's like here?" she whispered to him. "Can you see how the Spaniards make prisoners and slaves of us?"

"I see it clearly," he answered. "What Qoloq feared."

"Run, then," she urged him. "Run before it's too late for you. Find other land the foreigners haven't invaded over the mountains. Take Dolores along if she pleases you, to give you children and help you hunt food."

"She does please me." Massilili had a soft tone to his voice. "But she would never leave the mission."

"Run by yourself, then. Get far away to save your own life. I'll come with you."

"I won't leave the mission." Massilili shook his head. "Listen to me, Aunt. When I was lost and wandering in the high mountains a man saved me, a wild man. He was free to live wherever he chose yet he wandered from place to place. He was never in a place that was his home. He told me he missed the mother and father who raised him, and he missed the girl in his village that he loved. He had all the freedom a man could dream of but it wasn't good for him because he had no one to share it with."

Cayatu listened. She felt a tug on her heart and wondered, but she let the thought go. She nodded to Massilili. "I couldn't be happy being free without you and Tomas. But listen to me. There are people living on the other side of those mountains, the people our village traded with. Your man could've gone to live with them. You could. You would find a woman in the villages there by the big lake."

"My place is here. We can dance for First People here."

"Will you dance for First People when you kneel with Dolores in the church?" Cayatu's laugh had a mocking edge, but she held a stern look on her face.

Massilili stood silent, staring back at her.

"The priests will never allow it. They punish anyone who doesn't pray to their God. Punishment much worse than these stocks."

"They don't know. Many men and women here still thank Coyote of the Sky and Sup and the others for their existence. My father taught me the skills of a shaman—how to heal and how to listen when First People speak. I belong here—to keep our faith in First People strong."

Chapter Thirty-Three

Freed from the imprisoning stocks, Cayatu hurried to Tomas's hut the next afternoon. Finding it empty, she busied herself setting a small fire while she waited for him. Looking across the hilltop, she paused to marvel at the mission's transformation over the years since she'd first camped beside the stream in the canyon. New adobe buildings were replacing the original wooden structures now. Massilili had told her the missionaries planned to build a larger church in stone, a major undertaking that would take him and other stone cutters high into the mountains.

Circular huts in the *ranchería*, like Tomas's, were being torn down and replaced with one-room adobes. The Chumash people were being told to quit living in the old thatched huts, Tomas said, and live in a civilized fashion in the single-room dried-mud houses. Cayatu didn't understand how the dark, damp adobes could be better than their huts.

Waiting for him to come along the path, Cayatu imagined herself tending a fire outside her crude shelter in the valley near the ocean. She saw herself roaming between the shore and the low hills that stood like sentries guarding the higher peaks. She'd picked berries and seeds from secret places scattered about and hidden. How tough that life had been, she remembered, a constant struggle to find enough food, feeling helpless in the face of storms that attacked the valley each winter with winds that tore her shelter apart and rains that drenched her.

After a time, she saw Tomas, trudging head down, hurrying toward her. As Tomas neared, wiping the heat of the afternoon off his brow with the back of his hand, she thought what a kind man he was. What good was it to be free of the mission if you led a solitary life she asked herself, hearing Massilili's words again? With Tomas and Massilili close at hand she had all that was important in her life.

As her thoughts flitted back and forth, she formed a new resolve. Perhaps she could have both; the men she loved close around her, and freedom from the tyranny of the Franciscans and soldiers. She had to look at freedom in a new way. Freedom didn't have to be a life lived in the old valley. Freedom could exist right here, within herself. All she needed was a hollow space in her heart. A shelter in her soul where she could be free.

Clare," Tomas called out nearing the hut. "I'm glad you're here."

"And I'm glad to see you," she laughed. "But promise me, Tomas, never again to call me Clare."

"It slipped out," he said chagrinned.

"Say you'll try, Tomas," she said, turning serious and taking in a big breath, "and I'll promise never to speak of leaving the mission again." Cayatu looked for some sign from Tomas before going on, "If you'll still have me, I'll be your wife. Here in this hut."

No longer stone-faced, as he'd been in the canyon, Tomas's joy overflowed him. His mouth split into a smile so wide she could count his teeth.

Cayatu laughed again, moving to his side and throwing her arms wide open to embrace him. She exhaled the deep breath now, letting it out slowly, feeling a calm she hadn't known for a long time; a calm she'd only known lying beside Ysaga in the bower on the edge of their village. She thought she saw tears in the corners of Tomas's eyes but the mistiness in her own made her uncertain.

They stood in their embrace a long time. Neophytes nearby looked up from tending their own small fires to stare.

"Cayatu will marry me," Tomas shouted like a young boy. "We'll have the priests' ceremony."

The mission Chumash gathered around them. Women ran to their huts to tell their husbands the news, returning with foods for a celebration. Dolores gushed with approval when she heard the news. "May the Virgin bless you with children," she said, giving them a solemn look. Then she ran off to tell Massilili.

"How wonderful Tomas wants you for his wife," Massilili said when Dolores brought him back to the gathering. "He's a good man. He'll be a good husband."

Dolores fluttered at Massilili's side. "I had to search all over the mission to find him," she told Cayatu. "He was far down the path, almost to the corral when I caught up with him." She paused for breath. "This is God's way," she announced. "May the Virgin bless your marriage, Clare. All of us should be married and raise children." She stole a look at Massilili.

There was happy chatter around Tomas's hut, then all talking stopped abruptly. Heads turned in unison toward the mission. Cayatu turned with the others and saw Demetrio de Alba leading two soldiers as he strode into the *ranchería*, his sword swinging and jangling against his leg as he moved. Father Salamanca hobbled along behind, breathing hard in his effort to keep up. De Alba halted in front of the knot of celebrating people.

"What's going on here?" he said with dullness making his

voice sound hollow. Lifeless eyes jumped from face to face in the group.

Tomas stepped forward. "We celebrate," he said. "Clare—Cayatu—has agreed to be my wife."

Salamanca didn't smile. "A terrible thing has happened," he muttered. "God have mercy," he said, looking to the sky. "A terrible thing."

"Stand back, *Padre*." De Alba pushed the priest aside and planted himself in front of Tomas. "Jimeno is dead. Murdered," he said, holding his stony gaze on Tomas. He looked up, taking in the rest of the neophytes. "Do you all understand that? Jimeno lies dead at the corral—murdered."

Chapter Thirty-Four

Esteben Salamanca felt himself shriveling day by day, getting smaller as the time his God had allotted him slipped away. Each day he felt just a little less than the day before, less alert to the needs of his flock and less able to protect it. No sickness hovered over him, no threat to his health was likely to claim him, it was just that his life was winding down and he was slipping into a world with fewer imperatives. With greater frequency and greater clarity, Brother Esteben saw in his mind the family plot at his ancestral home on Majorca.

He knelt in the silent church, semi-dark because dawn and the rising bell were still an hour away. In his mind, though, he heard the magnificent choir in the Cathedral of Mexico City singing *El Cantico del Alba*, the traditional hymn of daybreak. What kind of day would this dawn bring him, Esteben wondered? The shiver that started deep within and ran the length of his spine wasn't due to the chill of the early hour, although chill was certainly in the air. His shiver was for the ordeal ahead. He prayed to his God for one more day of strength to defend the children under his care from the vengeance of Demetrio de Alba.

He stayed kneeling in prayer well past first light, then

pushed wearily to his feet, using his gnarled hands on the altar rail to pull himself up. He shuffled out of the church, back along the covered veranda to his cubicle where a solitary breakfast and de Alba's arrival awaited him.

Good morning, Brother Esteben. Christ be with you." Fermin Ortiz pushed open the door an hour later, greeting the old priest as he had on hundreds of other mornings.

Salamanca met the greeting, rising from his unfinished meal. "Another day without finding the killer could put the Comandante in a particularly foul mood, don't you think?"

"I do indeed." Ortiz moved to a straight-backed chair near the interior wall and seated himself. "What will he do if no one's found?"

"My guess is he'll want his pound of flesh some way."

Ortiz reached over to pick a crust of bread from Salamanca's plate.

"Take it all." Salamanca motioned with his hand. "I've no stomach for food."

"Jimeno was a bad man," Ortiz said with indifference. "De Alba knows that. His death is no loss. Perhaps we don't need a replacement. Vicente or Tomas could lead the others."

"In the name of God, show some compassion, Brother Fermin." Salamanca rose from his desk and came in front of it to stand over the younger Franciscan.

"I have no compassion for Jimeno." Ortiz worked over the scraps of food left on Salamanca's tin plate and set the plate aside. "He was a bully and a brute," he said between bites. "We're better off with him gone. Don't you support me in that?"

Salamanca stared at Ortiz, trying to understand his brother priest. After all their time together, Salamanca still thought of him as a stranger, a man outside the mold. He made note of Ortiz's humorless expression; his jaw set firm, with an expression on his fleshy face as blank as the room's adobe wall.

Ortiz gripped the wooden cross that hung from his belt, holding it as if it were a weapon to smite any man who challenged him.

"I left the cattle to you and Jimeno," Salamanca continued after studying Ortiz, still holding him firmly in his gaze. "I suppose you've done your job well enough, but I wonder at our poor record keeping. Explaining tallies that don't add up to our superiors has been hard for me. Do as you need to do today, but be wary of Demetrio de Alba. You weren't in San Diego to see the wrath of the commander of that *Presidio*."

"The head?"

"I can never get that horror from my mind. It stayed on the fence rail for months. Till the flesh rotted. I implored the Virgin to make it go away—"

There was a sharp knock on the door. De Alba pushed it open without waiting. He nodded to the priests but moved immediately behind Salamanca's desk and seated himself.

"I've decided," he began without any greeting to the Franciscans. "We'll call an end to this inquisition today. Now."

The two priests looked at each other surprised.

"Without finding the killer?" Salamanca asked.

"Without finding the killer," de Alba replied in a mocking tone. "We won't find one, I'm thinking. And I won't let these Indians make fools of us. They might think us weak."

"So they can go back to their work?" Ortiz nodded approvingly. "A good plan, *Comandante*. The mission needs tending. The cattle have strayed by now. My *vaqueros* can handle the work of rounding them up without a guard from the fort."

"We'll see about that." De Alba looked hard at Ortiz. "It's important to get the cattle together. For now your men can ride without escort. Call them together now and we'll give them a warning."

Salamanca tried to keep the benign expression on his face, a constant mask to his real emotions. He reached up to run his hand through the sparse tonsure of hair that circled his head, thinking something strange was afoot. What was happening here that he didn't understand? They treat Jimeno's life as if it had no value.

Two thoughts warred in his head. First, he wasn't sure he had the strength to find out what was propelling de Alba and Ortiz in the same direction of disregard. More importantly, he understood he was trapped in whatever drama was being acted out. If he acquiesced, he was as insensitive to Jimeno's life as they were, willing to throw it into the bone yard as easily as they might throw night soil from a bucket. No justice. No retribution.

If he brought them to account by insisting the hunt for the killer go on, he was putting all his neophytes at risk. Salamanca dared not do that. He understood that Jimeno had lived an ungodly life. Still, all life had value, didn't it?— if he didn't believe that, what was he doing in this outpost struggling to save souls?

"So," he heard his own voice interrupting, "The killer will go unpunished? Shall we all kneel down and pray to God Almighty for forgiveness for our callousness? Do we let it go as if a life is without meaning to our Lord?"

De Alba was in the process of lighting a stubby cigar. He spit the tip he'd bitten off onto the floor and let his eyes, hard as turquoise stones, bore into Salamanca. "You want a killer, do you, *Padre*? You want another execution like the one in San Diego? Do you really want that here in Santa Barbara? Again at *your* mission?"

Salamanca looked about the room with just the slightest nod of his head. He knew he was trapped, knew that while it no longer mattered to him what his superiors thought, he couldn't endure another nightmare. He backed off, throwing his sloping shoulders into a shrug of indifference. "Do what you must," he said. "I'll pray for you both."

De Alba ignored him. "Call all the *vaqueros* to the front of the mission," he told Salamanca. "They all hated Jimeno. Any one of them might be the killer."

"Not just the *vaqueros*," Ortiz interrupted. "Jimeno was hated by all the neophytes for his freedom with his whip."

"We'll strip the *vaqueros* and give each one ten lashes. Make an example of them. We'll tell them we know it was one of them who did the killing and if they don't come forward to confess, we'll whip them again. If one of them does confess, I'll administer the punishment; not you weak-kneed priests."

That night Esteben Salamanca passed on quietly into the next life. When his maker called him, Salamanca was kneeling alone at the foot of his cot in the small room that had served all his needs since coming to Santa Barbara. Wrapped in blankets against the dampness of the evening, he had recited the familiar words that had haunted him since joining the Order: "Have I done enough, Lord? Have I served you well all these years?

"Lord, I *haven't* done enough," he prayed in anguish. "For that I beg forgiveness. In your name I've sinned, show me your mercy. I didn't always have the strength to fight for you. I've failed these children you put in my charge. I've failed because of my weaknesses. They sicken and die, their children are stillborn, their numbers dwindle month by month. I didn't know how to save them. In your name I tried and failed. Do you take them in your loving arms? Or do they burn for my failure?

"I have no strength to tame the appetites of my countrymen. I stood by while Brother Ortiz's arrogance grew, without speaking out as St. Francis would have done.

Ortiz steals from you, Lord, steals from the neophytes in his care in your name. Perhaps he does worse, and I do nothing. I came ready to stand up to the soldiers, an evil I knew from before. De Alba is a small man, a frightened man. But the evil of men like Ortiz acting in your name—their arrogance and disregard for the lives of our children is something I wasn't strong enough to fight. I've written the *Padre Presidente* with my concerns about Brother Fermin. What else can I do? Find it in your merciful heart to forgive me my sins. I'm too old, too weak, too scared to continue."

His mind wandered from his prayers, as it had done more and more often these last few years, to scenes from his childhood in Petra. He saw himself walking by a stream with the young woman who had been his life at age twenty, until he was called to God. The image brought a sweet sadness to him that nestled close to his heart, clouding his eyes. Where was she now? And what kind of life had she led without him? Is it all in vain, he asked his maker? I see an innocent boy, joyful in the arms of his sweetheart. Are good intentions the frauds we use to cover our failures? Is a life in Christ a masquerade for our least noble thoughts? Show me my life has been worthwhile, Lord.

It was at that moment that Esteben Salamanca's Lord called him home.

After a special Mass was conducted by Father Fermin Ortiz, Esteben was buried in the floor of the mission church, in honor of all he had done at Mission Santa Barbara. Every Christian soul in the *Pueblo de Santa Barbara* made the journey up the hill to honor him. Demetrio de Alba wore his best old uniform.

A new Franciscan, Miguel Peralta, arrived at the mission in time to marry Dolores and Massilili. Father Peralta was a Mexican-born Spaniard, a *criollo*. He knew he was looked down upon by Demetrio de Alba and Fermin Ortiz because he wasn't born in the Mother Country. So Miguel busied himself writing reports and requisitions to Mexico City and conducting morning and evening worship services— leaving all aspects of secular mission life to Ortiz.

Chapter Thirty-Five

The last notes of the *Salve Regina* echoed off the adobe walls of the mission church and faded to quiet. The sound of her voice, mingling with other voices, thrilled Cayatu as she stood in the choir loft at the back of the church. She loved to sing this hymn, with its soaring notes and counterpoints of male and female voices, more than all the other hymns.

Hearing her own voice, sounding rich and pure, blending with the other women and contrasting with the deep-throated voices of the men, sent little chills up her spine. Father Salamanca had taught her to sing the hymn and explained its words. Now, he was gone. She missed the passion he had given to his music and his gentle ways of teaching. She thought of him when she sang.

After Miguel Peralta gave the final blessing, the kneeling congregation of townspeople and neophytes stirred, rose to their feet, and began to shuffle out of the church. Cayatu climbed down the ladder from the loft at the left side of the main doors and went outside where she waited for Tomas to join her.

"You sing with the voice of an angel," Tomas said as he came to her.

She smiled. "Like an angel, eh?" she said, giving him a

look. Then she turned to find Massilili in the crowd, acknowledging other friends who called and waved to her as she did. He stood a little ways off with Dolores, beginning to ripen with child, surrounded by other young women. Seeing her wave, Massilili left the group and approached.

"So, you sing the foreigners' songs for them," he started with no greeting. "You honor their God."

"Honor their God?" Cayatu laughed. "No, no. I sing to hear the joyous sounds our voices make, Massilili. Nothing more. If anything, I sing my happiness at having you and Tomas with me. And your new child coming. Sometimes I sing to the trees and rocks around us when I'm alone, giving thanks for our lives. Never to the God of the Spaniards."

"Still, the priests try to fill us with their stories."

"You knew they would."

"Just as I knew I'd find others here who honor First People. Many others. We meet secretly now. You should join us. You too, Tomas."

"What you're doing is dangerous," Tomas said. "If the priests find out…"

"—They won't. We're careful."

"Tomas is right," Cayatu said. "You shouldn't talk about this when the missionaries are so close. You shouldn't talk about it at all. It *is* dangerous."

"Men talk. I hear them talk about Giant Eagle coming back to save his people. Word spreads," Tomas said. "In time the whole village will know."

"Are you afraid, Tomas?—"

"—Clare. Clare, *ven aqui*," a woman's voice called out. "Come here, Clare, see how my baby has grown."

Cayatu turned to see Josefa sitting in the black carriage drawn up on the path to the *pueblo*. The memory of her ride with Josefa brought with it a tingling feeling in her stomach and a quick smile. She saw that Josefa held a small package in her lap wrapped in a cotton blanket. Holding her smile, she waved back.

"Come here, Clare. To talk."

Cayatu turned to Tomas. With her head she nodded slightly in the direction of the carriage. Tomas turned to see *Comandante* Demetrio de Alba standing next to it, speaking with Fermin Ortiz.

"Come with me," she told him. "You too," she said to Massilili.

Tomas hesitated, looking to her for support. Then he shrugged and turned to Massilili. "I'm not afraid," he said, "but wait till you feel the Spaniards' lash on your back. You'll know to be careful."

They walked across the plaza in front of the church, where Mexicans from the *pueblo* and Christian Chumash gathered in small knots talking excitedly to one another with happy voices. De Alba paid no attention as Cayatu, Tomas and Massilili approached the carriage, continuing his conversation with the priest in hushed tones.

Josefa beamed. "Your hair called out to me in this crowd," she laughed. "You cannot hide, Clare, can you? Your hair shines like a harbor beacon calling out to ships in the ocean."

Cayatu laughed back. "When I was younger I thought my hair was more beautiful than any of the other girls in my village, Josefa. I was so proud of it. I combed it every day to make it shine. My sister scolded me for combing it so often. She said I would be punished for my vanity one day." Cayatu laughed again. "Punished with white hair that makes people stare."

"They stare at your beauty. But look at my daughter—six months old now. She has the beautiful dark hair you used to have."

Beautiful black hair but strange eyes, Cayatu thought. Eyes the shape of my sister's, but so different. Her other features—the shape of her nose and chin—are those of a Spaniard. She glanced over at De Alba and Ortiz, heavy in conversation, then at Josefa, and finally at Tomas and Massilili who stood back from the carriage. Coyote has played a marvelous trick on us all, she decided, looking from face to face. He's done his mischief perfectly.

"Have you given her a name?" she asked Josefa.

"I have—" she paused to cast a sharp look at de Alba and Ortiz, who both looked up when she stopped talking. They saw her staring at them, and quickly turned their heads away. "—I'm naming her Delfina."

Cayatu took in a deep breath. "May I hold her?"

Josefa handed down the infant. Cayatu cradled her in the crook of her arm, lifting the blanket away from her face with her other hand so she could study the sleeping child. Delfina opened her eyes and cooed. Cayatu smiled. She put her hand down on Delfina's tiny hand. The baby reached out to take hold of a finger. Cayatu's heart beat in her chest. She whispered to the child, "You'll need those fists to fight for your place, Delfina. No one will make room for you."

Taking a step or two away from the others, Cayatu turned her back and began rocking Delfina in her arms. A lullaby she had sung to Massilili years before came back to her. She began humming it, gently rocking the baby. From the corner of her eye she saw a disapproving look cloud Josefa's face. She pulled herself back from her thoughts and covered the infant's face with the blanket so only the eyes peered out. She handed the baby back to Josefa, feeling a lump form in her throat that made her swallow hard.

Josefa took back Delfina, cradling her in her arms. "So, Clare, will you come to live in the canyon with me and help raise my daughter? The adobe in the canyon is almost finished."

Her words brought Ortiz and de Alba to an abrupt halt in their own conversation. They looked at Josefa then at each other without speaking.

"That would be good," Tomas said, coming forward to stand beside Cayatu. "We could live near Josefa and you wouldn't be lonely when I'm with the herd."

"Who is this man who wants to live with you?" Josefa asked.

"My husband, Tomas."

"So, your husband?" Josefa said, eyeing Tomas. "I didn't know. A *vaquero*—that would be perfect. You'd be together. We could build a small adobe next to mine. Is it decided then?"

"Perhaps we should pray on that for awhile and ask for the Lord's guidance," Fermin Ortiz spoke out. His look darted from de Alba to Cayatu and back to Josefa. "Clare is one of the best weavers we have. I don't know if we could let her move out so far to work for you."

De Alba showed Cayatu no sign of recognition. His eyes were distant, cold, fixed, holding her in his impassive stare. A chill ran inside her. She moved a step closer to Massilili. "She makes cloth for the fort, too, does she not?" he asked Ortiz. "I think her place is here, near mission and *Presidio*, where she can serve our needs. I wouldn't like to see her leave the mission, *Padre*."

Ortiz shook his head in agreement.

Josefa aimed an angry look at de Alba. "I need help with the child so far from the *pueblo*. Clare is a good worker and my friend. I want her out there with me."

"Stay here awhile until we find the right woman to help you," Ortiz said.

"Yes," de Alba agreed. "Stay in the *pueblo* where we can be close."

"It's my land," Josefa snapped back. "I'll live there as I please. And I want Clare with me. To help with Delfina."

"Perhaps in time," de Alba said.

"In God's good time," Ortiz echoed.

Chapter Thirty-Six

The wild man inched his way along the outcropping. To his left a solid wall of rock stretched above his head; on his right a chasm dropped off into the floor of a deep valley lost in the haze. One misstep or loose rock and he knew he'd be on his way to the Peaceful Place.

He told himself what he'd done was foolish and unnecessary. Yet he'd done it and he felt no remorse. It was his life that had been sacrificed after all. His heart beat against his chest as he edged his way around the rocks, his fingers complained as they grasped the jagged outcroppings.

Ever since Massilili had left him he'd been watching for his chance, waiting, thinking the idea foolish—that he'd never have the opportunity—but waiting nevertheless. Then his chance had come. He spotted Qoloq, struggling up the trail one day, topping the last ridge and slowly making his way across the barren plain to the sacred rocks. He'd waited, secretly watching from far off until the bear shaman was finished with his dreaming, his rock painting and his long night of solitary dancing. He waited until Qoloq began the arduous journey home.

"You're Qoloq, the shaman of *Mishopshnow*," the wild man had accosted him from behind a boulder on the trail, startling Qoloq so severely he dropped to his knees to keep from falling off the steep slope.

"Who are you?" Qoloq asked, regaining his feet. "How do you know me?"

"I've watched you a long time. You robbed my life."

"I've robbed no man," Qoloq answered, and then as an afterthought said, "All our lives have been robbed. We've been abandoned and we're waiting for the end."

"But it was you who took away my life."

The wild man came safely past the outcropping and followed the ancient animal trail into a clump of thick bushes where blue flowers grew against green bark. He thought back on the conversation with Qoloq and asked himself how it could have ended differently. Why had Qoloq cursed him?

Emerging into the open again, he was in a curving amphitheater carved into the mountain by ancient winds. A little meadow lay at the base of the rock, where shrubs and grasses sprouted from the pebbly soil.

As he neared the end of the meadow, he stopped short. A shaggy bear cub fed on low-growing branches a few yards in front of him. He watched the cub, admiring the free, wild creature that stood almost as tall as he was. The sound behind him startled him to action again.

The she bear had been foraging apart from her offspring. Seeing the man, she roared her alarm. The wild man took the measure of his situation: on his left, the cliff dropped off too steeply to allow any escape; the she bear blocked the trail back into the heavy brush. His only hope was to run past the cub. He knew he couldn't outrun the she bear for long, his chance of escape was slim but he had to try. Fear for his life drove him to action.

The bear was moving toward him an instant before he

started to run. He raced passed the cub and the she bear roared her anger. He rounded the bend, leaving the amphitheater behind him and ran along a long narrow stretch of trail with a sharp drop on his left. Already, he could feel the bear closing in on him. Small rocks and stones sliced into his feet as he raced along the trail. Once, he stumbled, but kept his balance and continued running. The stumble had cost him his lead, the bear was almost on top of him.

He saw a shallow depression in the face of the rock wall ahead of him, a narrow opening, with talus rock piled in front of it, forming a cave just large enough for a man to wedge himself into. It seemed a long way off. He gasped for breath. Too far, he thought, but he ran on. Now, he could feel the bear's sour breath on the back of his neck.

He arrived at the opening in the rocks just as the bear swung her giant paw at him. He was in midair, diving into the small space when her claws slashed his leg, shredding his flesh. Pain knifed him. The bear's claws cut all the way to the bone. He went over the rock barrier, barely missing an outcropping aimed at his head, falling hard on the stone slab, bleeding. The bear tried to get at him through the narrow space. Her teeth were bared and her breath seared him, churning his stomach until her stench and the loss of blood made him faint.

Chapter Thirty-Seven

Massilili ran through the *ranchería* calling loudly for Cayatu, "Come quickly," he shouted.

At the sight of his torn and blood-stained shirt, she rose from the fire outside the hut she shared with Tomas. Her heart beating against her chest "What?" she gasped.

Massilili stopped beside her. "A man is hurt. Come help me."

She hurried along the path through the village, running to keep up with him. Together, they raced along the trail by the stream, going past her old shelter, deeper into the canyon, to the place where the stream narrowed between boulders. Massilili stopped there.

Cayatu stopped, too, as if suddenly rooted to the ground at the far side of the rocks. She stared at the man lying in front of her, his left leg wrapped in bloody cloth strips. She knew him, but called her eyes liars. She was unwilling to accept the reality of the wild-looking man.

He grinned up at her from where he lay, his face barely masking his pain. "Speak to me," he pleaded, his words coming in short spurts. "So long since I've heard your voice."

She dropped to her knees beside him. "You? Is it really you?"

Massilili squatted down beside her and put his hand on her shoulder. "I found him on the mountain, aunt. In a cave. A bear tore his leg open."

"Will he survive?" Cayatu felt weak.

"He will."

"I haven't waited all this time to see you again to die now," the man said through tightly clenched lips. "I owe Massilili my life."

"—You saved *my* life before," Massilili interrupted.

Emotions swirled through Cayatu like leaves in a wind. She needed time to calm the pounding in her chest.

She raced back up the path to her hut, searching through the meager belongings she and Tomas shared, tossing clothes about, frantic to find something she could used to wrap the wound. She found nothing useful there but the whole time she searched, her mind was dizzy with memories.

Leaving the hut, she raced along the path that led behind the mission to the storerooms where cloth she and the other women wove was stored. She grabbed the door handle and pulled at it. It didn't open. She kept pulling, not seeing the lock. Tears blurred her vision as she wrestled with the door, panic and frustration took control of her so she couldn't think.

Seeing the lock at last, she ran to the field next to the storeroom for a stick or stone, something she could use. She stumbled about until she found a thick stick. Running back to the locked door, she looked around to make sure no one was watching her, and then hit at the lock two, three, four times. When it didn't break, she slid the stick between the hasp and the door. She forced it up with her arms, using all her strength. The wooden door groaned. Finally, the hasp flew away and the door swung open.

Cayatu found cloth on a table in a far corner and grabbed several *varas* of it. "My cloth," she said aloud. "I wove it." She gathered what she needed. Then, with a mean sweep of her arm, she threw the remaining pile off the table onto the ground and ran back out into the daylight.

Massilili stopped her as she ran back into the canyon. "Does he still mean so much to you?"

She looked away, trying to form an answer. "I don't know," she said. "You were just a young boy. I dreamt of what my life could have been with Ysaga. Then I knew it never would be. Now he's here. I don't know what I think."

"Tomas?" Massilili's voice held an edge.

"I love Tomas. Oh, Massilili…" Her voice quivered. "Ysaga was a boastful boy. He strode about the village boasting of his father's wealth, whining when he didn't get what he wanted. But he loved me. He wanted me to share his hut. I loved him back."

"When does Tomas return?" Massilili asked her.

"After the branding—Four, five days."

"Will you tell him?"

"I couldn't," she answered.

When Massilili left, Cayatu went to Ysaga's side. She knelt beside his sleeping form and very softly swept away his hair and kissed his forehead. When he didn't stir, she lay down beside him and wept.

With Cayatu's care and the herbal poultices Massilili applied, the fire was driven out of Ysaga's leg, but when the leg healed, it was obvious much flesh had been lost. His leg looked shriveled, smaller than the other. Massilili cut a tree limb for him to use as a crutch. Wobbly at first, he learned to walk with the stick.

When they were alone, Ysaga and Cayatu talked about days past, followed by long silences. It was almost as if they were unwilling to remember those days for fear they wouldn't stay pure in their minds. Talking about them might spoil them, or wipe them away altogether.

"How many nights did I think about you?" Ysaga said one evening as darkness embraced the wooded glen. "Did you think about me, Cayatu?"

"Always," she answered, avoiding his look. She busied herself tidying up little things in the crude shelter that needed no tidying. She stopped to look at him. "That was the best time of my life."

"We were lovers."

There were no more words between them. In the stillness of the canyon they shared a look. Cayatu struggled against her feelings but found herself drawn to his side. He stretched out his arms and she lay down beside him.

"Won't this hurt your leg?" she asked.

Ysaga's only response was to gather her into his arms, where he fumbled with her clothes. He kissed her and his hands roamed freely over her. Her breath came in short little spurts. She saw him wince as he tried to roll toward her.

"Don't," she said. "I'll come to you."

They lay in the darkness, the sounds of night creatures around them. A chorus of tree frogs rose and fell away, rose and fell away again. Small animals scampered through the leaf litter on the canyon floor as the two lay side by side, silently watching Evening Star watching them through the treetops.

Cayatu stirred. "What will you do?"

"The mountains are a mean place to live," he answered.

"Have you lived there all along?"

"Only these last few seasons."

Slowly, Ysaga spread the story of his life out before her as she lay by his side. He told about wandering in the valley in the days after Qoloq expelled him from the village, never knowing she had been cast out too. He'd walked along the beach to other villages but was driven away by the people in each one. Eventually, he struck out across the mountains, hoping to find a home with the Yokut people, but often he couldn't find enough food on the journey and had to sleep hungry in the snow high up on the peaks.

"I thought I would die many times then," he said. "Then one day I looked down into a giant valley with mountains in the distance even taller than the ones I'd crossed. But, oh, how I missed the ocean where we grew up," he told her. "I came back. One day I found Massilili struggling for water. He almost died before I cared for him."

Staring into the dark of the canyon, so Ysaga couldn't see the tears in her eyes, she asked, "Will you come to the mission?"

"What can I do? Look at this useless leg. Massilili says the only way for us to continue living along the ocean is to pretend to live the Spanish ways while holding on to our own. Should I come to the mission to be with you?"

"You'll never again have your freedom," Cayatu said sobbing. "From the day you're baptized you'll be told everything to do. They'll treat you like a child and never let you leave again."

"What good is freedom if I'm alone? The Spanish have conquered us. Without fighting. I think the life with the missionaries is my only choice."

"We're not the same," she said, feeling the lump grow in her throat so she had to force her words out. "Only a fool spends time dreaming of a past that's lost forever. The light-skinned people came and our world unraveled. Now there's no place for us. We're lost."

"Can we share the life that's left to us, Cayatu?"

She choked back her emotions. "I have a husband."

In the faint light Cayatu could see the pain sear across his face before he turned away from her. He looked into the black abyss of the sycamore trees, hiding his feelings. Finally he looked back and spoke with a steady voice. "Of course. How could it be otherwise? You didn't know if I were dead." He threw off another long sigh. "You couldn't wait."

She moved close to him again, looking into his sad eyes reflecting her own pain in the dim light from the rising moon filtering through the trees. Not physical pain but dumb pain, like the pain in the eyes of a doe dying with an arrow in her heart. "We can be close again, but we'll have to be careful." she said.

Chapter Thirty-Eight

Massilili threaded his way between boulders down the familiar path. Ever since his time with Ysaga, he'd roamed the mountains the Spaniards called *Santa Inés*, searching out places to quarry the yellow stone the missionaries valued for their new buildings. From his high vantage point, the ship swinging at anchor just off shore seemed like one of the small stick boats he carved for his son, Asunción.

He hated that name. He'd argued with Dolores to give their child a Chumash name, something strong, like Hew, the name of a powerful *tomol* builder in a story Qoloq told. But his wife wouldn't hear of it.

"The Franciscans won't baptize a child with a name like that," Dolores scorned him. "They want each of us to have a Christian name. I do, too," she added, putting her hands on her slender hips. "What's the purpose of our lives here unless we become Christians?"

Massilili hadn't bothered to answer. In all other areas of their life together he gave comfort and love to Dolores. They were good parents to their son, but only grudgingly did he use the boy's baptized name, and secretly he called the boy Hew.

Now Massilili was anxious to get back to Dolores and the

hut they shared. He was impatient to take her in his arms again, and hold his son. He looked forward to spending time with Tomas and Cayatu and their new baby. He'd been living in the mountains with the other stonecutters, robust men like him, almost five days. It was time to get home.

Reaching the bottom of the steep trail, Massilili hurried through the wooded section of the canyon along the stream, already thinking about lying with Dolores, thinking about how welcoming her arms would be and how her breasts would feel. He stopped only briefly to inspect the site where the missionaries said stone for a new dam would be needed.

As he strode into the *ranchería*, Dolores spotted him from the door of their adobe hut. She came running to him, calling, "Hurry" with a fretful tone he could already hear.

He quickened his steps till he held her in his arms.

"Asunción is sick. His skin burns," she cried, burying her face in his chest and going limp in his arms. "He can't swallow."

Massilili stroked her hair with his big hand, letting it drop down to rub along the curve in her back, trying to comfort her. "How long?" he asked.

"Two days. Cayatu's baby is sick too. There are others." Dolores clung to him, until he gently unlocked her arms from around his neck.

Asunción lay on a mat in the adobe. Beads of fever glistened like drops of fog on his forehead. Massilili knelt to sooth his son and recoiled when he felt the heat in the small boy's body. Asunciòn whimpered. His body was limp when his father lifted him off the mat. He gulped for air, his lips opening and closing like a fish out of water, taking short, quick breaths that made a scratchy noise. Massilili touched his hard and swollen neck. Fear coursed through him.

Carrying the boy in his arms, with Dolores trailing behind, he walked through the village to the hut Cayatu and Tomas shared. "How is it here, Aunt?" he called from the doorway. "Dolores says Joselito is sick, too."

"See for yourself," Cayatu answered. She picked up the infant and opened his tiny mouth with her finger so Massilili could see the thick, dark, coating on the baby's throat. The rasping sound came at intervals when the infant interrupted his crying to gasp for air.

Massilili turned to Dolores. Asunción? his eyes asked.

Her eyes responded, yes.

"Whatever sickens our children is spreading through the village like a mountain fire," Tomas said from a corner of the hut where he sat against a wall, his head buried in his hands. "Each day more babies and small children sicken. Now the elders."

Tomas told Massilili he'd gone for help in the *pueblo*. "The people there were sympathetic but held back," he said. "They wanted to help but kept their distance from me and shooed their own children into their houses. None of them showed signs of the sickness."

"Just here?" Massilili asked. Don't the Mexican children get sick?"

Tomas shook his head.

"Another disease the ship brought from *Nueva España*!" Massilili pounded his anger with one big fist against the doorframe. "We should take the children away, hide them from the sickness."

Dolores came from behind to put a restraining arm on Massilili's shoulder. "No," she said, "We won't leave. The priests will help us. Give me Asunción. I'll take him to Father Peralta. He'll pray for him. You come, too, Clare."

"A waste," Massilili said, holding the boy out of his mother's reach. "Have the priests ever cured anyone? No! They mumble prayers and say it's in God's hands, but their God doesn't cure our children. Maybe I can heal Asunción with Qoloq's medicine, or maybe he'll go to the Peaceful Place, but I won't give his life to the Franciscans."

Dolores moved quickly and snatched the child away from Massilili. She turned her back on him. "He stays with me," she said in a fierce voice that echoed her desperation. "The Virgin has always brought me comfort when I prayed. She'll cure our child. Come with me, Clare."

"Go alone," Cayatu said. "Tomas and I will care for Joselito here." After a pause she added, "You should listen to your husband."

Massilili glared at Dolores. He snarled like an animal, pounded his fist again, and stalked out of the hut.

Cayatu watched her baby hang limply at her breast, feeling so light in her arm she thought he might float away. She wiggled her nipple back and forth across his mouth. Joselito showed no interest. He was struggling to breathe. A tear run down her cheek as she looked across the hut at Tomas. "Is there nothing we can do?" she asked.

Tomas's look was sad and helpless. He didn't speak.

"He won't eat," Cayatu said, tasting her own bitterness. "I think it's too painful for him to swallow. He'll die soon if he doesn't eat."

Tomas only nodded and averted his eyes. Under his breath he muttered, "All the children may die."

"That would be the end of us, wouldn't it, Tomas? No children to take us to the future. Imagine, Tomas, all our people gone, like a breeze that blows down from the mountains and disappears over the ocean. Here, then gone. Unremembered." Cayatu was weeping, pushing her words out between sobs. "Where does this trouble come from? Is this the Franciscan God's doing? Or have First People abandoned us?"

Tomas lifted his head, showing Cayatu his own tears. "What does it matter? Our child is suffering. Dying. No God would bring this on a child, so new, so small as

Joselito. I hate all gods for this."

Our child. Cayatu wished she knew the father for certain. No doubt he was a Chumash child. Knowing that had given her a feeling of joy in the months she carried the baby. Not a half-breed. Joselito had been everything Cayatu had hoped for in the few weeks since his birth. The boy who would grow up strong and gentle like his father— whichever man that was made no difference to her, the child had a strong beginning. He'd grow strong like his grandfather, Muniyaut. Perhaps he'd become 'Altomolich like him. She knew that was impossible now, only a dream, but secretly she called the baby Silikset because she despised the Spanish name Tomas had picked. Like Massilili, she wanted her child to have a proud name.

Taking the infant off her breast and wrapping him in the fur of a rabbit skin, Cayatu pulled her *camisa* back to her shoulder and sat staring out the doorway of the hut at the mission buildings. "Would it be any different if we lived in a village away from the mission, Tomas?"

"No different." Tomas cleared his throat with a quiet cough. "We'll be fine after the sickness ends. It is so sad for Joselito…We can have more children. Don't speak of leaving the mission. You promised you would never speak of that again. We have to do our best for Joselito."

"He won't survive, Tomas. I can feel him fading away already. Preparing for his journey to the Peaceful Place." A deep sob wracked her chest. "He's so small for that journey, Tomas. All alone. He has no dream helper to guide him. So tiny and alone." She tried to stop the flow of her tears but they came in a flood. "I called to my mother, Sioctu, to guide him across. She'll be waiting for him."

"You still believe—"

"—Sioctu will take his hand. Muniyaut may come to him, too. We are Chumash, Tomas, our son is Chumash. I call him Silikset, not the missionaries' name.

Cayatu's hand brushed the tiny fringe of dark hair, wet with the fever sweat, off the infant's forehead. Then her hand went to the shell basket beside the sleeping mat. She touched the coils. She would teach the boy the traditional ways if he lived. Silently, she implored Sioctu to keep Silikset safe on his journey and show him the high place in which he rightfully belonged if that was his future. She tried not to think about the sadness, but for an instant she thought about Delfina, safely away from the mission, away from the sickness, healthy in the home of a Mexican woman.

Massilili walked through the village, stopping at huts where other children burned with fever and clung to life by the slimmest threads. Some adults—old ones—had the swollen neck and black throat, too. It was spreading. They coughed weakly and struggled for breath like the children. He urged the families to gather up the sick ones and carry them into the canyon.

Staying in the mission *rancheria* would be certain death, he told them. They should flee the village until the sickness was gone. The sickness was a punishment First People had sent them to show their anger, he told anyone who would listen. Sun would take them all home to his daughters; Eagle of the Sky had willed it.

Massilili left the sounds of coughing and wheezing behind and walked across the front of the mission to the steps of the church. He mounted to the top step and stared up at the bell tower and the cross, cast in silver moonlight. No emotion showed on his face. He rocked back and forth as the sounds of shell rattles and panpipes played in his head. Then he lifted a foot and put it back down. He lifted the other foot. He began moving his feet in a pattern. One foot then the other. Slowly at first but growing stronger and faster. His eyes moved from the cross to the stars above him, the only witnesses to his dance, each one speaking to him.

The music in his head played faster. His footsteps quickened to keep pace. No one watched Massilili dance, but dance he did. Faster, turning and twirling, now. Jumping and crouching. On the steps of the mission church time stopped. It was a dance of absolution and a dance of recognition. All alone, the spirits hovered close around him. Faster. On and on he danced and spun and leapt and twisted and jumped as the moon dipped low. On and on, hour after hour, with the stars tracing their paths across the heavens, until he fell on the front step of the church, numb, panting for breath.

Chapter Thirty-Nine

Asunción is dead," Massilili could barely get the words out as he told Tomas the next morning. "Last night Dolores held him as he went to the Peaceful Place."

"Little Joselito died in the night, too." Tomas's face was swollen with sadness. "Father Peralta took him from us this morning."

"I'm going to all the huts, telling people to go into the canyon with their sick ones. We'll stay there until the fever and coughing stops. We'll dance for First People. Come with us."

Tomas shrugged. "I have no faith in First People—they abandoned me long ago."

"Cayatu?" Massilili looked over at his aunt.

"I'll stay with my husband," she said.

"We may never come back."

"Come back if you can… Do what you must," she said indifferently.

Walking from hut to hut Massillili gathered a small band of followers, some sick themselves or caring for sick children and old people. When he returned to his own hut, Dolores lay on their sleeping mat grieving.

"We'll go into the canyon until the dying stops," he said, kneeling beside her and gathering her in his arms.

"Why? It makes no difference." She buried her face deep in the mat so he could barely hear her voice.

"To live."

"Asunción's gone. What good is living?" Dolores turned her head to the side and coughed.

When she turned back to look at him, Massilili saw the wetness of fever gleaming on her forehead. Pain stabbed at his chest, more powerful than any physical pain he'd ever felt. It pressed against his ribs so he couldn't breathe. "You?" he gasped, knowing the answer.

He lifted her into his arms, hugging her tightly. "I won't let you go," he promised her. "I'll give up my own life before I'd spend one day without you."

He walked out of the hut with Dolores in his arms.

"Where are you taking me?"

"To the canyon. We'll live there. You'll get better."

"Stay here," she said. "To have the rites for Asunción. If I die I want the priests to give me the rites." She mumbled a few more words and then fell limp in his arms.

Others were watching as he carried her through the village. She was light, too light, he knew. No burden. Villagers followed him. Soon there were fifty men and women walking behind him as he moved across the front of the mission aiming for the path into the canyon.

"—Stop there," a voice called out from the steps of the church. "Go back." Fermin Ortiz stood with hands on hips, shouting to the group. He gathered his robe about him and ran down the steps of the church, blocking their path. "Where are you going?"

"If we don't leave our huts, more will die," Massilili told him.

"You can't leave the mission. Go back," Ortiz said.

"We'll go anyway," Massilili said. "You can't stop us."

"It is not allowed," Ortiz said again. "Go back to your huts."

"Can you cure our sick children?" Massilili confronted Ortiz.

"We do our best," the priest said, "and pray for God's mercy."

Still holding Dolores in his arms, Massilili turned to his followers. "Don't listen to this priest," he shouted to them. "He can't save our children. Our only chance is away from the mission—"

"—Not allowed," Ortiz shouted again, more to the crowd than to Massilili. The crowd milled about, some pushing forward to stand with Massilili, but others in the back drifted off like smoke, hoping not to be recognized.

"Look at my wife." Massilili held Dolores in his arms, too weak to protest. "Look at her," he demanded. "Sending her back to the *ranchería* will kill her."

"God's will be done," Ortiz said. He looked around to see if anyone was coming to his support.

He heard sounds behind him and turned to see two soldiers coming up the path from the corral at a trot. "Go back to your huts before I have these men take the whole lot of you to the fort."

The smoke drifting away became a steady flow at Ortiz's words. People turned from Massilili and slunk back to the *ranchería*. In moments, he stood alone facing Ortiz. He stood straight, taller by a full head, looking down at the missionary who blocked his path. Ortiz stood his ground.

"Once more, I tell you to go back," Ortiz ordered. "If you don't I'll have you whipped. That's all I'll say."

"Look at this woman!" Massilili's pain was an angry shout. "She loves life at your mission. She's a Christian woman. She prays daily to the Virgin for guidance in her life. She worships your God. Look at her carefully, Father Ortiz, know her, because you're sending her to her death."

Chapter Forty

Death crept back to Cayatu's hut during the night, with only coughing sounds to announce it. It laid claim to Tomas. His fever began a short time after Joselito's death. His throat swelled shut. Cayatu gave him water, but she could see how painful it was for him to swallow. She hovered over him, mopping the sweat from his face. She watched him fade from life, helpless even to ease his suffering. His eyes were small sockets drilled deep in his head.

Through her tears, she saw the simple, handsome man walking up the hill from the *Presidio* the day they'd first met, so full of enthusiasm for mission life, proud to be a part of it. Over the years, his gentleness and caring had won her heart. Without her ever knowing how or when, her feelings had blossomed into a deep love for Tomas.

He motioned her down close beside him and started to raise himself up.

"No, Tomas." She eased him back down,

He resisted. "I must talk." His rasping whisper came in short breaths from parched lips, no more than a murmur on the wisp of a breeze. "Soon I'll go…"

Cayatu ran her hand through his sweat-soaked hair. "Talk a little, then lie back and rest."

"It's all so sad," he wheezed. "Is Ysaga sick too?"

"No, he doesn't have the fever," she answered.

"He's from your village?"

"He is." The stab at her heart was unbearable.

"Do you still love him?"

"You're my husband," she said. "I love you, Tomas. Please rest." Cayatu turned her head away so he wouldn't see her face.

Tomas rested for several minutes while his breath came in short rasps. She panicked he was slipping away, but he reopened his eyes. A flicker of life hung on. "You'll need Ysaga... When I'm gone."

"You'll be fine, Tomas. Only rest." Cayatu's tears flowed freely as she looked down on the wasted man. "Believe me, Tomas, I do love you. I loved Ysaga as a young girl. When he first came to the mission I got confused. Can you forgive me? Don't leave me, Tomas." She put her head on his chest. "Please don't die," She pleaded.

Her heart was already crushed by the loss of her baby, barely a month old and never baptized. Silikset was gone, hardly ever there. She'd wanted to tell him so much. About his grandfather's *tomols* and Sioctu's baskets; about his place in the Middle World. But he had left too soon. Looking down at Tomas, she knew soon no one would remember.

Tomas lifted his hand to touch her hair and smiled at her though dimming eyes. Another coughing attack wracked his body, shaking him with its violence. He closed his eyes for a moment. Blood trickled from the corner of his mouth. Cayatu wiped it away with a cloth. Tomas sank deeper into the reed mat with only the faintest glimmer of life left. A flicker of strength came back and he started to speak again. When she put her ear close to his mouth to hear, the smell of death engulfed her.

"I..." He struggled to find sufficient breath to continue. "... killed Jimeno."

"You, Tomas?"

Tomas came as close as he could to a smile. "An evil man... He hurt you... I cut his throat with his own knife."

She forced her words through her uncontrolled sobs so he would hear her. "I'm not worthy of your love, Tomas. I've done so many things to wrong you."

"The baby?" His eyes had a hopeful look.

She looked at him a moment, unsure of his question. Then she bit her lip. "Yours, Tomas," she said without hesitation.

He sunk deeper into the mat and his soul departed for the Peaceful Place.

Fatigued from ministering to the sick and dying neophytes, Miguel Peralta administered last rites. He took Cayatu's hand and spoke a few words of sorrow at her loss, and then prepared for the burial. Too many were dying for the usual funerals. Instead, Cayatu followed Tomas's body when it was carried to the cemetery. It was placed in a common grave with the others who had died during the night.

Hidden away behind the church, the cemetery was too small to hold the bodies of all the Chumash who had died at the mission. A few men were digging up bones at the far end, away from the new graves, taking them in hand carts to the stone house at the back of the cemetery to make room for the new dead.

For several hours she sat by the grave. All the sadness she felt spilled out. Gone was her husband, not bravely as her father Muniyaut had died, not given the honored funeral he deserved, as Muniyaut's had been, but thrown in a shallow hole with twenty others. She felt a heavy weight on her heart when she reflected on how she had wronged him. She knew, too late, that she had loved him far more than any other man.

Tomas and Dolores gone. Children gone, too. Others would be gone soon enough. Only two mattered to her now; Massilili, hardened to stone from his own losses, and Ysaga. Only the three of us now, she thought—and Tanayan.

Chapter Forty-One

Hey ahead, give us room. Move off to the side."

The voice of a Mexican man walking beside a *carreta* up the dry, rutted road broke the morning stillness. It was the same path over the hill on which Cayatu had followed Fathers Salamanca and Ortiz to the *Presidio* years before. The path was well trodden now, she saw as she reached the summit with Massilili and Ysaga. Horse hoofs and wooden wheels had rutted and grooved it, biting deep into the soil so that the approaching cart carried a trail of dust behind it that dimmed the clear sky.

The *carreta* made slow progress up the hill, with its wooden axle protesting every turn of its thick wheels with a grinding, scraping noise. The shouting man walked beside a tired-looking ox, urged it on with a length of tree branch that he slapped lightly on the beast's flank. Another man rode in the cart protecting the load of trade goods as it bounced over the ruts.

"Make room for us to pass, *por favor.*" The man smiled, showing yellowed teeth under his dark mustache, but his voice grew more insistent as the *carreta* struggled for the crest.

"We've as much right to walk the road as you do," Massilili shouted back at the man, moving to the middle of the path.

"Let's move off for these men," Ysaga said, leaning against his walking stick, watching the cart approach. "We want no trouble with them."

Massilili held his ground.

"We seek no trouble, either," the Mexican man said, heavy sweat visible on his forehead. "We've a big load here to trade with the *pueblo*."

"Sí," the man standing in the cart laughed, "This hill's a tough one on our sweet Dulcinea."

The Mexican leading the cart gave out a husky laugh of his own and brought the ox to a halt barely a length from Massilili. He was short, but built wide and soft, with his stomach hanging well over the rope he used for a belt. "A fine enough companion for a cold night by the side of the road, she is, but there's no romance in her."

"I'll take no insult from any man." Massilili stood face to face with the Mexican. His fists hung like stones at the end of his bulky arms, tight and ready.

"We've given no insult," the man in the cart said, surprised, "only asked you to move to the side."

"Let them pass," Ysaga urged Massilili again. "There's no insult here. Leave them be. We don't want trouble."

"Your friend's right," the short Mexican said. "Let us pass."

Massilili shot a look at Ysaga. "You never want trouble these days. You let the foreigners order you around and you spend your life trying to please them. You're not the man you were in the mountains."

Cayatu stood on the edge of the road, holding the shell basket and studying her nephew blocking the path. She understood Massilili's bitterness, born of his grief, but worried what trouble it would bring him.

The man in the *carreta* spotted her basket and called out,

"That's a fine looking basket you've got there. Not many of that kind anymore, *Señora*. No indeed, not many left. How about trading for something in our cart?"

Massilili and the ox driver still exchanged looks across the few feet that separated them—Massilili's was defiant, the Mexican seemed helpless. Then recognition crept over the Mexican's face. "Hey, Raul," he called to the other man in the cart. "This is the Indian who attacked us in the village that night. That was a long time back but I still remember."

"The other man jumped down from the cart to get a better look. "By Christ, you're right; yes you are. Been a long time. He's the one broke my arm. So, *Señora*," he called to Cayatu, "will you trade?"

"We want no trouble with you," the ox driver said again to Massilili. "We wanted none before but you hurt us both."

"You were drunk. You shouldn't have been in Qoloq's village stealing from us during our ceremony," Massilili said.

"No trade," Cayatu told the man.

"We meant no harm then nor any now," the Mexican said. "We're just traders. It's a tough life we have, going from village to village. Now will you let us pass by?"

"I can offer a lot for that basket. People will pay for a beauty like that one."

"This one is special," Cayatu told him. "I won't trade it away."

Massilili walked to the *carreta*. "They steal from our villages," he called out to Cayatu and Ysaga, pointing to baskets and stone bowls on the floor of the cart. "See. They loot our villages."

"We traded fair for these things," the man in the cart said, "The villagers trade with us because we're honest."

Cayatu walked to Massilili's side and took his arm, pulling him away from the *carreta*. "It's not our business," she said. "Let them go on to the *pueblo*. We have a long walk ahead and no time to stand here and look for fights that aren't real."

The three continued their journey down the hill. The Mexican slapped his stick against the ox's flank and moved off toward the *pueblo*. Massilili turned back to the two Mexicans as they separated. "You're thieves," he said, but continued moving away from them as Cayatu tugged on his arm.

Looking out over her valley from the hilltop, hundreds, maybe thousands of gray-white sheep grazed on the spotty grasses as far as Cayatu could see. The raw earth smells she remembered were replaced by animal smells. The village seemed inconsequential as they approached it, shoved out of the way against the beach.

Flapping sounds of loose tule fronds dancing on the breeze on the roofs of empty huts caught her attention as she walked into the village with the two men. In the distance, she could hear the moaning of the surf dying against the sand, and the gurgling noise the water made as it retreated back over the rocks. She could hear that sound because the village was still, there were no people sounds. The occasional man or woman she passed—mostly old ones tending their cooking fires—sat in silence.

Tanayan turned from her work, looking up as they approached. Cayatu saw a frail, old-looking woman, far older than her years, kneeling by her fire. Her black hair was streaked with white and her hands trembled as she patted acorn meal into flat cakes. Cayatu's breath caught in her throat at the sight of her sister's skin, splotched with dirt and grease. There were stains and rips and matted filth in her sea otter skirt.

"Are you my son and sister? Or is this some new trick to torment me?" Tanayan greeted them.

"We're real, mother," Massilili said, moving to her side and embracing her frail body in his giant arms.

"I never thought I'd see you again in this life. Qoloq told of you walking off into the darkness. We thought you had died."

"I let him down. You, too. The spirits didn't come to me then. I didn't want to shame you."

Tanayan turned her gaze on Cayatu. "My little sister has come back again," she said, "with hair the color of moonlight. Old woman's hair, like mine, but you're not an old woman."

"Neither of us is old," Cayatu said. "These passing seasons have been sad ones for me without you." She held out the basket for Tanayan to see. "Each night before I sleep I take out the shell basket our mother wove. I look at it and think of her." Cayatu had tears clouding her eyes. "When I'm sad I talk to her." She reached out to hold Tanayan's fragile hands in her own, forming words from her sorrow. "And I think of you, raising me with all the love of a mother. I hold the basket and I think of the time I lived here."

"Who is this other man?" Tanayan asked as if she hadn't heard Cayatu.

"Ysaga, the man Qoloq banished."

Tanayan recollected, "I remember him now. That seems so long ago. Why have you come back now?"

"The *padres* gave permission for us to leave the mission for as many days as we needed to visit you," Cayatu answered. "Without the permission, soldiers would have come after us and taken us back."

A puzzled look clouded Tanayan's face. She paused a moment, then went on, again as if she hadn't heard her sister. "I'm sorry. In my heart I've always been sorry for you, Ysaga. It had nothing to do with you, but you suffered. It was about Qoloq's dream. I often think of the days when we all lived here. You were such a pretty young girl."

Tanayan's eyes jumped from one to the other, her words came out without any order as her thoughts came to her. "You loved to watch Muniyaut work. Massilili would come to the hut at the end of the day and tell Qoloq and me how he would become a great canoeman. Ysaga, you were the most boastful boy in the village, always talking about how you would paddle the farthest and catch the biggest fish. I see those days clearly in my mind as I work."

"Qoloq's dream?" Cayatu said.

Tanayan nodded. "It frightened him. Coyote came to him after you were born. Qoloq worried you would have powers stronger than his—"

"Where is my father now?" Massilili interrupted.

"He's not in the village anymore," Tanayan said. "I don't know where he is or if he'll ever come back."

Tanayan stopped talking and put her hand to the side of her head, as if she were trying to remember. The others sat awaiting her words. "He was always angry," she started again. "He'd walk through the village shouting curses at all who wouldn't listen to him, and there were very few who did listen. He drank the momoy often.

"He decided to hold a ceremony before the great fish hunt," her expressionless voice droned on. "It was a silly idea—most of the men had given up fishing. No one came to the ceremony. There were no other *Antap* dancers so he danced all the dances himself, all night long."

"If I had been here, I would have danced with him," Massilili interrupted again. "It wasn't right for him to dance alone."

The look Tanayan gave her son was curious, but she didn't respond to him. Instead, she continued with her story. "It was so terrible the way people laughed and mocked my husband. He paid no attention. He completed the ceremony with dignity and came back to the hut. We lay together that night. It was the last time. In the morning he walked away from the village. Since then, I've lived alone."

Cayatu moved close beside Tanayan, putting her arms around her sister, rocking her gently. "We want you to live with us now," she said.

Tanayan looked surprised. "At the mission?"

"We should be together—to care for each other."

Tanayan reflected a few minutes, her face creased in thought. "I'll stay here," she said.

Massilili took her hands in his. "You won't survive here, mother. You don't have the strength to gather food—there's no one to help you. Come with us so we can care for you."

"My decision's made," Tanayan said, "made before you came. I watch others go but I'll stay here. I know you are right—it is harder to gather enough to survive now. The fields are trampled by animals and we can't burn them anymore—the soldiers forbid it. If Qoloq doesn't come back by the winter solstice, I'll do as our women have always done. The winter solstice, that's all. Perhaps I've waited too long already."

They sat silent in the darkness for long intervals, letting the fire die, sharing the sad reunion. When they did talk it was mostly about the days when they were all together in the village. After sitting with his head down in his hands listening, Massilili looked up. "I'll go find him," he said.

A ray of hope lightened Tanayan's face. "Where will you look?"

"I'll go over the mountains to the sacred place where he took me. I'll bring him back, mother. We'll do the dances together."

"That would make Qoloq proud," Tanayan said.

"I can do it. I'll start in the morning."

Ysaga stirred and looked at Massilili. "That would be a foolish thing," he said.

"Foolish? I won't make the mistakes I made the last time. I'll take food and water. I think I can go there and back in four or five days."

"Still it would be useless." Ysaga had an uncomfortable look on his face. "You would risk your life for no reason. Qoloq has been gone a long time."

Tanayan said, "He could be there. Living alone. Massilili could bring him back."

Ysaga avoided their faces. He stared up at the sky,

growing into blackness now. He moved his lips as if he were forming words that didn't come out. Then he looked back at Tanayan and Massilili. "Qoloq is dead," he said. "I know this to be true because I saw him die."

The others came alert, focusing on him as he continued. Massilili stiffened. He gave Ysaga a resentful stare.

"It was the day the bear clawed me. I confronted Qoloq. I asked him why he had banished me for loving Cayatu. He took my life from me, took me away from you, Cayatu. Qoloq began acting like a wild man, shouting and cursing. He pushed me, started hitting me with his fists, telling me I was part of Cayatu's plan against him. He came after me with his knife. I didn't know what to do so I pushed him away. When he looked at me there was a fire burning in him. The momoy was still with him making him crazy, I saw it in his eyes. He shouted curses at me. At you, too, Cayatu. Then, before I could act, he turned to face the chasm. He said nothing more. He spread his arms out like a bird and jumped into the air, as if he were trying to fly. He fell a long way."

Chapter Forty-Two

The courier came late in the night, reining his mount to an abrupt halt at the *Presidio* gate. He hailed the guard on the wall, demanding to be taken to the *Comandante* immediately. The sergeant on duty was reluctant, but the courier insisted it was an urgent message from the governor so the sergeant hurried across the quadrangle and knocked on the *comandancia* door. After several minutes de Alba appeared, groggy, wearing a long woolen nightgown and cap. "What is it?" he asked in a voice heavy with sleep and *aguardiente*. He took the offered envelope from the soldier's hand and pointed to a bench outside for him to wait.

Shutting the door, de Alba examined the seal pressed into the red wax. "Sola," he muttered. "That pretender." Then he slipped a long forefinger under the flap and pried it away from the seal. Taking up a candle from the table, he scanned the message. "Indians," he said aloud, and now he was fully awake.

He set the letter on the desk and dropped into the chair behind it, pulling the night cap off his head and tossing it on the table. He ran his fingers through his beard and then smoothed the hair on the back of his head. Lost in thought, he sat for several minutes before a faint smile crossed his face. "Perfect," he said. Then he got up and opened the door.

"In the morning get ten men ready to travel," he ordered the waiting sergeant.

"Yes, Lieutenant," the soldier replied. "Can I tell them the purpose?"

"We go to Monterey," de Alba said. "Full equipment and weapons. To support the governor"

The soldier saluted and started into the dark.

"Wait," de Alba called him back. "Tell the courier to wait. I'll have a message for him in a few minutes to take back to the governor. Give him food and a place to rest for an hour or so. Send our messenger to the mission. Have him tell *Padre* Ortiz to be ready to travel with us in the morning."

Closing the door again, de Alba lit several more candles. He selected a cigar and poured more brandy. He picked up a sheet of paper and took a quill pen from the inkpot. Holding the unlit cheroot in his mouth, he started to write.

Excellency,

I have received your summons. You do me the honor of allowing my men to support you in defending this land from the raiding heathens. My men and I will march immediately at full speed to your assistance. If it is God's will we will fight to the death for the king. We will not fail you.

As I join you in defense of Monterey there is another subject that brings me great trouble for which I will seek your counsel, Excellency, after the horse thieves have been defeated. I beg for your indulgence in this matter for I can do nothing without your approval, Excellency.

At Mission Santa Barbara there is a Franciscan, Padre Fermin Ortiz, who is stealing cattle from the mission herd and selling their hides and tallow to traders and whalers from other nations, even though commerce with foreigners is forbidden by His Majesty. On the one hand this is a matter for your Excellency's attention, but it is also a matter that should be brought to the Padre Presidente. Padre Ortiz will accompany me, so if you think it is an auspicious time, you might consider informing Padre Lasuen of this matter.

Your Humble Servant,
Leut. Don Jose Maria Demetrio de Alba
Comandante, Presidio de Santa Barbara

De Alba poured another glass and read the letter over several times, still smiling. He made several minor changes, then he recopied it onto a new sheet of paper and placed it in an envelope. Dripping hot candle wax on the flap, he pressed his seal into it. He went to the door where the sergeant waited, handed him the envelope and told him the courier must leave before dawn on his return trip. Back in his chair he lit the cigar and put his feet up on the desk, smiling.

So, *Padre*, this is where we part," de Alba said to Fermin Ortiz as they sat astride their horses at the junction of two trails on a hill overlooking the bay of Monterey. "You to pray with *Padre* Lasuen at San Carlos and me to fight the heathens."

"Yes, but puzzled I am about being summoned here," Ortiz responded. "I never did see the message."

"Pity." De Alba shrugged it off. "I destroyed the note after reading it as it instructed. Soon you'll know the purpose. It's just a league or so on this road in the river valley. The *Presidio* is still a good ride ahead so we'll say our goodbyes and spur our horses on, *Padre*."

Ortiz looked back at him. De Alba thought he saw a cloud drift over the priest's round face. "*Padre* Serra was wise to put so much space between fort and mission here. Would that we could have done the same in Santa Barbara," Ortiz said.

"Really, *Padre*?" De Alba gave the priest a disdainful look. "Had that been the case we might never have entered our profitable venture together. You would still be a mendicant." De Alba laughed hard but brought himself up short. "*Adios, Padre*, the governor awaits us. Pray we will not have to fight." De Alba spurred Esperanza to the head of the column of riders and waved his plumed hat as Ortiz rode off alone down the thickly wooded path.

Fermin Ortiz looked at the carved wooden doors of the basilica of Mission *San Carlos de Borroméo* and wondered what lay beyond them for him. The doors were set in a fine stone archway. Above the door a window, perhaps the finest window Ortiz had ever seen, was recessed in the wall. Formed artfully from stone hewn by Indian craftsmen, the window's frame resembled a compass with strong, carved lines at the ordinals. It sloped inward to a graceful scalloped glass, dark in the shadow of the stone. The beauty of it gave Ortiz a feeling of faintness and a tinge of jealousy.

He was greeted by an *alcalde* who led him to a courtyard surrounded by flowers and fruit trees. The *alcalde* told him to be comfortable, explaining the *Padre Presidente* would be along shortly.

But how could he be comfortable not knowing why his superior had called him to Monterey? He searched his mind for possibilities, as he had searched it on the three-day ride to get here, and could only come to the conclusion *Padre* Lasuen wanted to pay him a great compliment for his dedicated service in Santa Barbara or bestow some other honor on him. What else could it be? As he looked around the courtyard he tried to picture in his mind the courtyard he'd build for himself when he left the order. Ortiz tried the best he could to collect himself, but his feeling of excitement sent little shivers tingling the hairs on his arms.

"Brother Fermin," a voice called out from behind him. It startled Ortiz. He rose quickly and spun around to face Father Lasuen, *Presidente* of all the missions, standing there. "God granted you a safe passage to our mission?" he asked.

"Oh… yes, Father," Ortiz stammered, recovering from the shock of Lasuen's silent approach. "Safe indeed. And you, Father? God grants you good health, I pray."

"For the most part. Only when the fog drifts in do I feel my age. Come, sit. What brings you to our mission?"

Lasuen's question took Ortiz by surprise. He looked at his superior, trying to fathom what lay behind eyes sunken into his long, narrow face. Deep in the pit of his stomach, where the feeling of excitement had aroused him moments before, a small sense of worry began. His thoughts went briefly to Demetrio de Alba.

"I came at your request, Father. The *Comandante* of our *Presidio* sent a message you wanted me to accompany him here."

"Ah, I see," Lasuen said, a faint smile coming to his austere face. "Our soldier friends are having their fun at our expense, Brother Fermin. So sit, we'll talk awhile and you will tell me how things are at your mission."

The two sat on benches in the middle of the courtyard fragrant with flowers growing around a fountain. Ortiz gave Lasuen a report on the progress he and the new Franciscan were making in Santa Barbara. Lasuen listened, nodding from time to time or asking questions to elicit more detail. As they talked, the sun began to slip toward the ocean in back of the mission. Feeling safer now, Ortiz gave Lasuen much detail about life at Mission Santa Barbara.

"Now, about the cattle tallies," Lasuen said. "Brother

Peralta does his best—as Brother Salamanca, God's mercy on his soul, did before him—to explain, but still, we don't understand why your herd grows so slowly." The look Lasuen gave Ortiz was not benign. It had an edge. Ortiz saw it in the narrowing of his eyes and tightening of his lips.

"Perhaps you compare our tallies with those from other missions more conducive—"

"—Brother Fermin, it would be better if we didn't chase around this bush too long. Better if we spoke frankly with each other. Cattle have been disappearing from your mission. Do you know what is happening to them?"

"Perhaps they are straying deep into the canyons along the coast. Or through the passes to the Mission Santa Inés grazing lands."

"Brother Fermin, let me speak as plainly as I can to you." Lasuen's voice took on a sharp edge. "Cattle are missing from your herd. They don't stray and are not stolen. We have reports of bones—large piles of bones—near the beach seen by travelers coming north. Your cattle are being slaughtered. Brother Salamanca wrote us about that before he died. Now, *Comandante* de Alba reports the same thing. Both say you are the cause, so it is best if you are honest with me on this matter."

Fermin Ortiz trembled. Never before had he been caught in a lie. He felt sick in his gut that someone doubted his word, or rather felt sick that he had been found out in the lie. He gasped for breath, trying to conceal his anguish from his superior. He struggled to find words to defend himself, all the time knowing he wouldn't find any. He sat in silence, staring down at the shiny pebbles of the courtyard while Lasuen waited patiently for a response.

"I see," Lasuen said finally. "It's as the others say, isn't it, Brother Fermin?"

When Ortiz nodded, Lasuen sat absorbed in his own thoughts for what felt a very long time to Ortiz. In the silence he saw the face of Demetrio de Alba leering at him on the trail. "Our paths part here," he'd said. "...Soon you'll know the purpose." Bitterness choked in his throat, sending spasms through his body, tightening the soft muscles in his arms and legs into knots. How could this have happened? Inwardly Ortiz raged. How could he have allowed it? He had the vision, put the plan in action, made it work. He would have to deal with de Alba as soon as he got back to Santa Barbara.

Ortiz's thoughts raced to find an escape from this courtyard, from this mission and this man who controlled him too much. If he could just be back in Santa Barbara he could take the gold and silver coins he had hidden away there and flee. Start a new life with a cattle herd of his own in some place where a defrocked Franciscan might pass as just another settler. All he needed was to stand up, walk out of the courtyard, reclaim his horse and ride away. But he couldn't move. He waited for Lasuen to speak again.

When Lasuen did it was in a quiet and welcoming voice. "Brother Fermin, we have a room prepared for you here. We want you to join us for awhile. Soon, we'll have a new mission in the north, a place we've named for Saint Rafael. With your experience in mission work you'll be a great asset there. I'm sure in no time you will build it into a prosperous mission where we can train the local Indians in Christian virtues. Don't worry about your meager possessions in Santa Barbara. A benefit of being a Franciscan, don't you think? We'll have your things fetched from there and brought here. In the meantime make yourself useful. I'm sure there are chores the other Brothers would gladly share with you. The *alcalde* will show you a room. Then you can join us at dinner.

"One more thing, Brother Fermin." Lasuen got to his feet, shooting him a contemptuous look that stabbed Ortiz's heart. "Most of the missions along the coast are trading with the Bostonmen and other foreigners now. We need to do that in these difficult days in *Nueva España*. But you are the only priest among us who does so for his own profit, at the expense of his mission and his Indian neophytes. If it weren't a difficult time between Spain and *Nueva España*, I'd send you to Mexico City in chains for the thief that you are."

De Alba and his men took their time getting to their meeting place with Governor Pablo de Sola on the banks of the Salinas River. When the camp was established he sought out the governor, finding him in a tent in a triumphant mood.

"Excellency, it's good to find you happy and victorious, although I regret not getting here in time to fight. I heard the news."

"They're gone, Demetrio. The scoundrels melted back into the tules of the interior. Even if you had made haste to arrive here as I ordered and you wrote you would, you wouldn't have been in time for a fight. A pity, no? But it's good to have this chance to talk face to face. Tell the news of Santa Barbara. What is this you write about the Franciscan?"

"A great concern, Excellency. He breaks the king's law about trading with foreigners. He steals cattle from the mission to sell their hides to ships that land out of sight of my men."

Sola let out a bellowing laugh. "Come now, Demetrio. What he does to the Franciscans' cattle is no concern of ours as long as we're fed. If he breaks the royal law who suffers? It's happening at other missions."

"Oh, no, Excellency. I would not break my king's laws."

"Hmm," Sola's look showed he was already bored with the conversation. "At any rate, we have to look the other way when the missions trade for goods we no longer get from Spain. The king's grip is slipping and so are his laws. Soon *Nueva España* may gain its independence." Sola stopped, then gave de Alba a smirking smile. "I hear the women of Santa Barbara are some of the fairest in all of Alta California. I hear they have fine frocks and pretty ribbons for their hair. Do we accuse the priest of glorifying the women by himself?" Sola laughed again. "I think not. Be careful, Demetrio. Don't be too precious in your words or your actions. Someone will find you out. In any case, I passed your message to Lasuen. The Franciscans can wash their own laundry, no? I suspect that was your intent in the first place."

Chapter Forty-Three

The crows crowding the treetops surrounding the *lavandería*, watched the women kneeling at the stone basin scrubbing their families' clothes. They cawed back and forth, fluttering and hopping from branch to branch as each new bird flew in to disrupt their pecking order. The morning air was sharp and still. The musty smell of desiccating fields hung heavy over the mission. It was the unique smell that comes just before the rains begin when the land lies barren and the warm, dry summer days have turned sour. In an instant the birds took flight, climbing high and circling overhead.

The abrupt noise of their departure startled Cayatu. She set down a wet *camisa* she was beating against the side of the basin and looked up to see the trees begin to sway. A low rumbling sound started from deep within the earth. The ground beneath her began swaying with the trees. The shaking started slowly but grew and kept growing, growing sharper, growing more violent. The wide-eyed women looked at each other and began to scream.

A sound, like the moaning of a high wind, grew with the heaving of the land around her. Still on her knees, Cayatu could only watch as the mission church began to sway

slowly at first, right to left, then back, left to right, gaining
momentum. Small cracks opened on the adobe walls. Like
spider webs, they crept across the face of the buildings,
growing larger as they progressed, peeling off the thin skin
covering the building's adobe bricks. Other cracks opened
in the ground around her, opening then closing just as
suddenly. The water in the *lavandería* rocked from end to
end, splashing over the sides and soaking the front of her
blouse. A fissure in the earth directly under it opened,
splitting the basin in two so the water gushed out and
melted into the ground.

Women screamed trying to rise and run to their huts, but
the violent shaking tossed them about like leaves in a wind,
pitching them back to the ground. They hugged the earth
and cried their fear. Cayatu tried to get to her feet, thinking
of Ysaga and Massilili, thinking she had to get them all
together if they were going to survive the destruction First
People were raining down on them. On wobbly legs she
stood, holding the *camisas* and trousers she'd been
scrubbing. She took one tentative step toward the *ranchería*.
Then another. Then she was thrown down like the others,
unable to move. Coyote is having his revenge, she thought.

Massilili was far up the canyon when the shaking started.
He was working with other men placing heavy stones to
build the mission dam higher. With the others, he sweated
in the dry heat of the canyon. He stood up straight to steady
himself, thinking at first some dizziness had come over
him, maybe some small trick of mischief from a lurking
creature from the World Below. Then Massilili saw the
terrified faces of the other men. They all stood still, like the
stones around them, staring into the high mountains
already disappearing behind a giant dust curtain blotting
out the sun.

Through the dust, Massilili saw rocks and boulders crashing down, crushing shrubs and trees as if they were tules, crushing everything in their path. Here and there he could make out animals fleeing the onslaught of rocks. He saw a mountain lion lead two cubs along a trail he knew well, desperate to find a safe place for her brood. This is our punishment, he thought. We didn't listen to Qoloq. Now the serpents who hold up the Middle World are showing us their anger.

When he turned back he saw the face of the dam began to quiver, he shouted to the other men, "Jump. Get away from the dam."

The ground continued to roll. It was a storm-tossed ocean of earth growing angrier second by second. The big rocks in the dam slipped back and forth, left to right, shifting in unison, straining against each other. One small rock fell into the stream. It left a little hole where a trickle of water started. Another rock fell and the trickle became a gush. Then another and the gush was a torrent, racing down the canyon. Massilili watched the gap widen as stone by stone the dam tore itself apart. It's all lost, he thought. All we've built is gone.

Massilili found a safe place, clinging to a slender sycamore on higher ground. He motioned to the others to find safety. They did and watched, their mouths agape, as the dam broke apart. When it collapsed altogether, a cataclysm of water surged out. Massilili saw a body clad in the fragments of a leather jacket, wash over the lip and disappear downstream to the ocean.

Inside the mission, Father Rogelio Tapia, the crippled new missionary who had come to replace Fermin Ortiz, grabbed his crutch as the shaking began. He hobbled out the door of his cubicle and away from the building amid a rain of falling roof tiles as fast as his withered leg would allow. He got only a few feet from the veranda before he was tossed to the ground like an empty flour sack. Looking back he watched the building tremble, as if it knew its life was being snuffed out and it was grieving. Wooden posts that held up the veranda roof shook loose and fell. The roof crumpled, followed by a deluge of adobe bricks.

In horror, Tapia watched cracks running along the ground open and close on either side of him like giant jaws gnawing tough food. One opened a dozen yards in front of the church and crept toward it, stopping halfway up the front steps. The steps parted in both directions, tossed aside by an invisible hand.

Then, as Tapia continued to lie on the ground, praying for mercy, the cross atop the roof slumped. The roof crumbled inward, knocking the walls out as it did. Suddenly he was looking inside the church from the ground where he lay. He watched statues fall off the altar and smash on the floor. "God deliver us," he prayed. "Save the church we've worked so hard to build in your name. Save these Indian children who depend on us for their sustenance."

Just my miserable fate, Demetrio de Alba thought as he watched the *Presidio* walls falling around him. He could hear the wooden palisades splintering like firewood amid the stronger sounds of the rupturing earth. Wooden roof beams and building frames shattered around him as if they were small sticks. He crawled to the middle of the parade ground where he could only watch his fort twisting apart. I shouldn't be here, he complained. I should be in Mexico City. Better still, Andalusia. *I will not die here, so help me God.* I'll survive this horror.

But his *Presidio* was not going to survive. As de Alba watched, hot coals from cooking fires rolled about and danced through the air like fireflies, landing in piles of sticks, and logs and roof thatch. Flames sprung up and spread from building to building until an inferno blazed around him. Like an animal, he crawled out the open gates, unable to stand, unable to do anything to stop the conflagration.

When the tremors weakened some, de Alba rose and careened along with other soldiers fleeing into the *pueblo*, dodging pieces of brick that fell from all directions as they tore loose from the walls of houses. People huddled on the ground, protecting each other from the falling debris and de Alba pushed them aside as he tried to find a safe space. De Alba knew the flames from the fort would race through the town soon enough, but he cared only for his own safety.

As if in a daze, he looked toward the beach, wishing for a ship to sail him away from this purgatory. Two small coastal schooners anchored in the roadstead were careening wildly, still tethered to their cables so that they pitched like wild horses as waves tossed them about. One snapped loose in the roiling waters as de Alba watched. Waves pushed it shoreward until it rested on a sandbar and rolled on its side, like a beached whale.

The other ship, still anchored, was unable to stand the strain of the heavy waves. It rolled to one side until its twin masts were parallel with the water, pointing at the beach. It hung there for several moments. Then the schooner succumbed to the waves beating against its exposed hull and rolled farther until its decks were awash and everything that had been on them bobbed about in the surf.

The shaking was not as intense in *Cañyon de Corral*. Josefa's new house swayed, showing small cracks in the adobe, but stayed together. The dust cloud Massilili and the others had seen, hung like a beige blanket along the entire front of the Santa Inés Mountains. Josefa stood in the doorway, watching, transfixed for a time by the shaking ground and rolling trees, fearful, but unsure about what to do. Above the sounds of grinding earth, she heard another, more mournful sound. It confused her, scared her, too. She searched for its source, finally seeing the cattle coming together in bunches on the hillsides, moaning as they moved down the slope toward her. Startled back to action by the thought of Delfina, she raced inside the adobe. She took the sleeping girl from her bed, grabbed the icon of the Virgin of Guadalupe from a table, and raced back outside. Josefa stopped in the yard and sunk to her knees in prayer, still serenaded by the lu-luing of a thousand steers. On her knees, she saw the ocean begin a retreat from the beach, leaving a broad strand of pebbles and sand where fish flopped about in puddles. After a long time of pulling back, the water surged back in a series of waves, not high, but relentless ones pushing onto the beach and climbing up the draw between the hills, coming on and on until she thought the valley would flood. "Holy Mother," Josefa prayed, "I've come so far. Don't let me die. Keep your daughter Josefa and her baby Delfina safe from the destruction around us."

The water surged half a league inland up the gradually rising valley, then, having spent its fury, it started its return to the ocean in a rush, taking with it a hundred head of cattle that were never again seen or accounted for.

In the *ranchería*, men and women sat dazed among the rubble of their tumbled down adobes. A few—only a few—clutched children to their breasts, others sat like the statues that had been on the altar, staring vacantly at the destruction around them. Some moaned or howled their anguish. Dust hung in the air, catching in people's throats and blurring their sight. Ysaga watched from in front of the hut he shared with Cayatu—Tomas's old hut— holding a bloody rag to his forehead.

"Oh, no," Cayatu cried out, seeing him there as she stumbled through the rubble.

"It's nothing," he reassured her. "A chunk of brick hit me when a wall collapsed."

She wrapped a clean rag around his head and they sat together, silent, like the others.

Accompanied by two other dam builders, Massilili arrived shortly after.

"Everything's in ruins," he called out, coming toward them."

"We were at the dam," one of the men with him broke in. "It's gone. The water ran out. A body swept away."

Adraino, the other man, looked down at the ground. "An awful lot of work to rebuild, I think. The *padres* will keep us very busy."

They built a small fire, like others in the neophyte village, but there was no water and no food. Their blankets were buried in the rubble so they huddled close to the fire and close to each other for warmth. Cayatu dug through the ruins with her hands searching for food or things she could salvage. She rescued a few utensils and some clothes. She kept on digging until she recovered her shell basket buried in the dust and debris.

During the night the earth rumbled again several more times. Each time they doused the flames with handfuls of dirt. Other fires burned out of control in the Chumash village and crumbled mission buildings. The night sky over Santa Barbara was bright with flames burning in the *Presidio* and *pueblo*, lighting it like orange dawn. When dawn came the scene of devastation overwhelmed them. The air was heavy with choking smoke and dust. The sun shining through it cast a deadly pall over everything.

Chapter Forty-Four

They're rebuilding on our backs," Massilili mumbled. "On my back."

He stood bent over in a field east of the *Presidio* where men and women were making new adobe bricks and roof tiles in a mud pit. Bricks and tiles already dried in the sun were laid out along the ground. He loaded a tile in each of two buckets attached to a yoke across his shoulders and carried them back to the fort, straining under the weight. At the fort, he unloaded the tiles for workers who were putting on new roofs. On his return trip to the mud pit he filled his buckets with water from a stream running near the *Presidio*.

The sun beat on his back and the weight of the yoke cut into his shoulders but he continued the trips with tiles and water into the afternoon. He'd been chosen as a tile carrier, along with Adraino and two other men, because they were stronger than the others. Every morning, they worked rebuilding the mission buildings and from midday until dark, they worked at the *Presidio*, carrying tiles and bricks from the pit and water to keep the mud flowing.

Massilili knew he and the other mission Chumash worked at both mission and fort because *Comandante* de

Alba told the Franciscans he couldn't hire enough laborers in the village to rebuild fast enough to protect the *pueblo*. The priests, eager to rebuild their mission, had no choice, sending Massilili and others to work at the *Presidio* each day, telling them it would only be for a short time.

He dumped his buckets of water into the foul-smelling pit where men and women stood knee deep in mud, filling wooden forms for bricks. Other women brought bundles of straw to mix into the mud.

Straightening up, Massilili saw Adraino coming up behind him. He could see the weight of the buckets dragging the yoke down into Adraino's shoulders, pushing his whole body down so his knees were bent and on the verge of giving out.

"Take a rest, friend," Massilili called out to him and walked the few steps to his side.

"How much longer?" Adraino asked. "Each day is a new torture for me."

"And no end in sight," Massilili answered. "You need to take lighter loads, Adraino, or you'll be crippled soon enough."

"Remember how we fished?" Adraino said, halting to set the yoke down and rest, letting a far off look come over his face. "When we lived on the shore we were the men the other villagers looked up to. We were strong. We could paddle all day without tiring and land the biggest fish. The young women brought us food and fought for just a smile. I wish I could go back to those days."

"Tonight we'll go to the canyon," Massilili answered to console him. "There'll be a full moon and I'll dance. Coyote of the Sky and Evening Star will see our dance. Perhaps they'll bring back those days if our dance is strong enough."

Both men loaded new tiles into their baskets and began the walk back to the fort. Massilili stayed close to his friend, watching his steps shorten under the weight of the buckets. On the return trip to the mud pit, Massilili emptied his buckets and took the yoke off his shoulders in order to help Adraino. As he approached to pour his buckets into the pit, Adraino staggered. His legs gave out and he fell face down into the pit.

Some of the men and women near him in the pit laughed as they watched Adraino flop around in the mud, unable to find his footing. His arms flailed, flinging muddy water everywhere as he sought something to grab on to. They called him a pig and made oinking sounds as he floundered. Their laughter faded away when they saw he couldn't get to his feet, lying exhausted, covered head to toe in dark mud, choking on it.

Massilili jumped into the pit. Wrapping his arms around his friend's chest, he lifted him upright and pulling him out. He laid him down on the bank. The brick makers looked on in stunned silence as Adraino, desperate for breath, choked on the mud. Massilili looked for some way to help but he could only stand by helplessly as the choking continued. Then it stopped.

Everyone stopped work and turned to stare at Adraino who lay still on the ground, color drained from his face, his eyes rolled into the back of his head. A murmur went between them, spreading from man to woman throughout the length of the pit. Massilili dropped beside his friend, shaking his arm gently as if to awaken him from a long sleep. "Tonight you'll dance in the canyon with me," he urged his friend. "Wake up."

"What is going on here?" Demetrio de Alba rode up unnoticed on Esperanza, accompanied by his sergeant. "Why aren't you men working?"

The brick makers turned away, shrinking back to their work with somber faces. Massilili looked up from the ground to the mounted man. "He's dead," he told the *Comandante*. "His legs gave out from the heavy loads he was carrying. He fell in the pit and choked."

"Heavy? Not that heavy," de Alba said, seeming to take no notice of the dead man. "Life at the mission has made you soft. These loads aren't too heavy for men to carry, for women maybe."

Massilili felt the sting of de Alba's insult. He responded, "If these loads aren't too heavy, why don't your soldiers carry the water and bricks? Maybe they're weak like women."

De Alba fixed his stare on Massilili. "Who are you, big man?" he asked.

Massilili stared back and said his name.

"Don't you have a Christian name?" de Alba demanded.

Massilili didn't answer. He just kept his eyes on the *Comandante*. He stood half covered with mud, unflinching.

De Alba's pale face grew red under his beard. His eyes narrowed, still focused on Massilili. He spoke in a low, sneering tone. "You question my men?" he said. "You speak with disrespect? And disrespect for the king's soldiers?" He drew his sword from its scabbard. "I could kill you here for that insult." His words were spit on the ground, as if he were laying down a challenge.

Massilili stared steadily at de Alba, whose drawn sword caught the sun and flashed sparks. "The man is dead," he said. "Can't you see it?"

"I see it," de Alba replied. He turned to his sergeant. "Get a cart to haul the body back to the mission."

Massilili raised his eyes, looking past de Alba toward the mountains. Not far up the trail, just a short way off, he saw the mountain cat again, pacing back and forth in front of her cubs, looking in his direction. Massilili's eyes went to the *Comandante*, then back to the cat. She stopped her pacing and returned his look. Their eyes locked on each other briefly.

No one else saw the cat, all eyes were fixed on de Alba's sword, wavering in the air, and at Massilili who stood anchored to the ground.

"We do your work," Massilili said, breaking the silence.

"And you kill us with it." He pointed down at Adraino's mud-encrusted body.

De Alba turned to his sergeant. "The Indian thinks we're lazy. He thinks he's stronger than we are. He doesn't understand we could be attacked any time. We're defenseless until the fort is complete; pirates or these Indians could destroy us. We can't have it. Look at the other diggers in the mud. They watch to see what I'll do. Throw a rope on him. I'll show them who rules this land. I'll show the priests while I'm at it."

The sergeant dismounted and approached Massilili with a rope he took from his saddle. Massilili didn't flinch, still watching the mountain cat that sat in the field, staring back at him while her cubs played safely beside her. He didn't move when the sergeant dropped the rope over his head and fastened it around his waist and then handed the other end to de Alba.

Massilili had to trot the whole way up the hill to keep up. He was gasping for breath when the *Comandante* reined Esperanza to a stop in front of the mission. A crowd of neophytes began to gather. Summoned by the *alcalde*, the priests came down the veranda wearing shocked expressions. They implored de Alba to let Massilili go but the lieutenant told them to stand back. "This man is a troublemaker," he said to Father Peralta. "We can't have that. There are too many of them and not enough of us to allow their disrespect. They would destroy us if they got the upper hand."

De Alba spurred his horse forward and Massilili ran along in back until they were beside the wooden cross that stood on the edge of the hill. He dismounted and pushed Massilili against the cross, spreading his arms out along the arms of the cross and lashing his hands securely.

Massilili turned to look at the crowd that had formed behind him. He saw Cayatu, pale and shaking, pushing to get to the front. Ysaga limped behind her.

"No," she shouted, seeing him tied to the cross.

Demetrio de Alba dismounted and took his whip from behind the saddle. Uncoiling it he walked back from the cross.

"Stop!" Cayatu cried. She broke out of the crowd and ran to her nephew. She reached out her arms and embraced his back, shielding it from the lieutenant.

Over his shoulder, Massilili saw de Alba grab Cayatu.

"Out of the way, woman, or I'll flog you, too," de Alba said, flinging her aside. Then he stepped back and swung the whip over his head, unleashing its hatred in one continuous motion, like a striking rattlesnake. The lash slammed into Massilili's shoulder, biting deep. Massilili shuddered from the force of the blow and the sting of the tip. As de Alba withdrew the rawhide lash, blood rushed to fill the deep cut it had made in the raw flesh. Massilili gripped the cross tightly, preparing for the next blow that came quickly as the *Comandante* found his rhythm and put his whole strength behind it. In rapid order the whip splayed across his back, knifing deep cuts and slicing strips of skin with each stroke. He felt faint. He knew he couldn't endure these knife-like blows for long.

De Alba paused to catch his breath and calm himself.

Cayatu sobbed and tried to get to Massilili but the *mayordomo* blocked her path and grabbed her in his arms to pull her away.

Massilili saw it all through eyes grown dull, but he stood as straight as the flailed skin on his back would allow. He turned to the crowd. "Fight them," he called out, "fight them all." He shouted in the strongest voice he could find, "They are killing our children, killing us all."

Chapter Forty-Five

Andres, the new *alcalde,* hurried through the *ranchería* calling out as he went from hut to hut, "We're looking for Massilili. This man brings news from Mission Santa Inés, important news."

Cayatu looked up. Ysaga got to his feet, but Massilili stayed on the ground, carving on a stick of wood with his knife.

"What news?" she asked.

"We'll tell it to Massilili," the *alcalde* said.

"Say what you came to say," Massilili told them. "It makes no difference to me. I have no secrets."

Andres and another man hunkered down next to him. "A man was whipped at Santa Inés by a guard for a crime he didn't do," the *alcalde* said.

"The priest did nothing to stop the whipping so we captured him," the messenger added. "We locked the priest in a storeroom. Fighting started.We killed a guard and now we control the mission."

"Revolt?" Massilili questioned the runner. "Why bring that news to me?"

Andres gave him a knowing look. "We know your feelings toward the foreigners," he said. "I thought you would join with me to lead our people."

"True enough, I hate them, but why should I care what they do at Santa Inés?" he charged. "What business of mine?"

"We must act together," the messenger said. "We want all Chumash to fight together to destroy these Spaniards—priests and soldiers and townspeople—who have enslaved us."

"—Fine for you," Ysaga interrupted, moving closer to stand above the trio. "We know harsh treatment here too, but why should we do anything?"

"Wait," Massilili said, giving Ysaga a disdainful look then turning back to the *alcalde*. "Perhaps this is something."

"No!" Cayatu rose to stand beside Ysaga. She place her hands on Massilili's shoulders. "Let the people at Santa Inés fight their own foreigners."

"You're right, Aunt," Massilili reached up to take Cayatu's hands in his, "but this may be an opportunity for us."

The runner shifted restlessly, watching the others talk. After listening awhile he rose and pulled himself to his full height. "Our leaders told me to say to you if you don't help us, we'll attack you when we've beaten the foreigners."

"Don't dare to threaten," Massilili said, rising to confront the messenger. His voice was controlled but it held an edge. "We'll do what's best for us. In the end we'd lose a fight, and you will too, but perhaps there's another way." He turned to the *alcalde*. "Do what you want, Andres, but I say call the people together and we'll see what anger they have."

Massilili and the others waited while Andres went through the *ranchería* calling everyone to the front of the mission. When most had gathered, he explained what had happened at Santa Inéz. The people reacted intensely to the news. Massilili saw some shaking their fists. Murmurs passed through the crowd—"we're slaves," one man shouted, and "we'll be killed if we fight," another countered.

Cayatu saw *Padre* Tapia limping toward them from his cubicle at the front of the mission. She was startled to see Josefa trailing behind him, holding Delfina by the hand. "What's this about?" Tapia asked in his quiet voice when he came up to the group.

His face turned pale as Andres spoke. "I heard this morning," Tapia told the crowd. "Surely you won't join them."

The response was mixed. Men and women milled around, breaking into smaller groups, arguing and shouting at each other.

"Quiet!" Massilili shouted above all the other sounds to silence them. "Listen to me," he shouted again to command their attention. "Those of you who say it isn't our fight are right. It's not. The people at Santa Inés can do what they choose. But listen to me. Their fight gives us strength we didn't have before. Soldiers will go from the *Presidio* to Santa Inés. They're spread out. Now is the time to show them our own strength."

"Good God, what will you do?" Tapia asked.

Massilili looked straight at the priest. "We'll protect ourselves," he said, a mix of anger and disdain rising in his voice. "More than you do for us! You do nothing. You're powerless to stop the soldiers. You don't protect our women—look how many have been assaulted. Look how many of us have felt the whip. You and Padre Peralta—all you Franciscans—are powerless."

"What would you have me do to avoid a fight?" Tapia said, wringing his hands together.

Massilili answered, "You can do nothing for us unless you stand up to *Comandante* de Alba. Go to the *Presidio*. Make him come here to talk with us. We'll tell him ourselves what he must do to avoid a fight. Go to the fort— bring de Alba back with you."

Cayatu edged away from the group and went to Josefa, who stood with the little girl off to the side, near the church steps.

"You shouldn't be here," she told Josefa.

"I came to pray with the priest," Josefa said with a hint of anger in her voice. She gave Cayatu a questioning glance.

"I mean it might not be safe for you and the girl," Cayatu said, putting her hand on Josefa's arm. "Chumash at Santa Inés are fighting—"

"—I know," Josefa interrupted. "Demetrio told me. He sent men there. Will you fight?"

"I hope not, but you and Delfina would be safer away from here." Cayatu knelt down beside the girl, reaching out to touch her soft face with the color and smoothness of doeskin and stroke her dark hair. "You grow so quickly," she said to Delfina. "Our children are dead but you grow more beautiful each day."

The little girl smiled back but stayed quiet. Cayatu turned back to Josefa and saw the look in her eyes but ignored it. "It's been a long time since we saw each other, Josefa, and now she grows so fast."

"She's a handful, Clare, over three years old now," Josefa said, relaxing just a little. "I miss you, *mi amiga*. These last years since the earthquake and revolution in Mexico have been bad ones for us. The *pueblo* isn't the friendly place it once was. I still call you my friend, and I still want you with me at my home in the canyon, but others in the *pueblo* are angry. Come live out in the canyon with me and we can escape the anger."

"I'd like that," Cayatu said, holding Delfina's small hand in her own, studying her fine features.

She wondered how she could ever have been scared of this beautiful child. The girl returned Cayatu's smile, showing the round fullness of her baby face, but shuffled her feet, impatient for her mother to walk with her.

"I can't leave my men," Cayatu said finally.

"Men?" Josefa raised her eyebrows.

"My husband and nephew. Ysaga walks with a stick, like the priest. He needs me to help him."

"Your husband, the *vaquero*?"

"No, Josefa, Tomas died from the diphtheria two years ago. I had a baby boy who also died. Ysaga is a man from my old village."

"I'm sorry for you." Josefa embraced Cayatu. She held her for a moment, then backed away. "We could care for your men together. Find chores for them in the canyon, Clare. Please come live there with us."

"The missionaries won't let Massilili live so far away and I fear for him living alone here, Josefa. His wife and son died from the disease. He's a sullen man, an angry man now since he was whipped." Cayatu's eyes searched Josefa's face for a reaction. "He speaks little and broods much of the time, carving little boats out of wood, like the ones he used to make for his son."

Josefa shook her head, her lips pursed tightly. "Demetrio has a mean streak, I know that well myself. Best to stay away from him when he's in one of his moods."

Cayatu smiled at her friend. "I miss you, Josefa. You were the first in the *pueblo* to be my friend. You taught me your words and told about how you live. But now, it isn't safe for you here."

"Not safe for you either, Clare." The look on Josefa's face turned sad. "Things have changed since we first drank chocolate together. Many of my people resent you now. We have our own revolution, you know. The ships don't come anymore. The people in the *pueblo* grow poorer day by day. And angrier. There isn't enough food. The soldiers are starving, Demetrio says, and they blame it on the missionaries who give you too much. It isn't a happy time for any of us. Be careful my friend."

Chapter Forty-Six

So, they want *me* to come to them, is that what you're telling me, *Padre*?" Demetrio de Alba glared at Rogelio Tapis standing face to face with him in the *comandancia*.

"The faster we get back to the mission, the better chance we have to stop a revolt," The priest replied.

"You think so, do you?"

Tapis felt the arrogance in de Alba's voice knife into him but he stood his ground, looking squarely into the stone-hard eyes of the *comandante*. De Alba towered over him, but Tapis kept one hand on his cane, the other behind his gray robe clenched into a fist. His face was impassive.

"What right do your Indians have to summon me, eh? And what right do you have coming down here demanding my presence at your mission? I'm still the governor's representative here, not you. I still speak for him. You have no right to order me." De Alba turned his back on the priest and walked to the window, staring out over the parade grounds.

Tapis took a deep breath de Alba didn't see. "With respect, *Comandante*, the time for posturing is past. You don't intimidate me with your rank. No one questions your authority, but how we act now can prevent bloodshed. You need to bargain with the neophytes."

"Bargain?!" De Alba thundered, turning back from the window. "There is no bargaining to be done. We need your Indians to go back to work."

"Lieutenant, it's the way your soldiers and the Mexicans in the *pueblo* have treated them that has brought us to this terrible day. They complain your men are lazy."

"Lazy?"

Tapis saw the anger twist de Alba's face.

"What can you expect," de Alba said, lowering his voice. "My men haven't been paid. Look at their uniforms—ragged. Their families live in poverty. Without the food your mission grows, they'd starve. And it's hardly enough."

"And yet you treat our neophytes rudely," Tapis said with bitterness in his voice. Behind his placid exterior he was working hard to keep the fire that was raging within him from showing. "Ever since the earthquake, they've been asked to work too much for you."

"Ever since the revolution, you mean. My men hate your Indians, *Padre*, did you know that? They see them living better at your mission than they do. They don't think Indians ought to live better."

"They don't? Or is it you who doesn't, *Comandante?* We're no better off than you are, yet you place all the burden for food and clothing on us."

De Alba didn't answer. He went back to staring out his window. Tapis watched him finger his beard, then run his hand down the back of his head and neck.

De Alba turned back from the window once more and moved across the room to sit at his desk. "I don't think I should go to them," he said, calming down and looking at Tapis standing in front of him. "If I go, they might think we're weak. Look how they outnumber us, Rogelio. We could never control them."

"Demetrio, they have only requested to talk with you. If

they'd wanted to join the Santa Inés band, they could already have done so. "This is the time to talk with them in order to prevent a fight," the Franciscan urged. "They'll abide our rules if they're promised fair treatment."

"Still, it's a dangerous thing. They could capture me the way they captured the priest at *Santa Inés*. I wish I had word from the governor telling me his wishes on the matter. I remember when I was garrisoned outside Mexico City, Rogelio. We had superior officers nearby to tell us our orders. To take on the responsibility."

"Did you fight battles in *Nueva España*, Demetrio?"

"No, never. It was a good life there. If I do the wrong thing here, my career will be over. Already I've changed my allegiance. Now, this Indian revolt starts at one of my missions and who can say what the governor will do to me. If I could, I'd leave Santa Barbara tonight. I'd sail on any ship that would have me and leave this terrible land to you."

Tapia studied de Alba for several moments without speaking, studying his eyes and the tight set of his jaw for the information he was seeking. "That time has passed, too, Demetrio," he said finally. "We must face up to our responsibilities. You and me both. God commands us to be the guardians of these peoples, not their oppressors. I've looked in my heart and see that we've mistreated them. I pray, and a voice answers I should've been stronger in standing up to you. But I can't undo. We have to go forward, and that means you must meet with the neophytes. We should start now."

"In *Nueva España* we didn't have decisions like this to make." De Alba was once again up and moving to his window. Tapis followed his gaze and saw several soldiers moving about the parade ground. "We had an easy life," he said. "We had good food and drink. The women were friendly and there were no battles. But here, on this forgotten frontier..."

De Alba went to the door, opened it and called out to his

sergeant. "Jose, get my horse ready. Get a detail of ten to go to the mission. Have them bring their weapons—lances and muskets. We'll go immediately."

He turned back into the room and reached for his sword belt to buckle around his waist. Then he picked up his flintlock pistol from the corner of his desk and stuffed it into his sash.

"Demetrio," Rogelio Tapis said, limping over to stand directly in front of the commander, "this is not a good idea. Go unarmed to the mission. Leave your men here. You'll frighten my Indians if you take armed soldiers with you." He paused and then pleaded, "In God's name leave them here."

De Alba hardened his eyes again so Tapis finally saw the real emotion in them. "Frighten them we will," he said. "We can't let them have an advantage over us, can we, *Padre*?"

As Massilili and the others watched from the hilltop, the party of soldiers started the short journey from the *Presidio,* but the situation among the watchers had changed. They were no longer disorganized. First, the *alcalde*, Andres, ordered the women and children to gather up a few possessions and go into the canyon past the mission dam to wait.

"I will not go with them," Cayatu said, returning to the group after Josefa departed with the child. "My place is here and I'll stand with you."

Ysaga tried to change her mind but saw it was futile. Massilili judged it not worth trying.

As the solemn procession of women marched down the path into the canyon, Andres told several of the older men to take whatever food was necessary from the storerooms to accompany the women, but under no condition were they to touch the wine or *aguardiente*. Then he told a few of the younger men to get their bows and arrows and for the field workers to get their knives.

"Not a good thing to do," Massilili warned him.

"No, not a good thing," Andres agreed, "but necessary to protect ourselves."

"The soldiers will be on their guard when they see the weapons."

"Massilili, look how the sun glints off the barrels of their muskets as they ride. It's like it's always been—they'll come to show us how strong they are. You see, the *Comandante* brings men with him. Our only chance is to show them we have strength, too."

The Chumash men stood in a tight knot, waiting to confront the soldiers. They spoke in hushed voices or spoke not at all, watching the progress of the mounted men. Massilili paced off to the side, away from the group. He stood looking out over the *pueblo* at the aquamarine ocean, thinking how meaningless this all was. He thought about Dolores and Asunción and Adraino—all gone, so many others gone, too—Qoloq driven mad. He looked at the islands hovering on the edge of his world and wished he was there now trading acorns for arrow points. He shrugged, as if to clear himself of a weight on his back, throwing off his thoughts, and returned to the group as twelve horsemen breasted the hill and reined to a halt. He moved easily through the others, who parted for him, until he stood with Cayatu and Ysaga in the front rank.

For a few moments there was silence. De Alba let Esperanza prance from side to side, showing off the horse's power. *Padre* Tapis dismounted and separated from the soldiers, standing off to the side between the two groups. Massilili studied the looks on the soldiers' faces. He saw tough men, weather-hardened from their outdoor life, but thin and mean-looking.

"Disband." The single word coming from de Alba's lips sounded more like a curse than a command. His eyes swept over the Chumash and their weapons. Massilili saw a look that chilled him to his core.

"Disband," the command came again. "There is no reason for you to confront us with weapons. My men have not harmed you and we don't want to fight. But we will fight if you give us reason. Your *padre*"—he gave Tapis a disdainful stare—"says you would talk with me. Talk now and then return to your homes and put away your weapons."

Andres stepped ahead of the others. "We'll talk with you, *Comandante*. And you'll stay until you've heard us out." Andres forcefulness sent a ripple of words through the two groups of men confronting each other. "We don't want a fight any more than you do," he continued, "but if it's to be a fight we'll win. So listen to me when I say you must order your men to treat us with respect."

De Alba waited a moment before speaking. "All right, I've heard you," he said. He waited a moment longer then spat on the ground in front of him. He put his hand on the hilt of his sword. "Now put down your weapons and return to your homes," he barked. "Tomorrow I'll expect you to return to your work. I'll take my whip to any who do not. Understand?"

In the silence that followed—while the soldiers and their Spanish leader confronted the Chumash men, and the Chumash men stared incredulously at Demetrio de Alba—Massilili saw an arrow come from somewhere off to the side, floating through the air like a sparrow, looking for a safe place to land. It bounced harmlessly off the leather-covered shoulder of a soldier. The man pulled his mount back, more in surprise than from the force of the arrow. The other soldiers pulled back too.

Massilili searched the group for the bowman, but couldn't find him.

Andres shouted to his men, urging them to pull back. They retreated a step.

De Alba turned in his saddle, aiming back down the hill

as his men backed off farther.

Then another arrow took flight. This one nested in a soldier's leg. He shouted his pain. The soldiers turned back to face the Indians. No order was given but several muskets fired with muzzle flashes and loud reports. The smell of powder fouled the clear afternoon air. Stunned by their own actions, the soldiers turned and started down the hill toward the protection of their fort. Another arrow found a home in the flank of a fleeing horse.

Massilili stood dazed as a few of the neophytes started to pursue the soldiers down the hill. They stopped when they realized some of their comrades were wounded. Three men had fallen when the muskets fired. Blood soaked the ground beside them. Ysaga lay unmoving.

Chapter Forty-Seven

Horror engulfing her at the sight of the gaping hole the musket ball had ripped in his chest, Cayatu dropped to her knees beside Ysaga. Blood spurted from the wound with each heart beat. Ysaga was alive, but unconscious.

Massilili knelt beside her, encircling her in his arms while she cried over the body. His kiss brushed her hair and he held it there for a moment. Cayatu could feel him trembling as he hugged her to his chest. Then, abruptly, he stood and called to the men milling about.

"It's started," he shouted. "There'll be more fighting if we stay here, fighting we'll lose because of the soldiers' leather and muskets. I say we take food and go into the canyon with the others. We can wait there and watch what the soldiers do."

The men listened. As if coming awake from a dream, they nodded agreement and began clustering around him. They shouted questions.

"Will we ever come back?" one asked.

"Should we kill the priests?" shouted another.

"Can we take our old people?" from a third.

In turn, Massilili answered each: "It could be a very hard time. I've been in the mountains. If we have to go there, I'll lead you."

The men accepted Massilili as their new leader. After giving more instructions, he knelt beside Cayatu again.

"Ysaga's badly hurt, Aunt. I don't think he'll live if we carry him to the canyon."

"Carry him back to our hut," she begged Massilili. "I can tend his wound there. We'll come to join you when he can travel. Help me, Massilili. Hurry. Please." Deep in her heart, Cayatu felt pain. Tomas already gone and Ysaga slipping away. The hollow spot in her heart where all the love she had for her men was safely hidden away, ached beyond her ability to endure. She stayed limp on her knees.

Massilili motioned to two men who carried Ysaga to the *rancheria*. He lifted Cayatu and held her tightly against him as they followed. After the other men had laid Ysaga on his sleeping mat, Massilili held her at arm's length and looked down into her tear-stained eyes.

"Ysaga won't live, Cayatu. I'm sorry. Come with us. We'll see what the next days bring, but I think we'll never come back. We'll go to the big valley near the lake you used to talk about. We'll live out our lives there. I want you with me. We are alone now."

"I can't," Cayatu cried out her pain, "not now. Not until Ysaga can travel with us. I can't leave him." She sobbed against Massilili's shoulder. "Stay here with me, Massilili," she begged. "When he's better we'll go together to the big lake."

Massilili held her tightly while grief wracked her body so hard she knew she'd collapse if he let her go. For a long time he held her in silence as she grieved, then, slowly, he withdrew his arms. He stood, and when she looked up at him she saw the dullness in his eyes replaced by a rekindled fire.

"I can't stay," he said, his voice cracking as he choked out the words. "To stay here is to die—the mission destroys us. Our only chance is finding a new place far from the Franciscans and the soldiers. My heart breaks to leave you." The words caught in his throat. Tears slid down his cheeks. "I love you, Cayatu. My life will be bitter without you. I lost you once when you left the village. Now I'm losing you again."

Once more, Massilili embraced her and lifted her chin so that they looked into each other's eyes. He kissed her and then backed away. "Stay with your husband, I understand, but I go with the others…"

Cayatu turned her back on Massilili to tend Ysaga's wound. She sensed he stood a few minutes longer in the doorway watching her. Then he went out, shouting instructions to the men.

Ysaga fought for life, but the flow of blood from the sucking wound in his chest couldn't be stopped. It slowed to a sticky ooze, bubbling and foaming with air as he tried to breath. The cloths Cayatu bound around his chest were useless, soon soaked through. Ysaga wasn't conscious but delirious words formed on his parched lips. There was no breath to give them sound. She soothed him with cool water, and kept a constant vigil at his side. Deep in the night he took his last gasping, sucking breath. His eyes opened for an instant, then he died.

The night held an eerie stillness—no sounds came from the empty huts in the abandoned *ranchería*. As the sky lightened shade by shade with the coming dawn, Cayatu tried to clean Ysaga's blood from her face and hair. She washed his body, then her own. The hut stank from death. In a stupor, she moved to the doorway and sat in the still dawn air.

As the sun rose, she watched a few old ones—too old to travel—stirring in their huts. She waited for the familiar sounds of the mission bells but they didn't ring. There was no *alcalde* to ring them. The mission was silent. There was no smell of *atole* cooking in the mission kitchen drifting through the village and no aroma of wood fires outside the adobes. The mission was deserted.

She walked away from the hut, out of the *rancheria*. Beyond the village she walked through the small gardens where families had grown their own food. Still farther off, she walked into open land stretching down the side of the hill west of the mission. She wandered through the fields spotted with golden poppies, struggling with her grief; overwhelming grief now accompanied by her sense of loneliness.

In the distance, she heard the sounds of horses racing up the hill, and she knew the soldiers were coming back. She climbed to the edge of the village, but kept herself hidden where she could watch. A few soldiers on horseback crested the hill and dismounted in the center of the village.

She watched as they went into some of the deserted adobes and began pulling out the scant possessions of families that had fled into the canyon.

"Look here," one of them shouted to his companions, "They have more food than we do." He threw bowls and plates on the ground, smashing them into fragments. Others stomped on baskets they found, and flung the food in them to the dirt. Hut by hut, they destroyed everything they could find.

Cayatu watched them go into her hut and repeat the senseless destruction. She slammed her fists into the ground. Anger and sorrow and helplessness made her body tremble, but she kept hidden.

"There's a dead man in here," a soldier shouted to the others. "One we shot." He dragged Ysaga's body by the heels out into the light.

A soldier in a ragged uniform went into another hut and came out dragging an old woman by the arm. He flung her to the ground, shouting to his companions. She cowered at his feet. They gathered around her, mocking her. Cayatu could hear her faint pleas for mercy. She saw the woman try to crawl away, but the soldiers just laughed. Then one took his lance and drove it full into her belly. She screamed. The man put his boot on her chest to retrieve the blood-smeared blade. Cayatu turned her face away and vomited.

She turned back to watch the men comb through the village, destroying more possessions and hunting for other Chumash. When they found one—man or woman—they murdered. They continued killing and looting while she watched, sick from the horror. She tried to drive the dying screams from her head. Finally, their fury spent, the soldiers rode back to the *Presidio*. She heard them laughing as they rode away.

Chapter Forty-Eight

What will you do now?" a faint voice behind her asked.

Cayatu stirred from the place where she lay on the ground, exhausted from a night without sleep and consumed by the horror she'd watched. She looked around the field, but saw no one.

"What will you do now?" the voice came again, quiet but insistent in the stillness of the morning.

She sat up and looked again. This time she saw the old woman sitting with her hands in her lap a short distance from her.

"There is nothing left," she answered. "I'll join Massilili, your daughter's son, in the canyon. We'll leave here forever. Seek a new place where we can live the old ways again and die when our time comes."

"Leave nothing behind if you go, Cayatu," the Indian woman told her in a whispering voice.

"I have nothing to take. Everything is gone."

"Not gone, daughter. Go back to your hut and search."

Cayatu got to her feet and walked back to the desolate village. She moved Ysaga's body inside the hut, out of sight, feeling the hollowness deep in her heart again as she did. Coming back outside, she looked at her meager possessions scattered in the dirt. She found the shell basket, twisted and half buried in the ashes of the fire pit. She brushed it clean with her hands and clutched it close to her heart.

"Remember when Tanayan gave it to you?" her mother's voice spoke at her side again. "Remember what she told you?"

"I've always tried to live with dignity, Mother. The men who took our land from us took our dignity, too. Nothing remains. I'll go to join Massilili." "Leave nothing behind," her mother said again. "If you leave something behind it will always draw you back. You'll never be free."

"But this is all I have," Cayatu answered her.

"Not all," her mother said again. Then Sioctu's voice weakened. Her image faded. "Not all," her voice echoed.

Cayatu knelt in front of her hut a few more moments thinking about her mother's words. They spoke to her heart. A resolve formed. Holding the basket in her hand, she rose and started walking to the west.

Cayatu skirted the *pueblo* and joined the trail but kept well off it, out of sight whenever possible, moving quickly when she was in the open. She stayed on the alert for any movement. Once, two Mexicans came up behind her on mules and she ran into the chaparral, hugging the ground till they were far ahead and out of sight. Her stomach called out for food and water on the long walk but she only stopped once to sip cool water scooped from a stream in her cupped hands. She found berries to quiet her stomach, but the feeling gnawing at her was not from hunger. How could she do this, she asked herself? The answer wasn't clear but she knew she must.

As she walked through the afternoon, the western sky dissolved from vivid blue, into shades of pink and red, flaming orange and finally violet. By the time she neared her destination it was past twilight, the last of the hunting hawks had returned to their perches for the night. Sun was gone and the sky was coming alive with stars. A quartering moon was just cresting the eastern horizon. Evening Star guided her into the canyon. She saw two horses tied to a rail in front of the adobe. A roan mare stood docilely, head down, tethered to a rail fence, reminding her of Tomas's horse. The other, a gray stallion, pawed the ground at her approach and flared its nostrils. Through the window she could see flickering candle light. The smell of wood smoke hung in the still evening air, with only the buzzing sound of unseen insects and an occasional cry of sadness from a distant coyote disturbing the night.

She hesitated at the door, asking herself again—how can I do this?—but when she began to feel she didn't have the strength to go forward, she heard Sioctu's voice again: "If you leave something behind you'll never be free." She drew in a breath and without knocking pushed open the door.

Josefa screamed, then, recognizing it was Cayatu, calmed herself. "Aí, Clare, my heart stopped. I didn't know you at first. We're afraid of Indians today. I thought we were being attacked."

"No one is left at the mission," Cayatu responded. "They're all dead or fled into the canyon behind the mission."

Moving farther into the room, she stopped short. Demetrio de Alba sat at a table, finishing his evening meal. He turned to stare at her. Once again, she saw the pale blue eyes that seemed to slice through her and told nothing in return. She wanted to back away, turn and run out the door, but she stood her ground, returning his stare, keeping her feelings locked. Standing firm.

"Get rid of her," de Alba told Josefa.

"You killed us," Cayatu shouted at him, her rage surging to the surface. "Your soldiers killed old men and women."

Josefa turned to de Alba with a questioning look.

De Alba shrugged. "They fired arrows at us."

"Old men and women don't shoot arrows," Cayatu snapped.

"How could this be?" Josefa asked. "How could you allow—"

De Alba shrugged again. "The men were angry. I couldn't stop them. They paid no attention when I ordered them to halt. They rode to the mission this morning."

"You didn't try to stop them, did you? They killed old people." Cayatu confronted him.

"Demetrio, you are *El Comandante*. How could you...?"

De Alba rose from the table and faced the two women. "They were just Indians. There was nothing to be done. This one is lucky to be alive."

"You allowed the murders?" Josefa said, her voice quivering. "You are a vile man, a murderer, Demetrio."

Cayatu watched the color drain from Josefa's face. "I've come for Delfina," she said. "I've come to take my child."

"Your child? Oh, no, Clare, Delfina is mine."

"You know she's not, Josefa." Cayatu put her hands on her hips; she saw Josefa shaking. "The look on your face that day in the carriage told me you knew. I see that look now. Fermin Ortiz took the baby away from me the day she was born. He gave her to you."

Josefa looked at de Alba, her face drained of color. "Is that so?"

His face was stone. He shrugged but didn't speak.

Cayatu's gaze shifted from Josefa to see the look on de Alba's face. It was hidden behind the fair whiskers that covered his cheeks and chin, but the glint in his eyes was as steely-blue as the blade of his sword hanging from a peg in the corner of the room. She turned back to Josefa, sad in the knowledge she was about to hurt her friend. "Do you know who Delfina's father is, Josefa?"

Josefa's face still held its shocked look. She didn't answer. She stood motionless.

Cayatu's eyes flashed over to de Alba again. She saw his color rising behind the beard. His lips curled, showing just a glimmer of teeth. "The *Comandante* is Delfina's father," Cayatu said, bitterness gripping her. She baited Josefa,

"Look at you. All together. One family, father, mother and daughter. You're not the mother, but he is the father. She's my child and he's the devil who used me for his pleasure."

Cayatu took several steps closer to de Alba, fixing him in her eyes, but aiming her words at Josefa. "He lay on me every night when I was a prisoner at the fort, ramming me with his man-part, forcing his seed into me. Do you remember the day you came to the fort to ask about Guillermo? That's when the *Comandante* brought me to his bed every night, using me whenever he wanted. He gave me glass beads each time he thrust his man-part in me—worthless beads from a worthless man. He never asked. He took. He took me to pleasure himself and afterward I carried his child, the girl you call your daughter."

The horror on Josefa's face contorted it. She approached de Alba. "How could you do that, Demetrio? To her? To any woman?" She spit out the words.

He still stood in silence, penetrating both of them with his stare. Then his hand shot out with the speed of a hawk's screaming dive and slammed into Josefa's face.

Stunned by his viciousness, Cayatu saw tears forming in Josefa's eyes as she rubbed her cheek, already carrying the red imprint of his hand. Cayatu's urge to hurt her friend dissolved. She moved to Josefa's side to comfort her. "I've never told anyone, but seeing you now, I knew you should know the truth about this evil man."

A guttural laugh came from de Alba's throat. "You are a fool, Josefa. A fat sow and a fool. Look at you. How could I love you? Me! I've bedded the most beautiful women in Spain and Mexico. Do you think I would settle with a peasant woman here on the edge of Hell? You wanted a child, I gave you this baby. There she is, sleeping in the other room, and now I have the land. I fulfilled my part of the bargain, and I know you didn't hate the afternoons we spent on your mattress."

Josefa grabbed a pottery jar from the table and flung it at de Alba but it missed, crashing on the floor, shattering into noisy pieces. She ran to the table and picked up the knife de Alba had used to cut his food. She charged back across the room at him. "I'll kill you!" she yelled, "you brute!"

De Alba side stepped her charge and slapped the knife out of her hand. It clattered on the floor alongside the pottery shards. "Kill me, would you?" he taunted her.

Josefa began beating on him with her fists.

Cayatu stood watching impassively as Josefa's arms flailed, hitting the *Comandante* in the face and chest with a torrent of blows that had little impact.

"Enough," de Alba shouted. "I've had enough of you." He pushed her off and hit her in the face with the back of his hand.

She wobbled backward, stunned by the blow. A thin line of blood started at the corner of her mouth.

"I'm leaving here as soon as I can get a ship. Leaving you and the child, too. My career is finished. Keep your miserable land, it's made me rich enough. I don't need it any longer. Or you."

Filled with rage, Josefa charged into him again, swinging her arms wildly. De Alba hit her again, this time with his fist. Cayatu saw the steel in his eyes flash with anger as he punched her in the face and chest and stomach several more times.

Josefa had stopped hitting him and stood dumbly while he mauled her.

Cayatu dropped the basket she had carried from the mission from her hand. Her thought was to defend her friend. While de Alba seemed to delight in pummeling Josefa, Cayatu walked to the corner where his sword rested in its scabbard. She drew it out, feeling its heft, seeing sparks flying off the steel from reflected candlelight. She turned back at him.

"Stop!" she shouted, pointing the tip of the blade at him.

He looked at her, startled. Then he let out another of his

animal laughs. Josefa crumpled to the floor but De Alba paid her no attention, turning to Cayatu. "Put it down," he ordered her. 'You can't kill me. I am *El Comandante*. You're just an Indian whore." But the look on his face showed fear.

Cayatu took a step toward him and he backed up. She stayed just out of his reach with the tip of the sword pointed at his stomach. "You deserve to die," she said, words coming in her best Spanish now so that she knew he understood. "You're a devil sent to torment us. We were helpless to stop you."

Again, he tried to laugh, but it was weak. "Put down my sword. You won't kill me with it, you're too timid. All your people are." He reached out to take the sword away from her.

Cayatu saw the terror growing in his eyes as she held steady, the blade aimed at his belly. She paused only an instant. She drove the blade deep into Demetrio de Alba's stomach, looking straight into his face as she did. It took all her strength to drive it in. Then she let go of the hilt and backed away. Her eyes watched the pain come into his eyes. He staggered back against the wall. He looked down at the gold-hilted blade she had run through him. Blood flowed from the wound, staining his ruffled white shirt and dripping off the sword blade. It dripped on the dirt floor of the adobe. De Alba reached for the hilt, trying to pull the sword out, but his strength was already draining away. He sank lower against the wall until only his head was propped against it. His eyes grew dull. He made only a gurgling sound before he died.

Cayatu watched him die, feeling no pleasure in what she'd done, only relief. She felt unburdened, as if a weight had been finally lifted from her. She turned to Josefa lying on the floor sobbing. Her face was bruised, already swollen. Blood trickling from the corner of her mouth was now a fine line down a crease in her chin. Cayatu knelt to cradle her, holding Josefa against her own breast. Both women let their tears flow freely and held each other tightly.

Cayatu helped Josefa to sit in the chair by the table. She bathed her face in cool water. She found a blanket to throw over de Alba's body. As she was doing that she heard Delfina stirring in the next room. She went to the little girl and took her from her cradle, rocking Delfina in her arms, soothing her with a quiet song. Delfina looked at her through sleepy eyes, but seemed to remember her. She cooed at the sound of Cayatu's voice. With Delfina in her arms Cayatu went back into the other room.

Josefa's face twisted in panic. "You're taking my daughter away, aren't you?" she said.

"Not your daughter, mine."

"Where will you take her?"

"To live over the mountains."

"Oh, no," Josefa sobbed. "She can't live like an Indian. How can you be so cruel to me?"

"We've learned to be cruel to survive in your world."

Cayatu watched the tears start again and slide down Josefa's swollen cheeks. She dabbed them away with a cloth and handed Delfina to Josefa as her own sadness flowed from her eyes. "Hold her this last time, Josefa. There is one more thing I must say to you. It hurts me but I must say it. Your husband—Guillermo—I killed him. I'm sorry. I was hiding in the canyon when he found me. I hit him with a rock to make him let me go. I killed him with it. I didn't know he was your man."

Josefa soothed the child in her arms with trembling hands. "Oh, God," she sobbed, "you killed both my husbands."

"Two of mine are dead because of your people," Cayatu replied. "We've both suffered much, the two of us."

Tears flowed freely, but Cayatu saw no anger in Josefa, only her tired face, swollen with cuts and bruises from de Alba's fists, and seeming to sag with the heaviness of the last hour. After rocking Delfina in silence for a few moments, Josefa sighed. "Look how our lives are entwined, Clare. Guillermo, Demetrio, your men, Delfina. At each turn in my life you are there. I knew the baby was yours. I knew it in my heart. I could tell by the way you held her, how you looked at her, sang to her. I thought we could raise her here together. I begged you to live with me. Over and over. You, her real mother, and me, the woman who loves her and needed her to replace all the sorrow in my heart. I kept asking…"

Cayatu couldn't bear to hear Josefa any longer. She took the sleepy child away from Josefa and hugged her. Delfina tried to squirm away, looking back over her shoulder and reaching out her arms to Josefa. "Mama," she cried out.

Cayatu held Delfina tightly and walked to the door. Opening it, she looked out toward the mountains where Massilili and the others waited. Clutching Delfina, she took a step out into the darkness. In her mind the images were clear. She saw the oak grove where women gathered acorns, heard the waves lapping against the *tomols* on the beach, smelled the cooking fires and watched the hawk circling overhead. But only in her mind. That life was no longer real. She forced the images away. Cayatu knew she had to move on to a new life.

She turned and went back inside the adobe. She went to the table to pick up the shell basket from where she'd set it down minutes before. She walked over to the chair where Josefa sat sobbing, her face buried in her hands. The icon of the Virgin sat on the small table next to her. Cayatu looked at it for a moment, still holding the child and the shell basket.

She handed Delfina back to Josefa. The lump in her throat let her words come out as a whisper. "We are both mothers to this child. We'll raise her together. I'll teach her about her grandmother who wove this basket and her grandfather who built magnificent canoes and her aunt who lived with dignity," Cayatu told Josefa. "And you will teach me to drive the carriage and ride a horse to the *pueblo* and other things I'll need to know."

The End

Historical Note

Near the close of the 18th Century, California was a desolate land. The Spaniards, who had conquered Mexico in their quest for New World riches, judged Alta California to be without value and ignored it for two hundred and fifty years. California might have remained forgotten indefinitely if the Russians coming south from Alaska, and the English moving west from Hudson Bay, hadn't begun coming south into California, driven by their unquenchable appetite for furs. Fearful the security of Nueva España (Mexico) was threatened, Spain decided to create a buffer in California.

In 1769, leather-jacketed Spanish soldiers and gray-robed Franciscan priests, led by Father Junipero Serra, established Mission San Diego de Alcala, the first in a string of 21 missions that would stretch northward to Sonoma, California, over the next fifty-four years. After founding the first mission they marched up the coast toward Monterey, stopping at Indian villages along their route. At a village called Mishopshnow by the Chumash and La Carpinteria (the carpenter's shop) by the Spaniards, the soldiers and priests marveled at the tomols, sea-going planked canoes, being built.

Cayatu, a young Chumash woman, was born and raised in the village of Mishopshnow, east of Santa Barbara. Her father was the leader of the Brotherhood of the Canoe which built the tomols. He held a high rank in the village. Cayatu's mother was also high born, a daughter of the local chief.

The Royal Presidio of Santa Barbara was built in 1782. Three other forts were built at San Diego, Monterey and Yerba Buena (San Francisco). No more than 60 Soldados de Cuera (leather-jacketed soldiers) were assigned to the Santa Barbara Presidio and they were spread thinly among the five missions they were charged with protecting-San Gabriel, San Buenaventura, Santa Barbara, Santa Ynez and La Purisíma Concepción.

The soldiers who manned the Presidio came from northern Mexico with a party of settlers who were the original founders of the Pueblo of Los Angeles. Most of the men brought their wives and children with them because it was understood from the time they were recruited that they would settle in the new, virtually empty land and probably never see their homeland again. They marched across the parched Sonoran Desert and fording the Colorado River at Yuma, Arizona. Then they continued marching across the California desert to the coast. Josefa and her soldier husband, Guillermo, came to Santa Barbara with the other soldiers, with Josefa carrying their son Joaquin on the long march. The infant didn't survive the hardships of the journey.

After a four-year delay, Mission Santa Barbara was founded on Dec. 4, 1786, the Feast Day of Saint Barbara. Junipero Serra had died by then so the founding ceremony was presided over by Padre Presidente Fermin Lasuen. The mission priests immediately began seeking souls to save at the nearby Chumash villages.

The Chumash did not flock to the Santa Barbara Mission for religions reasons; they came to survive. European diseases like small pox, pneumonia, diphtheria and syphilis were spreading through their villages and some of the Indians believed they would escape death at the mission. Their food supply dwindled as the mission cattle and sheep grazed on traditional seed- and acorn-gathering grounds.

Once baptized, neophyte Christians were not allowed to leave the mission. Any of those who did leave without permission were hunted down by soldiers, returned to the mission and punished. Unmarried women were locked in women's quarters each night at the mission to prevent what the priests called promiscuity. The priests punished neophytes for other offenses too, such as lack of attention in worship services. They used whipping, confinement in stocks and other punishments they thought necessary to Christianize the Native Americans. It was the goal of the Spanish Kings, who were considered the protectors of the Pope during this period, to make all native people in the lands Spain colonized good citizens of the Empire, and being a good citizen meant becoming a good Catholic.

Until 1821, only Spanish ships were allowed to trade with Spain's New World possessions. People in Santa Barbara and throughout Alta California depended on the yearly ship that sailed from San Blas, Mexico, to bring them the supplies they could not produce for themselves. In some years the San Blas ship failed to arrive and soldiers, people of the pueblo and mission padres went without both necessities and luxuries.

With free Indian labor Santa Barbara Mission grew rich. Large cattle herds roamed the hills around Santa Barbara by the thousands and provided all the leather the mission and Presidio needed for shoes, saddles and other leather goods. Cow hides and tallow from rendered fat were the mainstays of the early economy. Traders from other nations soon found it profitable to smuggle goods into California to trade for the hides and tallow which were much in demand in eastern mills and factories.

The Mexican rebellion from Spain, which started in 1810 and ended in 1821, meant almost no annual supply ships came to California. Presidio soldiers, unpaid, with tattered uniforms, had to depend on the mission to keep them fed. The soldiers and settlers (gente de razón) directed their anger and frustration toward the neophyte Chumash under the protection of the Franciscan priests.

A devastating earthquake rocked Santa Barbara a few days before Christmas 1812, severely damaging both mission and Presidio. During the rebuilding period, soldiers and priests depended on the Chumash for backbreaking labor.

In 1824, the mission Chumash rebelled against what they thought was unfair treatment by the Spanish priests and soldiers. They captured Mission Santa Ynez and encouraged their brothers at Mission Santa Barbara to revolt. Rather than face a pitched battle, most of the Santa Barbara Mission Chumash fled over the mountains to the Tulare Lake region of California's Central Valley. After they fled, Presidio soldiers pillaged their village, killing remaining neophytes too old to flee with the others. Six months after the revolt, a party of priests and soldiers marched into the Central Valley and forced the Chumash to return. Most reluctantly came back, but Massilili and some others hid and never returned.

Readers of Dream Helper should note that while it is purely a work of fiction it is based on this historical record. The actual time period has been compressed to make a more unified and satisfying story.

Dream Helper

Questions and Topics for Discussion

1. Discuss your feelings about the Chumash people. What was their life like before the coming of the Spaniards? Why did they accept the newcomers without a fight? What motivated them to join the missions? What was life like for the Chumash who stayed in their villages or lived in the pueblo?

2. Discuss the Spaniards and Mexicans who came to Santa Barbara. What motivated them to move to an outpost far from their homes? What do you think their lives were like before coming to Santa Barbara? How did they feel about the Chumash? What do you think life was like for this small band of men with their wives and children?

3. What are your feelings about the Franciscan priests? Were they an overzealous group? A group of misfits? Why did they treat the neophytes in their charge the way they did? How was their concept of religion in the 18th and 19th centuries different than the concept today? Do you think the author treated them fairly?

4. The Chumash people saw spirits all around them; in the rocks and plants and animals. How did that differ from the Spaniards? The Chumash believed they had Dream Helpers that guided their lives; what guided the lives of the priests and soldiers? Discuss the differences and similarities in the two world views.

5. Discuss the plot hatched by Demetrio de Alba and Padre Fermin Ortiz. Each had different motives to begin with; what do you think they were? How did you feel about each of these characters?

6. Discuss Josefa's role in the story. Is she an important character or an insignificant one? Justify your opinion with specific instances from the story.

7. Discuss the ending of the story. What feelings did you have at the end? What motivated Cayatu's decision? What events throughout the story led to her decision? Was it a satisfying decision?

8. The author used a lot of symbolism throughout the story. Discuss some of the symbols and their use in advancing the story. What did the seed basket represent? The hawks? The mouse early in the story? What does the Dream Helper symbolize?

Contact info@rinconpublishing.com for book club pricing!

Willard Thompson's
Chronicles of California
Continue with

DELFINA'S GOLD

Coming Soon

With a weak Mexican government now in control of California, traders flock to her shores from New England in pursuit of cattle hides and tallow. Russian sea otter hunters eye the land covetously from their base in northern California and Englishmen from Hudson Bay grow bold in search of furs. When American mountain men crossing the Sierra Nevada Mountains are added to the mix, California is up for grabs.

Cayatu and Josefa must adjust to the ways of the foreigners while holding on to their own traditions. Courted by the sons of wealthy rancheros and the greedy newcomers, Delfina must look to her future while trying to deny her past. Aware her suitors will stop at nothing to strip the land she loves so dearly of its natural wealth, Delfina must protect Cañon de Corral, her inherited land grant, sprawling along the Pacific coast near Santa Barbara, from the men who pursue her. Only one man loves the land as Delfina does. He loves her, too, but struggles with his own demons.

When historic figures Thomas O. Larkin, Augustus Sutter and Major John Charles Frèmont enter the story the stage is set for a showdown of epic proportion.

Don't miss *Delfina's Gold*, book 2 of the Chronicles of California, available soon online and at your favorite book dealer.

Rincon Publishing

Dream Helper Order Form

Telephone orders: 805-565-7946
Fax orders: 320-215-6536
email orders: orders@rinconpublishing.com

Postal Orders:
Rincon Publishing,
P.O. Box 50235, Santa Barbara, CA 93150

Name: _____

Address: _____

City: _____ State: _____ Zip: _____

Telephone: _____

Email address: _____

Number of copies _____ @ $16.95 = $_____

Shipping: ($4.00 for first book; $2.00 for each additional) $_____

Sales Tax: California addresses please add
sales tax of $1.30 for each book ordered $_____

                                  Total Paid $_____

Payment
___ Check   __ Visa ___ Mastercard

Card Number _____

Exp. date _____

Name on card: _____

Contact info@rinconpublishing.com for book club pricing!